ALSO BY LUCRETIA GRINDLE

The Killing of Ellis Martin

So Little to Die For

The Nightspinners

LUCRETIA GRINDLE

 RANDOM HOUSE | NEW YORK

THE

Nightspinners

A NOVEL

This is a work of fiction. Names, characters, places, and incidents
are the products of the author's imagination or are used fictitiously.
Any resemblance to actual events, locales, or persons, living or
dead, is entirely coincidental.

COPYRIGHT © 2003 BY LUCRETIA W. GRINDLE

All rights reserved under International and
Pan-American Copyright Conventions. Published in
the United States by Random House, Inc.,
New York, and simultaneously in Canada
by Random House of Canada Limited, Toronto.

RANDOM HOUSE and colophon are registered
trademarks of Random House, Inc.

Library of Congress Cataloging-in-Publication Data

Grindle, Lucretia.
The nightspinners: a novel / Lucretia Grindle.
p.cm.
ISBN 0-375-50776-0 (acid-free paper)
1. Murder victims' families—Fiction. 2. Philadelphia (Pa.)—Fiction.
3. Georgia—Fiction. 4. Sisters—Fiction. 5. Twins—Fiction. I. Title
PS3557.R526 N64 2003
813'.54—dc21   2002069703

Printed in the United States of America on acid-free paper

Random House website address: www.atrandom.com

9 8 7 6 5 4 3 2

FIRST EDITION

Book design by Barbara M. Bachman

WITH SPECIAL THANKS TO MY FATHER AND MY HUSBAND

FOR THEIR RELENTLESS SUPPORT AND GOOD HUMOR,

AND TO MY EDITORS, LEE BOUDREAUX AND MARIA REJT,

FOR THEIR EXPERTISE AND PATIENCE, AND TO MY AGENT,

SLOAN HARRIS, WHO IS SIMPLY THE BEST.

The Nightspinners

SHOO FLY. THAT WAS WHAT MY MOTHER CALLED ME. SHOO Fly Pie. Shoo, Fly—don't bother me, I belong to somebody. I can hear her still in the southern nights of my childhood, nights that never seemed clear and clean like they do farther north but were instead heavy and alive with fireflies, and nightjars, and all of the things that move and wind through the dark.

When I think of those nights now, I hear my mother's voice. She is standing in the kitchen, the soles of her Keds firmly planted on the linoleum floor. Her hands, narrow and long-fingered, move rhythmically and without thought, like something programmed. She is canning. She ladles whole peaches, squishy and bright yellow, into jars, pours syrup that will stick to you and burn if it spills. She spoons piccalilli that is red and green and hot with peppercorns. And while she does this, she sings.

Her thin, hopeful soprano threads its way through our house. Sharp and not quite right, her voice is out of harmony with Georgia. It does not match the long green fields of the farm, the road, red with dust, the sun-blistered walls of the sheds, or the slow creak of our screen door. It is not some slow, rolling bass, nor the sweet arc and swoop of a Baptist hymn, nor a sad, slow sax note of the South. Her voice is not a knife wound. It is just something present and unseriously painful, like a paper cut that stings and cannot be forgotten.

"Shoo, fly," my mother sings, and sometimes in the night I feel that she's calling my special name. My mother didn't have a special name for Marina. I'm not sure why, perhaps because it was enough of a name in itself, enough of a distinction for Petamill, Georgia. We longed to be called Sue-Ellen. Carla-Louise. Mary. Daisy. Or best of all, Elizabeth-Anne. But no, there we were in that town with those names, Marina and Susannah, the living evidence of our mother's optimism, of her double-dog dare that in the face of circumstance we would "become something." It was as if, in naming us as she had, our mother had given us something grandiose, something to make up for the fact that we had no father. Or, to put it more accurately, that she had probably never been quite certain of who he was.

Not that our mother was wild anymore. Our birth must have cured her of that. With her bobbed dark hair and her pressed white blouses, the tiny gold earrings from the five-and-dime, and the midheight heels that she wore to work, our mother's wildness was a thing of the past. It clung to her only in half-remembered stories and hovered about her fine-boned beauty like a memory. I dream of my mother as a young girl, and when I do she is always wearing a candy-red dress with a wide skirt and little flat shoes that are black and have bows on the toes. Her waist is tiny. Her hair is a glossy cap. And I can hear her laughing. I dream of her in roadhouses, in those places by the side of secondary highways where the parking lot is crowded with pickup trucks and lit by a neon sign, and where the noise from the bar and the jukebox lifts everything up and floats it out onto the heavy dark.

But that is only my dream. I do not know what the reality was, and my mother never told me. As I have grown older, I have come to suspect that it had more to do with the backseats of Chevrolets, with beer cans and bottled cocktails. With truckers pulling through town. There was, of course, our hair, which was a color unlike any known in our family and distinctive enough to have been something of a clue, if we had been looking for clues. But, now that I think of it, Marina and I were peculiarly uninterested in the possibilities of our parentage. We had very little, if any, interest in who our father was. Our world was closed and complete. Night after night we spun the threads of a cocoon around ourselves while, upstairs in our room, we listened to our mother's song.

We lie stretched and still in our twin beds, and if our mother was to climb the stairs and look in on us, as she so often does, she could assume, from the sweet tilt of our heads and the motionlessness of our hands, that we are sleeping. But she would be wrong. On those nights Marina and I are not drifting high above the farm on a cloud of dreams. We are not sinking and innocently lost in sleep. Oh, no. We are busy.

Without so much as a motion or a sound, Marina and I are weaving words. We are sliding them along the bar of light from the hall that filters under the door. We are sending phrases, paragraphs, laughter, faster and faster, like flights of moths across the dark space of the room. Braiding the strands of our secret cocoon, we are nightspinning.

Not that our mother would know this. Not that anyone would know it. It is our secret. No one guesses that we are nightspinners. No one knows how much we talk, or about the web of secret words we stretch between us. We work in silence. And when our mother eases the door open, she rewards us for what she assumes is our sleep. She whispers, "You are such a good girl." She says it just once, to both of us, as if we were one. Which, in fact, we are. We are two peas in a pod, Marina and me. We are bright as buttons. Cute as pie. Mirror images. We are twins.

BY THE TIME WE WERE NINE OR TEN, MARINA AND I could carry on complete conversations without speaking. Our nightspinning that had begun in the dark had long since grown strong enough to withstand the light of day. I would feel a prickle on the back of my neck, a subtle rising of the tiny, soft hairs that grew there, and I didn't even have to look at her to know what she was saying. Marina would send entire paragraphs into my head, whether I wanted them or not. Permanently set to receive, I was a fax machine that never ran out of paper. My mind was a blank slate, and Marina could write on it any time she chose. Mostly, when she was nightspinning, she would not meet my eye. She would look in another direction, her gaze fixed on the wall or the fields, her chin set stubborn. And the tiniest smile of triumph would flicker across her face because I could not stop her, could not turn her away if I tried.

To be honest, most of the time I did not try. And neither, insofar as I know, did she. For I used my privilege as a nightspinner, too. I sent my share of messages across our private airway. But I do not know if the back of Marina's neck prickled, or if she came to resent me for my uninvited presence in her head. I presume that was what she felt, if only because it was what I felt. But I do not know, and since I never asked her, I will never know. My sister is dead. She was murdered eighteen months ago in Alexandria, Virginia. Now she is just a case number, an unsolved homicide. One of many.

IT IS GOING TO RAIN, I CAN SMELL IT. THE HIGH SASHED window that opens onto the balcony of my apartment is raised, and the sounds and the smells of the city drift into my room. There is not much traffic in this part of Philadelphia. Popular wisdom says the city is dying, and so perhaps that explains the quiet of it. It is only occasionally that I hear footsteps on the sidewalks below, or shouted laughter, or the rush of a car in the street like a great exhaled breath.

In the corner beyond the fireplace, the dog moves restlessly. He is a German shepherd, a leggy, two-toned wolf, black and tan with a bearlike snout and golden eyes. As I watch, he rises from his bed, stretches, and regards me seriously. It is almost midnight, and we are due to be abroad, to make our final patrol of the empty streets. He paces in front of me through the hallway and waits while I reach for my sweater and his leash.

We open the door and pause outside my apartment. Only five of us live in this building, and it is possible to imagine that the other three apartments do not exist, that the dog and I are completely alone, and that in stepping through the door and out onto the landing, we have crossed back over time, fallen through a hundred years.

The house is a brownstone, a dowager duchess of the Victorian past modified only slightly in order to greet the modern age. The wall sconces, once lit by gas, are flame-shaped buds of glass. A brass chandelier, adapted uneasily to electricity, hangs in the stairwell. One story above me, a great skylight glows faintly, its smoky panes suggesting an eternal blanket of snow or a Holmesian fog. The stairs, thick-carpeted in crimson, wind down four flights to the parquet floors below. The banisters are huge and ornately carved and far too wide for me to wrap my hand around. This late at night, in the quiet, I feel that I am a small child and the grown-ups are asleep.

The heavy doors swing shut behind us as the dog and I come down the front steps and onto the sidewalk. We pause to sniff the air, to listen, and then begin our walk, turning left and, a block later, left again. We have a routine, and it never varies. Along Delancey Place, the dog inspects each set of iron railings, considers each ginkgo tree. He stops to peer intently at several sets of the wide front steps that lead to glossy black doors with knockers of polished brass in the shape of claws or lions' heads. One particularly ornate lintel is supported by a pair of caryatids. The dog gives them a conspiratorial glance in passing, and they look benignly down on us, as if their thoughts have room to wander while they hold the house on their heads. Even in the coldest wind, or in the powdery pinpricks of the snow, the dog never hurries this ritual. Sometimes his leisurely pace, his lack of urgency, makes me impatient, but not tonight. We are having an Indian summer, and even though it is late September, the breeze is a warm breath that puffs in from the Delaware, bearing the promise of soft, overblown drops of rain.

On nights like this, I sometimes think I can smell the sea. The ports of Philadelphia are a long way from open water. Nevertheless, I like the idea enough that I often insist on it. "You are lying!" George would say when I claimed that I could taste the ocean, could roll its salt along the back of my tongue. He would smile, reach for my hand, raise his eyebrows at the horror of it, and exclaim, "You are such a liar, Susannah!" Born and raised among the small towns of the Midwest, George found mendacity both incorrigible and faintly erotic. Now I wonder about him, and whether he misses the idea of the sea, and my lies. Then I remind myself sharply that George is no longer my business. He has decamped to Paris, and I am not to wonder about him, not to indulge in fruitless speculation. I have given up keeping track of French weather and calculating time changes. That way lies the road to ruin. The dog turns left, and left again, and we are on the home stretch.

As I lock the door behind us, the clock in the entryway strikes twelve. I slip the dog's leash off and let him run ahead of me up the stairs. He is on the landing when the phone begins to ring. He cocks his head and looks at me, and I look back at him and shrug as I fit my key into the lock. He noses the door open, and I wipe my feet and drop his leash on the table and follow him into the living room, past my desk where the phone rings and rings.

At first I used to answer it. "Hello, hello," I would say obligingly over and over again. But there was never anyone there. I even dialed *69 a couple of times, but all I got was a beeping tone that the operator informed me meant my caller had "blocked" the line. Now I no longer bother about the calls. I have become used to them. Like the walk, this midnight call has become part of our routine. The phone will ring exactly five times, and then, just before my answering machine clicks in, it will stop. Even as I think this, the noise ceases, and the first splats of rain hit the balcony window.

The dog makes a quick patrol of the apartment and returns to his bed in the living room. He does not sleep in my bedroom; he likes to keep his distance. He is aloof in his devotion and not especially made to cuddle. His purpose is more serious, and he has chosen it for himself. He is the watcher at my door.

His yellow eyes follow me. I can feel his cool regard as I stop in front of the hall mirror, caught by my own reflection. I am the only one left now, and I think that I look both the same and not the same. It is as if, now that Marina is gone, I am more concentrated. I am both of us, doubled up, distilled.

I reach up to unclip my hair and stop in midaction as my hand moves in the mirror. It is my mother's hand, exactly. Bony and long-fingered, it reaches into the air, a blank space on the finger where she wore her ring. It is spooky and yet momentarily familiar, the claustrophobic way in which my mother and Marina have arrived to dwell in me. It is as if they have quit the game and left me the family representative on earth. I shake myself, push them away, and finish the gesture they have arrested me in. I remove the large clip and let the hair fall down around my shoulders. I am not a vain woman, but it is true that this lion's mane of bronze and red is my pride and joy.

I'm going to pour myself another glass of wine. The rain is picking up tempo now, bouncing on the lead wall of the balcony, spreading a thin sheen that glows dull orange in the reflected city lights. I relish these last warm nights even while I look forward to the tang of fall. Sometimes I think I moved north for the seasons. But on the other hand, perhaps I just got this far, just hit this city and stayed. Perhaps I have no good reasons for being here at all and I just insist on the idea of them, like the taste of the sea. Perhaps I make them all up. After all, Marina and I were both terrible liars.

We would make up anything, any old story or excuse, just for the sake of it. I could always tell when Marina was doing it. I would catch the slide of her eye, and without missing a beat, I would join right in. My grandmother was particularly easy prey. We would go over to her house after school and insist that we were getting a puppy, painting our bedroom turquoise, having nothing but angel food cake for dinner, and watching *Love American Style* on TV until midnight. Now that I think of it, she didn't really pay very much attention to us. Maybe we weren't actually very good at it, or maybe she honestly had better things to do than care about what we ate or watched on television. Or maybe she had heard it all before. There is evidence, after all, that our mother was no angel.

Momma herself always knew when we were lying. She would just look at us out of the corner of her eye or raise her hand like a policeman stopping traffic, the wedding band that she insisted on wearing flashing in the light. Or she would simply say, "Well, that's some tall tale," which was immediately deflating. There is nothing on this earth to stop a good lie in its tracks like the conviction that you are not being believed. But Momma aside, that was not usually a problem. Charlie and Dex Eames, and Sonny Delray, and Della Hervey, and Anne Louise Blakemore, and anyone else who cared to listen, all believed that we would be getting a puppy any day and that, when we grew up, we were both going to be ballet dancers.

We finally did start to take ballet lessons when we were ten. Our mother's "jam money" paid for them, along with her extra hours hostessing at the only fancy restaurant in town, the Coachstop. When the Coachstop got a liquor license in the summer of that year, it was a big deal because everybody made more money and all of the customers had a cocktail before dinner. I don't remember one reference, ever, to anyone in that town drinking wine. At home you drank beer, or peach cordial, or malt liquor out of long-necked bottles, and when you went out, you drank bourbon, with or without ice, or martinis, or sometimes something like a sidecar. If you were a lady, you might have a Tom Collins, or a sea breeze, or a whiskey sour.

I still love those names. I love the idea of Angostura bitters, and maraschino cherries, and all the little colored paper umbrellas that anyone who eats in one of my restaurants would choke over. That's what I do, by the way, I design restaurants. I call them "mine," but of course they're not. They are just my designs, my ideas and artistic vision brought to life. You would recognize them. They are those places that offer small, intricately designed towers of food on outsize plates and wildly chic seating arrangements where the size of the bill is diametrically opposed to the portions served. That is what I do, how I make my way in the world. I create the ambience, the look, the safe haven that you move into in order to be fed.

Anyway, that year when we were ten and our mother had a good year selling her jams and relishes and chutneys, we finally got our ballet lessons. The Shall We Dance studio, which was really a big room with a mirror and a rail fastened along one wall, was on the second floor of the hardware building. You got to it by a rickety set of wooden stairs that ran up the outside wall of the building and that I am 100 percent sure were not safe and legal. We went there every Wednesday after school. We pliéd, stuck our toes out like ducks, and whined for pink leotards and matching tights that our grandmother and Uncle Ritchie, who lived with her, finally bought for us. Our mother bought us kid-soled ballet slippers that were shiny black and soft on the bottom and came pressed together like hands in prayer bound by elastic bands.

At the Christmas pageant, we both wanted to be the Sugar Plum Fairy, but neither of us were. We were mice in the first part and candy canes later on, and I have hated *The Nutcracker* ever since. Marina said that it didn't matter. Lying in our beds one night after a particularly boring rehearsal in the church hall, Marina spun the words out to me. She said that it did not matter, that it was of no consequence at all, and that our day would come. She said that we would show them all, that one day we would be perfect swans.

We would dance *Swan Lake,* and one of us would be the black swan and one of us would be the white swan, each a perfect inversion of the other. "Look," Marina had commanded. "Look, you can see them." And I could. Just as she had promised, the swans were dancing in the shadows of our room. Leaping and fluttering, they never put a foot wrong, until finally the poor prince was so besotted that he never even noticed that they were not one and the same.

I think of those swans still. I had forgotten them for decades, but lately they have come back to me. I see them in the shadows of a different room, one as far removed from our twin beds and sash windows and patchy screens as can be. The bedroom that I lie in now is a period gem. Its Victorian moldings and ceiling rosette have been lovingly restored by the architects who own this building and live on the ground floor. This is highly desirable, this live-in architectural arrangement. Or so I am told. It is a guarantee of good taste, so we can all rest easy in the sure knowledge that the stairs will not be redone in a carpet of unfortunate pattern, or the etched-glass panels of the vestibule doors replaced by plywood.

The rooms of my apartment are painted in soft grays and mossy greens, colors I have always loved. Once, when I thought I might be getting married, I contemplated a gray wedding dress. Something very pale and gauzy, like a spiderweb. But I did not get married, and so I am alone in my bedroom, except for the swans. They come into the darkness, or rather out of it, those two identical divas, one black, one white. They pivot and flutter and pirouette. But now, as they go to leap, they hesitate and falter, stalled, like figures on a music box whose time has run out.

You don't think about time running out until it happens to you. And then you can barely get it out of your head. It is as if you are living with that hourglass and it is draining, draining, draining. All those grains of sand. You do not think when you are a child that your mother's hours may be limited, or that those long summers will not go on forever, or that there will not always be a second chance to make things right. You do not think of the not-so-slow corrosions of cancers, and it does not occur to you that on some March night, just as spring is seeping through, its colors spreading like a wash across winter, someone will ring your sister's doorbell, will step over the threshold.

You do not think of these things before they happen, and afterward you cannot stop. Or at least I can't. That is what I think of as I listen to the rain and watch the smeared glow of the city lights across my balcony. I think of nightspinning, and of broken webs, and of words that hang unheard in the dark.

THE NIGHT BEFORE OUR MOTHER DIED, I WAS WOKEN BY Marina. The insistent tone of her voice, punctuated by a loud banging on the door of my dorm room, dragged me out of sleep. When we went to the University of North Carolina, Marina suggested that we share a room, but I promptly vetoed the idea. College was my first real time away from home, my first break for freedom, and I was determined to make the most of it.

I was eighteen, and it had occurred to me that my mind might not be a piece of communal property that I was destined to share with my sister. By the time we packed our identical duffel bags in the fall of 1983 and loaded them into Momma's car for the trip to Chapel Hill, I had endured three months of Marina's hurt feelings and several lectures from my mother on the subject of cruelty. Neither had any effect. Within a week of my mother wishing me luck and kissing me good-bye, her eyes wide with hope and sorrow, I had cut off all of my hair. I looked like I'd had a close encounter with a pair of hedge clippers, but I thought it was marvelous. Never again would anyone start a conversation with me only to realize three sentences in that I was not Marina.

Now, in the predawn hours of this October morning three years after our arrival in North Carolina, Marina was hammering on my door, standing in my hallway, demanding my total attention. The moment I opened the door, she burst into the room like fury itself, the damp night smell of mown grass clinging to her. I watched as she began grabbing my things. Clothes and hairbrush and glasses and shoes were stuffed into a blue canvas bag, and even as she was saying, "It's Momma. Come on, we have to go!" I could feel my stomach constricting into a sour, bile-filled puddle of dread.

"How do you know?" I finally asked. She shoved a pair of jeans and a sweatshirt toward me and shook her head at my obvious stupidity, at the sticky slowness I was mired in.

"Uncle Ritchie called me," she replied. "And if you had a phone like any normal person, he'd have called you, too."

I felt as if a bucket of glue had been poured over me and was hardening. But by now Marina was pushing me toward the door, urging me on as one does a large reluctant animal, a cow or a mule that, given half a chance, might suddenly sink down on its haunches and lose forward motion altogether.

"I knew anyways," she added, as I had known that she would. My sister was still convinced of her psychic powers, of her ability to communicate with me and Momma and God only knows who else at will. I felt like pointing out that this was precisely why there was no reason for me to bother with a telephone. But I didn't argue. I was being hustled along the hall and down the stairs and pushed out into the street where Marina's old blue Honda sat like a Matchbox toy, pulled up at a rakish angle onto the grass verge.

It seems to me now that drives like that are always the same. They have certain characteristics in common, those moments in your life when everything is about to slip over the edge of change and there is not one single thing that you can do about it. There's an immediacy to every little detail. You notice with utter clarity the gas station that you pull into before hitting the interstate. You remember the neon sign with the letter missing, the attendant who slouches with the lethargic hostility of adolescence and smells vaguely of marijuana and spearmint chewing gum. And you recall the disappointment of the night air that rushes in through the rolled-down window and fails to bring with it the shock of coldness that you had hoped would snap you into feeling something.

I slouched down in my seat and undid my seat belt in a gesture of defiance, and I put both feet up on the dashboard. But when I stared out the half-rolled-down window, all I could see was my own reflection staring back at me and beyond that, trapped in the glass, Marina's profile as she drove.

I REMEMBER WHEN I FIRST KNEW THAT MOMMA WAS SICK. It was during the spring break of our freshman year in college, long before anyone said anything, long before anyone actually "knew" anything, in the diagnostic sense of the word. If I were Marina, I would probably insist that Momma had a black aura or some such thing, but I didn't need any supernatural indicators to tell me what was obvious.

I was standing in the dining room of our house, where I had been working on a project. I had come back to Petamill for spring break because I had nowhere else to go, and on arrival I had wasted no time in spreading my things over the entire dining room table, rendering it useless, and my mother and I had fought about it. It seemed like we fought about every little thing since I went off to Chapel Hill.

Turkey or ham for Easter, whether she did or did not have the right to send my high school clothes to the church charity sale, if I could or could not borrow her car, would or would not leave my shoes scattered around the living room. But it wasn't really the shoes or the car, and I didn't give a hoot about my old bell-bottoms or what we ate at Easter. It wasn't any of those things that I was fighting, it was Momma herself. It was her stoicism, her endless optimism, the way she just carried on, year after year, seating ladies at the Coachstop and recommending the club sandwich and the crab cakes, canning and jamming and saving pennies and hoping that somehow things would turn out and we girls would make something of ourselves beyond that tiny southern town.

Looking back on it now, I don't know what else I thought she could have done. But at the time, her resignation terrified me. I wanted her to do something. I wanted her to sweat, to fight, to struggle against circumstance. I was desperate for her to kick against the dusty, dirt-packed roads and the repetitive smack of screen doors, and the Sunday sound of Baptist hymns, and the billboard on the road out of town that said JESUS SAVES. But my mother did not believe in violent struggle. She believed that you played the cards you were dealt, that you took up your hand with good grace, and that that was just how life went.

The problem was that I didn't want my cards, I wanted a whole new deck. And I did not feel that my mother's message was one I could afford to hear. Mired in the arrogance and the myopia of youth, I believed that my mother had no dreams, or that if she did, she did not dare to fight for them.

On that particular spring afternoon, which must have been a Sunday because Momma wasn't at work, I was staring out of the dining room window when I saw her coming up the track that ran across the fields. She was walking very slowly, and her head was bent, and once she paused and looked to be catching her breath. She was carrying a paper grocery bag that was probably filled with canning jars that had been stored in Uncle Ritchie's basement, and she kept switching the bag from arm to arm, leaning it against her hip like it was heavy.

Suddenly I wanted to run out of the house and take the bag from her. I wanted to carry it back to the porch, walking beside her up the steps and chattering about my friends at Chapel Hill, and about my classes, and about all the plans that I did not have for the future. But I couldn't. I stood frozen to the spot, as if I had been turned into a pillar of salt like one of those ladies from the Old Testament. And as I watched her through the window, I felt a burning in my stomach and recognized the hideous knowledge that reaches beyond fear and into the certainty that nothing will ever be the same again.

The screen door banged in the kitchen when Momma came in, and I could hear her moving around. After a moment the noise stopped, and it seemed to take hours for me to walk out of the dining room and across the hallway to the kitchen door. The balls of my feet were tingling, and my ears were pricked like a cat's. I don't know what I expected to find. Maybe I thought she'd be dead on the floor. So when I pushed the door open and looked in and saw her sitting at the red-topped kitchen table, I was so flooded with relief that I picked a fight with her right off about whether or not I'd take a part-time job at the campus art store.

Marina came in right in the middle of it, and hard as I tried, I couldn't involve her. She got that stubborn look on her face and refused to say a thing, and finally Momma just stood up and turned away to the sink and started rinsing out jars. And then she looked at me and shrugged and said, "Oh, Shoo Fly, you just do whatever you want," and that answer terrified me so deeply that I stayed awake all night, listening to the peepers and staring into the hot dark.

BY THE TIME WE GOT TO THE HOSPITAL IN THE LATE morning, there wasn't much of Momma left. She died quietly that afternoon with no fuss, playing out the cards she'd been dealt. Marina and I didn't know what to do, so we just sat on either side of her bed, as identical and silent as bookends.

Momma was buried in the Petamill Unitarian cemetery next to Grandma. We probably talked about the idea of cremation, since both of us were big on making informed decisions, even if we already knew what we were going to do. Probably Marina brought it up while I was downstairs washing dishes and staring out of the kitchen window and she was up in Momma's room lying on the bed or going through drawers deciding what Momma should wear for her journey into eternity. Most likely she telegraphed the words right into my head, saying something like "I don't even want to think about burning her up, do you?" And I probably replied, "God, no. None of those urns and scatterings and ashes." "There aren't any ashes," Marina would have said. "At least that's what they say. They say it's more like sand. Kind of grainy and heavy." That's probably how it went, with us a floor apart and not a word spoken that any other living person could have heard.

Uncle Ritchie bought a new suit. It was light gray and vaguely shiny, and even though I'm sure it fit him, he looked uncomfortable in it. He looked squeezed and buttoned as tightly as if he were being garroted. I didn't need to be told that Uncle Ritchie wouldn't be around long. I don't mean that it was the great hereafter beckoning him. It was more like somewhere south of Miami, although the similarity between the two does not escape me. I pretty much knew that Uncle Ritchie had been biding his time, just like the rest of us. Ever since his wife, whose name I can't even remember, ran off with somebody-or-other a long time ago, Uncle Ritchie had been the ghostly pet of both my mother and my grandmother. Now that Momma was dead, the whole of Grandma's farm was his. The farm was nothing to write home about, but its sale would probably set him up for life in some halfway decent Florida trailer park where he could fish. Momma's house and its two acres, for what it was worth, were ours.

I couldn't look at that house with its white clapboard and its porch and screen doors without feeling something akin to a bout of panic. It was as if one day I might walk through the door and never be able to get back out again. To be in that house was to be fifteen or sixteen or seventeen forever, locked into that Georgia town, the flat mud-green lozenges of the fields and my mother's eternal hopefulness. So what I did next now seems inevitable, but it is not something that I am proud of.

There's a weird kind of silence that comes down on the day after a funeral. I felt as if I'd been to a party and was slightly hungover from it. Sometime in the late morning, I went out onto the front porch and sat on the glider, which had been there since about 1965 and whose springs were squeaky and potentially lethal. They gave you the distinct feeling that you might be gliding happily along when they would decide, entirely of their own volition, to let go of their springy little lives and shoot you forward, right off the porch and into the driveway. I was contemplating this, wondering how far I might fly, as my sneakered toe propelled me back and forth in a satisfyingly moronic stupor, when Marina came out and sat down on the porch step.

There were times when the sight of Marina still jolted me. Times when, no matter how much I ought to, I never could get used to the idea of a carbon copy of myself. No matter how short I cut my hair, or what I wore or how I spoke, I would always be her. If you ran an electrocardiogram on us, the peaks and troughs would match exactly. And so would the irises of our eyes, and the shape of our earlobes.

"What do you want to do with the house?" Marina asked after a while.

I stopped in midglide and looked at her narrowly. She wasn't looking at me. She was staring across the crabgrassy lawn and the track that led to Grandma's house—where this very moment Uncle Ritchie was probably packing his Bermuda shorts—and out into the field beyond. Her eyes were fixed on the crop of something that looked like kale, planted by the Herveys, who leased the land and all married one another and wore overalls and promised to buy Uncle Ritchie out as soon as he named the day, which would probably be tomorrow.

"What do you mean?" I asked.

"Well." Marina turned slowly and looked at me. She shrugged a little. "I was thinking," she said, "that after we finished school, we could just come home."

The words filled me with a distinct physical urge to leap up and start screaming and waving my arms in the air like a crazy person, but instead I waited a moment and then said, as calmly as I could, "What?"

"Come back here," Marina said, warming to her subject. "You know, live here. Like we used to. Everything could be the same again. We could both get jobs around here. It wouldn't be hard. It would be just the same." She repeated this insistently, as if it was a virtue, the main selling point of her master plan.

I stared at my twin sister, wondering if she was out of her mind. It was all I could do not to slap her or shake her, not to lower my face to hers and scream that we were grown up now, that we weren't the goddamn nightspinners anymore, and that besides, didn't she understand that I had spent practically my whole conscious life, at least since I could remember it, wanting, and then trying, and then succeeding in getting out of here? I wanted to scream at her that "just the same" was, to me, roughly the equivalent of dead.

Marina started talking about how it would be, about which of us could have Momma's room and how we'd repaint the downstairs and I could turn the garage into my studio. I would never have to leave at all, except to go to Piggly Wiggly and to collect my social security checks. I could see us sitting right here on this front porch, on this same glider, the two weird sisters creaking down into middle age. Eventually we'd stop talking altogether and just hold long conversations with each other through the telegraph wires in our heads. And maybe of an evening, Momma could join in, too. And then we'd start dressing alike, and local kids would stare at us when we went to the bank, and dare each other to ring our doorbell on Halloween.

I got up and went into the house, slamming the door hard behind me.

IT WAS LATE THAT NIGHT WHEN I CAME DOWNSTAIRS. I knew Marina had gone to bed because I'd heard her, and I'd waited for a good long time before I came out of Momma's room, where I'd been pretending to sleep, and sneaked along the hall without flipping the lights. I even remembered to skip the tenth step on the stairs where it squeaked. I had on my favorite red shoes, just like Dorothy in *The Wizard of Oz*. But mine were Keds, not ruby slippers.

In the kitchen I paused long enough to drop an envelope on the table. It wasn't addressed, but Marina would know it was for her. In it was as legal-sounding a letter as I knew how to write, in which I gave her my half of the house. I don't think that even then I could have fooled myself into believing this was an act of generosity. And instead of making me feel less guilty, as maybe I'd half hoped it would, it only made me feel worse. I was like a thief, except that what I was stealing was wrapped in an act of omission.

I was careful with the screen, easing it back so it didn't bang, like I'd learned to do when I was a kid, and in two steps I was on the back walk and tippy-toeing along the concrete path to the garage. Marina's Honda was parked in the driveway, and while it wasn't actually blocking the big barnlike doors of the garage, it wasn't out of the way, either.

I swung the doors back and saw Momma's icky green Impala parked right dead center, where it always was. One quick look reassured me that it had four inflated tires and a key in the ignition. I was counting on the fact that it would have gas in the tank, too, since Momma always took care of things like that. I opened the driver's-side door and threw my duffel bag onto the seat, and I was about to swing my big canvas purse in behind it when something strange happened.

The next thing I knew, I was out of the garage and running back up the path and darting into the kitchen like something behind me was on fire. I didn't need to turn on the lights. I went straight to the cabinet, the one to the left of the sink where Momma stored her jams and jellies and relishes that we'd always made such a fuss over having to eat and been so embarrassed by. And before I even knew what I was doing, I had the cabinet open and was reaching up for jars of red pepper jelly, and green piccalilli, and yellow corn relish, and sweet orangey balls of pickled peaches.

I stuffed as many jars as I could into my shoulder bag. They clinked and clanked, and the bag weighed about a ton, dragging on my shoulder. Then I grabbed a few more jars, as though they might be the last food in the world that I would ever have the chance to get my hands on. When I couldn't hold any more, I backed out of the kitchen, leaving the cabinet wide open and letting the screen snap like a gunshot as I hobbled down the path and into the garage, bent double over my booty like Quasimodo.

I threw the jars and the bag onto the Impala's long, slippery bench seat and climbed in. I said a prayer of grace and thanks to Momma as the engine turned over on the first try and the needle on the fuel gauge zoomed up to FULL, and then I put the car in reverse and went flying backward out of the garage, just missing Marina's Honda and driving a deep set of ruts into the soft earth.

I didn't turn on my lights as I shot out onto the road and made a three-point turn. Nor did I look up. I didn't need to. I knew what I would see. I knew that I would see the white-clad figure of my sister standing like a specter in the upstairs window, staring down at me from the darkened house.

I WAKE UP EARLY TO MILKY LIGHT THAT FILTERS THROUGH the curtains. The material shifts and breathes in the gritty draft of air that sighs from the window. The pattern is crossed with green leaves, and they appear to lift and float. The street below is utterly silent. I have dreamed of Marina.

When she was alive, I rarely dreamed of her. In death, however, she has infiltrated not only my waking hours but also my sleeping ones. There is almost never a night that goes by when she does not put in at least a cameo appearance. Last night I saw her standing in a circle of fire.

Uneasiness clings to me, but I do not know why. I can hear my heart, and on my tongue is the metallic aftertaste of fear. I lie very still, watching the dust motes in the new day. I concentrate on the row of pictures that marches across my bedroom wall. They are antique prints, aquatints of historic houses in Britain. I find them soothing. Tiny people populate their scenes. Women walk across long lawns shaded by broad oaks. Children run, their minuscule hands raised, their voices locked in silent shouts and laugher. Men stand under willow trees beside ornamental ponds and step in and out of carriages. Merton House. Haddon Hall. Lanhydrock. I was in England only once and never visited any of these places, but I like their names, and I repeat them to myself until I can no longer feel the beating of my heart.

I get up, and my feet feel for the grainy familiarity of my threadbare rugs. I invested early in shabby chic. Initially it was a design choice that was a function of poverty rather than trend, but now that I can afford to get rid of them, I have grown attached to my distressed tables and my blotchy mirrors in their gilded frames. I pull on my jeans and shirt, dressing quickly. The living room seems reassuringly normal when I open the door, and the dog is waiting for me. He watches me from his bed by the fireplace. He might appear relaxed, lounging in his large fur coat, but I know that he is coiled like a spring. He calculates my every move, waiting for the faintest sign that I am ready to go out.

The dog was a pup called Jaeger when George brought him home for me almost three years ago. But I do not speak German, so I changed his name to Jake. Jake the Snake, I sometimes call him. My Yellow-eyed Friend. The Young Man in the Two-toned Suit. I wondered if it was bad luck to change a dog's name, the way they say it is to change the name of a boat or a horse, and I worried that this might evidence itself through Jake hating me, or being stolen or hit by a car. I was sometimes afraid that I had bestowed misfortune upon him. And I feared that he would not understand words like "sit," and "dinner," and "ball." That he would feel lost in a foreign world, and would lie patiently on his bed, hoping to one day hear a word spoken in German.

But if this was the case, if Jake was lost and teaching himself English, he was a quick learner. Certainly he never misunderstood "walk" or "park," words that still throw him into a wild dance of anticipation. That is what he does as I gather his leash and his red rubber ball and a couple of the extra plastic bags that I steal from the vegetable section of the supermarket. He charges into the entrance hall ahead of me and stations himself across the door, reaching up to nose the worn Yale lock, urging me on, butting against me as I bend to tie the laces of my sneakers.

As we come out onto the landing, I can hear the stereo in Cathy Benotti's apartment. Our apartments share the top floor and are separated by the divide of the attic stairwell, so no noise carries from my kitchen to hers. This is merciful, because she plays Celine Dion, Oasis, or Hootie and the Blowfish every morning while getting ready to go to work. This morning "Up Where We Belong" filters out around the edges of her apartment door. I cast only a cursory glance at my mail from yesterday, lying in a small heap on the landing table, before I follow Jake, who is already bounding down the first flight of stairs.

Cathy is helpful by nature, and she often collects my mail from the front hall when she comes in from work and leaves it on the table in the top landing. I know she believes that she can lure me into active engagement with the "real world" through telephone bills and Williams-Sonoma catalogs, but I am uncooperative on this front and often leave my mail on the landing for two or three days before I take it inside. Cathy does not quit, though, and she would make a project of me if I let her. She knows there is misfortune in my past, and while she considers me both odd and irresponsible, she thinks that I am worthy of salvation. She demonstrates this conviction by inviting me to the parties that she gives and introducing me to all the single Northwest flight attendants and ticket agents with whom she works. "You have to kiss a whole lot of frogs," Cathy told me once, lowering her voice to the whisper that many people feel the imparting of wisdom demands.

When Jake and I step out of the house, the air is muggy. Far above, there may be a clear, crystalline blue, but you cannot see it: a thin veil of cloud whites out the sky. Jake and I start down the street. He stops beside me at the lights, and my fingers rest on the sleek familiar fur of his head as if he were a Seeing Eye dog. When the traffic stops, people surge toward us. The women wear suits and running shoes and glance at their watches with peeved expressions. The men look drifty and sad and carry briefcases. Jake and I weave through them as if we are negotiating rapids or driftwood on a river. We reach the other side in safety and continue down the five blocks that slope to the Schuylkill.

Jake's park was once the province of junkies and hookers, a meeting place for the less savory side of the city's gay scene. Now it has been rehabilitated and claimed for dogs. They come not just from this neighborhood but from all over the city. Cars containing Labradors, Rottweilers, and Jack Russells park along the opposite street, their inhabitants wriggling with joy at the promised opportunity to run free.

Young mothers push strollers and call to golden retrievers, and in the early morning and at sunset a fleet of veterinary students arrive and land like geese, all accompanied by the strays they have rescued.

Jake drops his red rubber ball at my feet, his eyes bright with expectation. Looking at him, I feel a terrible pang of guilt. There is no reason for me to stay in the city. I should not have moved into the brownstone a year ago, when George and I went our separate ways. I should have moved to Bucks County, or to the Brandywine, or to somewhere out along the Delmarva Peninsula. I should have gone then, and I should go now. I should not linger and instead should summon the energy required to step forward into my brave new future. This is what others tell me and, periodically, what I tell myself. I should not wait for George, and indeed, I am not. His intentions are declared, and he has moved on, into the young and tender arms of one of his graduate students.

I know this fact, and I am surprised by how little I care. I blame this on Marina. I am quite certain that it is her revenge on me. She has reached down from whatever netherland it is that she now inhabits and pulled some plug on my life. She has opened a valve, and then she has watched as feeling and color and even pain have swirled away. Jake gives a small growl of impatience, and I reach down for his ball and throw it, watching as he races across the scrubby grass and leaps to meet it in mid-arc.

"YOU HAVE AN ADMIRER," SHAWN CROWTHER SAYS AS I come through the vestibule doors. This morning he's wearing tight black jeans and a white T-shirt with PHILLY ROCKS lettered across his chest in a purple color that roughly matches his hair. Shawn's voice is high and singsongy, and he waggles his index finger at me as if I'm a naughty child. I have no idea what he's talking about, but I don't say so, and he forgets to elaborate because Jake pounces on him and is busy sniffing the bottom of his pants and his running shoes.

"Jakey!" Shawn squeals, and Jake hops with pleasure.

Shawn is a relatively new addition to the household. I guess he's been a friend of Cathy's for a while; apparently they met at the gym where Cathy hangs out, especially during the summer because it's air-conditioned and her apartment isn't. She told me she and Shawn became "workout buddies" because he has the best abs she's ever seen. "Uuun-be-lievable!" she'd said, rolling her eyes. I think she has a crush on him, but the evidence would suggest that not much is going to come of it. Still, I suspect that Cathy lives in hope, because last month she convinced Zoe Pellier, one of the architects who owns the building, to hire Shawn as some kind of secretary. Now he seems to be ubiquitous. I almost fell over him last week when I came out of my apartment and found him on his hands and knees polishing the bottoms of the banisters, but he made up for it by kissing my hand and explaining that he was "Zoe and Justin's new wife." "I can be your fiancée, too, if you want," he'd said.

In theory, this marriage will enable Zoe and Justin to spend more time doing drafting work in the studio that they keep uptown, while Shawn does things like call the plumber and organizes what Zoe calls the quagmire of her and Justin's paperwork. In practice, however, Shawn seems to spend most of his time dusting and polishing and rearranging the mail into little alphabetical piles that he stacks on the sideboard in the entryway. This last practice has already been the cause of some controversy. According to Cathy, last week Gordon Renski, who lives in the apartment below me, accused Shawn of opening one of his credit card bills. Shawn vehemently denied it, and now Gordon glares at him on the stairs, and Shawn is prone to sticking his tongue out when Gordon's back is turned.

Even so, Zoe says Shawn is a godsend. She told me this last week, and she widened her eyes and nodded as she said it, so I assume that his job isn't in jeopardy. "I have no idea," Zoe added, "how you do your thing all alone." I assumed that by "thing" she meant my so-called business, and I refrained from sharing with her that my idea of paperwork generally runs to a series of large brown envelopes. I label them and fill them up and stick them in a drawer. I'm sure the sight would make Shawn faint.

Now he's spraying Windex on the huge gilt mirror that hangs over the sideboard, and rubbing at it with wadded-up newspaper. "I just cannot stand fly spots," he announces. He glares at them in the mirror as Jake and I start up the stairs, then he raises his eyebrows in mock horror so his tiny spikes of hair rise and fall like a crown of thorns.

"I like the new hair color," I say. As far as I can remember, last week it was kind of blue.

"You should try it," Shawn says, attacking a fly spot. "It only lasts a couple of weeks, and it doesn't even trash your hair." He looks in the mirror and grins at me. "I don't know what I'd do without Miss Clairol."

A large florist's bouquet, shrouded in plastic and tied with a bright orange bow, has been carefully laid across the landing table outside my door. "These Came For You!!!" Cathy has written in swirly letters on a yellow Post-it note. Obviously this is what Shawn was talking about, and I can imagine the thrill it must have given both of them. Cathy has arranged the flowers so prominently that even I will not be able to ignore them, and when I take them inside and open them, two sachets of Flower Fresh plop into my kitchen sink. But I can't find a card. There's no hint of their provenance. They are lilies, a dozen stems in orange and yellow and a deeper, almost brownish red. They have been carefully arranged in a cascade, the darker colors at the bottom and the paler blooms reaching up like tongues of flame.

The colors clash and are faintly disturbing. On the whole, I really don't like lilies. When Marina and I were small, Momma planted a bank of them by the garage, and they grew like weeds. Their upturned orange faces were too sharp against the chipping white paint. Once Marina said she saw a copperhead in the lilies, but I knew this was a lie. Blacksnakes lived there, and since they're the enemies of copperheads, I didn't think we could have both. Even so, when I walked by the lilies on my way to the clothesline, the plastic basket biting into my hip and my feet bare in the saw grass, I gave them a wide berth. I watched for a sudden motion, for a bobbing of their bright faces or a ripple in the forest of their leaves that stood tall in the heat and were so dark and shiny that they might have glowed with sweat.

I cannot imagine who might have sent the lilies. It seems unlikely that they are from any of Cathy's coworkers. One of them asked me out several months ago, but I was evasive and rude, and he went away with the faint and consoling impression that I might be gay. I look at the calendar over the stove, but Thursday, September twenty-eighth, means absolutely nothing to me. I start to go next door and ask Cathy if she is certain she has not made a mistake, but then I realize that she will have gone to work by now. It would be pointless in any case. Before her present incarnation as a deputy supervisor for Northwest ticketing out at the airport, Cathy flew the wide blue skies. She eventually was promoted to purser. Cathy was the smiling flight attendant who kept track of the vegetarian meals and made sure that the economy fliers weren't using the first-class bathrooms. She may be terminally perky, but she does not make administrative mistakes.

I stick the lilies in some water and pour myself a cup of coffee. Then I call Beau.

"Did you send me flowers?" I ask.

"Why would I do that?" he replies, and I can hear someone in his office. I can see him raising his hand to them, index finger up, to say "Just a minute." I can see his unruly mess of blond hair, his tweed jacket hung over the back of his chair, his loosened tie. And I feel a small pang of disappointment. Even though I don't like the lilies, I realize that I was half hoping Beau had sent them.

"I have no idea," I say, "but somebody did."

"Well, sugar, I would have if I'd thought of it," Beau says. "Have a beer with me and tell me all about it."

I don't need to ask where or even what time. It will be at seven, because the first thing Beau likes to do when he gets home from work is watch *The Simpsons,* and we only ever go to one place. It's a mediocre bar called Sherlock's that serves pallid, elongated burgers, yellow-cheese nachos flecked with bright green pieces of jalapeño pepper, and cheap beer. There is guaranteed to be no live entertainment. "Twenty-two-b Baker Street," as Beau refers to it, has the sole advantage of being about four steps from his apartment. And since Beau is terminally lazy and not filled with the spirit of adventure, I always go there.

"Well," I say, "my dance card is free."

I SEE HIM THE MINUTE I WALK IN. BEAUREGARD WEBSTER. When George told me that one of his colleagues was dating some guy called Beauregard from South Dakota and wanted to bring him to our Christmas party, I laughed out loud. I didn't know that anyone from South Dakota could be called Beauregard. I had known Beauregards and Shelbys and Camerons up the wazoo, but they all came from my side of the Mason-Dixon. Until I met Beau, I'd never even considered that you could grow up in Spearfish and be called Beauregard.

The romance with the colleague hadn't lasted more than a couple of months, but Beau had. He'd struck up a vague guy-type friendship with George and used it as an excuse to wander over to our apartment on the weekends and play with Jake. Then, when George and I split up, I got Beau, just like I got the sofa and the wok. I had always known, in some secret part of myself, that Beau liked me better than George, and besides, I had Jake. I didn't fool myself about the real nature of the attraction. But even so, I was pleased when I moved into the brownstone and found Beau on my doorstep holding two tennis balls and a six-pack of beer.

I have pushed the door open and paused, not to search among the crowd or to scan the faces but to savor the comforting smell of beer and cigarette smoke, and the babble of indistinct words and jagged lines of laughter. Beau is leaning on the bar, his heavyset frame askew as he flirts with the bartender. She is petite and butch, with a nose ring and a slight air of menace. When Beau turns and sees me, his hair falls into his eyes. He pushes it away, yanks at his already loosened tie, and treats me to the cockeyed smile that nurses in the hospital where he works find so charming. This otherwise potent weapon glances off me. One of the more useful legacies of my southern past is that I am immune to charm. God has not created the crooked smile that can twist my hard heart, and Beau knows this. Even so, he never stops trying. It's one of the things I love him for, and he knows that, too. I slide onto a bar stool, and Beau orders a pitcher of beer.

"Suuusannah," he says. "Oh Susannah, don't you cry for me."

The first swallow is cold and familiar. I take my time, drawing it out, knowing that I am not meant to look forward to this as much as I do. Beau watches me and lights a cigarette.

"So," he says, "someone sent you flowers?" I nod, liking the cool way the glass fits into my palm, watching our reflection in the wood-framed mirror behind the bar. The bartender catches my eye, glances at Beau's cigarette, and scowls in disapproval. I smile at her, reach for Beau's pack, light one, and blow a quick stream of smoke in her direction.

"So who?" he asks. "Who is your suitor?"

"No one," I say, "probably. Must be something to do with work. They're testing a new arrangement for the opening and they forgot to include a card." Actually, this idea had not occurred to me until this very moment, but it seems by far the most obvious explanation.

"How is it?" Beau asks. "Cambodia, or Laos, or whatever the hell it's called."

"Indochine," I say. "It's good."

Beau and I have laughed long and hard over my current restaurant project. It's a big and expensive job, one of those East-West fusion places where everything is gussied up with lemongrass and ginger. The tension is rising because it is due to open on the Friday before Christmas, and the contractors, who were out on strike, have only recently returned to work. The owners often send me things in the mail, swatches of material, sample menus, lacquered red chopsticks, and forget to tell me their purpose or origin. I ignore these, leaving them in sad heaps on my study floor while I continue with the finishing touches of my designs.

When the owners initially explained to me that they wanted the concept to be "steeped in the heritage of Southeast Asia," Beau suggested that they call the place My Lai. I thought that the pictures from *Life* magazine would be an highly effective motif, and Beau pondered the possible ingredients of a house cocktail called the Lieutenant Calley. The idea did not come to pass, and instead Indochine is black and white, startled by only the occasional livid burst of color. Huge lithographs of a woman who looks suspiciously like Catherine Deneuve cover the three-story dining room wall. She will gaze down on miniature plates of tempura and spiky arrangements of elephant grass and orchids.

In all likelihood, the lilies have been sent as a test run for my approval, a down-market alternative to birds of paradise. Beau begins to tell me a story about the hospital funding office that he runs, but I have become distracted. I pour myself another beer and wonder if I can make all of Indochine's waitstaff go barefoot and wear black pajamas and coolie hats.

IT IS ELEVEN O'CLOCK BY THE TIME I LEAVE SHERLOCK'S. Beau tries to persuade me to take a cab, but after a second pitcher of beer and a plate of nachos that neither of us was interested in eating, I wave him off, telling him I need the walk. At first there are people on the streets. Voices bubble around me, snatches of conversation wash up and recede. The gas lamps in front of the opera house are flickering, giving the illusion of wind on this still night, and the lights of the tall buildings are silver streaks on the sky.

As I head downtown, the streets empty. The more obvious theaters and bars cluster toward the historic district. Down here they are more discreet. They are tucked in behind the facades of the once great houses, squirreled away in storefronts, recessed beyond courtyards and awnings on the side streets. I skirt Rittenhouse Square, where at night the homeless congregate and sleep on the ornate benches that old ladies occupy by day. I can feel eyes watching me as I cross the street. For just a moment I imagine that I feel someone moving behind me, and a cold prickle dots the top of my shoulders, then I turn the corner and hear a snatch of music ahead of me.

There is a restaurant on the block that was one of my first projects. It seems dated now, but I still stop to look at it. I know that beyond the doors are bare tables, wicker-seated chairs, stainless-steel buckets of flowers, round blue plates. A group spills out onto the sidewalk, two couples with arms entwined, and with them comes a burst of light, a clatter of conversation, and the splurge of a saxophone. I walk on, heels tapping the pavement, bearing me along on the sweet, jazzing riff of the city.

My block is darker. I have passed the little antique shop, the newspaper stand, and the video store and quite suddenly the heavy familiar blocks of the brownstones rise around me. My building is the last one on the corner, and I must run the gauntlet, weave under the trees and slip from streetlight to streetlight, in order to reach it. Jake will be expecting me, and I am reaching for my keys, swearing yet again that I will clean out my bag, when the hairs on the back of my neck stand up.

It happens without warning, and the sensation is so powerful that I stop in midstride and almost lose my balance. My body tingles and goes very still. I can hear nothing beyond the dim murmur of traffic, streets away. A swath of shadows stretches out in front of me. I take two steps forward, and I am sure that I hear two steps that are not my own. I stop and they stop. I know I hear breathing. I have just passed a streetlamp, and I do not want to turn around. Suddenly I'm too afraid of what I'll see. My throat begins to close, and I cannot decide whether to spin and face the circle of light or run.

Then, one house ahead of me, a door opens and two men in jeans and polo shirts burst down the steps. A taxi whizzes down the street and stops as the lights turn to red. The men, whom I have seen before, raise their hands in greeting as they pass but do not break their stride. In my bag, my hand closes over the cool lump of my key ring, and I step forward, shaking my shoulders, letting out something like a sigh, as if I have been holding my breath.

Jake is waiting for me as I come through the apartment door, and I pause only long enough to grab his leash. The sound of footsteps seems silly now that I see Jake again. He's my shield, my magic sword. No matter how late it is or how dark, the streets never frighten me if I am with him. I am euphoric, unreasonably lit up, and biting back a powerful desire to laugh. Jake tumbles down the stairs, and as I follow him, I imagine that I can feel the house quivering with life. Soft music comes from behind Cathy's door. On the next floor down, I can hear the TV playing in Gordon's apartment. Gordon works in a bank and is deeply attached to Jay Leno. Someone has put flowers on the sideboard in the front hall, and the etched glass in the vestibule doors looks made from spun sugar.

I let Jake take his time. There is a parrot who lives in a basement apartment on Delancey, and sometimes it sits in the window and talks to people's feet as they walk by. Tonight, from behind its sheer white curtain, it talks to Jake, yammering like a fortune-teller at the fair. Jake stands on the pavement looking from me to the shadowy figure of the bird, cocking his head and raising his eyebrows in amazement. It is just before midnight when we get back, and I am standing on the balcony when the phone begins to ring.

In the pause between the shrill tones of the fourth and fifth rings, I hear the front door of the house slam closed, and a moment later Zoe and Justin appear on the sidewalk below. They are carrying neatly arranged bundles of rubbish. Tomorrow is Friday, garbage day. Anytime after midnight, black plastic bags and neatly folded newspapers and cardboard boxes may be piled on the far side of the street. There is an unwritten rule that if you have anything particularly good to get rid of, shoes or an old overcoat, leftover party food or an uneaten pizza, you do not wait for the morning but take it out the night before. You arrange these things carefully, allow them to protrude from the corners of bags, place them discreetly on altars of bottles and tin cans so that in the deepest hours of the night, they can be picked over, adopted, accepted, or rejected.

Zoe and Justin have left what looks to be a hat, a torn blanket, and a box, possibly containing food. Halfway up the street, another door opens, another couple appear bearing bags. I realize that this week I have nothing to leave, no broken-handled saucepan, worn-out jeans, or single gloves. I step back into the apartment, leaving the balcony window open, and decide I will take down the ordinary rubbish anyway; then I won't have to worry about missing the collection men in the morning.

I have tied the two bags and collapsed several wine cases and tied them with brown string when I notice the lilies. Their inky, dark leaves glisten, and for half a moment I think I see them quiver. I still have the big ribbon they came in, and I snatch them out of the vase, letting them drip on the hardwood floor while I bind their stems and crimp the edges of the bow.

Outside, Jake and I dart across the street. Other people are coming out of houses carrying boxes and bags of trash, and the atmosphere is almost festive. Jake and I place our bags beside Zoe and Justin's, and then I lay the lilies on top. I set them gently, as if they are the centerpiece at a funeral.

Back upstairs, before I close the window, I step onto the balcony again. In the shadows and under the trees, all the bags are dark lumps, but I can pick ours out. It is topped by a paint splash, by the flame-colored streak of the flowers and the burst of the orange bow. I turn away and close the window, quite certain they will find their home, that my offering will be accepted, and that long before dawn, the lilies will vanish into the night.

"AND SO?" ELENA'S VOICE COMES TO ME FROM A LONG WAY off, as though she is calling out from behind a wall or speaking from the end of a long hallway, instead of from the smooth leather armchair where she sits not six feet from me. The sleek Swedish lines of the chair do not suit Elena's bulk. The paisley of her skirt and the layered brocade of her jacket threaten to spill over its slim arms, to break free of the dour lines of tubular steel and flood across this room where we sit bounded by bookshelves and watched over by the mandatory dusty ficus tree and the smudged dirty window that looks down onto the quiet street below.

"You should get bars," I say, prying my eyes away from the window and looking at Elena. "It really isn't safe."

She smiles, her heavy, aging face creasing and bending at all of its accustomed points. "Are you still so worried, Susannah," she asks, "about safety?" There is a light in her eye, a glint of mischief as sharp as the high-pitched ring of a bell. The question is a joke, a self-parody. I am the doctor, you the patient. The cigar is not a cigar, and your slip is showing.

"Of course," I say. And I am tempted to add, "Aren't we all? Shouldn't you be?"

I have been coming to Dr. Elena Schulberg for just over a year now.

A psychotherapist of the old school, she is a genuine Viennese, the widow of a professor at Penn. She is a big woman, and in her luxurious clothes she looks like something designed and painted, an aging Klimt or the sculpture of a woman made by Gaudi. This image is enhanced by the fact that Elena often sounds like an imitation of Anna Freud. Even after years in the United States, her accent is pronounced enough to be hokey. In fact, everything about Elena could appear to be fake, a self-dramatized concoction, except that she is real. In fact, there have been times when Elena has seemed more real to me than I am to myself. Every Friday for the last thirteen months I have sat in this room and asked her to make sense of the tangles in my mind. Sometimes she has been more successful than others. Today we have been talking about one of our favorite subjects, an old saw we return to again and again. We have been discussing Marina's death.

It happened in the spring, on March 19, a Friday. In the evening, to be exact. Or at least that's what they think. That's their guess, the best they can do on the evidence, which—surprisingly, given the gruesome nature of the crime—is slim.

It was, by all accounts, a beautiful night. The moon was half full, and the air was soft and warm. Cherries would have been in blossom, their petals drifting down and landing on the cobblestones, dotting the water of newly filled fountains and the windshields of the cars parked along the streets. On a night like that, at the end of a long winter, people would have been going out, walking to the restaurants that sit on the piers along the Potomac, buying a bottle of wine, collecting a pizza, lingering on their doorsteps to sniff the air. Or so you would have thought. You would have thought that in a courtyard of fancy town houses like the one where my sister lived, people would have been around. You might have thought they would have stopped to talk, to greet one another, to comment on the flowers that had recently been set out in window boxes and stone urns. You might have thought they would have noticed a stranger. But on that count at least, you would have been wrong. Apparently they did not.

She wasn't found for several days, and by then it was hard to fix the time of death. She was seen at six-fifteen that Friday, shortly after she garaged her car. She was carrying a briefcase, wearing a suit. Her winter coat was still flung over her shoulders. She said good evening to several people, and smiled, and walked into the courtyard and, presumably, through her front door. And it was not until she did not turn up at a dinner on Saturday and the hostess in question had called five times and gotten no answer; not until she failed to appear at her job as an analyst at World Bank on Monday morning, that anyone became truly alarmed. By the time the homicide detectives of the Alexandria police force called me on Monday night, they figured that Marina had been dead for as many as three days. She fought hard, they could tell that much. But he slit her throat, and in the end he stabbed her more than twenty-five times.

I say "he," but it's a generic form. I have been assured that there is no reason to assume the killer might not have been a woman. This idea, naturally, does not go down well. Most people don't like to think of women killing other women, and especially by such a gruesome method. But nothing can be counted out.

"Everyone is concerned about safety, my dear," Elena says gently. She is not joking now. "At least everyone who thinks," she adds. "But we have to live in the world, after all, don't we? We ride the bus. We cross the road. We even walk our dogs at night. What happens if we allow our fears to govern us?"

"We become cripples," I say, rewarding her with a smile. "We become prisoners." I know these responses well. Elena nods, pleased with my progress.

"And, so," she says, "what else? What is it, Susannah, that is bothering you?"

"Nothing," I reply. "I'm sorry."

"George is back?" Elena asks. "No?"

"Yes, I guess so. I mean, I don't know." In fact I do know. I know perfectly well that he's back, because Beau has told me, and because the term has started, and that means George will be teaching again. Fresh from his year in Paris, he will stand behind the lectern and perhaps occasionally affect an accent not unlike Elena's. He has brought with him the wife he acquired on what Beau terms his "Junior Year Abroad." She is very young, and very gamine, and speaks with an accent of indeterminate European origin. Beau suspects her of coming from Oklahoma.

I know this because he ran into them on his lunch break. In the bookstore. In the philosophy section. Holding hands.

Beau was briefly introduced and insists that the wife's name is Vignette. His rendition of this story, delivered earlier this afternoon by telephone, made me laugh, which was the point. But it was also a warning. The devil is abroad, and Beau doesn't want me to be taken by surprise.

"And what do you think about that?" Elena asks. She cocks her head to one side, encouraging response. She's finding me heavy going today.

"I don't care," I say. "Really, Elena. I do not give a damn, and that's God's honest truth."

"Good," Elena says.

"It's brought things back, that's all," I say. "But it was bound to, wasn't it? I mean, everything happened when George was here, and then he was gone, and now he's back again."

"So it takes you back to what happened before he left?"

"Of course," I say. "I mean, Marina, and everything falling apart. And then the fight."

At the mention of the fight, Elena and I both smile. It was the fight that brought us together, the fight that propelled me to her door. And as usual with things like that, it was the catalyst, and turned out to be the least of my problems. Now I can smile about the fight. At the time I believed it was conclusive evidence that I was going out of my mind.

This thesis was suggested by George one August night a month before he was due to leave for his year in Paris, when he told me that I had become "as crazy as my crazy fucking sister." Shortly afterward, I slapped him. And then he slapped me back, and then I broke a lot of things that either we had purchased together or I had given him as gifts. And then he packed a bag and went to a hotel and called the next morning to tell me that I was going insane, that my rage at being left behind while he went to France for a year was conclusive evidence that he had both made the right choice in deciding to go alone and was now making the right choice in leaving me. And incidentally, he added, since Marina had been killed, and actually, probably for some time before that, I had been as crazy as a bat. Given the way I had behaved toward Marina even before she was dead, and the fact that I had refused even to speak to her on the telephone, I had probably always been as crazy as a bat. George just should have seen it earlier.

His argument had seemed persuasive at the time. Elena, having listened patiently to the details of the fight, had shrugged at the broken china and asked me about Marina. "What could you have done?" she had asked, after I told her about the knife wounds, the lack of evidence, the front door that was not forced, the blood smears that said nothing, the fingerprints that could not be matched, the startled look on the detective's face when I arrived to identify the body, and the joke I had made, asking if he needed verification that I was next of kin.

"How could you have saved her?" Elena had asked after I told her how I had stood and stared at Marina's ruined face. "What do you think you could have done?"

"Talked to her," I finally replied. "I could have talked to her."

But I hadn't. On that count, George was right. In the end, I refused even to pick up the phone.

Although we had been almost completely estranged in the years since Momma's death, in the weeks before she died Marina had tried repeatedly to reach me. The first time she called, I really was on my way to a meeting, and I spoke to her only briefly. But from the moment I heard her voice on the phone, heard her demanding my attention and my time and possibly my entire life, I felt something close to panic. I recognized the insistence in her tone, and I felt her sense of ownership, this thing she believed she held over me because my heartbeat was the same as hers. I felt it as surely as a hand laid across the back of my neck. And in that instant I knew that if I let Marina back into my life, she would nightspin her web around me until I was paralyzed.

So when she called again, I said I was too busy, or promised that I would call back. But I never did, and she kept calling. Finally I told George to say that I wasn't home, and when he wasn't there to lie for me, I stopped answering the telephone altogether.

She caught me only once, on the Saturday before she died. It was in the evening. I was making dinner. George had taken Jake to the park, and we were expecting guests. When the phone rang, I reached for it without thinking. My sister's voice was edgy, high-pitched, and angry.

"For Christ's sake!" she exploded across the telephone line. "What the hell is the matter with you? You just don't return phone calls?" A glass of wine was sitting on the counter, light glimmering off of its liquid surface, and as I reached for it, I could feel my pulse begin to hammer. "Dammit!" Marina was saying. "You can't do this! You can't block me out, and you know it. You have to talk to me!"

"No," I said, hearing my own voice, hard and flat. "No, I don't. I don't have to talk to you." There was a silence before I heard Marina's voice again. This time it was quiet. Not much more than a whisper.

"It won't do any good, Shoo," she said, and I could see the beginnings of her smile. Over hundreds of miles, I could sense the slight, twisting rise of her lips. "You know it won't do any good. You know that if I want you to, you'll hear me anyway."

And then I leaned over and pulled the phone plug out of the wall.

IT IS FOUR O'CLOCK WHEN I LEAVE ELENA'S OFFICE. I follow her down the narrow back stairs of her house and along the hall to the front door, where she lets me out onto the street.

"Remember," she says, standing on the step, her heavy hand resting on the cut glass of the doorknob, "I will be here next week, and then I am gone. To Austria, for a month."

"I won't feel abandoned," I say.

Elena goes home for a month twice a year to stay with her sister, and this is another of our jokes, that I will become an orphan, that I will seethe with quiet rage because she has abandoned me. I have read enough contemporary fiction to know that this is what patients often feel, and I have heard that when all the Manhattan therapists decamp to Long Island and upstate Connecticut for the month of August, the steaming city is populated by the grieving, the orphaned, and the angry. However, I have previously assured Elena that in my case, this is not a concern. By now I know she agrees with me, and what truly worries her is not that I will be enraged at her desertion but that I will simply forget to come again on her return; that in her absence I will drift away, will slip my moorings and float, unguided, out toward the flat plate of the horizon that is the edge of the world.

———

THE FIRST HINTS OF TWILIGHT THICKEN THE LATE AFTER-
noon as I weave my way downtown along the narrow streets of the historic district where Elena lives. It's just after five, and things are
closing. Normally I would walk from Elena's, but today I have brought
the car. I have a meeting at Indochine that even now I am late for.

The car's big engine hums, and for half a moment I close my eyes
and breathe in the comforting smell of its leather seats. I do not need
an old Mercedes-Benz. I could easily make do with a Honda, or any
number of small, fuel-efficient vehicles that would require less care,
take up a smaller and cheaper space in the garage, be easier to park. But
I love my car. I bought it from a secondhand dealer, a shyster mechanic
in a dubious part of town who assured me that it once belonged to his
mother. It is a big old sedan of the deepest midnight blue, a color that
they do not make for the American market anymore.

I pay my garage to wash the car regularly, to polish its beveled
chrome lines, wax its doors and roof and hood. I know this is vanity,
and that it may seem incongruous given how I look myself. But I am
fussy on this score. To me my car is akin to an ocean liner, large and ungainly, verging on ugly, but grand, and I treat it with all the care ac-
corded to a species on the endangered list. The garage attendants agree
with me. They are sick of rounded Saabs and tanklike SUVs. "That car
has style," one of them has told me. When they see Jake jump into the
backseat, they shake their heads in disapproval, even though he sits on
a folded blanket.

There is a parking space of sorts in the alley behind Indochine, and
I pull in beside two dumpsters full of plywood under a sign reading NO
TRESPASSING—DANGER ZONE—PRIVATE PARKING. Lolly's white Lexus has
already taken the prime spot, and I am forced to the outside, blocking
her in. This doesn't actually matter, since we'll be leaving at the same
time. There is no sign of Lolly herself, and I assume that she's already
inside talking to the construction manager and feeling superior because
I am late.

Lolly is one half of the partnership that owns Indochine, and there-

fore my employer. This is not the first time I have worked with Lolly
Bailey and Richard Thomson, who may or may not be her husband. I
am not entirely clear on the status of their personal relationship, and
they have never cared to explain it to me. They were married, or are
married, or might be about to be married. The difference to me is minimal. Bailey Thomson, Inc., pays its bills, avoids bankruptcy, and occasionally makes money, all of which could be considered a rarity in this
business. They own another city restaurant that I designed for them.
On the top floor of an old warehouse looking out on the Schuylkill, it
is a martini bar with red leather couches that serves Cal-Mex nibbles,
baby lobster tacos, crab and black bean enchiladas, and hollowed-out
limes filled with margarita sorbet. Basically it's a safe place for single
bankers and the younger Penn professors to hang out and feel they are
hip and marginally dangerous. Indochine will be Bailey Thomson's up-
scale showcase.

"Put a hard hat on," Lolly says as I approach her, sitting with the
construction manager. "We're underinsured."

She is wearing a pale pink suit that hints of a pearly dawn. The skirt
is midcalf length, a wraparound that she has made no attempt to se-
cure. Her long stockinged leg emerges from the resulting gap and ends
in a high-heeled shoe of the same pink. I have seen this before, this
predilection of Lolly's for perfectly matching footwear, and I have always assumed that she has her shoes specially dyed. I envision them two
by two, lining her closet shelves. Baby blue, pearly pink, buttermilk
yellow, they're every color of the pastel rainbow. She glances up at me
and taps her head reprovingly. Lolly likes swift adherence to the rules.
The hard hat that tops her silver pageboy is a spotless white and has the
word BOSS lettered across the front in red.

"Go look in the front room," Lolly says when I join them. The construction manager smiles at me and shakes my hand. "Lookin' sharp,"
he says, and I assume that he means the front room of the restaurant,
not the too-large hard hat that I have put on and must hold with one
hand to prevent it from slipping down over my eyes.

I leave Lolly and the construction manager, whose name I vaguely
remember as Earl, or maybe Al, in what will one day be the restaurant's
reception area, where they are absorbed in some sort of wiring dia-

gram, and pick my way down the short hall into the main dining room.
The hall makes a sharp dogleg turn at the end. I had specified this particularly, insisted on it. I pulled a minor artistic tantrum when it looked
briefly as if it might be too difficult to do. The point is that this way, the
entire back wall of the two-story room will be intact, unbroken by
doors.

The impact on turning the corner and entering the room is what I
had hoped for. There she is, my black-and-white lithographed lady.
Head and naked shoulders only, she stares out from the wall. She's
replicated eight times in her series of panels, four on top of four,
spreading from the ceiling down to six feet off the floor. The wall has
been lacquered black, and the tables and chairs, when they are set in
place, will match.

"What do you think?" Lolly asks. She has sneaked up behind me.
"Please, dear God," she adds, "tell me they got the lighting right. It cost
a fortune. If they didn't, I'll have to slit my wrists."

"They got it right," I say. "It looks good."

"She's not too creepy, is she?" Lolly has raised this question before,
as if she's mildly afraid that the woman's blank eyes will put people off
their food.

I shake my head. "No," I say. "And even if she is, by the time we get
this room finished, get the tables and chairs and the bamboo tree and
everybody in here, believe me, she'll only be background."

This seems to reassure Lolly, and we spend the next hour and a half
sitting on metal folding chairs in the reception area going over orders
for plates and cutlery. Not for the first time, I talk Lolly out of knives,
forks, and spoons with bamboo handles. I also put my foot down on the
issue of square plates. I do, however, allow her round ones in the lacquered deep red that she favors.

By the time we've reviewed the linens, it's near seven o'clock.

"I don't suppose we could hire only Asians?" Lolly asks as she
squares the edges of her papers and fits them neatly into her document
case. "No," she says, glancing at my face. "I didn't think so."

We switch out the lights, leaving on only the night lamps, and Lolly
removes her hard hat and slips it into a plastic bag. I leave mine where I
found it, lying on a trestle table by the entrance to the kitchen, which

is virtually finished and already slated for inspection. The heavy steel door that leads to the alley shuts behind us, and Lolly sets the site alarms.

"I never would have believed it," she says as she punches in the last numbers on the electronic pad, her manicured hand swift and sure, "but I think that this thing is actually going to be done on time."

"Don't jinx it."

She rolls her eyes at me. "I guess you knock on wood all the time, too," she says.

"You bet," I say. "Doesn't everyone? Don't you?"

"Susannah! I was born in Jersey. How can you be born in Jersey and be superstitious?"

By this time we are walking toward our cars, and Lolly laughs, her voice high and unexpectedly girlish. She is still saying something to me, something about sending me swatches for napkins, and I am nodding in reply as I cross the front of my car and reach the driver's door. There is a security light mounted on the building across the alley, one of those yellowish sodium lights that give the aura of eternal fog, or malaria, and throw strange shadows, so at first I do not see it. Lolly is already getting into her car when I begin to swing the driver's door open and then freeze. She looks up and sees me.

"Susannah?" she calls. "What is it?"

But I cannot answer her. I cannot move. I am embarrassed as tears begin to prick behind my eyes.

"Oh shit!" Lolly says. She is standing beside me now, and together we stare down at the beautiful, lustrous blue of my driver's door, where someone has carved deep, long scratches to engrave the single word BITCH.

"I'M NOT SURE WHAT IT IS THAT YOU EXPECT US TO DO, ma'am." The cop's voice is low, unexpectedly melodic, and accentless, as though he has been trained at a drama school or to speak on the radio. He is young, black, and handsome, and for an absurd moment I picture him playing Othello, his long-fingered hands holding Desdemona's handkerchief instead of his police notebook and a blue Bic pen.

"She doesn't expect you to do anything, she just needs the police report for the insurance," Lolly says. Her voice is shrill, and she stresses the words "do" and "insurance," as though she's said this four times before, which she has, and as though she's talking to an idiot, which she isn't. Her tone isn't lost on the cop, who glares at her and focuses his attention on me.

"You arrived at five-fifteen and didn't come out of the building again? Didn't come to get anything from your car? Until you came out at approximately seven P.M.? And that was when you noticed the door? Is that correct, Ms. . . ." He has given up on "ma'am," and his voice fades off as he hunts among the scratchings in his notebook for my name. I am beginning to feel faintly ridiculous.

"DeBreem," I say. "Susannah deBreem, and yes, that's right." I don't even know if Lolly is right about the insurance, although it has the ring of truth. Presumably, if I don't get this in writing from the police, my insurance company will posit the theory that I did it myself in order to get a new driver's door.

"A boyfriend?" the young cop is asking. "Someone you recently broke up with? Could this be personal? Someone who would have a reason to do this to you?"

"Like what?" Lolly asks. I shake my head. I can hardly believe that this is one of Cathy's friends feeling snubbed, and the idea of George creeping around back alleys in order to carve the word "bitch" in my car door is almost enough to make me laugh out loud.

"No," I say. "Look, it was probably just some kid."

Lolly is fidgeting behind me, and I want badly to get out of here. Over the cop's shoulder, I can see his partner sitting in the cruiser that they've parked on the far side of the alley. He's a big, heavyset Irishman, and he looks as though he would be pissed off with all this if he could spare the energy.

"Okay," the young policeman is saying to me. "I don't see that there's anything more we can do. I'm sorry about your car, Ms. DeBeers. We'll file the report."

"Great," I say, "thanks very much." I start to say that it's deBreem, that DeBeers is a diamond company, but it's a losing proposition, and instead I stick my hand out. When the cop shakes it, his grasp is weak, and his fingers feel floppy. He takes an awkward step back and then turns away.

"There goes Philadelphia's thin blue line," Lolly says as the cruiser slides out of sight along the canyon of the alley, leaving nothing in its place but the sickly yellow light of the streetlamp falling on brick and potholed tarmac. "I'd take you out for a drink," she goes on, "but I have to be in a meeting fifteen minutes ago. It's the symphony ladies, and if I don't get there, they'll screw up the catering for Yo-Yo Ma, and there'll be hell to pay."

For some reason, it always surprises me when I remember that Lolly is the head of a high-powered volunteer group that seems to be responsible for virtually everything that happens at the Philadelphia Symphony. Already she has opened her car door and is stretching one long, high-heeled leg toward the well of the driver's seat.

The Lexus's lights flare up in two white beams as I unlock my door, sliding my eyes over the deformed panel, trying to avoid looking too closely at it, as a lover might avoid a new scar. I back out into the alley, and Lolly whizzes past me.

After she is gone, I sit in my car without moving. There is an unnatural calm in the alley after the strobe of blue lights, the cop's questions, and the streak of the Lexus. The engine hums, and I cannot hear any other sound. I try to imagine the scrape, or was it more of a rip? I envision a sharp edge or a pointed tool running down through the layers of buffed wax and the deep blue of the paint. It bites metal and spells out a B, an I, a T, the hissing sound of CH. I imagine that if I held my hand against the letters on the car door, I could read them as if they were Braille, could read the hatred that must rise up from them and would brand my palm like a burn.

JAKE THREADS HIMSELF BACK AND FORTH AROUND ME, urgent and sinuous as a snake, nearly knocking me off my feet as I reach into the closet for his leash. While Lolly and I waited for the cops, I used her car phone to call Beau and ask him to come over and walk Jake. But there had been no answer, and clearly he didn't get my message. Now it's past eight-thirty, and Jake has been sitting alone in the darkness, waiting for me. When I open the apartment door, he rushes out onto the landing and flings himself down the stairs. I trail after him, glad that no one seems to be around. I run my fingers along the banister, trail them across the fruit and leaves carved into the newel posts. I let the leash drag behind me on the new crimson carpeting, and its heavy brass clip falls from step to step in a drumbeat.

Jake and I make our escape onto the street without being seen, but when we come back from our walk, we are not so lucky. We step into the front vestibule, and through the frosted panels of the inner doors, I can see that figures are standing in the entry hall. I can hear the sharp, high ring of Cathy's laugh. I don't know who she's talking to, whether it's Gordon or Shawn or Justin or Zoe, but I do not want to meet any of them. I am in a terrible mood, and I want to be alone. I consider retreating, dragging Jake down the steps and onto the sidewalk. But they will have seen me by now, and besides, it is way past Jake's dinnertime and I am dying for a drink.

"Hey!" Cathy says as we come through the doors, stepping from the faintly grimy marble of the vestibule onto the polished parquet of the entry hall. "How was your day?" Jake wriggles away from me and goes to greet Gordon, who is sorting through a stack of mail that is piled on the high, polished sideboard. He's thumbing through Shawn's neat piles as though he's certain that something of his is missing.

"Lousy," I say. "My day was lousy." My voice is louder than it should be. Gordon turns to look at me, and Cathy's face collapses. The words came out more harshly than I had intended. Cathy looks as if I have slapped her, as if she has made my day lousy. A swell of guilt and irritation rises in my chest. It's a familiar sensation, this resentment at the weight of other people's feelings. Elena insists, however, that the guilt is sometimes good for us. It keeps us kind, she says, when by instinct we might be otherwise.

"I'm sorry," I say. "My car door was gouged."

"Oh!" Cathy exclaims. "Oh, no. Not your gorgeous car! I love that car! Was it deliberate?"

"Yes," I say. "Very."

"You're sure?" Cathy asks. Crystals hang in the windows of her apartment, and tiny cherubs armed with bows and arrows dot her notepaper. Pointless vandalism is not part of the world that Cathy wants to believe in. "It couldn't have been an accident?"

"Not unless someone accidentally wrote 'Bitch,' no." My voice has become waspish.

"Oh my God!" Cathy says, her eyes widening. "You're kidding. In your garage?"

"No, uptown. It was my fault for leaving the car on the street."

"Wow," Gordon says.

"I can't believe that," Cathy says. "Poor you." She is anxious to offer me her sympathy, to salve my wound.

"I'm fine," I say. "It was just stupid, that's all."

The doorbell rings, and I realize that Cathy must have given up on Shawn or is hedging her bets, because she's obviously waiting for a date. The blue coat she has on is new—she came in and showed it to me when she bought it on sale a week ago—and she is wearing black trousers. Her dark hair is slick with gel, and she smells vaguely of fruit chewing gum.

"I have to go," she says, "or else we could have a drink. I'll call you!" I nod as she slips through the glass doors. Gordon and Jake and I stand listening to the rise of her voice and to the lower rumble of the man's as they greet each other and then disappear out onto the street, the heavy front doors clunking closed behind them.

"Well," Gordon says. I am not sure if he is referring to Cathy, or to my car door, or to the pile of mail he has assembled.

"Are you missing something?" I ask, nodding at the mail.

"No," Gordon says. "Just checking. After last time."

"Did he really open your credit card bill?" I'm not even sure why I'm asking this, except that I don't want to talk about the car door anymore.

"Damn right," Gordon says. "He's like goddamn Tinker Bell, all at once he's everywhere with his feather duster."

"I guess he does a good job for Zoe," I say. I can't imagine why I'm defending Shawn, unless it's because I don't like fly spots, either. Gordon makes a humphing sound, and I decide to drop it. Jake's hungry, and he's already halfway up the stairs.

"Is there anything there for me?" I ask.

"Nope," Gordon says. "Maybe the good fairy already took it up for you." I ignore this and begin to climb the stairs behind Jake. Gordon follows me.

"You know," he says, "that kind of thing, I mean that someone wrote that on your car door, that's really kind of scary." I cannot see Gordon as he speaks, and his voice rises from behind me as if broadcasted over a loudspeaker. "You're a woman in the city," the message says, "be afraid." I understand that it's well meant, but I'm already pissed off by the way he's talked about Shawn, and I feel my hackles rise.

"No, it isn't scary," I hear myself saying. "It's just really stupid and a big pain in the ass."

We have reached the first landing, and I turn around as Gordon stops in front of his door. The doors on this floor are huge. Once they must have led into the upstairs parlors and the master bedrooms of the house. Their lintels are heavy with mahogany vines, fruit, and leaves.

"Do you want a drink?" Gordon asks. Standing in front of his door, he looks momentarily dwarfed, although he is not a small man. From where I am, two steps above him, I can see the smooth wave of dark hair across the top of his head and the slightly thick set of his neck, which is still tanned from the summer and exposed where it meets the collar of his plaid shirt. He pulls his key out of his pocket and slides it into the lock without a sound. "I have a bottle of wine open," he says. And suddenly I feel bad that I've been so short with him. If I thought that somebody had opened my mail, I'd probably be nasty about it, too.

I hesitate. I have glimpsed the front room of Gordon's apartment on the odd occasion when I have been passing and he has left the door ajar. I have seen the large bowed window with the mahogany window seat and caught sight of the side of the fireplace, which is of the same carved wood, dark and masculine, and utterly different from my apartment's delicate moldings and moss greens and grays. I imagine the feel of the wineglass in my hand, the half-hushed music from the stereo. Then I remember that Gordon would be there, too, and that I would have to make conversation and behave myself. I decide I prefer my bad mood and go up another step.

"Thanks," I say, "but I have to feed Jake." Gordon looks at me, and I can feel my face getting hot. Then he nods and steps inside, and without a sound the heavy door swings shut.

"Dr. Doom has a crush on you."

The words float down from above, and at first I can't tell where they're coming from. Then I look up and see Shawn's face. He appears disembodied, as though he's become one of those cherubs that the Renaissance painters were so fond of, nothing but wings and a head hovering above me.

"What are you doing up here?" I ask, and I wonder how much of the conversation he heard.

He ignores my question and grins at me. "Want some popcorn?"

I can see that the door to Cathy's apartment is open, and I smell the fake buttery scent of microwave popcorn.

"My TV's dead, and Cathy, bless her little heart, said I could use hers," Shawn explains. "Don't worry," he adds. "I'll lock up on my way out. Cathy gave me keys. I got your mail." He bounces back into Cathy's apartment and reappears a second later with a copy of *Architectural Digest* and a couple of bills. "Great article on the Georgians in Dublin," he says as he hands me the magazine and the envelopes. "I knew you wouldn't mind if I peeked."

I start to say that I do mind, actually, but it seems too petty, even for me, and so instead I reach for my keys. Jake is sitting at our door, looking at me beseechingly.

"There's a *Star Trek* marathon on 56," Shawn adds, glancing over his shoulder into Cathy's apartment, "but my guess is you're probably not a Trekkie."

IN MY EARLIEST MEMORY, I AM LOST. BEFORE THIS I RE-member fragments, a door, a window, a patch of color. But this is my first real memory, the first whole story where I played a part. We must have been on a picnic, or on one of Momma's excursions. These were typically trips to a battlefield or a state park. Momma and my grandmother would sit on a blanket on the grass and eat sandwiches, and Uncle Ritchie would bring a portable deck chair of yellow webbing, and his fishing line, and the tin cash box where he kept lures, and pieces of wire, and cutters, and the tiny flies he made from tufts of feather.

I do not remember exactly where we had gone that day, but I do remember the heat, because at lunch Marina and I had had a fight over which of us should get the last cup of the lemonade that Momma had made fresh that morning and put in the cooler with plenty of ice cubes and slices of sugared lemon. We had both refused to share, insisting on all or nothing, and the fight had nearly reached the hair-pulling stage when Uncle Ritchie settled it by flipping a coin. Marina chose heads, and I chose tails, and I won. I drank the lemonade in one long gulp, and then I licked the sugar off the lemon and slurped out all the pieces of pulp right in front of her.

Later, when everyone had finished eating and the grown-ups had fallen asleep, I wandered off by myself. I remember that one of my feet hurt, as if I had a stone in my shoe or had been bitten by a spider, and I sat down. I bent my head back, and the light seemed to spin above me. I could smell pine and the soft scent of scrub grass. There was no suggestion of fear in this perfect moment, just a sense of weightlessness, and I know now that what I felt but could not then name was freedom. Reveling, I watched the patterns of light above me, the fractured lines of blackness and the greens that twinkled and revolved like stars.

Then, suddenly, the world went still. The light stopped dancing. The boughs of the trees grew thick and heavy, and the sun turned white. It was very hot, and all at once I knew that if I got to my feet and started to run, I would not know which direction to go in order to find my mother.

I sensed Marina's presence like a smell, and when I looked around, I saw her standing in the forest, not four feet from me. She was wearing a yellow T-shirt and the same pink shorts that I had on, and the same pink dime-store sneakers with beads tied into the laces. Utterly immobile, she was framed by the undergrowth that brushed at her bare arms and legs. We were five or six at most, and my sister's face was narrow and freckled, her hair tied back in a neat ponytail. She was staring at me the way a cat stares at a bird that is wounded: with great interest and a significant measure of detached malice. I wanted to say her name, but the words dried out and died in my throat.

"They all love you better," Marina said quite clearly. "But I hate you." And then she turned back into the bushes and was gone.

I was screaming when my mother and grandmother found me. I had worked myself into a frenzy, and although I was probably not more than a hundred yards from them, I had been unable to find my way back. Frantic, I had thrashed at the bushes, scratching my arms and face. I had lost one of my pink sneakers and was streaked with dirt. "Shoo Fly, Shoo Fly," I can hear my mother say. And I can still smell the sweet scent of her bath soap as she wiped my face with the edge of a napkin dipped in ice water and smoothed the tangled hair from my eyes.

THE YELLOW SWATCH OF WATERED SILK THAT I AM WORKing with is exactly the same color as the T-shirt Marina was wearing that day. I did not realize it until now, until I held it up here against the paper of this color board that I am composing, and saw that it was not warm and golden, as I had hoped, but sharp, a thin sunshine yellow. Looking at it, I hear Marina's voice. It is clear, as a child's voice is, but each of her words is as complete as a pebble dropped into a glass of water. I. Hate. You. It was quite dispassionate, obviously something that she had considered. She never said it to me again, but I never got the feeling that she was sorry, either. Neither my tears, nor my subsequent hysteria, nor the loss of my pink sneaker had moved her.

The color board is my first gesture toward the project that will follow Indochine. It is a tea garden, a glass-topped pavilion in the courtyard of a small museum where students in black leather jackets and ladies who appreciate art can purchase herbal infusions by day and white wine by night. I have put off working on it for so long that I am behind with the designs, and I cannot procrastinate any longer. Such is the faith of the board of directors that they gave me carte blanche, so I have no one to blame but myself for the yellow, which was entirely my idea. I wanted to pair it with mint greens, with something cool and faintly Edwardian. The result is a failure. The swatches of material and blobs of paint remind me of nothing so much as waterlogged petals or colonies of algae, things that grow and float on dead water.

I reach for my glass, realize that it is empty, and get up to pour myself another drink. My back and my knees are stiff, as if I have been exerting myself or just sat through a long flight. I drop three ice cubes into my glass and swirl them in the amber whiskey, listening to the satisfying cluck-cluck they make as they knock against one another. Returning to the living room, I silently curse Marina.

There was nothing wrong with my design. I had been happy with my colors until she emerged in her child's T-shirt and gazed upon me from the shadows, dropping her words like stones. Now I will have to start over. I will have to find a combination, a pattern and colors, that Marina has no claim on.

"Crazy," I say out loud. Anger boils up in me. It rises through my body like mercury, burning until I have to blink in order to focus, have to take a breath and step back. I close my eyes, take a deep swallow of the Scotch, and the phone rings.

My reaction is so fast that I am not even aware of it. It's as if something inside of me is exploding. I don't know if it's midnight, or ten-thirty, or one A.M., but I grab the receiver from my desk and scream into it, "Leave me alone!" And then I send the phone sailing across the room. It hits the arm of the couch and bounces back onto the thick pillows.

I am shaking all over, trembling with rage and surprise. The Scotch has spilled out of the glass in my hand and is running down my wrist, and I am staring at the phone as if it is a living adversary. When I go to pick it up I hear a voice coming out of it.

"Susannah? Susannah?" the voice is saying. "For Christ's sake, are you there?" It's Beau.

"Yes," I say, raising the phone to my ear. "I'm here."

"What in God's name is going on?" asks Beau. "Are you okay?" A moment passes before I say yes. And then I add, "I thought you were someone else."

"Who?" Beau asks.

"I don't know," I say.

Beau clears his throat. "Well, then," he says, "do you want some Chinese food?"

Ever since I moved into the brownstone, Beau and I have kept keys to each other's apartment. We assure ourselves that this equal access is necessary in order to subvert disaster. What we have in mind is heart attack, epileptic fits, fire, sudden death. I read an article once about a woman who choked on a plum stone and lay dead for a week. In the wake of George's departure for Paris, I occasionally viewed my new apartment as a potential mausoleum. It was this as much as anything that drove me to surrender a set of my keys to Beau, who suggested that I steer clear of unpitted fruit.

In reality, our comings and goings have been more geared to the collecting and depositing of mail, and to the occasional delivering of dry cleaning, than to emergency intervention. The greatest beneficiary has been Jake, whom Beau often walks or feeds if I am held up with Lolly or kept late working at a site.

Therefore, rather than hearing the front door buzzer, I learn of Beau's arrival from Jake's squeal of welcome, followed by the distinctive smell of Chinese food. Then Beau himself is leaning around my kitchen door. He thrusts a large brown paper bag toward me and says, "Beware of hospital administrators bearing Kung Pao chicken."

We spread the white cartons across the kitchen counter and perch on my two high stools. We swing our feet in the air, like children at a soda fountain. Yellow and orange patches blossom on the sides of boxes that hold pineapple shrimp and chicken. Beau picks one of them up and roots in the bottom with his chopsticks. He reminds me for all the world of a cartoon bear peering into a discarded can.

"So you don't know who the creep is who calls?" Beau asks. After shrieking at him on the phone, I have been forced to tell him about the phone calls and about what has happened to my car door. It seemed thinner in the retelling, filled with the potential for self-dramatization.

"Nope," I reply. "I don't even know if it's the same person. They don't always call, either. This week they've slacked off."

"He, she, it hasn't called tonight?"

I shake my head, and as if on cue, we both turn to look at the wall clock, which reads twelve-twenty. If the telephone was in the room, we would probably stare at that, too, but it isn't, so we can't. Instead Beau puts down the sticky container and reaches for my beer.

"That's mine!" I say.

"I know," he replies, and winks at me. "What about star—six—nine?" he asks, making it sound like a game-show introduction.

I shake my head. "I tried that once, but I got a weird tone that the operator says means the line is blocked."

Beau shrugs. "Well, I guess if I was into making pervert calls, I'd block my line, too," he says. "Actually, you can buy those things at Radio Shack for twenty bucks. They're called the Phone Zzzapper or something. They work on caller ID, too."

"How do you know?" I ask.

"It's the kind of cool stuff that cool guys like me know," he says. "What you should do is change your number."

"I know," I say, "I know. But everybody I know has this number, and so do all the contractors and everybody from work." I get up and get myself another beer from the fridge, since Beau is drinking mine.

"Excellent point, Watson," Beau says. I flip the cap off the bottle and throw it at him.

"I figure they'll just get bored," I say. "Eventually."

"It's a telemarketer gone berserk," Beau announces. He considers this, rolling the neck of the beer bottle between his palms. "I love the word 'berserk.' " Then he treats me to his best grin. "Suuuusannah," Beau asks, "if I walk the dog, can I get really drunk and sleep on your couch?"

BY THE NEXT MORNING HE IS GONE, VANISHED AS IF HE never was. The dishes are scrubbed clean of duck sauce, and of the gummy shreds of dumpling and the bits of hardened rice. "Dog fed," says a note taped to an empty can of Alpo on the counter. "If he says otherwise, he lies." A similar note is taped to Jake's leash, which has been looped through the handle of the refrigerator door. It says, "Dog walked." Both of the notes are illustrated, and I study them as I pour my first cup of coffee. On the first note, a stick-figure dog eats a hamburger that he holds between his front paws. On the second, a stick-figure man and dog walk arm in arm while a round child's sun shines overhead.

I don't find the third note until I go to rub Jake's stomach as he lies on the living room rug. I come face-to-face with the square of paper as I bend over. This one is taped onto the pillow that Beau used, which is in turn on top of a neatly folded Hudson's Bay blanket that I bought long ago on a college trip to Montreal. A stick-figure man is jumping in the air. "Thanks!" the note reads, and then, "Don't forget—church concert tonight—7:30."

I had forgotten. Beau has never invited me to go to a church service with him, and even if he did, I would not want to go. Every day as a child, I sat on the school bus and read the billboard on the road into Petamill, Georgia, and I still do not think that Jesus saves. The church concerts, however, are an exception to my rule of abstinence.

Beau's choir gives three a year, and every time he sings a solo, and every time I go to hear him. I have a routine now. I linger outside the door until the music starts, and on the first strains of the organ, I slip inside. Sitting in the back pew in half darkness, I raise my eyes to the lurid stained glass above the altar, where a yellow-haired Christ tends his lambs on a pasture of neon green. The choir begins, and I tap my foot to the familiar words. "Rock of ages cleft for me." "The Lord is my shepherd." Then I wait for the moment when Beau steps forward, his ungainly bulk shrouded in the sky-blue nylon of his choir robe, and as he reaches the lectern and draws himself up, I close my eyes. Sometimes I think I hold my breath until I hear Beau's voice, and then I feel it lift me up, and I surrender. As Beau sings, I rise beyond the dull gray walls of the church. I let him carry me away, and we spiral above the city, borne upward on his soaring, hopeful notes of praise.

CHAPTER 6

"SO HOW THE HELL DID THIS HAPPEN?"

It is as much a statement of outrage as a question, and Benjy scowls at me over his shoulder when he asks it, as if I might have taken a screwdriver and done it myself. His dark, beetle-browed face compresses into a frown, making him look fierce, like the Billy Goat Gruff in a fairy tale. I shrug, but Benjy has already turned back to the car. He bends down, examining the door and muttering to himself. The garage smells of oil and the black sludge at the bottom of the Mr. Coffee machine on Benjy's old wooden desk. A stack of semiclean-looking Styrofoam cups sits beside the machine, and I consider helping myself but then think better of it. I am mildly hungover after last night's Chinese-food fest, and I am not sure if the thick toxic liquid would kill me or cure me.

"I don't know how it happened, exactly," I say. Although I have a pretty good idea. The mechanics of the act, the how and the what, so to speak, are not terrifically difficult to figure out. "I've parked it there before," I add, as if this is some measure of self-defense. Benjy sold me this car, and he takes its well-being personally. "Can you fix it?"

"No, I can't fix it." Benjy straightens up and wipes his hands down the front of his coverall, which is so filthy that it's hard to imagine what it might have once looked like. It is the only thing I have ever seen him wear, and while I suppose that Benjy must have clothes on underneath, I can't swear to it. "What I can do," he says, "is try to find you a new door, but it'll take a while."

"How long?" I ask. The idea of being without my car makes me feel stranded and vaguely panicky.

"I dunno. It's vintage, and it's not the easiest color in the world to match. And it'll cost, Miss Cheap." I'm not sure exactly what I've done to deserve this nom de guerre; probably just coming to him in the first place instead of going to what Lolly would call a "real" garage. Benjy has few illusions about the nature of his establishment. He goes to the desk and pours himself a cup of coffee, then pours a second one and hands it to me. It's lukewarm and feels furry against the roof of my mouth.

"Where's Jake?" Benjy asks, sitting down in a chair with wheeled feet and scooting himself backward toward a dented filing cabinet that is stacked with phone books. I point out that I have to take a cab back, since I presumed he would be keeping the car.

"So cabbies won't take mutts?"

"Not big ones, no."

Benjy considers the injustice of this before he digs a pair of thick-rimmed glasses out of his pocket and perches them on the end of his nose. The heavy black lines of the frames make him look like a cartoon character. Regarding him over the edge of my coffee cup, I imagine that I have drawn the glasses onto Benjy's face with a Magic Marker and that I could lean forward and add a mustache, or pointy ears, or small curly horns.

"All right," he says, "so in the meantime, until I can match up the door for you, I'm gonna put a new one on. I know you get jumpy without your wheels, and you can't drive around town with that written on the side of your car, people'll think you're a pervert. It won't look great, but I'll try to find a dark color until we come up with the real McCoy."

"Thanks," I say.

"For you, doll, anything." Benjy winks at me. "What can I say? My mother was a redhead."

I finish the coffee and drop the cup into a trash can that is filled with balled-up candy wrappers and Dr Pepper cans. Benjy has already embarked on his search for a 1972 Mercedes door. He's ferreting through a pile of papers and reaching for the wall phone that lurks behind an outsize NASCAR calendar. He waves to me, and just before I leave, I ask, "Do you see a lot of this kind of thing?"

"All the time, doll," Benjy says. "All the time." I'm not sure if this reassures me or not, and I think it over as I step outside into the afternoon sunshine.

I have to walk almost as far as the museum before I see a free cab, and by the time I've gone that far, it seems pointless not to walk all the way. It's Saturday, and the city is busy in a different way than usual. People are out on the streets, but they're wandering, slowed down, feeling the last of this warm autumn sun on their shoulders. The parking lot of the big new Fresh Fields supermarket is jammed. A couple of cars cruise around like predatory fish, waiting for spaces to open up, and a child squeals as his mother loads him into a cart and pushes it, running, toward the sliding door.

I pass by the small, solid block of the Rodin Museum and come up short, stopped by a river of traffic. A flock of runners pound along the opposite sidewalk. They're all guys, six or eight of them. From the easy way they bunch together, you can tell they're office mates, friends, a set of buddies who egg one another on and together fight the dreaded paunch and the first gray hairs. George used to run with a group like that, a covey of the suddenly not so young professors from the university. Every Saturday morning he would leave just before ten, yelling to me from the front hallway as he laced up his shoes, the last words muffled as the sweatshirt went over his head, and cut off altogether as the door slammed.

These guys are lawyers or bankers, though. They're better dressed than the Penn professors. I can see their mouths move as they talk, passing words back and forth, laughing, until the light changes and the cars come to a halt. Then the men move forward in one compact body. At the same moment, I step off the curb into the street. We meet, and they divide and flow around me. As they pass, I hear laughter and smell the slight mingled scents of aftershave and sweat.

———

THE SHADOWS LENGTHEN THROUGH THE AFTERNOON UNTIL the tree that spreads above my balcony casts a long, dark pattern that falls like a spiderweb through the window and onto the living room floor. Jake is snoring. It's a comforting sound, a soft, slow drawing in and out of breaths that shudder at the end, as if he cannot quite bear to let them go. He occasionally yips in his sleep and scrabbles his paws against his bed in a little running motion that sounds like mice. I watch him as I stand with the laundry basket balanced on my hip. Earlier in the day, I gave him a long run in the park, and now he is so peaceful, so absorbed in his dreams, that I tiptoe away and slip through the door without him, turning the handle slowly, so the latch falls silently back into place.

The lamps on the landings have not been turned on yet, and the frosted panes of the stairwell skylight seem to glow. I can hear music playing in Cathy's apartment, a soft thud-thud overlaid with the tinkle of piano keys. Far below me, Zoe crosses the entryway, and her heels clack on the parquet. She calls out the beginning of a question to Justin, and the words are lost as she goes inside and the door of their apartment swings shut. Gordon is listening to the TV, or to the radio, I am not sure which as I pass his door and make my way downstairs, my slippered feet whispering on the carpet.

The laundry room is in the basement, down a warren of corridors that run under the house and converge on a metal door that leads into the back garden. The half window of the door is crisscrossed in wire mesh, and though we all have a key to it—so in theory we may bring our bicycles and skis and boxes in and out—I cannot remember ever seeing it used. Now, as I stand at the top of the steep stairs that lead from the entryway down into this Minotaur's maze, I see that the lights are already on, and I can hear the swoosh and growl of the washer and dryer. I hold the laundry basket out in front of me, which means that I cannot reach for the banister and must feel my way, lowering each foot in turn, swinging it back and forth, dusting for the hard surface of every narrow step.

At the bottom of the stairs, a hatchlike doorway is set halfway up the wall. On my inaugural tour of the house, Zoe informed me that it was a laundry chute. A whole system of chutes runs through the walls of the house, and they are wide enough to hold a small child. Zoe showed them to me with great pride, pointing them out as part of the house's collection of period features. She assured me that they had not been blocked up, that domestic authenticity was still intact in the wake of restoration, and that each of the original bedrooms still had a hatch similar to this one, a mouth that once swallowed soiled sheets and damp bath towels and spat them out down here. The one in my bedroom is behind the bathroom door, but I have never opened it. It is tastefully painted to match the molding, and I imagine that if I shouted down it, or even whispered, anyone standing in the subterranean hallways could hear my voice.

I am tempted to put down my basket of dirty socks and jeans and lift the iron door of the laundry hatch. Perhaps I could hear Gordon's TV. I could shout back up the chute in French or pig latin and make him blink, spin around, wonder at the voices. I smile at the idea, but then the noise of the washer rumbles and dies, and I turn away from temptation, realizing that I must seize my moment or lose the opportunity to Cathy's towels or Zoe's Marimekko sheets.

A bare bulb hangs in the long corridor. Its lack of any shading is another of Zoe's gestures toward authenticity. The end of the hallway disappears in shadows, and I can just make out the square of dim light that is the window in the garden door. I take only a few steps toward it before turning right down another passage, then left into the windowless box of the laundry room. A year ago, when I first moved in, I wondered if I should leave a trail of bread crumbs when I came down here, or tie a scarlet thread to the bottom of the banister in order to find my way back, but over time I have grown fond of the basement. Now I think of it as the honeycomb, the secret terrain of the worker bees who labored here, who once scrubbed and mended amid shadows and ugliness, so delicacy and fine manners might flourish above them.

The bulbs in the laundry room do not have shades, either. There are three of them, and they are each at least a hundred watts. I stand in the doorway and blink, wondering if Whirlpool white enamel can induce snow blindness. The strength of the bulbs suggests Cathy's handiwork, and so do the new folding laundry table, the iron, and the bottles of spray starch ranged along the ironing board. "Anyone can use these!" a Post-it note stuck to the wall says. A smiley face beams out from below the exclamation mark.

In light of this generosity and goodwill, I have no choice but to be helpful. I take a load of pink and baby-blue towels out of the dryer and dump them on the table. Then I transfer the white wash that has just finished into the warm drum of the dryer. I stuff my own washing higgledy-piggledy into the machine and pour in the detergent, deliberately ignoring the manufacturer's advice and handy measuring scoop. I do plan to fold the towels, but first I peruse the various dials on the machines, wondering if the air supplied to delicate is really warm enough, and if cold will actually clean my clothes. I make my decision and am leaning over, about to push the appropriate buttons, when the lights go out.

At first the darkness freezes me. Like a sci-fi character hit with a stun gun, I'm stuck on my tiptoes, bent across the washing machine with my arm thrust aimlessly into pitch black. It is so dark in the room that I cannot see even my own hand. I withdraw it slowly and rock back onto my heels, placing my slippered feet fully on the stone floor. I straighten up, and then, although I cannot actually see it, I turn instinctively toward the door. And that is when it happens. My shoulders tense. My fingers go stiff. The back of my head is suddenly cold and feels electrified. I am not alone. Someone is standing in the doorway.

My first impulse is to close my eyes, to play possum, to block out this world. But I can't. Instead I am riveted, staring and unable even to blink, as if I do not dare take my eyes off of what I cannot see. The person is facing me. I know it as surely as if there is a taut string running through the space between us, carrying the vibration of a heart. A surging sensation pulses through me, and at the same time my muscles lock and turn solid. This is what it must be like to die of electric shock, to feel voltage coursing through you and yet be unable to move.

I don't know if I am breathing. I'm not sure because I can't hear anything. I'm suddenly conscious of the fact that there's not a rumble of traffic, not a drip of water, not even the whisper of breathing. The air between us is thick, and I cannot draw it into my chest. There is not so much as a glimmer or reflection of light, but I know with absolute certainty that if I could force my feet to move, if I could step forward and stretch out my hand, my fingers would travel through nothingness and meet the density of human flesh.

We stand there for seconds or minutes, I don't know, and when the noise does come, it is just a rustle. It is so small and so slender that it might not exist, except that I know now the doorway is empty. Then, from the hall, I hear something else. Slow and very deliberate, it is the sound of humming. The voice caresses the tune. It is high-pitched and faintly mocking, and it takes each note and lingers over it, making it full and fat, before releasing it and moving on. Leisurely and insistent, the voice takes its time. It rolls out the little song, allows it to swell, pushes it to become louder and louder, stronger and stronger, until I scream.

My eyes are closed tight, and the screams go on until they are broken by the sound of running feet, by clattering and bright lights. I hear Cathy's voice and feel someone trying to put his arms around me. But I push the arms away. I can't be touched. I am doubled over.

People shout my name, and finally, when the screaming slows and draws itself out to nothing but an embarrassing gasp, I hear a babble of voices, Cathy's, Zoe's, Gordon's, and Justin's. They have all come running. They are all here, gathered around me in the too-small laundry room, jostling the ironing board, tipping the folding table, knocking the towels and the bottles of spray starch onto the floor.

When I tell them what has happened, they look back and forth at one another. And then Justin and Gordon search the basement. They carry a tire iron and a hammer. They tell us that they opened old cupboard doors, looked behind bicycles and skis, forced themselves to walk into the ancient meat locker and to stand underneath the iron hooks where hams and dead birds were hung a hundred years ago. What they found is that the door to the garden was open.

It was not wide open, Gordon says. It was just cracked; only a thin line of light down its edge gave it away. It was as if someone took his time, was leisurely about departure, careful to pull the door closed.

The police come, but not for an hour and a half. On a Saturday night in the city, an open basement door is not a priority. No one can remember quite when it was used last, and no one can swear to turning the locks. At some point Justin swept leaves off the patio, and Zoe planted bulbs. But both of them thought they had used the doors that open from their own living room onto their sliver of a deck with its four little steps. Cathy remembers seeing them out of her window, but she cannot say on which day, or which door they might have used, or even if it was last week or the week before that.

"Garden wall," the policeman says. This time he is white, tired, and middle-aged. "Any kid could climb that garden wall." He suggests that we consider a roll of razor wire, and Zoe scrunches up her face in disgust. Or possibly broken glass. We could break wine bottles and slather cement along the top of the old brick wall and stick the pieces in. Then the shards, brown and bottle green, would stick up like rotting fangs, their tips showing above the climbing rose and the grapevine that Zoe plans to plant. Twice the policeman asks if I could identify the suspect, and twice I have to say no. Twice I have to tell him that I saw nothing.

"Then how do you know someone was there?" the policeman asks.

"I heard them," I reply. "After they stood in the doorway, I heard them humming."

The policeman writes this down and shakes his head. "In the future," he says, "be more careful with that door."

THE BLANKET THAT I HAVE WRAPPED AROUND ME NOW IS old. It is crocheted, a pattern of gaudy flowers in the bright oranges and cheap greens of acrylic wool. I push my fingers through the holes in the weave, and when I bring the material up close to my face, I smell mothballs and the vague, musty scent of things locked away in suitcases. My grandmother made this blanket. It is one of a dozen that she hooked and gave to us. They lay over the back of every chair, along the arm of every sofa, across the beds in the house that Marina and I grew up in. It is phenomenally ugly, and I do not know why I kept it. Since Chapel Hill, it has stayed in the bottom of my suitcase. Tonight, if I stretch out my arms, it hangs from my shoulders like a cape.

I have called Beau. I left him a message saying that something had come up, lying and making it sound as if I have urgent work to attend to. He will not call back tonight. I have told him not to, led him to believe that I will not be here. He will go to his party after the concert and drink beer and eat chips with a clear conscience, sure that he is not abandoning me.

Gordon offered to walk the dog with me, obviously longing to extend the wing of his protection over me, but I would not let him. I dug my hand into Jake's ruff, ran my fingers along the saddle on his back where the hackles rise, and told Gordon that I had my guardian. Earlier I had accepted Zoe's tea, and later, Cathy's wine. Now I am sated with concern, and all I want is to be alone.

It is past midnight now, and the phone will not ring. I walked Jake early, at eleven-thirty. I made sure I was back in time, just in case. Tonight, of all nights, I wanted to answer. I wanted to shout into the telephone, to scream that I refuse to be cornered like this. But no call came, and as the hours pass, my anger has faded into fear.

Sitting on the sofa, my hideous flowered wings wrapped around me, I replay the darkness. I wonder if I heard the flick of a light switch. If there was the faint sound of a footstep that I have forgotten. If I had turned, spun away from the dials, in the second before the lights went out, would we have come face-to-face?

My own bottle of wine is almost empty, and I cannot sit still any longer. I gather the blanket and stand up. I walk carefully, counting eight steps to the carpet's edge, and then four steps beyond to the cool of the windowpane and the gray of my balcony. Its colors shift in the mottled shadow of the tree and the city lights. I turn and count six steps back to the phone that will not ring, to the question that no one asked.

"Where were you?" the policeman asked, and "What time was it?" and "Were you alone?" and "Do you know who it was?"

He asked me all those things. But there is one question that he forgot.

"Humming, Miss deBreem?" the policeman had said, and I nodded, holding my breath. But he never thought to ask the next question. He never thought to ask me if I recognized the tune.

And I did. Until this afternoon, I had not heard it for over twenty years, but even so, I could sing it now. I could sing it just the way I remember it, in that same high southern voice of my childhood. "Shoo, fly," the words go, "don't bother me. Shoo, fly, I belong to somebody."

CHAPTER 7

THE TOUCH OF HIS SKIN HAD BEEN COOL AND UNEXPECT-
edly smooth when he shook my hand. A moment later, when he passed
me his card, I noticed that his nails were pale and clipped. I had noticed
his cuffs, too. They were bright white and stiff with either starch or the
sizing that comes in men's shirts. I remember thinking that altogether,
he looked too clean for his job.

"Homicide Division, Special Detective Mark Cope," the card says.
Embossed above the words is the seal of the city of Alexandria, and at
the bottom of the card, in the small, scratchy letters of Special Detective Mark Cope's handwriting, are the numbers of both his office extension and his home telephone. "You call me," he said when he handed
it to me on the day of Marina's funeral, "Miss deBreem, if there is anything at all that I can do for you." He had been the officer in charge of
the investigation into Marina's death, and I could tell even then that he
felt bad. That he had no words of reassurance to give me.

I have considered Special Detective Cope's offer over and over
again since I took the card out of the envelope where I've kept it for the
last eighteen months. Now I pick it up and bend it back and forth, as if
the feel of it in my hand will suggest to me what I should do. At times
his invitation seems more attractive than others. At times I imagine that
he could rescue me. And then I stop and ask myself, "From what?" Will

Special Detective Cope rescue me from a telephone that rings and a caller who does not speak? Will he save me from the word "bitch"? Will he defend me against a nursery rhyme? And how, exactly, am I supposed to tell Special Detective Mark Cope of the Alexandria Homicide Division about what I heard last night in the basement?

I loosen my fingers and let the card fall to the floor. It flutters, drifts like a snowflake on the way down. I have had far too much to drink. My mind feels soft and blurry at the edges, and the sharpness of everything, even the terror that I felt in the laundry room, is dulled. Only a few things still stand out. "We're the nightspinners," I hear Marina's childhood voice say. And then I hear her again, but this time she is older. "You know it won't do any good, Shoo," she whispers. "You know that if I want you to, you'll hear me."

"Marina is dead." I say it out loud, and I like the sound of the words. They have a shape and form of their own. They are tangible, and I can reach out and hold them in my hand. Marina is dead, and there are no such things as ghosts. "No such things," I say.

I am repeating assurances that were offered on a regular basis by both my mother and my grandmother, neither of whom believed in the shining, or in spectral figures of Confederate soldiers, or in any of the other stories I heard when I was ten, and eleven, and twelve. In the summer twilight, groups of kids would gather in the haylofts and the shadows of the barns and trade ghost stories before running home across the fields, giddy with fear.

"Nonsense," my mother would say when I woke with nightmares, when I ran along the hall in my bare feet and begged her to let me climb up into her high bed and seek sanctuary there for the night. "Nonsense," she would repeat even as she pulled back the soft linen sheet and let me climb in beside her. "I don't understand, Shoo," she would say, stroking my hair, "where these nightmares come from. You know those stories are silly." And I would nod, letting her believe that it was some stupid story of Della Hervey's or Sonny Delray's about a headless cavalry rider, or a ghostly slave that had awakened me and left me staring into the dark, heart hammering, while Marina lay still as death in her bed across the room.

I pull Grandma's blanket around me, covering myself with her flowers, and listen for the echo of my mother's voice. "There are no such things as ghosts," she says. I lie down on the couch, and my head hits the soft pile of cushions with a poof as their down collapses. In the corner, Jake shifts and stretches and falls asleep again. "There are no such things as ghosts," Momma says. "There are only memories, and they cannot hurt us."

WE MUST HAVE BEEN FIFTEEN IN THE SUMMER OF THE fires. They began, I think, in May or June, and at first they were so inconsequential, so likely the result of dry lightning strikes or of courting couples throwing still-lit cigarette butts out of car windows, that no one paid them much attention. They were just circles of hot orange light and blossoms of white smoke that punctuated the early-summer nights. And they seemed to disappear before the fire engine was ever called, and to leave nothing but a round devil's footprint blackening the corner of a local farmer's field.

By July they had become frequent enough to elicit comment from the fire chief, who was also our school principal, and he wrote a column in the *Petamill Times,* warning his students to be careful and urging farmers to keep a sharp eye out for wandering strangers or hippies who might be camping in the woods. The fires became a topic of conversation, and as the weather grew hotter and the nights thickened into full summer, people grew jumpy. After dark they took to peering out of their windows, to scanning their fields or the back lines of their woods for anything brighter or larger than a firefly. And by August, as the fields dried and the rains stopped, farmers began to sleep with one ear listening for the low, cackling laughter of spreading flames.

Yet the fires were infrequent enough that it was still possible to dismiss them as a series of accidents, to think of them as nothing but a strange chain of coincidence. One of those inconvenient flukes of nature, like a year of heavy ticks or a fall when too many deer get hit on the road. This theory was backed up by the fact that no real damage was ever done, until the morning when the Eameses' barn burned to the ground.

In other circumstances, that barn fire might have been a routine kind of tragedy, the sort of thing every farm both necessarily courts and dreads. But in the edgy atmosphere of that summer, and in light of what happened afterward, the fire seemed to take on special significance, as if it were a climax that we had all somehow been expecting.

I was never sure, even at the time, which came first, the acrid whiff of smoke on the heavy August air or the screech of the farm whistle that meant somebody on our road was in trouble. What I do remember is that it was hot, and that a faint uncharacteristic breeze ruffled the heart-shaped leaves of the lilac bushes and ran its hand across the tops of the alfalfa that was just coming into second crop in Uncle Ritchie's front field.

Momma and I were in the vegetable garden that ran out from the side of the house. The plot spread itself in a patchwork of purple-veined beet greens, thick splotches of red radish, and thin, wavy fronds of carrot tops. Momma and I were standing in a cloister of vines that morning, picking out the crop of runner beans and dropping them into brown paper bags from Food Lion. Dilly beans. Beans packed into jars with slivered almonds. We would eat them all through the winter. I was contemplating this fact, silently ridiculing Momma's emphasis on what she called homegrown goodness, when the single shrill note split the morning.

I turned to my mother, seeking confirmation of what we had just heard. The whistle was the sound of calamity itself. It could mean that a tractor had turned over, trapping Lou Delray or Tom Hervey or even Uncle Ritchie, compressing his chest against the rock-hard summer soil, squeezing the air out of him while someone ran for help. It could mean that a man had caught his hand in a baler or a wood chipper. It might announce that a child had stumbled on a dead log and surprised a copperhead or, worse, had wandered into the muddy shallows of the creek and come across a cottonmouth.

When the whistle sounded, Momma stopped picking, her hand raised in mid-motion. Then, as I watched, she tilted her face to the wind, scenting, like a dog. By the time she swung toward me, I could smell it, too. The whistle shrilled again. "Fire!" Momma yelled, her voice melding with the high, urgent note. And then she was running down the bean row, tipping the bag as she went, spilling shards of green onto the newly watered soil.

When I caught up with her, Momma was standing on the front lawn, and Marina was beside her. They were staring at the dark band of pine that ran along the far end of Uncle Ritchie's front field and marked the boundary of our grandmother's land. I could see, rising from beyond the trees, a gray haze of smoke that seemed to shimmer and coalesce even as we watched. There was something mesmerizing about its density, about the way the smoke formed itself into a cloud and puffed itself out at the edges, the way it wavered in a mass, rippling when the breeze hit it.

"It's the Eameses' barn," Marina said. Her voice was barely a whisper, and if our mother heard, she did not acknowledge it. I looked at my sister, inclined to argue, to point out that it was more likely to be the hay shed that Uncle Ritchie shared with the Delrays, but the look on her face made me stop. While Momma and I were beaded with sweat, our foreheads creased and our bodies fidgeting in the anxiety and excitement of disaster, Marina was absolutely still. A smile twitched the corner of her mouth, and she did not so much as slide her eyes toward me. Instead she watched the cloud of spreading smoke. She concentrated on it as if it were alive, as if she could mold it, cause it to blossom against the limp blue of the summer sky.

A pickup raced by, and another followed it. I saw Uncle Ritchie in the first, clutching the wheel with both hands. His soft bulk bounced and met the wide front seat again as he hit the pothole opposite our driveway and sped on. The second truck was the Herveys', and I had just enough time to glimpse Della and to be jealous of the fact that she was standing up in the truck bed, clutching the back of the cab, her hair blown straight back from her head, before the plumes of dust rose in the road and swallowed them.

"Come on, girls, come on now. Hurry!" Momma called. I had not seen her move, but when I looked around, she was trotting toward the garage, grabbing the big door with both hands and swinging it open, and a moment later our old Country Squire was flying backward out of the dark. Momma slammed on the brakes and leaned across to open the passenger door, yelling at us now to get in. I went first, and despite the cool of the shadows it had been parked in, the station wagon's front seat was warm and stuck against the back of my thighs as I scooted along it to make room for Marina.

We followed the pickups, veering past the hay shed, which was not burning, and down the old county road that was in even worse shape than ours and dead-ended at the Eames farm. As soon as we came around the corner, we could see the feathers of fire that were waving from the barn's roof, and the heat hit me even before I slammed the wagon's door and followed Momma and Marina as they wove through the collection of cars and trucks that had pulled up in the yard.

A bucket chain had been started from the house, and I saw that Grandma was already there. She was toward the back with the other old ladies, while younger people had joined in in the middle of the line. They were passing heavy black rubber buckets hand over hand, trying not to slosh the water out, while the Eames boys, Charlie and Dex, grabbed the empties and ran back up to the house with them. The men were closest to the wall of heat, which seemed to move steadily outward from the barn. Each man would throw a bucketful and then jump back, cursing and hopping as if the ground itself were scalding his feet. Marina ran to help Dex and Charlie, and when Momma and I joined the line, we felt the heat press itself toward us, reaching out and stroking our faces.

It wasn't until I heard a shout and looked up that I realized people were on the roof of the house: Mr. Eames and his brother, Royce Jr., and Joe Cappel, who did odd jobs for Uncle Ritchie and whose wife took in laundry and sometimes gave Marina and me hard candies when we walked past her yard on the way home from the school bus. They had rigged up a hose and were spraying the roof, soaking it as best they could so that when the barn finally went, maybe its sparks wouldn't set the house on fire, too. Down below, Mrs. Eames was watching them, her hand shielding her eyes as she looked up. The thin material of her dress fluttered against her shoulders as people ran back and forth around her.

At some point the fire engines arrived, and the bucket chain stopped, and we were all commanded to move back. They were still running out the big black hoses and yelling about getting water from the cow pond when the silo caught and went up. The torch of flame was so bright that the day dimmed around it, and even the firemen stopped to watch.

I could feel everyone around me holding their breath as the huge burning pillar seemed to lift off and hover above the earth. It paused as we watched, looking briefly as if it might take flight, as if it might continue to rise and then spin like a giant Roman candle. Momma reached out and clutched my arm. Her fingers dug into the flesh above my elbow, and I was about to complain when she let go to cover her mouth with her hands as the silo tipped sideways and crashed onto the barn roof.

There was something like silence. Then the barn let out a great sigh, as if finally giving up, and a terrible cracking, like hundreds of bottles breaking, made me reach to cover my ears before it was drowned in the sudden thundering of the barn walls as they fell in on themselves and lit the noon sky with a storm of sparks.

After the barn collapsed, Momma walked over to Mrs. Eames and put her arm around her shoulders. They had grown up together and been best friends in school. Momma rubbed little circles below the back of Mrs. Eames's neck the same way she used to when Marina and I were little and had heatstroke or a headache and would still let her touch us. The men were coming down from the roof of the house, and the sun caught the drips from the gutters and spangled them with colored prisms of light. Behind the crowd, the firemen moved in on the collapsed timbers and crisscrossed them with high, arching jets of water. The crackling of flames died to a hissing sound, and the plumes of smoke turned darker and rose in columns from the embers and the ashes and the soggy blackened piles that had been the new harvest.

Mr. Eames was the last of the men to come off the ladder, and when his work boots hit the ground, he stood still, holding the wooden rungs as if he could not bear to turn around and face the barn or the neighbors and friends who stood watching and pitying him. He was a tall man, and gangly, with a neck that seemed too long and arms that seemed too narrow to support his pawlike hands. No one came near him while he rested his forehead on the ladder's rung, but out of the corner of my eye, I noticed Charlie, who was a year or so older than Marina and me. He sidled up to the edge of the crowd and stood beside Marina. She did not look at him, but she moved her hand in a slight beckoning motion, as one might to a well-trained dog. It was almost unnoticeable, but I saw it, and Charlie sensed it. Without taking his eyes from his father's back, he ran his fingers quickly down her wrist and across her palm.

The sight fascinated me. It was no more than a brush, a quick, furtive stroke, and it might have been a mistake, except that it wasn't. The gesture was as intimate, and as full of history and promise, as a kiss. I felt myself flush under the layer of dust and sweat that rimed my body. I was suddenly and inexplicably embarrassed, and yet I could not look away from them. Until that moment I had thought that I knew everything about Marina. It had never once occurred to me that she might have secrets, that someone could be close enough to her to touch her that way without my knowing about it, or that some part of her life could be going on without me. But clearly it was, and I felt the flush on my skin deepen with confusion, for in the next second, as Charlie bent forward, leaning down to tie his shoelace, the bright coin of a medallion swung away from his neck.

He grabbed it almost instantly, shoving it back down inside his collar, but he had not been quite fast enough. I had seen the bright gold chain, seen the scalloped edge of the disk clearly, and even from that distance, I had recognized it. I would have known it anywhere. It was a Saint Christopher medal, and I had saved for four months to buy it for Marina on our fourteenth birthday.

"It's for safe journeys," the saleslady in Jordan's Quality Jewelers had told me when I first noticed it in the glass case by the window. Her name was Mrs. Pease, and her daughter, Danna, was two years behind Marina and me in school and picked her nose. I had gone into Jordan's with my mother, who was getting the clasp on her pearls fixed for the umpteenth time, and while she discussed this with Mr. Jordan, Mrs. Pease had lifted the Saint Christopher medal off of its velvet pillow and dangled it in front of my face. It was the size of a quarter, with ripply edges, and on it was a big man wearing what looked like a miniskirt standing knee-deep in the middle of a bunch of wavy lines, holding a baby on his shoulders.

"That's Saint Christopher carrying the baby Jesus across the river Jordan," Mrs. Pease informed me. "It's a real nice thing to give someone you love. It means they'll always travel safe." When I had asked her how much it cost, she replied, "Twenty-five dollars with the chain, which is solid gold." And then she put the medal back on its velvet cushion and snapped the glass lid down, turning the lock with a little silver key that was chained to her wrist. By that time my mother was done, and as we stepped out of the store, I said to her, "Do you think Marina needs to be kept safe?"

At this, Momma gave me one of her looks and said, "Shoo Shoo, you are wise beyond your years," which annoyed me and was really no answer at all. But all the same, I decided then and there to buy Marina the Saint Christopher medal.

I did it partly because I could tell by the way Mrs. Pease had locked it up that she figured I'd never be able to afford it, and partly because I was in one of my semi-Baptist fits and I feared that Marina was godless. The M that I had engraved on the back cost me an extra seven dollars, which meant that I'd taken Grandma's garbage out a lot more than I'd wanted to.

Now the sight of that medal swinging back and forth around Charlie Eames's neck was almost more than I could bear, and I willed Marina to look at me. I stared at her with every ounce of concentration I could summon, until finally she turned slowly toward me. She did not want to meet my eyes, I could tell. Her jaw was stubborn and set, and she was as intent on blocking me out as I was on prying her apart, cracking her open like a clamshell. Furious, I spun words out across the hot, muggy air. But the contest between us never got going, because in that instant, just as Marina presented me with the defiant, blank mask of her face, Mr. Eames let out an unholy yell.

It was like the sound a bull makes when it is pawing and lowing in rage, a deep rumbling that rises to an incoherent bellow. Mr. Eames raised his head and made the sound a second time, and then he swung back from the ladder, pushing it away so that it fell and clattered against the porch rail, and turned toward us. The third time he bellowed, the sounds formed themselves into words.

"Boy!" Mr. Eames screamed. "Boy, I'll kill you!" And before any of us understood what was happening, Charlie Eames was running, skirting the burning debris of the barn and making for the open field beyond. He tried to vault the high board fence of the paddock and failed. Stumbling and too frantic to think of turning to the gate, Charlie threw himself at the gray splintered timber, scrambling, his feet and arms moving like an overwound toy. But he could not move fast enough, and he was able to climb only a few feet when his father caught up with him.

The two huge hands fastened on the boy's scrawny shoulders and Mr. Eames held him up, dangling him by his overall straps and almost showing him off, like a possum or a rabbit he had just pulled from a snare. Then he flung his son down to the ground, roaring again with rage. Drawing his foot back, Mr. Eames aimed for the boy's head, but Charlie twisted in the puddles of water and ash and raised his arm in time. Even so, Joe Cappel and Mr. Delray, who had almost reached them by then, said they heard the bone in Charlie's arm snap like a gunshot.

It wasn't until an hour or so later, when we got in the car to go home, that I realized my mother was crying. Joe and Mr. Delray and some of the other men had pulled Mr. Eames off Charlie, and shortly after that his uncle Royce and his mother and our grandma, who had once been a nurse, had taken him off to the hospital. Mr. Delray and a few other men had walked off into the fields with Charlie's father, and everyone else had milled around, too startled and embarrassed to know exactly what to do.

"You know, the chief came and talked to Charlie and to some of the other boys. He warned them about those fires," I heard Mrs. Hervey say to my mother. And then I saw her shake her head and mutter while my mother shook her head and said, "That's no excuse, Ruth Ann."

It was well past noon when we finally got back in the station wagon, and the long bench of the front seat was so hot that it was hard to sit on. At first I tried to hold myself up with my hands, pushing my palms against the squishy plastic so I could raise the backs of my thighs where the skin felt as if it might be peeling off, but Momma turned the key hard in the ignition so it made a grinding sound, and then she backed up too fast and jerked the car around into the road, and I tipped over sideways. I looked at her to complain, but the words stopped in my mouth. Tears were pooling above the high ridges of her cheekbones and leaving pale stripes as they ran down her face. "Dammit," she was muttering. "Damn that son of a bitch." And she stepped on the accelerator so that the car bounced forward, and I fell against Marina, who was staring straight ahead and still refusing to look at me.

If the heat was burning the backs of her legs off, she did not seem to care or notice. Without watching what she was doing, Marina fiddled with the button on the door lock. She was pushing it down and plucking it up again with increasing savagery, until I was afraid that she was going to accidentally open the door and fall out of the car and into the ditch. I looked at my mother, who did not usually approve of this kind of behavior, but she was intent on the road and still shaking her head, twitching it from side to side as if she had a bug caught in her ear. Then Marina stopped. She sat quite still with her hands limp on her knees, and I could hear her humming to herself, singing the notes of a tune that I couldn't quite make out. They rose and fell and were lost in the wind that blew through the open window and whipped Marina's hair across the sharp angles of her face.

ELENA LEANS BACK IN HER CHAIR AND GAZES AT ME WITH all the detached interest and impersonal attention to detail that I imagine painters and pathologists reserve for their subjects. At first I found this scrutiny unsettling. But now I have grown used to it and usually just stare back at her, waiting for her to deliver the pearls of insight that her not insignificant fees suggest she keeps handy at her fingertips. But not today. Today I lean forward, anxious.

Elena looks at me for a long time and then finally says, "So, you are frightened in the dark by someone you cannot see, someone who is humming a song that was familiar to you as a child. Then you tell me a story. It is a terrible story that is very frightening, about a fire, and about violence, and about betrayal. The violence is to a child your age, by a man, in this case his father. The betrayal is that of your sister beginning to live a life that is separate from yours. As you realize that this is the case, that she is moving away from you, that she is in some sense abandoning you, she sings. I am sorry"—Elena raises her hand, and the dusty glow of her amber ring catches the sunlight that filters through the window of her study—"she hums."

Elena drops her hand to her lap and studies it. Then she says, "Fear is a strange thing. Of all the human emotions, it is perhaps the most powerful and often the most apparently irrational. It is also the most insidious. It can stay with us for years and arise with all its power when we least expect it. And the irony is, of course," she adds, smiling, "that so often our fear says more about what is inside of us than the thing outside that we perceive to threaten us."

Our hour is over, and Elena leads me down the narrow back stairs. I will not see her again until early November, and although I have reassured her that I will be fine in her absence, I am not so sure. All at once I feel reluctant to leave her, to walk out of the door and turn my back on the comforting bulk of her tapestried jackets. Standing with my hand on the doorknob, I already miss the familiar jangle that her jewelry makes when she moves, and long for the reassuring opiate of her perfume. Elena knows this, but there is nothing she can do about it. So she smiles and says, "Nothing will happen to me," as if she can read my mind, which is, after all, what I pay her for. "I will see you at four o'clock on Friday, November the third."

"Go safely," I say, and I open the door.

"Susannah," Elena says, "nothing will happen to you, either. You are fine. You know that."

"I know," I say, and I wish that I believed her.

"Tell me," she asks, "what happened? To the boy?" She is trying to focus me, to bring me back to the reassurance of the real world, and even though I recognize this, it takes me a moment to realize that she is asking about Charlie Eames.

"Oh, nothing," I say, trying to play along with her. "I mean, he ran away. And everybody knew after that that he'd been setting the fires. No one ever saw him again."

"November third," Elena says. And then she closes the door behind me.

IT IS NOT ENTIRELY TRUE, WHAT I HAVE JUST TOLD Elena. It was not intended to mislead, but it is an abbreviation. It's the sort of jumping from A to C that we all indulge in from time to time in order to get to the point. Because to say that no one ever saw Charlie Eames again does have a kind of accuracy, in the long run. In the short run, however, in the final hours before he boarded a Greyhound bus and set out for the oil fields, or for the flat, pale waters of the Gulf, or for wherever it was that he went to find his future, it couldn't have been further from the truth.

After all, Charlie did not run away from the hospital where I gather they set his broken arm. He came home. We heard later that he braved his father, who had cooled off enough by then to walk out into the field and stand there smoking cigarette after cigarette and staring at the ruin of his barn and silo until Mrs. Eames went out and took him by the arm and led him back inside for supper, where he sat as docile as a child with Dex and Charlie and his brother, Royce. And after supper, Mrs. Eames later told Momma, her head shaking and her voice faltering on the memory, Charlie's dad sat on the steps and offered him some bourbon "to kill the pain," which was the closest he could come to apologizing to his son for accusing him of burning down the barn and for breaking his arm. So, all of those people saw Charlie Eames before he went. And I know for certain that two others did. One was Sonny Delray, who loaned Charlie the fifty dollars he had saved up and "borrowed" his father's pickup truck to drive him to the bus station. The other, of course, was Marina.

As soon as we got home on the day of the fire, Marina jumped out of the car and went up the porch steps and into the house, moving as fast as a scalded cat. Momma herself went straight into the kitchen and picked out one of the ice-cold Miller beers that she kept lined up in the refrigerator door for Uncle Ritchie when he came by. I heard the bottle cap click onto the counter, and as I came through the hall, I saw her take a long drink without even bothering to pour it into a glass. This in itself was so unusual that I was tempted to stop and see what she would do next, but that would have meant abandoning Marina, who was already halfway up the stairs, and whom I was determined not to let out of my sight.

All the way home in the car, I had been sending her words, demanding to know what was going on between her and Charlie Eames and how she could possibly have given away my Saint Christopher medal. But she had blocked me out with her humming. She had used it like static or a radar scrambler, and I hadn't even been able to get her to glance at me. It was the first time she had ever tried this trick, and I was almost as intrigued as I was enraged.

The rebuff had only increased my determination to get her to talk to me, so I took the stairs two at a time until I was right behind her and could see the dark half-moons of sweat that had formed under the arms of her T-shirt and the bumpy outline that her bra straps made over her shoulders. She must have all but felt my breath on her back, and her long braid hung inches from my nose, swinging like a pendulum. I was sorely tempted to grab it and pull hard, but I knew that if I did, she'd hit me, and I didn't want to get in a fight while we were on the stairs and she had the advantage of height.

She grabbed the newel post at the top of the banister and swung around it into the hall. She was almost running now, and I think she would have sprinted for our room if part of ignoring me hadn't required not running, not acknowledging I was there at all. I knew that once we got into our room, I would have her cornered and she would have to face both my presence and my demands, so I may have slacked up a little in the last few steps.

What I didn't count on was her shutting me out. We had chased each other before, and when cornered, we always turned and fought. The pursuit was just a preliminary drama, a sort of ritual whereby we got as far away from Momma as we could, then jockeyed for an advantageous position before striking or receiving the first blow, which might be either verbal or physical. So it never occurred to me that Marina would simply refuse to engage. But that is exactly what she did. When she reached our bedroom, she stepped inside and, very slowly and deliberately, turned around and stared at me. I had to stop abruptly to avoid running into her, and I might have pushed past her if it hadn't been for the look on her face.

Long ago, Marina had mastered the ability to render her face utterly immobile, as if it were suddenly no longer flesh but a solid, cold substance, something like plasticine or agar gel that had been poured into a mold and left as a decoy while the soul inside retreated. She did this now, but the look in her eyes carried not contempt, which I had seen many times before, but something completely new. This time it was a warning. With all the power of her being, my sister was telling me not to come one step closer.

Despite the heat, I felt cool and slightly sick, and I stepped unsteadily backward. We stood there staring at each other for a few more seconds, and then, very slowly, Marina closed the door. I heard the latch click as she turned the handle, and I waited to hear her slide the bolt of the lock home. But we both knew that was unnecessary, and she did not do it. I stood waiting to hear her footsteps as she moved away from the door and into the room. But they did not come, and finally I turned away and went back down the stairs, straight across the entryway, and out the front door into the sunshine.

I finished the beans that afternoon. I picked up the ones Momma had spilled when the farm whistle went, and I stripped the rest of the vines clean of everything except the few late weanlings that wouldn't be ready for another week or so. And all of the time I was doing this, I kept an eye on the upstairs windows of the house, half expecting to see Marina looking down at me or at least to catch her figure moving behind the screens. But I saw nothing, and at dinnertime, I was surprised when she came downstairs as usual and laid the kitchen table and helped Momma make chicken on the barbecue as if everything was perfectly normal.

It was late that night when I heard her moving around. I knew better than to roll over or to even try for a peek at what she was doing. Besides, I didn't need to. We had sneaked out of the house hundreds of times together, and I knew perfectly well that she was pulling on her jeans underneath her nightgown, which she would wear all the way downstairs and possibly out to the garage, so that if she was caught she could say she was getting a drink of water or, in the worst-case scenario, that she had heard a strange noise or been sleepwalking. I heard her reach for her sneakers, which she'd tucked under the edge of her bed. And then there was the almost imperceptible swoosh of the door opening and closing again, followed by the soft pad of feet on the hall's bare boards and the conspicuous absence of the squeak from the tenth step of the stairs.

I waited until she was downstairs before I got up and tiptoed to the window, and I made sure I stayed to the side, in the shadow, so she would not see me if she looked up. I didn't hear the kitchen door open, but I saw the white flash of her nightgown as she darted into the darkness of the garage. I guessed that she must have left a T-shirt stuffed into one of the toolboxes on the shelves, or in one of the buckets that Momma used to store her gardening trowels. A few seconds later she emerged. There was a little moonlight, but I couldn't make out what color she was wearing, or if she had put on anything extra fancy. Even so, I was certain by now that she was going to see Charlie, because she had unbraided her hair. That was what Marina always did when she wanted to look special. In the pale white light of the moon, it hung in a sheet that fell down over her shoulders and reached almost to the center of her back.

When she reached the middle of the driveway, Marina stopped and looked back, as if she had sensed someone watching her. I ducked, but I could still see the white triangle of her face as it turned upward, searching the windows of the house. She paused, catlike, and then, apparently satisfied, she walked to the end of the drive, passed our mailbox, and broke into an impatient trot. By the time she crossed the road and hopped the ditch into Uncle Ritchie's field, she was running. I knew there was no danger now of her looking back, and I knelt on the window seat, pressing my hands and face against the screen, watching my sister as she moved away from me, following her receding figure as she ran through the new alfalfa and slipped into the far shadow of the trees and was lost in their long band of darkness.

She did not come back until just before dawn. The fields were lit in a wavering gray half-light when I saw her. She must have left the tree line sometime before, and she was in the middle of Uncle Ritchie's field when I picked her out. I pulled back from the window and withdrew myself into the shadows. I stood in the darkened bedroom and watched her approach the house, hovering just far enough back from the screen so I could see her but she could not see me.

She made her way across the field, her hands in her pockets and her head down. She had tied her hair back with something, but some of it had escaped and hung down across her shoulders. She stopped once, suddenly, as if she had heard something, and looked back toward the woods and then out at the road. My eyes followed hers, and I thought I saw it, too, a darker bulk where the bushes rose in a tangle. For barely a second, a light burned. It was an orange pinprick, so small that it could have been the flaring of a cigarette. Most likely it was nothing but a late firefly sparking in the darkness before dawn, and when I looked away from it, I saw Marina shrug and pick up her pace a little as she walked on. And then she hopped the ditch and came on down the road toward the house.

I got back into bed and kicked the sheets around and made sure to throw the neatly folded coverlet half onto the floor so it would look as if I had been dreaming. And then I closed my eyes and waited.

I had begun to wonder what she was doing, and I was nearly caught watching the door when I heard the tiny click of the latch. She had been so quiet that I hadn't heard her in the kitchen or on the stairs, and as the door swung open, I lay as still and as hushed as a rabbit with its ears folded back when it senses the approach of a cat.

She stopped just inside the room, and then I heard her footsteps again. But they did not pad to her bed, as I expected. Instead I felt her come toward me. Her breath made a soft puffing sound, as if she had been running or as if the effort of so much silence had exhausted her, and at first I thought she might snatch the sheets away or say something to me. But she didn't. She just stood there looking down at me, commanding me to look at her. But I turned stubborn to the core and refused to open my eyes and give her the satisfaction of sharing her adventure.

IT WAS MONDAY BEFORE WE HEARD THAT CHARLIE WAS gone. On Sunday morning Momma had finally rousted us out of bed and marched us off to help Grandma chip paint off the outside of her house. Our family had given up going to church long ago, which at times I almost regretted, because now, instead of observing Sunday as a time to do our duty to Jesus, we observed it as a time to do our duty to whatever Momma and Grandma decided to get done. As a result, we not only had to get up early but, more often than not, had to spend the day raking, or weeding, or painting, or doing some other job that was almost odious enough to make getting dressed up and singing "Rise and shine and give God the glory" look good. Even so, I half dreaded getting my driver's license in a year's time. I could only imagine how much that would widen the scope of Momma's ambition, and how she'd have me and Marina spending all our free time driving back and forth to the dump and doing good-deed things like delivering meals to old Mr. Marmion, who clacked his teeth and spat at you when he talked.

As the result of our paint chipping, Marina and I didn't get a chance to see anyone or hear anything at all that Sunday. Sonny Delray did not even stop by to make fun of us, which in itself was somewhat unusual. I kept an eye on Marina, but she didn't do or say a single thing out of the ordinary, and she was even friendly. So much so that I might have forgotten Charlie Eames even existed if I had not seen a path of broken stalks in the alfalfa when we drove back past Uncle Ritchie's field at dinnertime.

Nothing unusual happened that night, either. I set the table while Momma and Marina made dinner, and later all three of us washed the dishes. It was hot, and while Marina watched television and Momma did things at her desk, I went out and sat on the porch steps and watched the stars and tried to shake off the uneasy feeling that was clinging to me like the muggy, still air. Finally I got up and walked away from the sound of the TV laughter and the lights in the house. I turned out of the driveway and onto the road until I reached the thick tangle of wild berry bushes and old rose that still stood by the ditch. Grandma said roses meant a farmhouse had been here once, and that if you dug down far enough under the alfalfa field you might find goodness knows what, a silver spoon, a broken dish, some fragment from the lives that had been passed here.

Turning around, I saw our house with the lights shining yellow, and Uncle Ritchie's alfalfa field spreading away to the right of the road. I dropped on my hands and knees, and spreading my palms across the flat edge of the road and the dusty band of scrub grass, I searched. When my fingers hit the soft, spongy cylinder, I knew exactly what it was. I picked up the cigarette butt and dropped it in the pocket of my shorts.

Marina read *Jamaica Inn* in bed that night and fell asleep with the light on so that the moths batted themselves against the screen and I had to get up and take the book out of her hand. I knew from looking at her that she was not going to move again. So I turned off the lamp and got into bed and half listened through the night, skimming the tops of dreams and wondering who had stood by the old rosebush, smoking and watching my sister come home in the dark.

I WAS STILL THINKING ABOUT THIS IN A HALFHEARTED way on Monday afternoon, when we found out about Charlie Eames. Sonny Delray was the unlikely bearer of the momentous news. I saw him coming down the road while I was sitting on the glider pushing myself idly back and forth, wondering how long I could put off mowing the lawn. He swung around our mailbox, rapping the top of it with his knuckles, and I could tell just by the way he was walking that he had some big news to tell.

For as long as I could remember, I had never heard anyone call him anything but Sonny, and although I must have been vaguely aware that he had another name, I had no idea what it might be. He was a big boy, heavy with puppy fat that had lingered through adolescence and padded his body, making him look soft and squishy. Sonny was one of the people who never could tell us apart, and over the years Marina and I had occasionally amused ourselves by confusing him deliberately. He had a terrible crush on her, when he could figure out which one of us she was, and at the Memorial Day picnic that spring, we'd actually gotten him to kiss me when he thought I was Marina. Under the scent of the bleach that Mrs. Delray must have used in their laundry, I had smelled a distinct whiff of cow while he whispered that he loved me. In the midst of this clinch, which I had submitted to only after significant bribery, Marina and Della Hervey and Charlie and Dex Eames and a bunch of other people had jumped out from behind some trees and all but landed on top of us.

Sonny had been so mad that he'd run off and barely talked to any of us until after the Fourth of July fireworks. But by that Monday afternoon in late August, all had been forgiven, and as I watched him come across our lawn, I thought that he looked as if he'd been plumped up like a down pillow. He was positively bursting with importance and completely forgot to try to figure out which one of us I was.

"I came over to say how real sorry I am," Sonny announced.

He had come to a halt right in front of the glider, and I had to put my bare foot down hard in order to stop it from ramming into his knees. The sun was behind him, but in the shadow of his baseball cap, I could see that his face was creased with the kind of exaggerated concern that means people are secretly happy about bad news. A flicker of interest tickled my chest, but I had no intention of giving him the satisfaction of asking what he was talking about.

"I mean, I did ask him if he wanted to leave anybody a letter or anything," Sonny went on. "But he was in one real hurry, and I knew he'd told you himself anyways."

At that moment I felt Marina come around the side of the house. I couldn't see her, but the dense summer air had been disturbed, and I knew she was there.

"I tried to talk him out of it," Sonny was saying. "I surely did. I said, 'Charlie, you're crazy, man.' But he said there wasn't a single thing in this damned town that he cared about, and that all he wanted was never to see this place or anyone in it again."

"What are you talking about?" Marina asked, and Sonny's head swung around, making him look like a surprised tortoise. His face registered the momentary confusion that came with understanding he had not known to whom he was talking, and he blushed deeply at being caught out again. Then he said, "Well, Charlie Eames, of course." His embarrassment made him aggressive, and the words came out like a challenge. "I drove him to the bus station yesterday morning."

Something like a smirk began to creep across his face, and I saw Marina stiffen.

"I was at home taking care of that heifer when he came over," Sonny said. "Everybody else was at church. Except you, of course, since you guys don't go to church. I told Charlie that we could go by your grandma's, where you were probably working, if he wanted. But he said he was in too big a hurry, so we took Daddy's old truck. Charlie drove over 'cause he has his license. But I drove all the way home by myself."

He flopped down on the grass at my feet. Smiling up at us, he took off his cap and ran his hands through his hair, reliving his moment of glory in driving the six miles back from the bus station without a learner's permit. I was secretly impressed with this, since the only place I'd ever driven was up and down the road in front of our house, or around Uncle Ritchie's farmyard, and that was always with Momma and Marina in the car yelling instructions and grabbing the side of the seat or the door handles.

"I knew nobody would catch me," Sonny said, "because everybody was in church, including Dickhead." "Dickhead" was Dick Burns, Petamill's local cop. He was actually an all-right guy who cut most of the kids in town a lot of leeway in buying cigarettes and drinking beer, but we felt like we had to call him some kind of bad name anyway.

I had to admit that Sonny had been exceptionally daring, and he was so pleased with his retelling of the adventure that he and I had nearly forgotten Charlie Eames altogether. We were discussing the route Sonny had taken, and what it had been like, and what he would have done if somebody had recognized him, when Marina said, "But when is he coming back?" Her voice was higher than it should have been, and Sonny and I stopped talking and looked at her. "When did he say he was coming back?" Marina asked.

Sonny stared at her, then said, "He isn't coming back." And for a change he looked at Marina as though he thought she was stupid. "Don't you get it? He's gone. He left, man. He's history."

The words hung in the air. And suddenly I wanted to tell Sonny to shut up, but the sound died in my throat, and I couldn't. I just sat there with little waves of excitement lapping at my stomach while I watched Marina.

"He borrowed my fifty dollars," Sonny was saying. "That was all my summer money."

There was a pause, and then Sonny started pulling up the dandelions that grew around the legs of the glider and popping off their heads with his thumbnail. "He promised when he got a job he'd mail it back," he said, and then he added, "It wasn't the first time his dad hit him, you know. That's why he burned the barn down."

Silence hung in the air.

"Firebug, firebug," Sonny said, and a funny little smile played around his mouth. I might as well not have existed. He was staring right at Marina. "Crackle, crackle," he said.

I thought she was going to say something. She opened her mouth and closed it again. And then Sonny shrugged and pulled up another dandelion.

"Said he was going on down to Baton Rouge, or maybe to Texas." The head of the dandelion went flying into the air. "I've thought maybe I'd do that myself after high school. They say that—"

"Shut up!" Marina shouted. She glared at us as if it were our fault that Charlie Eames had burned down his father's barn and then decided to leave without telling anybody.

"Just shut up!" she yelled again, and then she turned on her heel and started down the driveway.

Sonny looked as if he'd been slapped. "Marina," he called after her. He began to get to his feet, pushing himself up in an ungainly motion, like an old dog that is too big. "I'm sorry," he called. "Hey, I—"

"Shut up!" she yelled again, without looking back, and then she started to jog.

I stood up then, and Sonny and I watched as she went up the road and jumped the ditch and started to run across the field, heading for the band of trees just like she had two nights before. Sonny's round pudding face was as hurt as if she had thrown something at him, and when he finally turned to look at me, I said, "What did you mean about the fires?"

But Sonny just shook his head as if he didn't understand me and threw the last dandelion he was holding onto the grass. "Nothin'. Nothin', Shoo," he said. Then he started to walk off down the driveway, his head all hunched down and his hands dug in his pockets, and he left me standing there feeling like I didn't understand anything at all.

AS THAT MONDAY AFTERNOON WENT ON, I FOUND I WAS secretly pleased by Sonny's news. I liked the drama of it, but even more, I liked the fact that Charlie Eames was gone. As I looked back over the summer while pushing the mower across our browning front lawn, I still could not tell when Marina had abandoned me. I could not pinpoint the day or even the week when she had entered a world that I was not allowed into. And although I was still not sure of the exact nature of the exclusion, I could smell the betrayal of it like a hound smells a skunk. The bright coin of the Saint Christopher medal, which was even now probably hanging around Charlie Eames's neck, speeding him in safety to wherever he was going, was proof enough of that. And to make things worse, even fat old Sonny Delray seemed to be a part of it.

In fact, not only had I been denied the vicarious thrill of Marina's love affair, and whatever else she and Charlie had been up to—which probably included firebugging, if Sonny was to be believed—but I hadn't even been able to figure out that I was being excluded. This in itself presented problems of a logistical nature. I felt like a general betrayed by his allies and ambushed at the same time. How could this have happened, I asked myself as I stopped the mower and pulled a plug of grass clippings out from between the rotors. I had been outmaneuvered as well as suffering an absolute failure of intelligence. I had been totally unaware anything was even going on. The net result was that Marina had betrayed me and made a fool out of me. And that, I thought, as I started up the mower again and lunged it dangerously close to Momma's flower bed, added insult to injury.

And so I hoped that Charlie's vanishing act would inflict upon Marina the rash of betrayal and the sting of humiliation that she had inflicted on me. And I was glad that her heart was broken, too. I was glad because right then the only thing I was interested in was revenge. And because I smelled the possibility of power.

If I was the only person who knew Marina's secret, I thought to myself as I wheeled the lawn mower into the garage, then I was the only person who could comfort her for the loss of it. Aside from Sonny, whom I knew damn well Marina wouldn't turn to if they were the last people left on earth. So I decided then and there that I would exact my revenge by being extremely kind and generous to Marina. I would bestow my pity on her. And then, sooner or later, I told myself, whether she liked it or not, she would be grateful.

I DIDN'T LOSE ANY TIME PUTTING MY PLAN INTO ACTION. The idea of Marina being beholden to me was too sweet to squander. She was back in time for dinner, and when Momma asked her twice what she had done that afternoon and twice she did not answer, I leaped in before the question could come up again. I said that we had trimmed the edge of the flower border and weeded around by the garden, but Marina had gotten a headache and gone to lie down. I went on with great confidence, rambling about the corn and about how I'd had to pick nine ears just to get these six we were now eating because there had been weevils and corn worms in almost every other one. I did not glance at Marina even once as I said all this, but I knew she was looking at me out of the corner of her eye. In ordinary circumstances, she would have been highly suspicious of this impromptu defense, but I could tell by the look of her that she was all wobbly inside and had been crying and could not be bothered to suspect my motives.

She went upstairs before I did, and it wasn't until after *Charlie's Angels* that I followed her. She was sitting up in bed reading again, or pretending to, her book propped on her knees. I watched her until she looked up, and then I said, "I'm sorry. You know, about Charlie. I'm sorry he left."

She started to shrug and go back to her book, to let me know that neither Charlie Eames nor my apology mattered to her, but then she stopped. She watched me, tugging on her braid, wrapping its long coil around her hand and pulling to see if it would hurt.

"I don't know why he didn't tell me," she said, and the misery and need in her face were so strong and so unfamiliar that I felt suddenly uncomfortable. "Why didn't he tell me?" she asked, and this time I shrugged.

"I don't know," I said. "Maybe he didn't have time."

She was still looking at me, and I began to fidget. Despite the fact that this was exactly what I had wished for, the situation was nowhere near as rewarding as I had thought it would be, and I began to wish that I'd never even noticed her and Charlie Eames, or that I could go get Momma and get her to take care of Marina. I stripped off my T-shirt and wriggled quickly into my nightgown. Then, before she could ask me anything else, I turned off my light and rolled over. I could tell that she was watching me, that she was contemplating saying something else, and I was relieved when I heard her close her book and turn out her light and no words came fluttering at me through the darkness.

It was hot, and I had rolled my coverlet all the way down to the bottom of my bed. When I heard Marina get up, I thought perhaps she was taking hers off altogether or going down the hall for a glass of water or to talk to Momma. But instead she stood in the middle of the room and whispered my name.

"Susannah, are you awake?" Her voice was quavery, and I knew that she was almost crying again. "Shoo?" she asked.

"Uh-huh," I said without turning over.

"I'm sorry I gave Charlie the necklace," Marina said. "I know I shouldn't have done that."

"That's okay," I grunted.

"Can I get in with you, Shoo? Please, just for tonight?"

When we were very little, we had often slept in the same bed. No matter how many times Momma separated us, she would find us in the morning curled into each other, our hair spread across the pillow, our hands sticky with sweat where our fingers had locked together. Now the sound of the night peepers filled our room, and from somewhere across Uncle Ritchie's field, I thought I heard an owl.

"Please," she said again. And without speaking, I threw my sheet back, and Marina slipped into my bed.

9

UNTIL THE BARN BURNED AND HIS FATHER BROKE HIS
arm and he ran away, until I viewed him as a cause of Marina's behavior,
I really never thought of Charlie Eames much at all. And after all that,
after he disappeared, I viewed him mainly as an object. He was a thrill
I had been denied, a secret that Marina had kept from me. Charlie was
on a par with a five-dollar bill that she had once hoarded, with eye
shadow that she had stolen from Woolworth's and didn't share. He was
like the dirty jokes that she sometimes whispered to Della Hervey on
the bus and refused to let me overhear. So I remember the fact of Charlie Eames but do not recall him as a person. I do not remember the way
his hair might have fallen, or the sound of his laugh, or the shape of his
hands and face.

What I do remember is the feel of Marina's body on the night when
she came into my bed. It was too hot and too heavy. She was a weight
that was tied to me, bound to me by arms as slender and supple as
vines, and by tendrils of need that wound themselves around me, and
by all the webs that we spun in the darkness.

I feel her sometimes still, and on these mornings I wake panting
and lie there slick with sweat, even though the room may be cold. The
air I am conscious of breathing on these occasions is particularly sharp
and clean. It tastes to me as it must to a swimmer who has been trapped,

fettered and tangled by weeds, and has struggled to rise and crack the shimmering surface of the water. On mornings like that, when my body finally cools and I have caught my breath, I feel a buoyant sense of freedom and release. This morning it lasts until I look in the mirror.

"Go away," I say to the face that looks back at me, and I feel instantly embarrassed, although there is no one to hear me but Jake. "I don't have time for you," I tell Marina. And then I open the medicine cabinet with more force than is necessary. I brush my teeth and braid my hair and get ready for the morning meeting I have with Lolly.

MINT GREEN IS THE COLOR FOR TODAY, A SHIRT AND headband and flat shoes that match. The headband and the collar of Lolly's shirt have tiny fake pearls sewn on them, and although I understand that the intent is something along the line of strewn stars, the overall effect is of bits of rice or confetti, as if she has just come from a wedding or a parade.

"The napkins have arrived," she announces as soon as I open the door and before I even have a chance to get out of the car. "I'm sure they're going to be totally fabulous. I can't wait for you to see them!"

I don't point out to Lolly that I have seen them, that in fact I designed them and this is what she pays me for. Instead I get out and stand on the sidewalk, scrabbling in my bag for my glasses case. We are on our way to the Design Center, which is housed in a strange windowless block of a building that hangs over the edge of the Schuylkill. There is a lurid mural of whales and dolphins painted on the side of it, which is justified by the fact that it was originally intended as an aquarium. The only available parking for the Design Center is along the University Bridge, where we are standing now. Lolly must have arrived seconds ahead of me, because the Lexus is tucked in two cars back and she was waiting when I pulled up, gesturing to where I should park, as if I might not be able to figure it out for myself.

"Oh," she says now. She has just noticed my new car door, which is blue, sort of, but nothing like the blue of my car. It's obviously spray-painted, the best Benjy said he could do in the circumstances. "Well,"

Lolly says, "that's not too bad." Which means, of course, that it's awful. "When is the new one coming?" She glances over her shoulder as she asks this, as if she's afraid that someone she knows might see her standing beside my disfigured car.

"Soon, I hope," I say, gathering up my briefcase and locking the car. "Don't worry," I add, "in the meantime I won't go around telling anybody I work for you."

This causes her to grimace and take me by the elbow. She marches me along the sidewalk as if I am a naughty child. "Come on," she says, "we can't keep the Dragon Lady waiting."

The Dragon Lady is actually Mrs. Koom Wai, a diminutive and terrifying Korean woman who owns one of the best textile places in the center. This morning she has received a new shipment of tapestried silks, and if Lolly weren't with me, I could easily spend several hours pawing through them, feeling their smooth, cool weight, watching the flash of their gaudy turquoises and magentas, and tracing the paths of their tiny embroidered figures, who scurry across bridges, racing from pagoda to pagoda. As it is, I wink at Mrs. Koom Wai, meaning that I will be back, and she fetches the tablecloths and napkins that I have chosen for Indochine. On her return she lifts each one, neatly folded, and then, like a magician, she releases the fabric with a snap of her wrist and sends it rippling in a wave of black and scarlet across the broad, polished surface of the display table. A "ten out of ten" is Lolly's verdict, and she takes me upstairs to lunch on the strength of it.

"This is to make up for the car, because I didn't have time the other night," she insists as I protest, and when the menus arrive, she orders us each a dry martini. "Just show it the vermouth bottle," she says to the waiter, "and for God's sake, no olive."

The drink leaves me feeling light-headed and irresponsible. I should be hurrying home to work, but after Lolly leaves, kissing me incongruously on the forehead, since she cannot be bothered to lean down far enough to reach my cheek, I linger for a cup of espresso and then wander downstairs. The center is laid out like the interior of a big hotel, and I stare idly through the thick-paned display windows of the shops that line the carpeted hallways.

I drift aimlessly and finally come to rest in front of a window that says, ULTIMATE KITCHEN. Beyond the glass is a riot of Provençal fabric. Dishcloths, oven gloves, tea cozies, and bread baskets are all made up in vivid yellows and electric blues, dotted with small red flowers. Dried boughs of olive and grapevines climb a central pillar, and copper bowls and pans and molds in the shape of hearts and fishes hang from racks along the ceiling. Below them are stacks of wicker baskets. But what draws me, what catches my eye, is the bright glint of stainless steel, the polished gleam of the knives.

Like jewels, they are locked behind glass and backed by black velvet. My request to touch requires a key, the opening of a padlock, and hovering supervision. The blades range from long, rounded at the end, and paper-thin, for slicing smoked salmon, to a fine eight-inch boning instrument with a point sharp enough to etch glass. There's a short, stubby serrated blade whose twist will zest a lemon or curl frozen butter into a ball. The handles are ebony, molded in the grip, and somehow already warm and welcoming to the touch. When I pick up the knives, they lock into my grasp with the familiar solidarity of a handshake.

The girl offers me a cutting board and a sacrificial tomato, but I don't take her up on her invitation. I'm feeling fickle, and I've been lured away by the poultry shears. My old ones disappeared some time ago, and the scissors I've been using since then are fine for snipping chives and worse than useless for anything else. Deboning a chicken is out of the question.

But this would not be true of the shears before me. Two pairs are laid out in the display case, and I lift them both. I snap at the air, hearing the quick swish, the delicate click of the blades as they meet. One set is serrated, the other smooth, and it is these I am drawn to. When I run my finger along their edge, I can feel how precisely, and how quickly, they will cut.

"I'll take them," I say. And the salesgirl slips the shears into a plastic sleeve and wraps them carefully in tissue paper that she ties with a raffia bow. She tucks a little piece of lavender into the knot. I can smell it as I take the package, and when I leave the shop, the shears sit in my shoulder bag, giving it a new and satisfying weight.

Outside, the wind has picked up. The overripe mugginess of the Indian summer has been chased away, and for the first time it feels like fall. The slight metallic tang of autumn clears my head, and I pause in the middle of the bridge to watch a train creep along the tracks on the far side of the river and disappear into the tunnel that runs under the Penn hockey rink and skirts the tall white buildings of the university.

I used to know them all, those buildings. I used to know their names, used to weave in and out of them expertly, dropping George off or picking him up, or going to meet him for lunch or a drink. But this information has begun to fade, and I am no longer certain I would know which alleys are one-way, which parking lots are safe, or which gates close at dusk. It is as if a part of me has slipped away while I was not looking, and like amputees who sometimes feel pain in a limb long after it is gone, I feel a sudden lurch of sadness.

All at once I'm caught in a short, sharp riptide of regret for all the things that I would wish undone, and for all the moments that I would wish rewritten and relived. The feeling is so all-encompassing, so complete, that it takes my breath away. But then I force myself to walk on, to put one foot in front of the other, and to feel for my keys and think of Jake, who will be waiting for me. I reach the car and have just decided that this afternoon we will go for a long walk in Wissahickon Park to celebrate the coming of fall, when I look up and see George. He's not ten yards away and coming straight toward me. I wonder momentarily if my thoughts have actually brought him into being, if I have somehow inadvertently conjured him up from some deep, hidden pool of longing and nostalgia.

The sight of him is at once so completely familiar and so utterly strange that I freeze. I knew that he was back from Paris, and that one day, inevitably, I would run into him. I have envisioned our meeting. I've played it out carefully and run through the possibilities, the coming around an aisle and seeing him in the grocery store, the bumping into him at a bar or a party, the unexpected sound of his voice during an intermission at the theater. Even so, I feel unfairly trapped, bullied, as if the past has broken through its barriers and elbowed its way into the present. I'm not ready for this sudden spinning sense that life has gone nowhere, that the last year has crumbled and I might as well be standing on another sidewalk, under streetlights this time, two days before he's due to leave for Paris, wishing him good luck and then watching him walk away.

His hair has grown a little. The wind lifts it up and blows it sideways. He's still wearing his old tweed jacket. It's one of several that he adopted as a uniform after he started teaching at Penn. But he's switched from khakis to black pants, tightish jeans, which, I guess, must be the influence of his new wife. He is, thank God, alone. And since I have seen him before he's seen me, I have a chance to take in the look of his face and to compose my own. I have the chance to arrange my mouth and eyes, to rest my hand on the car door so he will not see it shaking, before I say, "George?" His step checks at the sound of my voice, and he looks up to see me standing in front of him.

"Susannah!" His voice hasn't changed. He doesn't sound like Inspector Clouseau or Vincent Price. But I can't tell whether there's any pleasure in it or just surprise.

"How are you?" We both ask it at once and stop at once, sounding like a badly scripted sitcom.

"Fine," I hear myself saying, and I know I'm nodding like one of those dog things that sit in the back window of trashy cars and nod their heads up and down. "And you? And Paris? How was—"

"Great," George says. "It was really great." He's nodding, too. "I mean, it's just a whole different scene."

I ask George more questions, almost without realizing it, appropriate things about his book and his teaching. But I'm not really listening to his answers. Instead I'm slipping away. I'm wallowing in the sound of his voice, drifting on the memory of his touch, and catching the half-forgotten echo of his breath against my skin.

I want him to keep talking so I can watch the planes of his face a little longer, but he's stopped. I'm vaguely aware that he might have asked me if I'd read something in *The New York Times* about the Pompidou Center, and so I shake my head, which seems to satisfy him. Then he looks around, reaching for another subject. "Is this yours?" he asks, pointing at the Mercedes, and I realize he's never seen it, that I bought it as a treat for myself after he left.

"Yeah, I'd always wanted one. Well, an old one."

"So work must be going well?" George runs his hand along the car's roof, then looks up at me and grins. "Shame you couldn't afford all four doors, though."

"Well," I say, "just a casualty of city life."

George furrows his brow in concern. "Accident? I hope you're okay. Or should I see the other guy?"

"No, no," I say too fast. As much as I'd like to, I don't trust the concern in his voice. I'm beginning to feel uncomfortable, and I start to fumble for my keys. "It was just some little jerk being artistic. Letting me know what he thought of me."

"Somebody wrote on your door?" Perhaps things like this don't happen in the City of Light. George's voice sounds incredulous.

"Carved." I get the door open and throw my briefcase across the console and into the passenger seat. " 'Bitch,' to be exact," I add, straightening up and smiling. I expect George to laugh, but he doesn't. He's staring at the door as if he could see the word, and furrowing his brow again. His face is creased in concern, and I know him well enough to know that this time it's for real.

" 'Bitch'?" he asks. "That's really weird," and I feel a hollowness blossoming in my stomach, because now there's something else moving across George's face. It's like a shadow on water, almost not there but unmistakable at the same time. It's a slight shimmering suggestion of fear.

I don't want to ask, but I know that I have to.

"What? What's really weird?"

The bridge seems to have gone quiet, as if the people walking past us are bouncing on air, and finally George says, "Marina." He looks right at me, and the space in my stomach collapses in on itself, it implodes like a star.

"What about her?" And somehow I know the answer to this even before he says it.

"Somebody did exactly the same thing to her," George says. He looks at me. "Don't you remember?"

"When?"

My voice sounds croaky, like something's stuck in my throat. George shakes his head and looks at his feet. Like a kid, he's drawing a little circle on the pavement with the toe of his shoe, tracing it over and over again.

"George," I say, "when?" My hands are dug into my pockets, and it's everything I can do not to reach out and shake him.

"Maybe I didn't tell you," he says. "I can't remember. You guys weren't really talking at the time." He stops the circles and looks at me, shrugging. "She told me about it once when she called. When you wouldn't talk to her. She was pretty pissed off." He shakes his head as if he could clear it of the memory. "She said it was going to cost her a fortune. Some asshole had carved the word 'bitch' in her car door. It can't have been more than a couple of weeks before she died."

10

I PRESSED GEORGE AFTER THAT. STANDING ON THE BRIDGE yesterday, I grilled him, my voice unnecessarily shrill, demanding to know whether he could remember anything else, anything at all, that Marina had said. But he couldn't. Or so he claimed. It was probably the truth. His eyes had begun to flicker by then, and he just wanted to get away from me, to dart like a fish through reeds back into the unsullied waters of his new life.

The mention of Marina's name had curdled the momentary warmth between us. It had always been like that, even when she was alive, and George and I had already discovered once that being murdered in no way diminished her powers. By the time he kissed me good-bye, leaning forward and pecking each of my cheeks quickly, à la française, George's lips had not felt welcome, as I had expected they would, but dry and foreign. They brushed like paper against my skin.

Now I play George's words back in my head while I watch the flat glare of the light on the interstate. "Some asshole carved the word 'bitch' in her car door. It can't have been more than a couple of weeks before she died."

Jake lies in the backseat, and from time to time I can hear him snuffling. Occasionally he sits up and looks out of the window, and I catch a flash of black and sable in the rearview mirror. The road ahead is a soft gray strip, and the fields that border it have not yet turned fallow and dead. Soon blue-green wetlands will appear on our right, and shortly after that, Jake and I will get our first glimpse of the Chesapeake.

Kathleen Harper's directions were extremely accurate. She detailed churches that I will pass on the left or right, and roads that have county numbers and animal names like "Fox Way" and "Mallard's Lane." If the woman who was Marina's best friend in Washington had been surprised to hear from me when I called her last night, she gave no hint of it. There was nothing in her voice to suggest that she had forgotten me or that she found the fact of my calling in any way strange. Instead she had been ready with her directions, treating my request to come and talk to her about Marina as if it were the most natural thing in the world. She had sounded, in fact, as if she had been waiting for me.

I have met Kathleen Harper only once before, at Marina's funeral, a dingy affair at a crematorium somewhere near Reston. Fewer than a dozen of us stood in a modern white stucco chapel and sang "All Things Bright and Beautiful," which was the only hymn I could think of at the time, while my sister's coffin was propelled, as if by magic, down a sort of conveyor belt and disappeared behind a navy blue curtain. Kathleen had come up to me afterward, and I remember her as brunette, well groomed, and tall. She introduced herself as a colleague and friend of Marina's from World Bank, and like Special Detective Mark Cope, she gave me her card. She, too, had scribbled her home number on it and murmured, "If there's ever anything." And now it suddenly feels as if there is something.

THE HOUSE IS BIG, AND MODERN, AND ON THE WATER. Jake watches me from the backseat as I stand on the terra-cotta steps and ring the doorbell, which chimes three times like something out of Edgar Allan Poe. I can't hear footsteps inside, and if it weren't for the tail end of the car that I can see sticking out of the open garage, I'd think that the place was empty, like a house waiting to be sold.

I try to remember what I know about Kathleen Harper and come up with not much. I'm pretty sure I remember the mention of kids and

a marriage, or maybe of a divorce. But beyond that, I don't know anything about her. So when the door swings open, catching me by surprise, the woman who stands in front of me is a complete stranger.

I was right, she is tall and dark. She's also big-boned and too thin,
so the immediate impression is somehow two-dimensional. She looks
flat, as if she's a cardboard cutout. This illusion may also have something to do with the blank sheet of light that floods in from the glass
wall behind her, backlighting her like a prop on a stage. She had mentioned last night that she now works from home, and freed from the
obligation of going to an office, she is no longer well groomed. Her
skin is pale, as if she's a recluse or an invalid, and her hair is cut short,
almost like a boy's. She brushes it back from her forehead in a choppy,
nervous gesture, and I notice that she chews her nails. Two livid spots
of color appear on her cheeks as she stares at me. She opens her mouth
and closes it, then gives herself a visible shake.

"I'm sorry," Kathleen Harper says, "I don't mean to be rude. It's
just that sometimes I forget that there were two of you."

The house seems to be a series of glass rooms, some of which look
into each other and some of which look out over the water. There are
only a couple of small rugs on the floor, and all the couches are low and
rectangular and very Bauhaus. In the center of the living room is an upturned tea crate with a bowl of jelly beans and some magazines on it,
which suggests that her husband got the coffee table. I follow Kathleen
into the kitchen, turn down her offer of a sandwich or coffee, and then
accept a beer when she says she's going to have one.

"It's after two," she says. "I don't usually drink in the afternoon, but
it is one of the pleasures of being at home."

The kitchen, which is predictably sleek, is made almost entirely of
blond wood and stainless steel. A row of narcissus bulbs sits on the windowsill above the double sinks, and a child's pink knapsack with pictures of Barbie on it lies on the edge of the island beside a knife block
and a halogen stove. Pots hang from a rack on the ceiling. They're
highly polished and graduated in size and show no sign of having been
used in the recent past. It's not hard to see this room as a bastion of
take-out sushi and white wine in minibottles, and children who nibble

chicken fingers and other tubular things that go into and come out of the microwave on plastic trays. Kathleen opens the refrigerator, and when the door swings out, I see the picture of Marina.

It's one of several family photos that have been slipped into plastic sleeves and stuck in place with magnets in the shape of sunflowers. In it Marina is sitting on the steps of a deck, which I guess must be at the back of this house. Her arms are looped around two small girls, and she is smiling. One of the children holds a brown Labrador by the collar, twisting its head around in an attempt to make it look at the camera. Despite myself, I'm fascinated. The picture looks like my sister and not like her at once, as if someone else has invaded Marina's body.

"They adored her," Kathleen says. She's watching my face intently, and I feel myself color, as if I've been caught peeking through a keyhole or listening at a door. She flips off the tops of two bottles of Rolling Rock.

"She used to spend a lot of time here. This was our weekend house, predivorce." Kathleen hands me one of the beers. "We taught her to sail," she says. "You know, we'd have cookouts, go over to the marina, all that sort of stuff. The girls got a big kick out of that. Her name. Marina and marina. I told them it was a car accident." Kathleen adds this quickly, and a little half-smile plays around the edges of her mouth, as if she's both confessing and apologizing to me for this whitewash of Marina's death.

"I know you shouldn't lie to kids," she goes on, "but I could hardly tell them the truth. That's one of the reasons I started working at home after it happened, so I could be here for them. Poor little guys. They were having a hard enough time as it was, with the divorce." Kathleen takes a quick swallow of the beer. "Would you like to go outside?" she asks. "We could walk."

JAKE RUNS AHEAD OF US DOWN THE LAWN. KATHLEEN watches him with the combination of nostalgia and envy that is usually reserved for old boyfriends who have moved on to other women.

"I miss my dog," she says as Jake finds a stick and then drops it and heads into the tawny band of tall grass that fronts the water. "My husband took him and the boat. I kept the kids."

"That must be hard," I say. I don't know her well enough to add "I'm sorry," or to know if she'd rather have had it the other way around. Jake erupts from the long grass and hops over a stone wall at the bottom of the lawn, racing back toward me to make sure I'm still in sight. A dock runs out over the water, and by the time we reach it, he has trotted out ahead of us. I can hear his claws making little ticking sounds on the weathered silver planking.

Kathleen leans against the railing and watches the water, which is still and smoky in the late afternoon. " 'Treasure the Chesapeake,' " she says, quoting the license-plate slogan, the one that has a picture of reeds and a loon; you see it mostly on the back of four-by-fours. "It's polluted, you know." She stretches her hand down toward the water, as if to stroke it with the tips of her fingers. "They say they're trying to clean it up, but every time they do, you read about another company pouring crap into it. Marina loved this place. She said it was peaceful. I worry about that." Kathleen pauses. "I worry about whether she's at peace now." She finishes her beer and sits down on a board locker box where boat fenders and single sneakers and tangled fishing line probably end up. "So," she says, "you drove two hours down here. What is it you want to ask me?"

The question comes out as a demand, and when Kathleen looks up at me, her expression has changed. All at once it's a mixture of inquiry and defensiveness, like a child's, as if she expects me to accuse her of something or to hurt her feelings. Marina had perfected this look in her teens, this same guilt-inducing combination of nakedness and hostility, and with a flash of clairvoyance, I can see why she and Kathleen were such good friends. I can read it on Kathleen's face. The two of them must have recognized each other instantly. They must have realized that they'd each found a buttress, a sister-in-arms in their battle against the world.

I'm unprepared for this weird sensation that I'm talking to Marina by proxy, that I'm right back in a place I've run so far to escape. And I'm equally unprepared for my response to it, for this old resentment I thought I'd left behind forever, the one that's ballooning in my chest. I open my mouth and then close it again. I have to stop myself from stepping backward.

"I'm sorry," I say, and then I'm annoyed with myself for saying it. It's not, after all, as if the woman can read my mind, but she's thrown me totally off balance. Suddenly I think that this might not have been such a good idea, and I'm tempted to just put down my beer bottle and leave. Then I remember how deep the scratches on my car door were, and the look on George's face, and the darkness of the laundry room that was as thick and perilous as the river that runs underneath us now. So I pull myself together. I tell myself not to be ridiculous. And finally I just spit the words out.

"I need—" I start. "I mean, I want to know what happened before Marina was murdered."

Kathleen looks at me for a moment. "Before she was murdered?" she asks. She seems genuinely surprised by this, and slightly disappointed, as if she'd expected me to ask something else entirely.

"In the days before, the weeks before." I'm talking faster now than I want to, shoving urgency into the words until they sound as if they're piling up. "Someone wrote on her car. I need to know if there was anything else like that. Letters or phone calls. A break-in, maybe. Anything."

Kathleen is watching me. She looks incredulous and vaguely sly at the same time. The uncomfortable thought that I'm being an idiot, and that she may somehow be able to turn that fact to her advantage, occurs to me. When she finally speaks, there's something close to disdain in her voice.

"You don't know?" she says. She draws it out, and I realize suddenly that for some reason I don't understand, Kathleen Harper dislikes me intensely. "I can't believe that you don't know," she says again. She's going to make the most of this. "Marina went to the police and the whole nine yards. I mean, you're her sister, I assumed that she told you all about it. She called you, didn't she?"

"Yes," I say, and the word is tight in my throat. It's barely a sound. It's choked off by the memory of Marina's voice, and by the popping sound that the phone plug made when I pulled it out of the wall.

But I'm sure Kathleen knows all this. I'm quite certain she knows the whole story but wants to hear me tell it. It's important to her to humiliate me, and she's been planning this for a long time. What she wants is to hear me confess to total ignorance of the facts of my sister's life, to indifference in the face of her anguish, or worse, to willful abandonment. I can smell Kathleen's jealousy as surely as if it's perfume. She's desperate to hear me admit that in the end, Marina was closer to her than she was to me.

"She called, but we didn't get much of a chance to speak," I say.

Kathleen glances at me sideways and gives a sour little smile and a knowing nod. "There were phone calls," she says. "Chocolates. Flowers. Sometimes she thought somebody was following her. At the end there was the car. And somebody broke into her yard, threw garbage all over the place. It had been going on for months. Marina was being stalked."

I sit down on the locker and close my eyes. I can feel splinters through my jeans, and I imagine that a person wouldn't want to sit here wearing shorts in the summertime. The edge of the railing bites into the back of my head, and I push against it, welcoming the distracting line of pain the way you do when you dig your nails into your palm to stop yourself from sneezing or laughing in church. The heat has gone out of the sun, and the world seems utterly silent.

"She must have tried to tell you," Kathleen says.

"She did," I say. "I didn't feel like listening."

"Marina wasn't always the easiest person in the world." Kathleen's voice is modulated. She's scored a couple of points, and now she's willing to demonstrate her intimacy with the workings of my sister's soul. "You just had to understand where she was coming from."

In this moment my urge to slap Kathleen Harper is almost overwhelming, but I refrain. Instead I sit up and finish my beer. I don't have the energy to be interested in the vendetta that Kathleen seems to be conducting on Marina's behalf. I just want to get what I need and get out of here.

"Look," I say, trying to keep my voice even and neutral, "could you tell me what happened, Kathleen? Please. I'd really like to know." I attempt to sound like a supplicant, as though I'm eager to atone, on a pilgrimage that has nothing to do with self-interest.

"I can't see why it matters to you," she says. "It's a little late now."

She pauses, but I don't say anything. I have the distinct feeling that Kathleen knows, or at least suspects, exactly why it matters to me, but I'm not going to give her the satisfaction of saying so. I'm beginning to dislike her intensely, but I really need to hear what she has to say. She's the only person I have access to who knew my sister in the last months she was alive, and she'll talk to me because her desire to show off is even greater than her desire to punish me. As far as Marina goes, I'm the best audience Kathleen Harper is ever going to get, and she knows it.

"It started," she says, "I don't know, maybe six months before Marina was killed. At least that's when she started to notice it. At first it was nothing, really. Phone calls, nobody saying anything when she answered, that kind of thing. To be honest, at first I thought maybe she was being paranoid, except that Marina wasn't particularly paranoid. She got caller ID, but it wouldn't work. The line was blocked or something. I finally told her to change her number, and she did, but the calls kept coming. Then he, or she, whoever it was, started sending her things."

"Things?" I ask. "What kind of things?"

"Well, I know there was a bottle of champagne. And then some flowers. It was like she had a secret admirer. In fact, I teased her about it. There was a valentine." Kathleen stands up and puts her hands in her pockets. "One of those frilly satin hearts with chocolates inside." It's a second before I realize that she's crying. She quickly wipes away the tears with the back of her hand. "I didn't take it very seriously," she says. "And neither did she. She didn't even call the police until the car."

"And that happened when?"

"After Valentine's Day. The end of February, maybe."

"Was she scared?" I'm not sure why I ask this, but it seems important.

Kathleen wipes her eyes again and shakes her head. "No," she says. "That's what was weird, looking back on it. Even after the car, even after it got ugly, it was more like she was really annoyed, not scared." She sits down on the bench next to me, and I find the closeness of her vaguely repellent. Jake has come back down the dock and flopped at my feet, and when Kathleen leans forward to rub his ears, it's all I can do not to knock her hand away. "It was more like that after she came back from Georgia," she says.

"Marina went down to Georgia?"

The shock in my voice must be unmistakable, although the news shouldn't surprise me. I knew that Marina had hung on to the house, but somehow it never occurred to me that she actually went down there. After she died, the property reverted to me. I never wanted to set foot in the place again, and I sold it to the Herveys, along with all the contents, lock, stock, and barrel, through lawyers and without ever setting foot out of Philadelphia. Now the idea of Marina going back there, of her sitting on the porch by herself or sleeping in Momma's bed, seems at first macabre and then almost unbearably sad.

"Not too often, but sometimes," Kathleen is saying. Her voice makes me jump, as if I'd forgotten that she is sitting beside me. "She went there when she wanted to get away." Kathleen's voice slows down, caresses these last memories. I'm irrelevant now. She's just drifting, playing out this particular loop of the past. "The last time, she took a week off from work. It was in early March. Just after the car thing happened. I didn't know until she got back that she'd even been in Georgia. I guess she went down on the spur of the moment. She'd do that sometimes. She just left me a phone message saying she was going away."

Pictures are swirling around my head like snow in a snow globe, and the only thing I can hold on to is that she must have been there the last time she called me. When I unplugged the phone, Marina must have been standing by Momma's desk in the living room or staring out of the window above the kitchen sink. I can see her twisting the old yellow cord in her free hand, concentrating on the dark rings that Momma's jam jars had left on the countertop linoleum, or watching the tall, smooth fronds of the lilies as they threw spiky swords of shadow in the back-door light.

"I only saw her once more after that," Kathleen adds. "It was about a few days before she died. The kids were on spring break. We went shopping at Crystal City, and then we took them to a movie." She's staring out across the water now, and I can see the tracks her tears have made on her cheek and the slight smudge where she wiped them off.

"What was she like?" I ask. "When she came back, when you saw her that last time?"

Kathleen thinks for a minute.

"Determined," she says finally.

"Determined?"

"Yeah," Kathleen says, "like she was very focused on something, very preoccupied. She could do that. She could just close you out." She looks at me for confirmation, for reassurance that Marina could hurt, that she could turn herself to stone.

"But she wasn't scared?" I've ignored the question in Kathleen's eyes. I don't want her wheedling her way through the doors of my memory. She shakes her head. "Did she tell the police?" I ask.

"Oh, sure," Kathleen says. "They didn't do anything."

Kathleen's eyes are wide and green, and she's so close to me that I can see where her bottom lip is dented and cracked, as if she's been chewing it. "You know," she says, "I read this piece a while ago, in *Harper's* or *The New Yorker*, about this woman who was stalked." She doesn't take her eyes off my face. "This guy followed her. He called her, and sent her stuff, and broke into her house. She went to the police, and they said there was really nothing they could do. Finally she gave up her job and moved to another city and changed her name. The article said that the case was considered a success because he didn't kill her."

FEAR IS A RIPPLE ON WATER. ANY PEBBLE DROPPING, ANY tiny thing—the ring of a telephone, the slam of a car door, the shift of a shadow—can start it off. And when it's not like that, when it's not endless spreading rings, it's an undertow, a swift current that runs, lethal and unseen, below the surface of the day. Just now I can feel its pull, feel it teasing at me, trying to swallow me whole.

I stop the car and take deep breaths. It's late afternoon, and Jake and I are about five miles from Kathleen Harper's house. We're parked in front of one of the churches that she listed as a way marker in her directions. It's small and brick, and most important, it appears to be deserted. Which, right now, is crucial. Because I don't want anyone to witness this panic that's gathering inside me like a storm.

I get out, and Jake hops over the seat and scoots past me into the churchyard. I follow him and sit down on the grass and put my head between my knees, the way teachers at school used to tell us to do if we threatened to faint. When I look up, Jake is weaving among tombstones, pausing occasionally to sniff the ground or to study them as if he can read the inscriptions. The overgrown lawn that stretches out under the old trees has the reassuring smell of damp earth and old leaves, and the blankness of the tall white-framed windows promises anonymity. I can guess what's behind those windows, the plain rectangular room, the lines of dark wood pews, the pulpit and the hymnals, and the stone baptismal font, and I wonder if I can be cleansed. If so, I want the memory of this afternoon rinsed off of me. I want to be washed clean of it the way you want to be washed clean of a hangover or an unwelcome kiss.

I close my eyes and see Kathleen Harper's face. She's up too close. She's bending down to look into the car window, and her cheek is almost touching mine. She's completely determined that I understand how important she was to Marina. When she speaks, I can smell the stale warmth of her breath.

I dig my hands into my jacket pockets, feel the worn material, and let my fists unclench. Overhead a jet cleaves the late-afternoon sky, but it's high up and silent. I squint to watch it, and in my mind, I fasten Kathleen's voice to it and will it to diminish. I will her words to get smaller and smaller, to spread themselves thin and fade away like a vapor trail. But they're stubborn and won't go. They hang before me in the autumn air.

"Aren't you going to ask me?" Kathleen Harper demands. "Isn't that what you really want to know, whether or not Marina and I were lovers?"

IT'S DARK BY THE TIME WE GET HOME, AND I'M TIRED. I feel drained, worn out by Kathleen's anger, and by her insistence, and by my own fear. Part of me thinks that if I came face-to-face with Marina herself at this moment, I'd hardly care. I fumble with my keys and forget which one fits in the front-door lock, and then I drop them and have to start again while Jake sighs and sits down on the steps to watch me.

Now that I am home, I want to block the afternoon out. I want to have a long shower and wash Kathleen Harper off my skin. Maybe, I tell myself, I've settled something. Elena would probably say that I'm exhausted because in facing Kathleen, I've finally somehow faced Marina. And maybe she would be right. Maybe just by hearing the story, even if it is eighteen months too late, I've atoned, laid to rest the ghost that has been trailing after me, or at least appeased it.

It certainly feels that way, and strangely enough, Marina seems quite close. She's been with me all the way home, and for once I'm glad. This is not Kathleen's Marina, this is another one, a private childhood Marina who had special names for the stars, and whom I see too rarely. This is the nightspinner who could make swans dance, the little girl Grandma called Brave-as-Lion. She does not visit me often, but this evening something has brought her.

I undo the Yale lock on the apartment door, and Jake trots in ahead of me. I don't bother to switch on the lights. I like the glow of the streetlamps and the dusky light that filters into the apartment. I'd like to capture this light, with its woolly yellow softness, and I wonder if it would be too dim to eat by, and if not, how exactly one would reproduce it.

In the bedroom, I take off my jacket and drop it across the bed. And then something happens. It's almost nothing. It's just the tiniest motion, just a quaver, as if the air has been disturbed. And that's when I realize that someone else is in the apartment.

THIS TIME NO ELECTRIC CURRENT PULSES THROUGH ME, maybe because I can see, or because this time I'm not cornered in the basement, not boxed into the darkness like an animal brought to bay. Up here in the half-light, I'm on my own home ground. I strain to listen, trying to pick up the signal that alerted me, but there's no specific sound, nothing in particular beyond the slow purr of six o'clock traffic in the street below. And unlike last time, I can't tell how close this person is. I know only that he's here.

My shoulder bag is on the dressing table, and I inch toward it, sliding my feet over the rug, trying not to lift them and give myself away with a step. I keep my eyes on the bedroom door, the patch of gray wall, and the corner of a picture frame beyond. It's important not to be taken by surprise. The mouth of the bag is open, and my hand snakes into it. I'm watching the hallway and holding my breath while my fingers move slowly, carefully past my wallet and my hairbrush. It's an act of will not to scrabble. Not to grab or to scream. And then my fingers find the tissue-paper package, and something inside me relaxes as my hand closes around the blades.

There's a faint smell of lavender as I raise the shears level with my shoulder, adjust my grip, and step into the hallway. It's empty. The archway to the living room and the kitchen beyond is four paces ahead on the left, and that's the space I have to get past. I can see the glint of my keys on the half-moon of the hall table, but I know I won't need them. I hadn't yet thrown the bolts on the door or placed the chain. It will take me only one second, one turn of the wrist to open it and erupt onto the landing, to scream for help. But one second can be all it takes. I remember the white sheet in the morgue, and what was left of Marina's face.

I know I have to move. I have to take a first step, and I tell myself to resist the seduction of panic. It won't help me now. I'm quite certain that my life rests on my next ten steps. I raise the shears up and back, straining my arm as if it's a spring and I'm priming it for maximum thrust. Out. Down. Hard. And then a shadow moves at the edge of the arch, and a man steps into the hall.

A noise rises in me, something unplanned and loud, but my mouth goes dry at the same time. I can't move forward or backward. My lungs feel as if they're going to burst. And then Jake scoots into the hall, races toward me wriggling with pleasure, and Beau says, "Susannah?"

"Don't!" I'm yelling. "Don't, don't, don't! Don't you ever do that again!" I'm banging on him, hammering at his shoulders with my fists, and he's trying to apologize, trying to explain that he let himself in and fell asleep on the couch waiting for me. Jake's circling us, whining in distress and confusion because Beau is the person he loves best in the world after me.

"Susannah! For Christ's sake," Beau says. "Calm down!"

It's the wrong thing to say. I'm seeing Kathleen Harper's face, feeling her nasty little smile, and remembering the morgue in Alexandria, and the phone ringing, and the crackle of cellophane around lilies. Marina runs through high grass. Yellow light falls on the word "bitch." George shakes his head. The lights go out. It's as if someone has busted open a box inside my head and a slew of pictures has come spilling out, all mixed up and all linked together.

"Get out!" I yell at Beau. "Just get out and leave me alone!"

I see the words hit him, and he recoils from me. He drops my wrists, steps backward, and opens the front door. Even as it swings closed, I know I've made a terrible mistake.

"Beau," I call, "wait." But my voice has gone limp and useless, and suddenly I feel limp and useless with it, as if I've been dragged under by a wave and spat back up, waterlogged and bedraggled. Jake is turning in circles in front of the door, whining, and the sight of him makes me start to cry. The shears are underfoot where I've dropped them, and I kick them aside as I open the door. I call Beau again, and when I lean over the railing, I can see the top of his head. He's a ball of blond hair and black shoulders growing smaller, hurrying down, and he's not about to listen to me. Jake sets off after him, tumbling down the stairs. I follow two steps at a time, which is almost too much for me, and I nearly fall over when I crash into Gordon emerging from his apartment just as I reach his landing. For a second I'm in his arms, and then he backs up a little, concern written all over his face.

"Susannah," he says, "are you all right? I heard——" I'm embarrassed at being so close to him, and at the fact that he's heard me yelling, and now he's seeing me crying. He starts to say something, to reach out toward me, but I don't want Gordon's sympathy, and in that moment I hear the sound of the front door closing and jerk away. "I'm fine," I say as I push past him more roughly than I mean to, and I don't look back or say "Sorry" as I run down the stairs.

When Jake and I get onto the sidewalk, Beau is already across the street. He's only a few yards away from us and walking with his head down. This time when I call him, his step falters, and then he stops and turns around. Jake and I wait for a cab to come by and slow down for the light, which is turning, and then we dart across the traffic.

"I'm sorry," I say as we come up to him. "I'm sorry, I'm sorry." I'm saying it like a kid, fast, throwing it out as I approach him.

"It's okay," he says, but his voice is dull and flat. "I have no business letting myself into your apartment without asking you." He recites this as if it's something he's memorized, and then he bends over and strokes the top of Jake's head. The sight of his big hand between the dog's ears is such an ordinary gesture that it fills me with relief.

"It's not you," I say. "I was just so scared."

"I'm not surprised." Beau looks up at me, and I realize he's angry. "Why the hell didn't you tell me?" It takes me a second to realize that he's talking about the laundry room, but I don't have time to wonder how he found out because he's saying, "I mean, for Christ's sake, Susannah, some lunatic breaks in and terrifies you in the basement, I can't believe how scared you must have been, and you won't even tell me? Me. Beau, Susannah. I love you, and you call up and you lie to me. How am I supposed to feel about that?"

He straightens up and crosses his arms, and I have no idea what to say. We stare at each other until, finally, I stutter, "I meant to—"

But Beau cuts me off. "No, you didn't," he says. "You weren't going to say anything, the same as you didn't say anything about the phone calls, the same as you wouldn't have told me about the car if I hadn't called that night. You were just going to deal with all this by yourself, just like you always do. You like to think that means you're strong, but it doesn't. It just means that you're too goddamn insecure to trust anyone. You certainly don't trust me."

The words have come out in a rush, and I'm stunned, partly because they're true, and partly because of Beau's hurt and anger. I've never seen him mad before. I expect him to turn on his heel and walk off now. But he doesn't, and that makes me feel like crying again. He just stands there on the sidewalk with his arms crossed, staring at me, waiting for me to say something, while Jake gets tired and sits down, and people walk past us and give us knowing little sideways looks because we're fighting in public.

"How did you know?" I finally ask.

"Captain Bubbles told me," Beau says. "Captain Bubbles" is what Beau's taken to calling Cathy since he found out she used to be a flight attendant, and as he elaborates, he's torn between telling his story and holding the high ground of being mad at me. A smile sneaks up on the corner of his mouth. "It was a classic guerrilla action," he says. "I made the tactical error of taking too long getting the key into the door, and she and her boy toy ambushed me. They told me all about it. Full-flight update. They were both dressed in spandex. It was ugly. Early Sarah Brightman was playing in the background, 'I Lost My Heart to a Starship Trooper.' "

"It was not," I say.

"Okay," Beau admits, "I made up that part. Actually, I think it was *Yanni Live at the Acropolis*. But they were both wearing muscle-man outfits, including headbands."

"He's her workout buddy," I say.

I can see Cathy popping out of her doorway in the gym gear that she sometimes wears after work. The sweatshirt is red with an airplane on it, and the leggings are silver and emblazoned with NORTH-WEST in big scarlet letters down the sides of the thighs. She has red slippers that match, and I imagine her telling Beau all the lurid details of my adventure in the laundry room while Shawn looks on, nodding, behind her.

She would have impressed upon Beau the drama and the gravity of the situation and summed him up as potential boyfriend material for me at the same time. Probably she saw it as doing me a favor, bringing out Beau's protective instinct, casting him as the white knight and me as the damsel in distress. Cathy reads articles in *Cosmo* with titles like "Five Steps to Being More Vulnerable" and "How to Put the Pride Back in Your Lion!"

"She says I should take better care of you," Beau adds, and I snort. "Come on," he says, "I'm getting cold. Let's go have a beer." He puts his arm around my shoulders as I reach for Jake's collar.

"Beau," I say before we cross the street, "what you said before? About you love me? Is that true, or did you say it just to make me feel bad?"

"It's true, and I said it to make you feel bad." Beau is looking up the street for a break in the cars, and I can't see his face.

"Well, I love you, you know," I say.

"Damn right," Beau says, and then we step off the sidewalk and weave through the stopped traffic.

The air between us is fizzing. Beau keeps his arm around my shoulders, and by the time we get to the front door, both of us are giggling. It's not until we try to get inside that we realize that neither of us has keys. I left mine upstairs, and Beau's are in the pocket of his jacket still draped over the back of my couch, so we buzz Gordon. After my earlier performance, I feel like a complete horse's ass when I have to ask him to let me in. He does, of course, and when we get to his landing, he pokes his head out of the door while I apologize for being rude earlier. He looks as embarrassed as I feel, and the soft red tinge of a blush begins to creep above his collar. To make it worse, he tries to reach out and pat Jake, who skitters away and hides behind Beau, giving him a doe-eyed look of adoration and leaving Gordon's hand hanging in midair.

"So much for enhanced security," Beau says as we come up the stairs and see my apartment door wide open. We're both feeling giddy by now, and we laugh at this as if we've made an elaborate joke.

"Hi, lovebirds!" Shawn says. He leaps out of Cathy's door and onto the landing just as we get to the top of the stairs, and I think he might end up in Beau's arms. "I was just going to come downstairs and let you in," he announces, "but Dr. Dirty got there first." Shawn's in his gym gear, too, just like Beau said, and dancing from foot to foot like a kid who has to go to the bathroom, when Cathy appears and demands that we come out and have pizza with them.

"We've been lifting weights," she announces, "so we deserve a treat!"

She flexes her arms above her head like Wonder Woman, and I notice, not for the first time, that she's in impressive shape. So, for that matter, is Shawn. I'm not exactly sure what being a workout buddy involves, but I can imagine them being incredibly competitive at the gym, running beside each other on those machines, going faster and faster, or lying on their backs side by side pushing huge dumbbells into the air.

"What do you guys like best?" Cathy is asking. "Quattro Stagioni, or those Mexicali things with roasted corn? We're going to Mario's, they have awesome margaritas."

"They don't want to eat with us!" Shawn says, turning to her. "They want to be alone. Just look at them!" He gives us an exaggerated wink and takes Cathy by the shoulders, pushing her back through her door. "Say bon voyage," he commands.

The door closes behind them, and Beau and I stand in silence. I wonder if I'm embarrassed by what Shawn said, but then I look at Beau and decide I'm not.

"Do you think they're, you know?" I whisper, nodding toward Cathy's door.

"No!" Beau whispers back. "He's her lapdog, that's all."

"I don't know," I whisper back. "I'm not sure——"

"Oh, Susannah!" Beau hisses, and then he pushes me through my open door.

"SO WHY DID YOU COME OVER, ANYWAY?" I ASK.

The question is less than gracious, but it doesn't matter. We're sitting on the living room floor in front of the gas fire. We've finished off some Thai takeout and are working on a six-pack of beer. On another night I might light candles, but not tonight. Tonight we've left all the lights on. Jake's lying on the rug with us, and the stereo is playing old Beatles songs. "Yesterday." "All My Loving." "I Wanna Hold Your Hand."

Beau looks momentarily sheepish at my question, which makes me more interested.

"What?" I ask. "What?"

"You didn't come to my concert," he says. "You were busy with the ax murderer in the basement."

"Norman Bates," I say, "please. Show some respect."

"Yeah, right," Beau says, "doesn't his mother run a hotel?"

"No, a laundromat."

"Ah," Beau says. "But you missed my solo. So I was going to give you a private performance."

"You were going to sing? Just for me?"

Beau has never offered to do this before. In fact, I've never heard a note come out of his mouth except in church. He plays the piano, but it's as if he needs that lurid blue choir robe and the doleful eyes of Jesus on the neon-green meadow in order to find his voice. Now he's looking at me out of the corner of his eye, gauging my reaction to this gift.

"Will you?" I ask. "Please. For me and Jake?"

I lean over and switch off the stereo. John Lennon's voice stops in midword. I curl my legs underneath myself, and Jake puts his head in my lap, and both of us watch Beau. He's thinking this over, and when he finally makes up his mind and gets to his feet, he's as awkward as a bear. He stands above me and straightens his shoulders. He gives his arms and hands a little shake. And then he sings.

" 'I looked over Jordan, and what did I see, coming for to carry me home?' " His beautiful voice swells and fills the room. It balloons around me and Jake and Beau himself and rises up until we all seem to be rising with it. " 'A band of angels,' " Beau continues, " 'coming after me, coming for to carry me home.' "

I'VE WRITTEN "KATHLEEN HARPER" IN BIG BLOCK LETTERS on my graph pad, and I'm filling them in, shading the sides and making them cast a shadow across the little blue boxes on the paper, while I listen to the phone ring two hundred miles away. It rained last night, and a bright watery light plays over the living room floor. The puddles on the balcony shine white and ice blue, as if a mirror has been flung down and its broken pieces lie faceup to the sky. The phone has rung fifteen times, and I'm about to hang up when somebody answers.

I can tell right away that it isn't him. I remember his voice quite clearly, and it was measured, low, and precise. The words were as clean as the bright white cuffs of his shirt, as neat as the card that I have in front of me. "I want you to feel free," he'd said, "to call me. Anytime, if you have any questions. If there's anything you think of or anything I can do for you." I remember the words clearly, even eighteen months later, and I can't imagine the voice that spoke them ever sounding as staccato as the one I'm hearing now. This one barks. It sounds both harsh and matter-of-fact, and it spits out "Alexandria, Homicide," as if I've called a taxi stand or a sports bar.

When I ask for Detective Mark Cope, I can feel a pause come down the line and I imagine him dead, shot in an alleyway while in pursuit; or retired, moved to the Midwest to become a police chief in some suburb outside of Fort Wayne or Des Moines, where his kids can ride bicycles in the driveway and walk to the White Hen Pantry. But neither of these things is true. Detective Cope is in court for the day is all, and I can call back tomorrow or leave a message.

I choose the latter, partly because I promised Beau this morning before he left that I would do this, and partly because I'm afraid that if I don't leave a message, I'll lose my nerve. I'll decide that just because somebody vandalized my car and Kathleen Harper is a headcase, there's no need to waste Detective Cope's time and patience. I'll decide that this is stupid after all, that maybe what I really need to do is get on with my life, go out to dinner and buy a new dress. And if I do any of those things, I'll never call again. So I leave my number, area code first, and spell "deBreem" twice, just to be certain that there's no mistake.

I devote the rest of the day to the museum tearoom. This time I'm trying a light blue, two shades short of turquoise, and a lot of silver gilt. It's like Elgar played on electric instruments. I want the result to be both refined and tangy, to go with the lemon tea and cold white wine that these places demand, and I wonder if all the chairs and tables could be made of bright stainless steel but with curlicues.

I don't think of Marina, which is a relief, and it's midafternoon before I take a break. Jake is asleep on his bed, stretched out like a rag doll, his head flopping slightly onto the floor. Beau took him to the park very early this morning while I was still in bed. They came back with croissants, and I find buttery flakes of pastry in the sheets when I make the bed.

Beau circles around the edges of my mind, but I don't let him come all the way in. Everything between us has shifted. We're lovers now, and I'm not sure I want to think about what this might mean. At least not yet. I make the bed, put some clothes away, and fold up the Thai food cartons that still sit by the sink. And then, for some reason, I picture Kathleen Harper.

It's her height that comes back to me, the way I looked up at her when she opened her front door. And it's the loose-jointed power that swung through her stride and echoed in her arms that I find suddenly disconcerting. Like the Cheshire cat's, her smile materializes in front of me, the curving of her mouth that couldn't wipe out the way she looked at me, couldn't counterbalance the shadow behind her eyes, or the chapped, mottled skin of her lips, or the pungent smell of jealousy that rose off of her like steam.

I know, I'm absolutely certain, that I turned the deadbolt and latched the chain on the door after Beau left this morning, but all of a sudden I'm out of the kitchen and crossing the living room. I'm almost tiptoeing, as if I'm afraid that the air might jangle if I disturb it. And I'm hurrying. I'm tugging the chain, pressing the screws that hold the lock plate with my thumb, testing how much weight they'll take, and then I'm turning the key. I release the deadbolt and put my ear down and listen as it turns over. And then I unlock it and lock it again. Just to be sure.

BY LATE AFTERNOON THERE'S A TAUT SILENCE IN THE apartment. Every particle of air seems charged with possibility, and none of it pleasant. Detective Cope still hasn't called back, and as much as I'd like to call Beau, I don't want to tie up the phone for even a minute. Finally I can't concentrate on the tearoom at all anymore, and I decide to give up and take Jake to the park. Reaching the street is like stepping back into real time. I feel as if I'm reentering life after being trapped in some kind of suspended animation. Jake and I pause at the top of the steps above the sidewalk while I clip his leash on and arrange his selection of tennis balls in my pockets.

It's four-thirty, and children are coming home from school. Mothers walk by in pairs, grasping children by the hands and talking, their glossy heads nodding and their long woolen dress coats flapping open to reveal blue jeans and running shoes underneath. At the lights, a long line of little kids, all holding hands, comes to a halt. The two women shepherding them clap like cheerleaders and nudge the children into order, bending to adjust flopping backpacks, and pick up drawings of pumpkins and black cats that have slipped out of mittened hands and wafted onto the sidewalk like leaves.

I don't think it's going to rain, but a mist seems to be descending on the city, as if a cloud is slowly lowering until its underside rests on the peaks and spires of the buildings. The sound of footsteps always seems to be slightly muffled in this kind of weather, and as Jake and I head down toward the dog park, turning away from the busy cross streets, we seem to be moving in silence. The people we meet, men in business suits coming home early, women with grocery bags balanced on their hips, pass by us in a whisper, accompanied by only a rustle of clothing or the newspaper. Invariably their heads are bent, and sometimes I think I recognize people, only to find as they come closer to me that they are total strangers.

The dog park is alive with activity, and even before we cross the street, Jake is straining at his leash. This is one of the busiest times of the day here. Mothers and kids bring their dogs after school, and the vet students from Penn arrive with their foundlings. The instant we get across the road, Jake begins to hop with excitement. When I do not let him off his leash immediately, he turns and sits, staring at me imploringly, his gaze shifting from my face to my pockets where the tennis balls rest. When I release him and throw one, aiming it in a long lob at the top of the closest little artificial hill, Jake gives a squeak of delight and bounds after it, his ears flattening in anticipation.

I see several people I know, a sculptor accompanied by his St. Bernard, an accountant who practices tai chi on the tennis courts watched by his Old English sheepdog, and a woman whose name I can never remember who has an Airedale called Elsa. We greet one another and form a little circle of talk. We walk a circuit or two around the park together, discussing the weather or the likelihood that the leash law might actually be enforced, the absurdity of the advance marketing for Thanksgiving and even, someone says, Christmas, which has already started.

A pack of dogs whirls around the central patch of grass, chasing the tennis balls that someone inevitably throws for them. They race back and forth and around in circles, shifting their pattern and direction like a flock of ungainly birds. We watch them while we talk and are only dimly aware of where our own dog is in the group. So, when I am finally ready to go home and call Jake, it is not surprising that I can't find him immediately.

Occasionally, if Jake's having a good time, he pretends to ignore me. But I still expect him to peel off from the main body and come to me eventually, and I'm a little irritated when he doesn't. I whistle again, scanning the dogs, and it's a second before I realize that I don't see him. I can't pick out his tall pointy ears or the black tip of his tail from the midst of the woofing herd that surges past me, then spins around and surges again.

"Jake!" I call. "Jakey!" The sculptor and the Airedale woman have located their dogs and are brandishing leashes, and I've walked down the path a ways, wondering if Jake's gone off under the stand of squat little blue spruce trees sitting beside the boundary fence. I keep calling him and clinking the end of his leash, as if he might hear and recognize it.

Small petals of anxiety are beginning to unfurl inside me when I finally see him. He must have gotten sidetracked and gone after a squirrel. He's coming around the edge of the tennis court, where he knows he's not allowed to go because the tarmacked yard beyond is derelict and edged on one side by heavy scrub and on the other by a warehouse. He looks suitably abashed. In fact, he looks so sheepish that he might have committed a serious sin, like going after a cat. But I know that this is unlikely, if only because no kitty in its right mind would come within a mile of this place.

"Jaake," I say as he comes close to me, drawing the A out into a question, and he flattens his ears down on the sides of his head, the way he did when he was reprimanded as a puppy, the way he still does when he hears thunder.

We make it home in record time, because I want to watch the six o'clock news, and I just manage to mix Jake's food and slap his bowl onto the floor and pour myself a drink before I hear the sober tones of Jim Lehrer issuing from the living room.

"Today," Jim says, "the attorney general appointed an independent counsel—" and I leave the cupboards swinging open and abandon the kitchen, making for the couch, where I slump and stretch my legs out in front of me and take a first cool sip of wine.

An hour later, after a round-table discussion on the Balkans and a piece about geese migrating, I notice that Jake hasn't eaten his dinner. He hasn't even moved. After we came in, he followed me into the kitchen and then flopped down on his bed, and he's still lying there, curled up like a giant fox, his nose tucked in between his hind paws and his tail. Something makes me say his name, and even as I say it, I'm getting up, I'm crossing the room toward him, moving too fast because something is wrong.

Jake just barely lifts his head, and his eyes are dull and glassy. Beads of white foam are coming out of the corners of his mouth. I grab him and force his jaws apart to see if there's anything in there, although I'm not sure what I should be looking for. I try to lift his head up, but it's heavy in my hands, as if it's stuffed and weighted, and when I pull on his collar and call him, my voice high and frantic, he gets up, takes a couple of steps, and flops back onto the floor with a thud so hard it must be painful.

My fingers turn fat and rubbery when I punch Beau's number, like in one of those bad dreams when you're trying to call the police but can't hit the right buttons no matter how hard you try. Then I hear ringing and expect to hear Beau's voice. But when I do, it's the answering machine.

"Beau!" I shout into the phone. "Beau, it's me!" I realize he must be watching *The Simpsons,* and that's why he hasn't picked up, and I know that if I shout loud enough, if I tell him what's going on, he'll hear me and answer. His phone is on the table right next to the couch, so even if he's asleep, the ringing must have woken him.

"Beau!" I shout. "Beau, there's something wrong with Jake!" But Beau still doesn't answer, and in a couple of seconds, I hear a long beep that cuts me off. I don't know where he can be. At Sherlock's? Still at work? I have never known Beau to work a minute after five-thirty, but I start to punch his work number anyway, then remember that he has a new extension and I don't know it. As I reach for my address book, scrabbling in my desk drawer, I glance at Jake and realize I don't have time for this. Instead I call the garage and ask them to get my car out. Then I grab my keys and I'm racing down the stairs.

Tony, my night garage man, raises his eyebrows when he sees me running up the sidewalk. It's only four blocks and around the corner from my front door to the converted carriage houses that once held pony carts and four-in-hand coaches and now hold a cross section of Saabs and SUVs with the occasional Volvo and Audi thrown in.

"There's something wrong with Jake," I say by way of explanation for the fact that I'm not even wearing a jacket, although it's begun to rain, and not handing him the usual two-dollar tip that I give him when he has my car ready and running.

"Don't you worry," Tony says. Jake is a big favorite at the garage, and Tony's concern is all over his face. He closes the door for me as I pull out into the street, and I say a prayer to the god of parking that there'll be a space in front of the house. There is. I see it as soon as I turn the corner, and I slide the car into it, hugging the curb with no space to spare on the first try.

Jake doesn't want to get up at all now, and I have to drag him to his feet. There's more of the white foamy stuff along the edges of his mouth, and he hangs his head as if he's about to be sick. I half pull and half shove him out onto the landing, and I only just remember to grab my shoulder bag before I slam the door. The stairs are easier, but he's still like a big floppy toy. He goes a few steps and then wants to sit. When I push him from behind, he wobbles and looks as if he's going to stumble and fall all the way down, so I have to grab him from in front and try to hold him up and pull him at the same time. I'd pick him up if I could, but at a hundred pounds, Jake is too big. At some point I think that I ought to get help, but there's no noise from behind any of the doors, and I'm afraid that explaining would take too long.

Zoe and Shawn come in through the front door just as we reach the entryway.

"Susannah!" Zoe says. "My God, what's the matter?"

"I don't know," I say. "I'm not sure. I have to get him to Penn. The car's right outside." Zoe drops her briefcase and moves to grab Jake, who is three steps up and has started to wobble again. But before she can reach him, Shawn jumps up the stairs and catches the big dog up in his arms. Jake doesn't like to be cuddled by strangers, and he tries to struggle, even giving a little growl as Shawn lifts him. Zoe grabs Jake's head, which is hanging at a horrible angle, and I can't help but notice that dog hair is getting all over the front of her pretty black overcoat.

"Where's your car? Right out here?" Shawn asks, and I nod and open the vestibule door, and together the three of us cross the cold damp marble and go down the steps to the sidewalk. I get the car door open, and when Shawn tries to slide Jake onto the backseat, his legs drop and drag, and his nails make little screeching sounds against the wet stone. Zoe and I run around to the other side of the car, and as traffic whips past, we lift and pull Jake onto his old folded blanket. By now his eyes are closed, and his lips are twitching up in a funny little snarl. I turn down Zoe's offer to come with me and ask her instead to call the vet school and tell them I'm on my way. She obviously thinks that Jake is dying, and I do, too.

She leans in the car's open window and grabs my hand on the steering wheel. Tears are pooling on the rims of her wide blue eyes. "I'll tell them you're coming, I'll call right now," she says. Then she lets go of my hand and runs back up the steps. Shawn stands in the road and raises his arms like a traffic cop. A car skids to a halt, and the driver swears, and I just see Shawn swearing back at him as I pull out and slot myself behind a cab and catch the tail end of the yellow light.

I make it to the vet school in eight minutes flat, and by the time I get there, I don't think Jake's breathing anymore. Zoe's been as good as her word; a bunch of people are waiting for me. When I stop, they come running with a doggy stretcher. A vet is asking me questions while two people lift Jake out of the car and take him away. The last thing I see is his tail. Just before they go through the big swinging doors, it flops off the stretcher and hangs down like something dead.

I SIT IN THE WAITING ROOM. I'VE FILLED OUT FORMS GIVING permission for Jake to be anesthetized and operated on, but I have no idea if he's even still alive. The wall opposite me is papered with posters giving information on worming, and pet care, and adoption, and I stare at them as though I'm memorizing every word, but the letters slide into meaningless jumbles. In my mind, I go over and over the contents of the cupboards under my kitchen sink. There are bottles of Ajax and Lysol and possibly tiny cartons of rat poison. I keep my paints and solvents in a box in the hall cupboard, and I'm not careful with it.

I often leave the door open when I get a jacket or boots or even Jake's tennis balls. And for that matter, the balls could have rolled in something in the park. God knows what. Drugs. Poisons. Anything.

When Shawn comes in and sits down beside me, it takes me a second to realize that it's him. It's not until he offers me one of the Starbucks cups he's holding and says, "Here, this is for you," that I even look at him. He's wearing a black leather jacket and a baseball cap, and having dyed his purple hair back to brown, he looks pretty much like everyone else. I want to ask him what he's doing here, and possibly to tell him to go away, but he doesn't give me the chance.

"You shouldn't be here by yourself," he says, and I take the cup from him. "Mocha latte," Shawn whispers, "with a shot." He winks at me and opens the pocket of his jacket so I can see a little silver hip flask nesting there. "Never want to be without it. It's good for the soul."

The faint whiff of brandy curls toward me as I raise the cup, and he's right, it tastes good. "Thanks," I say.

Shawn nods without looking at me and takes a sip from his own cup. "Do you know anything yet?" he asks, and when I shake my head, he doesn't say anything else. He just sits there beside me in the waiting room, staring at the worming posters and sipping his coffee.

"You don't have to stay," I say finally. "This could take a long time."

Shawn shakes his head. "If you don't mind," he says, "I'd like to. I had a dog once, a retriever. Her name was Jess," he adds, as if this explains his desire to sit here with me in the vet-school waiting room, which, in a way, I suppose it does.

From time to time, I glance at him out of the corner of my eye, and the familiarity of his face is reassuring. He's a bigger man than he seems on first glance, and the bulk of him seems more solid, somehow more real, now that he's not camouflaged in one of his muscle-man outfits. I wonder where he came from and why he's here in Philadelphia. Some other time I might ask him about this, and about Jess, but at the moment it doesn't seem to matter very much.

When my name is finally called, I hand Shawn my empty cardboard cup and follow a young vet who is tall and pale and sounds Russian through a set of swinging doors that say PERSONNEL ONLY in chipped red letters. I think at first that I'm going to get to see Jake, and that he's going to be dead, but instead the vet leads me down a corridor and into what is clearly his office.

The room is tiny, with just enough space for a desk and two chairs. It doesn't have a window. Instead of daylight, an X-ray box glows behind the vet's head. A nameplate on his desk reads DR. VINCENT GUREWICH, DVM. He gestures for me to sit down.

"Jake is in shock," Dr. Vincent Gurewich says. He is holding a clipboard with papers attached to it, and he looks at them, not me. "We don't know exactly what is wrong with him. We've pumped his stomach, but he seems to have had some kind of seizure. We're trying to stabilize him now."

Dr. Gurewich speaks in very precise sentences. When he finally glances up at me, he looks exhausted, and I wonder how long he's been here, stitching up cats and dogs and telling people that their pets are dead. "It's possible," he says, "that he could have had a stroke, although at five, he's very young for that."

"What?" It sounds unbelievable.

Dr. Gurewich shrugs. "It's possible," he says. "It could have been brought on by some form of poisoning, or he could have a congenital heart defect that there would be no reason for you to know about. And nothing you could do about. On the other hand, it could be colic. It happens more frequently with horses, but also with large, deep-chested dogs. Their intestine becomes blocked and can twist and turn septic. Does Jake bolt his food?"

"No," I say. "At least I don't think so."

"Do you remember when he last drank?"

I think back. Usually Jake has a long drink and spews water all over the kitchen floor when he comes back from the park, but this evening I can't remember whether he did or not. "Maybe at two or three this afternoon," I say. "I'm not sure."

Dr. Gurewich nods as if this has been helpful, and then he stands up, so I do, too.

"They should be X-raying him now," he says. "If there's a blockage, it will show up, and we'll operate on him to remove it. He couldn't have gotten into rat poison? Anything like that?" I remember the little cardboard tray of d-Con that I'd placed under the sink pipes at the back of the cupboard right after I moved in, but in order to get to it, Jake would have had to plow through a whole collection of cleaning fluids and old sponges and unused shoe-polish kits, and I'm sure I would have noticed.

"I really don't think so," I say.

Dr. Gurewich nods and almost smiles as he opens the door for me. "There's nothing more you can do for Jake, Miss deBreem," he says. "Go home. We're sending the contents of his stomach to the lab for testing, and we will call you as soon as we know anything."

I feel as if I'm being dismissed, which I am, and I can't think of anything else to ask or say. I'm just about to step past Dr. Gurewich and into the hall when he darts back into his office.

"Oh, I nearly forgot," he says. He reaches into one of the drawers and hands me a large manila envelope. When I look inside, I see that it contains the dark leather coil of Jake's collar.

SHAWN STANDS UP EXPECTANTLY AS I COME THROUGH THE swinging doors. At the sight of him, I feel a quick, mean stab of irritation. I tell myself to grow up. He's only trying to be kind. He didn't have to bring me coffee or sit here wasting an hour. I tell myself I should appreciate the gesture. And then I try to convince myself that I do.

"They think he might have had a seizure, and they're keeping him for a while," I say as blithely as I can. "They think he's going to be fine, though. I'm sure he will be." But Shawn doesn't smile. He can tell that I'm lying about Jake being fine, and that half irritates me and half makes me like him.

"Come on," I say, "let's get out of here." I figure the least I can do is buy the guy a beer.

Bruges is a dark, wood-paneled place with stained-glass windows and pewlike booths. They specialize in Belgian beer, and the pitcher on the table between us is filled with something I can't pronounce. Shawn ordered it. He picked this place out. It's only around the corner from my garage and the house, and although I've walked past it probably a million times, I've never been inside before. I wonder if Shawn and Cathy come here, if they sit in these booths and eat moules frites and squeal together over the *Inquirer*'s style section. Now Shawn takes off his baseball cap and runs his fingers through his short, spiky hair so it stands straight up on end.

"Here's to Jake," he says, and raises his glass. We clink edges, and I take a mouthful of the tepid amber liquid. I don't like the taste much, but the color's beautiful.

"Do you live around here?" I ask.

"Kind of," he says, "about ten blocks away. It grows on you," he adds, nodding at my glass. "I thought it was gross, too, at first. Now I'm a convert. Actually, I think I'm just proud of the fact that I can pronounce the name. I always wanted to be a European."

"Have you been there a lot?" I ask. The question sounds ridiculous, but for some reason I have begun to feel incredibly awkward, as though I'm on a high school date. This makes me wonder again if I've got Shawn wrong. Despite the skintight jeans and the hair, despite the rhinestone earring, which he isn't even wearing right now, I've never been entirely convinced that he's gay. Maybe Cathy's on to something and he's straight after all, I think. Or hell, maybe he swings both ways. Who knows? But it does occur to me to wonder if he's making a pass at me and I just hadn't noticed.

Then he says, "Not a lot. I mean, I went on the postcollege-grand-tour-Eurailpass-trip. You know, backpack, Paris, Berlin, London. But a couple of years ago, we spent some time in Italy. Me and Bill. He was my partner," Shawn adds. "He died last year."

"Oh," I say, "I'm very sorry." Now I feel horrible.

Shawn shakes his head and actually smiles. "It's okay," he says, "well, I mean, it isn't. Especially not for Bill. What I mean is, it wasn't AIDS. He had a heart attack. It had been coming for a while. He was a lot older than me." I'm not sure what I'm supposed to say to this, but Shawn rescues me before I have to worry about it. "Yeah," he says, "Florence was incredible. Have you ever been there?" I shake my head. "Amazing," he says. "Bill and I only spent a week or so, but, man, would I love to go back there. You know, get an apartment for a while, just live? It's like, if you could do that, you'd become a whole 'nother person. You know?" He reaches for a beer mat and pulls a pen out of his pocket.

"Well," I say, "lots of people think that about moving somewhere." The specter of George in a beret is hovering above my head. "Sometimes maybe it's even true."

Shawn looks up at me and grins. He finishes the little drawing he's been making on the beer mat and pushes it toward me. "Here," he says, "for you. In case you don't ever get to Florence. That's the Palazzo Vecchio, the Medici palace where they hung their enemies out of the windows."

"Cool," I say. The picture is of a square castle with a tower.

Shawn pours more beer into my glass. "I mean," he says, "I happen to think that people can reinvent themselves. If they want to. I'm trying it next in Mexico, but I'll have to be quick, I only have a week down there. Zoe's stingy with vacation."

"Oh yeah?"

He nods and puts his glass down. "I'm going down for the Day of the Dead, it's on November second, and it's kind of like Halloween but not really. It's basically a big party. They take all this food to the cemeteries and lay tables and have feasts out there with all their ancestors and their dead friends. It's as if, once a year, the dead aren't really dead anymore. You can sit down and have dinner with them and work out all the stuff you didn't work out before they died. Sort of like an annual second chance."

I have a sudden vision of myself sitting down to a big meal with Marina. I wonder if we'd be our adult selves or our childhood selves, if we'd be eating roast lamb and a spinach soufflé or hot dogs and dilly beans. If we're grown up, I can't decide if she'd look like she did before she was murdered or after, and this bothers me. Either way, I think, it's not my kind of thing.

"Sugar skulls," Shawn says.

"What?" I ask.

"Sugar skulls," he repeats. "That's what they make for the dead. With black licorice holes for eyes. I'll bring you back some."

I realize that he's been going on about his trip to Mexico and I haven't heard a word. Now his face collapses, as though I've been a terrible disappointment. "Look," I say, "I'm sorry, I—"

But Shawn cuts me off. He leaves my apology, if that's what it was, hanging in midair. "That's okay," he says quickly, "really, Susannah, that's okay. You know, you've had a lot of shit to deal with lately. First your car, then the laundry room thing, and now the dog. It must be really scary." I realize that this is virtually the same thing Gordon said to me, and I wonder why it is that men need to convince themselves that women are frightened all the time.

"I don't really think they're related," I say. But even as the words come out of my mouth, louder than I mean them to be, my stomach shifts.

Shawn shakes his head. "Of course not, I didn't mean that," he says, even though we both know he did. "It's just that, well, you should be careful." He laughs and grabs my glass again. "Hell," he says, refilling it, "we all should. Did you know that Cathy went on, like, some airline-sponsored assault course? So she could jump hijackers and that sort of stuff. You would not believe what that woman can bench-press." Shawn raises his eyebrows and flexes his muscles. "She's probably the only one of us who could actually defend herself if she had to."

I look at him over the top of my beer. I'm wondering if he's going to tell me now how much he can bench-press, but he doesn't. He doesn't have to. He lifted Jake up like he was a powder puff. Beau and Gordon may call him Tinkerbell, but the guy looks to me like he's one solid muscle. He smiles at me, and I avoid his eyes and concentrate on my beer. But it's too late, he already knows what I'm thinking. To my horror, I feel the heat of a blush creeping up my neck, and I hope it's dark enough in here so he can't see.

"I mean, I don't see Zoe or Justin standing up too well," Shawn says, laughing. "Their idea of being attacked is somebody taking the sugar off their table at Starbucks without asking, and as for Gordon, maybe he's really Superman, but I still don't want to see him in his long underwear."

"Did you really open his credit card bill?"

The words are out of my mouth before I even realize I've said them, and I stare at Shawn, mortified, my hand frozen with my glass half raised.

He looks at me and laughs. "The expression on your face is worth a million bucks," he says. "Sure I did. Opening people's mail is fun."

"Fun?"

"Sure," he says. "You know, with a kettle and steam, just like in the movies." He grins. "I bet you never did anything like that, did you, Susannah? I bet you were always a good girl. Besides," he adds, "I wanted to know what Gordon was up to."

"Shawn!" I put my glass down. I can see him, bending over the electric kettle in Cathy's apartment. "Do you open my mail, too?" I ask. "And everybody else's?"

"Naw," he says. "Cathy shows me all hers, and it's my job to read Justin and Zoe's. You don't get anything interesting." He winks at me, but I'm not entirely sure he's joking. "I only opened Gordon's 'cause he's such a putz. Besides, I wanted to know what he does in there in his apartment by himself all the time. I thought maybe he was putting call girls on his MasterCard, or spending all night jerking off to those nine-hundred numbers."

"Is he?" I can't believe I'm asking this.

Shawn shakes his head. "Nah," he says, "nothin' that good. Our Gordy is a strange one, though. But maybe it just takes one to know one."

Shawn is still talking. Now he's asking the waiter for a menu and announcing that he bets it's years since I had a good meal. I don't want to have dinner with him, and I stand up too fast. My full glass of beer spills and pools across the table.

"Oh," Shawn says. He stops in midsentence. The waiter comes over with a big cloth and starts making clicking noises with his tongue, and I grab the beer mat with the picture on it and try to blot it against the leg of my jeans before the ink on Shawn's castle runs.

"I'm sorry," I say. "I'm really sorry, but I have to go. They're going to call from Penn. Maybe some other time—" I gesture at the beer being sopped up by the waiter, and at the half-empty pitcher.

"Don't worry, Susannah," Shawn says. He smiles at me. "I understand, really. I hope Jake is okay." I nod mutely and back up a step. "It's okay," he says again. He waves at the table. "It's just water and grain."

I smile and nod, my head wagging, and then I turn and start for the door, and it seems as if my boots make way too much noise on the dark, polished floor.

Back at the house, I sneak through the entryway, hoping nobody's home, and run up the stairs like a coward. When I pass Gordon's door, I try not to quicken my pace, but I can't help it. There's no sound coming from inside, and I'm glad. I don't want Gordon to be home. A get-well card addressed to Jake and signed by everybody has been left on the landing table, and I take it inside and prop it against my cookbooks. Part of me feels like such a heel for bolting out of Bruges that I actually consider going all the way back there to apologize to Shawn again, but I don't know what I'd say.

I tell myself that I should go and thank Cathy for the card, but I don't think I could stand her sympathy just at the moment, and I even feel half guilty for having a beer with Shawn behind her back. What I do, finally, is pick up the phone and call downstairs, because I promised Zoe that I would. But she and Justin aren't in, so I leave a message. Some very mundane part of my brain still seems to be functioning, and as I hang up, I remember the mat of pale hairs on Zoe's coat and wonder if I should offer to have it dry-cleaned.

The light on my answering machine is blinking, and the little red number two is lit up. The messages must be from Beau, and I start to call him, but when I'm halfway through punching in his number, I put the phone down. I know it's not fair or even particularly rational, but some part of me is really mad that he didn't somehow figure out where I was and come down to Penn, and instead I had to listen to Shawn talk about sugar skulls and dinners with dead people. I'll call him tomorrow, I think, when I can trust myself to be nice.

I pour myself a drink and sit on one of the high kitchen stools. The Scotch burns slightly in the back of my throat, and when it hits my stomach, I can feel it glowing, flickering against the darkness inside me like a little bonfire. On the counter beside me is a picture of Jake in a silver frame that says WOOF on the bottom, and I take another sip and promise that if he lives, I'll leave this city.

I should have left here a long time ago. When George went to Paris, I should have made a clean break. This is my punishment for not doing it. This is my punishment for penning Jake up in an apartment, for making the high point of his day the worn grass and paved paths of the dog park. This is my punishment for hanging on. I have money in the bank. I'll move to the Blue Ridge Mountains or the Great Smokies. Or maybe to a farm on the banks of the Shenandoah or the Potomac. I'll turn my back on this place. I'll walk away from the heavy facades of the brownstones, from the lacy spread of the trees in Rittenhouse Square, from the memory of George's touch, and from the lights that reflect at night like fireworks on the black, oily water of the Schuylkill. I'll leave it all behind if Jake lives. I swear. And we'll go somewhere, just the two of us.

THE PILLS ARE RIGHT WHERE I LEFT THEM, STUFFED IN an old cosmetics bag at the back of my top drawer. Elena prescribed them for me after I moved in here over a year ago, when I was having trouble sleeping. The truth was, I didn't really mind being awake, so I never used them much. But I didn't throw them out, either, thinking that sleeping pills might come in handy. These are small and pale blue, presumably to conjure up the picture of dreaming on puffy white clouds in innocent skies, and I'm shaking two of them out into the palm of my hand when the phone rings.

At first I think it might be the vet at Penn, but as I'm about to answer it, I look at my bedside clock. It's midnight. I watch the phone. It rings five times, and just as my machine is about to come on, it stops. I stand there, then give it the finger and pop the pills into my mouth.

THE PHONE IS RINGING AGAIN, AND THAT'S WHAT WAKES me. Shrill and long, it feels like a thin, bright chain yanking me up from thick darkness. My hand finds the receiver before I open my eyes, and it takes me a minute to understand that I'm hearing Dr. Gurewich.

"Not colic," he is saying, "and so there was no need to operate on him. It was very lucky, really——"

I've opened my eyes now, and I'm focusing on the tiny figures running across the pale green lawn in the picture of Merton House that hangs opposite my bed, and that is when I say, "Lucky?"

"Yes," Dr. Gurewich says. He pauses as though he's slightly annoyed with me for being so slow. "In cases like this, we don't always get to pump the stomach fast enough, but as I was saying, Jake didn't ingest much of whatever it was. We don't think there will be any long-term damage internally, but I'd like to keep him here for a few more days, until we get the full toxicology reports."

My brain feels as if it's been doused in syrup. It's sticky, and nothing seems to connect very well. "Did Jake eat something?" I ask.

"Probably," Dr. Gurewich replies. "We won't know what, exactly, until after we get all the tests. I wish I could tell you that would be today, but the lab is very backed up. Of course, I'll call when I have the complete results. But for now I would like to keep my eye on Jake. It's not cheap, I'm afraid. The cost per day—"

"It doesn't matter," I cut him off. I'm remembering Jake's picture in the frame that says WOOF, and the manila envelope with his collar in it. "I don't care what it costs. I want what's best for Jake."

"I'm glad," Dr. Gurewich says. "We'll call you tomorrow, Ms. de-Breem. I'm sure Jake will be fine," he adds, almost as an afterthought. And then he hangs up.

I lie in bed, holding the phone. The sleeping pills have made me feel as if I've grown enormously fat overnight, and I keep blinking. It would be easy to slide back down into sleep, but I decide to get up. I should call Beau, who will be worried by now, and besides, I want to tell someone the good news about Jake. The bedside clock says seven-forty, and I switch the radio on to hear the news. Someone on NPR is talking about farming as I get out of bed and turn on the lights and walk into the bathroom.

My eyes feel distinctly gummy, and I'm still blinking like an owl when I lean over to turn on the cold water. It's odd that my new kitchen shears are lying on the edge of the sink. I don't remember leaving them there. The pills have made me groggier than I thought, and I splash cold water on my face. Then I reach for a hand towel and look up.

The hair is long and copper-colored. It's a thick strand, half a handful, what the Victorians would have called a lock, and it's mine. It loops over the tape that holds it to the mirror and hangs down like a tail. And now I understand why the shears are here.

My own face comes into focus slowly from behind the hair, as if I'm far away and getting closer. I watch my hand in the mirror as I raise it to my forehead. I watch as my fingers find the fringe that is little more than a bristle. They brush the spot, feeling for a nick or a scrape on the skin. But there isn't one.

It was done carefully, and thanks to the sleeping pills, I probably didn't even move. I probably didn't even sense the person standing beside my bed in the dark. Or the hand that reached down and lifted my hair. Or the shears that came so close that they must have whispered against my face as the blades made their sharp, clean cut.

CHAPTER 14

"SO YOU'RE NOT ACTUALLY CERTAIN THAT YOU LOCKED the door?"

This time the police officer is a woman. She's about my age, and she's not wearing a uniform, which I assume means that I've moved up in the world. Her partner isn't wearing a uniform, either, and he's prowling around the apartment jiggling window frames while she talks to me and writes things in her notebook. Her name is Detective Rebecca Aaronson. Now she raises her eyebrows and inclines her head toward the front door. She's asked me this question before.

"I think I did," I say, "but I'm not sure. My dog was—"

"Right, right"—she waves her hand in the air—"your dog was sick."

Her partner has raised the living room window and stepped out onto the balcony, where he's examining the tree and peering over the balustrade. Detective Aaronson walks past me, and I follow her as she goes down the hall and into the bathroom. The lock of hair is still taped to the mirror. She looks at it and then flips through her notebook.

"So," she says, "let me just get this straight. You arrived back at your apartment at approximately ten last night and saw no one. The phone rang at midnight, but you didn't answer it. Shortly afterward, you went to bed and fell asleep. When you woke up this morning, you found the kitchen shears by the sink and this piece of hair taped to the mirror. Then you called us."

"That's right," I say.

"And you heard nothing in the course of the night? You didn't wake up at any time?"

"I'd taken a sleeping pill. Well, two, actually."

"And is that normal? That you take sleeping pills?"

"No. I was upset because of my dog."

Detective Aaronson and her partner have already examined the bathroom, and I have already told her all of this once, but she seems to want to hear it again. She flips through a few more pages in her notebook and nods to herself, as though she's come to some kind of decision. Then she glances at me, and her eyes are hard. They're a flinty blue and ringed by lush, dark lashes that seem somehow unnatural. The eyes are an extravagant ornament in her otherwise unremarkable face.

"Miss deBreem," she says, "approximately three weeks ago, the police were called to an alley off Chestnut Street where you claimed that someone scratched the word 'bitch' on your car door. Two days after that, you claimed that someone broke in and sang to you in the basement. There were no witnesses to either of these events. Now you claim that you've been receiving phone calls, which you've never reported, and that last night someone entered your apartment, cut off some of your hair, and taped it to your bathroom mirror, although there is no evidence of forced entry, nothing was taken, no harm was done to you, and you are not even certain whether you left the door open."

A wave of anger rolls through me, and I feel myself begin to tremble, which I do not want to do in front of this woman. "What, exactly, are you suggesting?" I try to keep my voice even, to stop it from creeping up above the red line that registers distress. "That I'm making this up?"

She doesn't reply, which is obviously a technique that she learned in cop school, or from watching *Law & Order.*

"Are you seriously suggesting that I cut off my own hair?" I realize that I'm sounding hysterical now. "That I carved 'bitch' on my own car door? That I made up someone coming into the basement? Why the hell would I do that?" I stop and take a deep breath. I'm trying to regain my cool and failing.

Detective Aaronson studies me and then says, "You have a drunk-driving conviction, Ms. deBreem, from October of last year. Is that correct?"

"Of course it's correct," I snap. It happened about a month after George left. During a period when, to put it mildly, I wasn't doing too well. I'd been out to dinner with Lolly and drank too much, which was par for the course at the time, and on the way home, I ran a red light. Luckily, I was only marginally over the limit, and it was two A.M. and the cruiser was the only other car around. In less auspicious circumstances, I might well have killed someone or at least lost my license. As it was, since it was a first offense, the judge accepted my plea and a hefty fine. "I don't see what that has to do with anything," I add.

Detective Aaronson consults her notes again. "At the time, you told the court that you were under extraordinary stress, your husband had left you and—"

"Fiancé," I say. "He wasn't my husband, he was my fiancé."

"And that you were seeing a therapist, a Dr. Schulberg. Are you still seeing him?"

"Her," I say, "and I don't see what that has to do with this."

"Have you ever heard of Munchausen syndrome, Ms. deBreem?" She asks the question so fast that I'm not sure I've heard her correctly.

"What did you say?" I ask, and I can hear my voice beginning to quiver.

"Munchausen syndrome," she repeats. "That's what it's called when people hurt themselves in order to attract attention." It's her trump card, and she almost smiles when she says it, as if she took Psych 101 and is proud of herself. Suddenly I hate this woman with an intensity that startles me. I'd like to fling myself at her, to scream into her patronizing, supercilious face. I'm literally speechless, and before I can recover, she tacks off onto another course.

"Do you have a boyfriend?" she asks. I shake my head. "Any exes? Anyone who might have reason to—"

By this time I must look like a dog with a flea in its ear. No, no, no, I'm shaking my head. I can't believe she's treading up this path, especially after I've already told her about Marina, which I did practically the moment she walked through the door.

"You don't understand," I insist now, and this makes her look pissed off, which actually pleases me, although I barely have time to think about it. I feel as if I'm awash with words, as if they're rising through me, propelled upward by a tide of anger and frustration and fear, and spilling out of my mouth in no particular order. "I told you already," I say, knowing that I sound like a kid about to cry. "I had a sister, a twin. Identical. She was murdered. Stabbed. Someone came into her house and killed her. Nineteen months ago. In Virginia."

Detective Aaronson is staring at me impassively, which so far has been her reaction to just about everything; from the hair to the shears to Marina's murder. Maybe she has only two emotional levels, this patronizing stare and sleep. Maybe she isn't real. Maybe if you cut her, she'd ooze hydraulic fluid instead of blood.

"My sister was being stalked before she was killed." I say this slowly. I'm trying to catch my breath, and I want the words to sink in. I want them to penetrate, to make ripples, waves, any kind of froth on the calm surface of Detective Aaronson. "Someone was calling her, following her. Don't you think—"

But I don't have a chance to finish, because Detective Aaronson's partner, who is tall and very pale and looks sort of like an albino vampire in his long dark coat, appears in the bedroom behind us and says, "Could have been the balcony, easy. Window wasn't locked when I tried it."

This is presumably further evidence of the unlikelihood of my story, one more fact to convince Detective Aaronson that I'm doing all of this, cutting off my hair and vandalizing my own car, making up men in the basement and murdered twin sisters in order to attract attention to myself. She steps past me and follows the vampire up the hall and into the living room.

"How many people have keys to this apartment?" Aaronson asks while she rattles the window frame. She's already gone out onto the balcony and looked over the edge. She's asked me this before, too. It was her first question. I didn't give her Beau's name then, and I'm certainly not going to now.

"No one," I say, just like I did the first time, and she can tell that I'm lying. She smiles slightly and shakes her head.

"You might consider getting the locks changed," the vampire says, and they begin to move toward the front door. I can't believe they're simply going to leave after being here less than fifteen minutes.

"Don't you want the hair?" I ask. "Or the shears? Aren't you going to try to take prints?"

They exchange glances. "Strictly speaking, ma'am," the partner says, "there's no evidence that a crime has taken place here. There's no sign of a forced entry, nothing stolen, and no threats have been made."

"No threats?" I'm practically yelling. Aaronson is buttoning up her coat. The partner nods sympathetically; clearly he's the good cop. "Look," he says, "most likely it's a practical joke that got out of hand." He reaches out to touch my arm, but I jerk away from him. He nods again and looks both sympathetic and slightly hurt. "If you can think of who might have done this," he says, "we'll be happy to talk to them."

Tears of rage and humiliation flood up and blur my vision as the door clicks shut behind them. I can hear their murmuring voices from the landing as they start down the stairs, and I don't even want to think about what they're saying. I close my eyes, resisting the temptation to sink to the hallway floor or beat the walls with my fists. I can hear Kathleen Harper saying, "She went to the police, but they said there wasn't anything they could do."

"No," I say out loud. And I open my eyes. I'm stuck with Marina's face and with her body. The same dips and valleys charted the beating of our hearts. But I'm damned if I'm going to share her death.

The card crumples in my hand when I grab it, and I hope I haven't creased the number or rubbed out the name. On the stairs, I take two steps at a time, and once I land sideways on my slippers and almost twist my ankle.

Aaronson and the vampire are just opening the vestibule doors when I come flying down the last flight, and he starts to say something, but I don't give him a chance. They've turned around to face me, and I shove Special Detective Mark Cope's card into Aaronson's hand.

"Here," I say. "Since you don't believe me, call him."

As hateful as she is, I know she's the one I have to convince. She stares at the card and starts to ask me something, but I've already turned my back on her.

"Just call him," I say.

"DONE IN A JIFFY," THE LOCKSMITH SAYS.

He keeps glancing at me nervously as he works on the living room window, as if he's afraid that when he turns away, I'm going to foam at the mouth or leap at him, springing across the room like Catwoman. I can hardly blame him; my appearance probably isn't reassuring. I've wrapped a scarf around my head like a turban, and I can't sit still, so I walk up and down the hall, and back and forth across the living room, and in and out of the kitchen, patrolling the rooms of the apartment. The only place I don't go is into the bathroom, where the hair still hangs from the mirror and the shears lie by the sink.

The phone has rung three times since the locksmith has been here. Once it was Lolly, and twice it was Beau. I don't answer it. I just stand beside the message machine and listen while Lolly asks where I am, and Beau asks about Jake. His voice is increasingly worried, swinging between anxiety and anger that I won't pick up.

The first time this happened, the locksmith was in the bedroom or the hallway, but the second time he was in the living room, and he watched me out of the corner of his eye while Beau pleaded with me to either pick up the phone or call him back. By now I'm sure the locksmith thinks that Jake is our child and Beau is my husband who's done something terrible to him, which is why I'm locking him out of the house and wearing a scarf on my head and refusing to answer the phone. I don't make any effort to enlighten the man.

Now he finishes the window and picks up his toolbox. "Okey-dokey," he says. "What do you want on the front door? New locks? Everything changed?"

"New locks. Everything changed," I agree. "And then some."

I manage to perch on the arm of the couch, but I can't stay there, so I get up and walk back and forth across the rug while the locksmith opens my front door and examines it. He whistles as it arcs out onto the landing. He appreciates the possibilities. He swings the door back and forth, testing the hinges and the weight, and then he nods and says, "Some of these old interior doors in conversions do that, open outward. And you've got some depth in the frame here. I can mount an inner grille if you want." He turns and looks at me. "I've got one in the truck that should fit. It'll cost you, but nobody gets in or out of here."

Zoe will have a fit. Vault-type grilles will hardly go with her idea of sympathetic conversion. If I live through this, I'll have to take it down. Then I think of Marina. Against the courtyard light, the person who rang her bell that Friday night would have been just a dark figure, nothing more than a shadow on the threshold. She probably couldn't even see the face. I imagine her opening the door slightly, and then I imagine it pushed. I imagine the quick thrust of a hand, the sudden step, a shoulder shoved through the gap.

"I don't care what it costs," I say. "Go ahead and do it."

I wait until after the locksmith has left to examine the windows and the door. I didn't want him watching, didn't like the thought of his eyes on me as I run my fingers over the solid brass locks that he fitted onto the window frames. I caress the door's edge, weigh the new key in my hand, and listen for the smooth whir, the deep click of the bolts sliding home when I turn the key in the lock, which I do again and again, my ear pressed against the varnished wood as if I'm listening for movement in a pregnant animal's belly.

It's only three o'clock, and the house is still empty. I can sense it when I step out onto the landing and check for shadows moving below. I listen. But there's nothing. There's no muffled radio or television. No slam of a door. No footstep cracking against the high gloss of Zoe's parquet. There's not so much as the distant hum of traffic. Satisfied, I turn and admire my door.

It looks exactly the same from the outside. No one could possibly guess what lies behind it. I'm the only one who knows. When I swing it open, the grille is dark and heavy-looking. It's as if someone has drawn a grid, hung black lines in the air to separate my world from the world out here. The squares are big enough to fit a hand through, and maybe an arm, up to the shoulder, say. But nothing more. A face could press against the squares. It could stare in at me. It could get as far as the eyes and the hands. But no other pieces could follow.

I select the right key and unlock the grille carefully. It's a little stiff, but I like the feel of it. When I push it, it swings inward on silent hinges. The grille meets the wall and makes a dark graph against the pale gray paint. Then I pull it toward me. I give it just the merest tug, and it swings back. It's perfectly balanced. The tongue meets the groove. The lock sets and drops home. Nobody gets in or out.

FIRST I CALL LOLLY'S OFFICE NUMBER, NOT HER PAGER, since I don't actually want to speak to her, and leave a message saying that I have to take Jake to the vet and I'll be gone all day. Then I call Beau. I try to make my voice sound as normal as possible when he answers the phone, and I know that if I do this well, he won't suspect that I'm lying. Beau doesn't lie himself, so he's not very good at figuring out when other people are doing it. Besides, he's too busy asking about Jake to be suspicious of me. It was nothing, I tell him. Just me being ridiculous. Just a worried mother overreacting.

"The way women do," Beau says, and I can see him smiling.

"The way women do," I agree, and I smile, too. If my face falls into the appropriate mask, my voice won't give me away.

When Beau asks me if I want to meet him at Sherlock's after work, I demur. I say I'm going out to dinner with Cathy, and as much as I'd like to get out of it, really, I can't. Beau says that those are the breaks, and he'll live with being stood up. Will I call him tomorrow, he asks. And I promise that I will. I even say something about the weekend, about how maybe we could take Jake for a run at Wissahickon, then go for a beer at the Valley Green Inn. I'm drawing it out. I'm giving Beau plenty of time. Ample opportunity. But still he says nothing, and after he hangs up, I admit that I've won my bet with myself, but it doesn't make me happy. Instead my stomach dips, and the light in the room seems duller. Beau never told me where he was last night. "You don't trust anyone," Beau had said to me two days ago. "You certainly don't trust me." And he's right. On both counts. I don't, not anymore. I can't afford to.

———

THE CALL FROM DETECTIVE AARONSON COMES JUST BEFORE five o'clock, which is, frankly, sooner than I'd expected. She doesn't apologize to me. She doesn't say much at all. Her voice is clipped and businesslike, and I can tell she's pissed off at having to make this call. Then again, I knew she would be. I knew that humble pie was not her favorite dish. But I also knew she'd eat it.

There's a distinct whiff of sarcasm when she asks if it would be convenient for me to come down to the station. Say, tomorrow? Nine A.M.? And after she tells me where to park and which desk to sign in at, I ask her if there's anything I should bring. A lock of hair? A pair of shears? She pauses for a second, then says no. Someone will be over to collect those. In the next hour.

It's the vampire, but this time he comes with another man. They flash their badges, and when the vampire sees the grille, he gives a small whistle. "Good girl," he says, as though I did it for him. "That was fast."

They go down the hall and into the bathroom, and this time I don't follow them. I don't even linger in the bedroom watching them. I just sit on the couch waiting for them to be finished. It doesn't take long. When they come back, the new man is carrying a brown paper bag. He holds it carefully and a little away from himself, as if he has a dead rat in there. A white tag attached to the side of the bag says EVIDENCE in square black letters, and below it I can see initials written in red ink, and the time and date.

The vampire comes into the living room, and without even glancing at me, he goes to the window and checks the new locks. He jiggles the window frames, which barely move now. He peers out onto the balcony. He's feeling proprietary. "Good," he says. "Very good." Then he gives me a big smile. "You take care of yourself, Ms. deBreem. Don't you hesitate to call us if you need anything."

I stand in the doorway and listen as they go downstairs. The policemen aren't talking, but I hear someone come in, and from the voice, I realize it's Gordon. He says hello to the two cops, and there's a little expectant pause after it, as if he expects them to explain themselves, but as far as I can tell, they don't. Still, I can tell Gordon's wondering who the hell they are, and I duck back inside and close the door and the grille before he can catch sight of me and decide to come up and ask about them or Jake.

As it turns out, Gordon doesn't come. But Cathy does. She knocks on my door and calls my name about a half hour later, as soon as she gets home from work. Shawn is with her, I can hear him.

"Susannah?" Cathy calls. "Do you want to come and have dinner with us?"

I stay very still in the hallway, which is where I'm standing at the time, as if I'm playing statues. I don't even rattle the cleaning bucket that I have in my hand. It's full of Windex bottles and Ajax cans and old wadded-up pieces of paper towel. I've been cleaning. I've been disinfecting and scrubbing and polishing. I've been rubbing and rubbing, then using a razor blade. I've been scraping away the gluey band that the tape left in the middle of the glass, the line that sat on my cheek like a brand, imposing itself like the mark of Cain every time I looked at my face in the mirror.

When I don't reply, Cathy waits and then calls my name again. This time I hear Shawn say, "She's really upset about the dog." I can almost see Cathy nodding in agreement. I can sense the glossy crown of her hair dancing back and forth. A second later their footsteps cross the landing, and I hear the jingle of Cathy's keys, then the heavy click as her door swings shut.

The phone rings just before ten, and as soon as I hear the vet's voice on the machine, I answer it. He is calling to tell me that the toxicology reports have come back on Jake. He was poisoned. But I already know that.

"It could be almost any kind of commercial stuff," Dr. Gurewich says. "It's widely available in any hardware store. The only contents of his stomach were a couple of uncooked sausages. Luckily he wolfed them down and didn't chew too much. The casings probably saved him."

A POLICE CAR GOES BY, AND WAVES OF BLUE LIGHT PULSE across the ceiling and wash up against the living room walls. When they're gone, the sound of the siren lingers. I can hear it wailing down the streets of the city. It's after two A.M., and I keep my eyes fastened on the dark lines of the grille. I watch the polished brass orb of the doorknob. It picks up light from the window and glows a little, like a magic egg in a children's story, one of those things that comes alive at night and grants wishes.

I've pulled an armchair into the corner of the living room beside Jake's bed, and from where I sit, I can see through the archway to the front door and watch the window and the edge of the balcony. I've been waiting for some time now for the doorknob to move. I expect it to twist silently. I expect to hear the faint scrape of a key in the lock, and then I expect to feel a vicarious frisson of disbelief, a jolt of frustration, when the bolts don't turn. Failing that, I expect a shadow on the balcony. I've memorized the pattern that the tree branches throw, and I'm alert for any change. There's no wind, so the first thing I may see is motion, or possibly just a thickening of the darkness.

Whichever it is, I'm ready. I opted, in the end, for the stiletto of the boning knife rather than the hatchetlike carver, and its long blade lies in my lap. Occasionally it glints, almost sparkles, in the dark. The blade is paper-thin and very sharp. I've already run my finger along it once and drawn blood.

Earlier, I'd heard the faint thud of Cathy's stereo as I stood in the kitchen, and I'd found myself drawing the blade back and forth against the whetstone in time to it. For a moment that was comforting. And so was the murmur of Gordon's TV. I could hear it occasionally, too, filtering up through the heat vents from the floor below in a sort of warm mumbling. They'll hear me scream, I'd thought then. Of course they will. If I get the chance.

CHAPTER 15

HIS HAND IS AS SMOOTH AND COOL AS A STONE.

"Miss deBreem," Special Detective Mark Cope says, "I want to thank you for coming in to talk to us."

He's flown up from Washington this morning. Another man, introduced to me only as "Phil Dorris, who has been helping us with our investigation," is with him. Dorris is thin and olive-skinned, and his long horselike face has trouble breaking into the obligatory smile when he meets me. The vampire is here, too, and Detective Aaronson, since presumably this is her party. She merely nods in my direction when I come into the room. She's wearing a blue pantsuit, and she's folded her hands in front of her so she looks peculiarly demure, like one of those ladies who work as guides in the art museum.

The room isn't small and dark and cramped like those featured on *Law & Order* or old reruns of *Hill Street Blues*. There's not a leaky radiator or a piece of watermarked plaster in sight. Instead, it's more like a conference room at a bank or an advertising agency, and the walnut-veneer table and matching chairs make me feel slightly underdressed. I have the surreal sense that I've come here to pitch a project to a bunch of backers, to discuss seating numbers and color schemes, instead of the similarities between the events that led, on the one hand, to my sister being hacked to death with a butcher's knife and, on the other, to someone creeping into my apartment to cut my hair off and tape it to the bathroom mirror.

Even as I think this, my fingers move toward the brim of my hat. So far I've been unable to stop this involuntary reaction, this need to feel the short bristly fringe that rises above my forehead in a ragged arch. I've given up the scarf for this meeting and opted for a hat instead. It's black felt with a narrow brim, and once it had a pink daisy pinned to it. I removed that this morning and threw it out. Flowers hardly seemed suitable for the occasion.

As I sit down, I realize that Mark Cope and Phil Dorris are watching me intently, as if the expression on my face or what I've chosen to wear might give some hint, some vital clue, as to why all of this is happening. Detective Aaronson moves down the table and sits on her own, while the vampire takes the chair next to mine. He gives me an encouraging little smile as he sits down, as if he's a coach and I'm a not particularly promising athlete about to enter the arena.

"It's the same person, isn't it?" I say. "That's why you're here?"

At this, Mark Cope and Phil Dorris exchange glances with Detective Aaronson. The vampire studies the edge of the table. The point seems elementary, but all the same, their discomfort suggests that I'm not supposed to have mentioned it.

"We can't be certain of that," Phil Dorris says. He makes a tent out of his fingers and wiggles them back and forth. Then he says, "But given the nature of the circumstances, it's a possibility that we have to consider, yes."

"Because Marina and I were identical?"

Dorris nods. "That, and the pattern that's developing."

He's clearly the front man on their team, and now I understand who and what he is. He's a shrink, a profiler, one of those guys they make TV series about. He specializes in psyching out serial killers and rapists and every other sort of criminally inclined weirdo. I wonder if he's from the Alexandria police or the FBI. Maybe he's been drafted specially from Quantico now that we've crossed state lines. If this is the case, I guess it means I'm privileged. But his presence doesn't make me feel better.

"There are similarities," Phil Dorris says, "which I'm sure you've already recognized." It's my turn to nod. "It's exacerbated, of course," he adds, "by the fact that you look alike. Most people like this go after a type, but in this case, it may be something a little different. If it's the same guy, he may be trying to re-create some scenario in his head that centered on your sister."

"Like what?" I say.

"I don't know." Dorris shakes his head. "The telephoning, the flowers, even coming into the basement. He's letting you know he's there. It may be a kind of courting ritual. It looks like he did the same thing with Marina. Then things started to go wrong. Probably she didn't respond the way she was supposed to. In a lot of cases, these people are convinced that their target is in love with them, and they're very deliberate. What they do may seem random to you or me, but it isn't to them. They have scenarios, ways they need things to work out. And when the picture doesn't play right, they feel like they're losing control. And then they get mad."

"So he's doing this because I'm Marina all over again? Because he sees me as a second chance?"

"It's possible," Dorris says. "Given the parameters of this case, it's certainly something we have to consider."

I'm trying to digest this. The suspicion that had fluttered in my stomach when I ran into George on the bridge, that had unfurled and grown in me as I spoke to Kathleen Harper, now seems intent on spreading its wings, on stretching and flexing until I split open and fly to pieces.

For the first time, I understand clearly that I'm going to die and that there's nothing I can do about it. It's inevitable, like being diagnosed with MS or Parkinson's or any other fatal genetic disease. It's no fault of my own, it's what I carry inside of me. I'm going to be carved up by some maniac with a butcher's knife because I was born with Marina's face.

"Miss deBreem. Susannah." Mark Cope is leaning across the table toward me. "We need your help. That's why we've come up here."

I look at his earnest face and feel laughter rising, exploding like fireworks inside of me. I want to point out to him that that's my line, but he starts talking again before I have the chance. I'm only half listening. I'm spending most of my energy trying not to squeal. I'm trying to preserve some shred of dignity by not doubling up over the table and laughing until the tears run down my face.

I can imagine Marina watching me, daring me to meet her eyes, and I hope she's here somewhere, flying around this blue carpeted room with its fake walnut table and chairs and reveling in what a joke all of this is. But of course she's known the punch line all along. This is what she spent her life trying to make me understand, that no matter where I have my dorm room, or how I live my life, or how far I run, we're always together. We're two peas in a pod. In life, and in death, we're one.

"As I told you at the time," Mark Cope is saying, "we're convinced that Marina was killed by someone she knew, at least well enough to let into her house. She may have been expecting them, or they may have just dropped by. It's even possible she invited them, although we can't find any trace of that in her phone records. So we need to look for anyone who has a connection to you now, however slight, and who your sister could have known then."

I shake my head. The laughter seems to have dried up as quickly as it sprang to life. My voice sounds perfectly normal. "We weren't friendly like that, Detective. I told you. I didn't know her friends. I really didn't know much at all about her life in Washington."

"So you haven't thought of anyone," he asks, "anyone at all?"

"I told you at the time, there's George, but——"

"Who's George?" This is Detective Aaronson. She's pounced on his name like a cat, and her pen is poised in midair.

"George Collier," I say. "He's a professor at Penn, and he was my fiancé when Marina was killed. She met him a couple of times, years ago, when he and I first started going out. But it's ridiculous. For a start, we were living together, and we were up here the whole weekend Marina was killed." She glances at Cope, who nods, but she asks for George's address anyway. I give it to her, even though I'm not sure it's right anymore, because I know she's going to find him if she wants to. Penn is hardly shrouded in mystery.

"Ms. deBreem," Phil Dorris says, "there's a good chance, in fact a real likelihood, that whoever this person is, he knew your sister. But that doesn't necessarily mean that you'll recognize him."

"Then how could I possibly identify him?"

"We can narrow the field a little," he says. "Whoever it was who killed your sister was probably living in or around Washington eighteen months ago. Or, if he wasn't living there, he may have traveled there regularly for work."

Lolly travels all the time, I think. And Beau goes to conferences. So do Elena and virtually everyone else I know.

"What else?" I ask.

"The method of attack"—Dorris pauses—"the, well, frenzied quality of the stabbing. That's rage. Pure and simple. And rage usually stems from the personal. A spurned lover, someone your sister perhaps unwittingly insulted or damaged in some way. Take the fact that her face was disfigured, that's a classic indicator of a connection that the attacker at least perceived as intimate. White, I'd guess. Male. Between twenty-five and forty-five. Possibly professional. Possibly affluent. But not necessarily any of those things."

"Oh, great!" I say. "Great. That really narrows the field! That leaves approximately, what? Two thirds of the population of Philadelphia who may be trying to kill me? Or is it only twenty-five percent? And by the way, are you so certain it's a man?"

"All we're certain of," Phil Dorris says, "is that whoever killed Marina was taller than she was and right-handed."

"So it could have been a woman?"

He considers me before he replies. "Yes, it could have been a woman, if she was tall enough and strong enough."

I lean back in my chair and close my eyes. For some reason, I feel as if I've won an important point here, as if we're scoring against each other rather than pulling on the same side.

"It's not that bad," Mark Cope is saying. "The police here are going to do everything they can. They need you to give them your address book, your business contacts, a list of everyone they should cross-check for any possible link with Marina." I open my eyes and stare at him like an obnoxious pupil staring at a teacher. He stares back at me, and then

he says, "In the meantime, we need you to be very, very careful, Susannah. This guy is close to you, and he wants you to know it. He's playing
a game here. He's got a plan, but we don't know what it is. Yet. So you
need to keep your eyes open. You need to look for a face on the street,
a delivery boy, a postman, a guy in the video store—anyone you see
more often than you should."

I glance at Detective Aaronson, but she's not looking at me, and I
know right then that they're not going to do a damn thing. Despite
Mark Cope, and Phil Dorris, and the fact that they flew up here, I'm
sure Aaronson is less than convinced that I'm in mortal danger. She's
probably still betting on Munchausen syndrome, or PMS and the power
of coincidence. And even on the off chance that I'm wrong, I'll bet that
the Philadelphia police are just as understaffed and overstretched as
everybody else. Even if they are convinced I'm about to be killed,
there's probably precious little they can do about it. All that giving
them my address book means is that I'll likely never see it again, and
they'll have it handy after I'm left chopped into little pieces in a
garbage can somewhere.

All of this is too real, and suddenly I think of Jake, and of the soft,
dark triangle between his ears where he still smells like a puppy when
I bury my face in his fur.

"Ms. deBreem?" Phil Dorris is saying. "Susannah? What is it? What's
the matter?"

"My dog," I say, and I can't finish the sentence because my voice is
jumpy and unreliable. Like an electric current with a bad connection,
it seems to be flickering in and out. Phil Dorris is sliding a box of
Kleenex across the table toward me, and when I reach out to take one,
my hand shakes and the white tissue waves like a surrender flag before
I can get it to my face.

"We'll get him," Mark Cope says. He's probably one of those men
who can't stand to see women cry. "I promise you, Susannah, we'll get
him."

The vampire makes some reassuring noises, too, and Cope is leaning toward me, trying to get me to look into his eyes, but I can't. I can't
stop watching Phil Dorris's long, horsey face and noticing that he and
Detective Aaronson aren't saying a thing.

———

ALL I WANT TO DO IS GET OUT OF THIS GOD-AWFUL BUILD-ing. I surrendered my Filofax to Aaronson, and I pulled myself together enough to shake everyone's hand and thank them, although I'm still not certain for what, and I'm walking across the lobby, making for the three sets of revolving glass doors that give onto the street, when Mark Cope catches up with me. I hear him call my name, and when I stop and wait for him, I see that he's slightly out of breath. He must have missed the elevator and run down three flights of stairs. I can't decide, watching him in his starched white shirt and his red power tie, whether it's his pride or genuine concern that made him come after me. Maybe my obvious fear is a blow to his ego, since it implies that I have less than 100 percent faith in him.

"Why didn't you call me?" he asks when he finally stands in front of me. "Why didn't you call me as soon as this started happening?"

"I called you after I went to see Kathleen Harper," I say. "I left a message."

He shakes his head and looks away from me. "I wish you hadn't waited," he mutters. "This guy——" He doesn't finish the sentence, and I want to ask him "What? This guy what?," but the words die in my throat. "Look," Mark Cope says, "back there, when you asked Phil if it could be a woman, did you have anyone in mind?"

"How closely did you check Kathleen Harper's alibi?"

I can see her standing on the step above me, see the shoulders that would have been powerful a year and a half ago from a summer's worth of sailing on the Chesapeake. I can see her flipping the bottle opener up in the air after she gave me the beer, and catching it again with her right hand. Mark Cope is watching me.

"I think you should check her out," I say. "Carefully. I think she and Marina were close. Really close."

"We did," Cope says. "Her and her husband. But there was nothing concrete. Her fingerprints were all over Marina's town house, but she says she used to visit all the time, and her kids' prints were there, too. We can't pin her down for all of the Friday, but we haven't turned up a sighting in the area, either. No sign of her car or anything like that. Of course, the window is big, which is a real problem. It's really anytime between six P.M. on Friday and eight P.M. on Saturday, when Marina didn't show up for her dinner date. We assume she was dead by then, but it would help if we had been able to make a more accurate time of death."

I look out through the glass doors. A thin drizzle has started to fall, and the sky looks white and fuzzy. The doors whoosh when they spin around, and people drop out of them and land in the marbled lobby. Some of them are clutching their coats and carrying briefcases as if this is an ordinary business office, and some are in jeans and sneakers with their hands dug deep into pockets and their faces turned down. It seems to make no difference that it's the weekend; the doors never stop. They could almost be automatic, the way they keep picking people up and spinning them out onto the sidewalk, scooping others up and dropping them back into the lobby, as if they're candy pieces in a machine or cogs in a wheel.

"Just after eleven-thirty," I say.

"What?" Mark Cope's voice seems indistinct and far away. People walk past us. A group divides and flows around us as though they're borne by a current and Mark Cope and I are two stones in a river.

"When she was killed."

I'm not watching Mark Cope as I say this, but I can hear him take a deep breath, I can almost feel him resisting the urge to reach out and grab me, to stop me as if I might flee, as if I might slip into one of the door's glass cubicles and vanish with a whoosh out onto the street.

"How do you know?" He asks it very carefully, and when I finally meet his deep brown eyes, I almost feel sorry for him.

"Because I heard it," I say.

THE SCREAM WAS HIGH-PITCHED AND VERY LOUD. IT EX-
ploded without warning inside my head, detonated in a blinding fire-
ball of sound that quite literally knocked me sideways. For a split
second it seemed to gather pace, to rush toward me, bearing down like
the whistling roar of a night train. And then it stopped. The shriek hung
in the air, ringing, before it died away and echoed into a ragged, gasp-
ing squeak.

I later understood that the squeaking sound was because her throat
had been cut, because the blade had bitten into her larynx and severed
her vocal cords even as they still attempted to protest. But at the time,
as I grasped the edge of the kitchen counter, hung on to it like the rail
of a pitching ship, and watched the glass that I had dropped shatter, and
the wine pool on the floor, I knew only that I had been winded. I felt as
if someone had socked me in the stomach or grabbed me by the throat,
and I was choking.

As the sound faded and the room came back into focus, I looked for
her. I absolutely expected to see her feet planted on the brick-
patterned linoleum. I knew that as my eyes traveled up, I would see
Marina's legs, her body, her face, as she rose above me like a pillar. And
when I found that she was not there, I spun around, certain that she
must be behind me, that she had somehow arrived at the apartment and

come into the kitchen. But the room was empty. There was no trace of her. There was nothing but the high ring of her scream and the dying echo of a gurgling sound, something like water running and bubbling down a closed drain.

I felt as if I had been momentarily deafened. It was the same sort of sensation that Uncle Ritchie warned about when he was shooting doves, the tinny ringing and the breathlessness that comes from being too close to the crack of a shotgun. A few seconds passed before I could hear the ticking of the big yellow clock on the wall above the stove, or the rhythmic drip of the faucet. Then I was aware that the slightly fuzzy sound of voices was coming from the living room, and I remembered that George had just put a tape in the VCR.

"Aren't you coming?" he called, and I realized that he hadn't heard a thing.

"Suze?" George yelled a minute later, as I was stooping to mop up the spilled wine. "Are you okay?" When he finally appeared in the doorway and saw the glass and the wine on the linoleum, he laughed and said, "Oh, thank God. I always hated those glasses." As he threw the broken crystal stem and the petal-shaped pieces of bluish glass into the trash, he added, "One down, five to go." And then he grabbed the open bottle and a new glass and said, "Come on, the beginning's the best part."

When I came out of the kitchen, he was back on the living room couch watching Tom Hanks struggle toward the Normandy coast on D day. I almost opened my mouth to say something, but George glanced up and patted the cushion beside him and said, "Come on, or I'll eat all the popcorn," and the moment passed when I might have been able to explain to him that I had dropped the glass and spilled the wine because I'd heard Marina screaming.

My telepathic conversations with Marina were not something I had ever tried to explain to George. I had told myself at the time that those were not the sort of ideas that interested him, but the real motive for my silence on the subject was more complex. He didn't like Marina, for a start, and beyond that, I didn't want him to think I was out of my mind. The truth was that I was just as happy to forget about them myself. I was delighted when, in secret, I looked up studies on identical twins that said this phenomenon was not entirely uncommon and almost always ceased after the onset of puberty.

In our case, this had been more or less true. And by the time we were in our thirties, we rarely had conversations at all, never mind ones that ignored the banalities of speech. The era of our private communication had really only lasted until the summer when the Eameses' barn burned. Or at least that was when I first became aware that Marina had figured out how to deploy some kind of scrambling device to keep me out. And by the time we graduated from high school, it was over. Along with our old ballet tutus and our dreams of being swans, the nightspinning was finished.

Or so I thought. Until the night she died. Then, in her last moments on this earth, Marina screamed for me. And just as she had promised, I heard her. Loud and clear.

Much later on that Friday night, after I had sat for three hours on the couch beside George, after we had drunk the wine and gone to bed and made love and fallen asleep, I woke up again and asked myself if I had really heard anything at all. Lying in the shadowed room with George beside me, I tried to convince myself that it had been nothing. I told myself it had been the television, or a siren. Or a smoke alarm downstairs, or tomcats fighting on the fire escape. I told myself what I wanted to believe, that the sound was nothing more than the city at night.

Unable to sleep, I got up and walked into the living room. Gray light wormed its way through a crack in the heavy curtains, and I slipped between them and opened the window and leaned out to breathe in the first soft greenness of spring that you can smell in the city only in the early hours of the morning when everything is still. I closed my eyes and thought I caught the faint, sweet scent of my grandmother's lilacs drifting up from the street, and the fecund odor of the dark earth that had been broken and turned under Uncle Ritchie's plow.

I almost turned back into the room to reach for the phone and call Marina then. In that moment, I felt a sudden urge to wake her up, to ask her if she remembered the smell of the farm at night and the way the moonlight turned the stunted pines behind the barn taller and spikier than they could ever claim to be in the daylight. For the first time in years, I yearned to hear her voice. I longed for her to spin out some old story about the Delrays, or about Della Hervey, or about the ghost of a white horse that she once swore she saw galloping in the moonlight and flying over the rotting, snaggletoothed rails of Uncle Ritchie's paddock.

But instead, I closed the window and told myself not to be ridiculous. I was far away and grown-up now. I went back to bed. I lay there and listened for a while to the soft blow and whistle of George's breathing. And then I fell asleep, unaware that my connection to Marina had been so completely severed that in the moment when I had missed her the most, I had not even realized that she was dead.

SPECIAL DETECTIVE MARK COPE IS WATCHING ME. WE'RE sitting in a tiny hole of a cafeteria across the street from the police station, and he's holding a Styrofoam cup of coffee with both hands. Steam rises out of it in a little tail. I have a cup of coffee, too, and when I lift it to my lips, the liquid is so hot that it burns the roof of my mouth and I don't taste a thing.

I have told Mark Cope the whole story now. Sitting here in this booth, watching cops and old men come and go through the steamed-up door, I have explained that Marina and I were nightspinners. I have described how we could send each other words, even dreams and nightmares, and how each of us could tell what the other was thinking. I've told him all of this. And I've told him about that final, ripping scream.

Now he sits staring at me. His dark, handsome face is as still as a statue's. He's trying to decide whether or not he thinks I'm completely crazy. He's weighing up the possibility that Detective Aaronson might be right. He probably wishes Phil Dorris were here, and that they could exchange a look or a secret hand signal. Or better yet, that Dorris could take over completely and he would not have to say anything to me at all.

"Susannah," Mark Cope says finally, and I have to give him credit for the fact that his gaze does not shift from mine, "why didn't you tell me all this before?"

I begin to laugh. "Would you have believed me?" I ask.

THE APARTMENT IS EMPTY. IT HAS NEVER FELT LIKE THIS before. Even when I first walked in and saw its unfurnished rooms, it didn't feel so totally uninhabited, so completely devoid of any kind of life. It's as if, in the few hours that I've been gone, someone's switched off a current and deprived this place of some unseen element that allows for the clack of footsteps, the shuffling of paper, water being turned on and off, the phone ringing. Perhaps, ironically, it's the grille that's done it. Or the new sets of locks. But I can't imagine music, or laughter, or even the sound of the radio here now.

I move carefully. I don't want to disturb anything. I feel as if I have to slip through the air in these rooms without displacing it. There's a thin rime of dust on the surface of my dressing table, and although it's probably been there for weeks, I notice it now, as well as the drip of the kitchen tap, which makes it sound as if nobody lives here.

Anger hits me, and it's as hot and vibrant as lightning across a darkened sky. I know that if I could get my hands on this son of a bitch, whoever he is, I'd kill him. I'd get him before he could get me. "Come on, you fucking coward," I want to scream, but the words choke on the still air of fear, and I have to hurry. Despite the change of the locks, despite the grille, despite Shawn and Cathy and Justin and Zoe, and yes, even Gordon, despite all of them so close around me, and despite Mark Cope's best assurances and the three copies of his card that I now have in my shoulder bag, I can't stay here a second longer.

I get my duffel bag down from the hall closet and open it out on the bed. And then I stand staring at my clothes. I have no real idea what I might need or how long I'm going to be away.

"What should I do?" I finally asked Mark Cope after he'd heard the whole story and we'd finished our coffee. "It's great if you believe me," I said, "and that knowing a closer time of death might help, but while you're trying to find out who this guy is, what do I do? Send him a message? Ask him to wait?"

Mark Cope shook his head. "No," he said. "What you do is disappear."

NOW, SITTING IN THE BACK OF A TAXI GOING UPTOWN, I'm surprised at how much better I feel. At least I'm doing something. I have a plan that I've worked out with Mark. That's how I think of him now. No more of this "Detective" stuff, we're on a first-name basis. He and Phil Dorris are flying back to Washington. They're in the air this very moment, recharged, reenthused, determined to go through every single alibi, every move of Marina's. "With a fine-tooth comb," Mark Cope had said, and, "We'll find something. We'll nail him. I promise."

My part of this plan is to not get killed, and in order to facilitate that, I'm checking in to the Marriott. Only Mark and Phil Dorris and Detective Aaronson and the vampire know this. I'm not allowed to tell anyone else. I'm not even allowed to talk to anyone else until Detective Aaronson tells me that the alibis of all the people I know, Zoe and Lolly and Beau, even Mrs. Koom Wai and Tony at the garage, have been checked, one by one. Only after we know that none of them could have been in Alexandria on that fine spring night am I allowed to return phone calls or put in the occasional appearance. In short, only then am I allowed to emerge from this dark wood into which I've wandered.

It won't take long, Detective Aaronson has promised me. In our second meeting of the morning, after Mark Cope and I sat in the diner, and then made our way back to police headquarters, she regarded me with something close to grudging sympathy. I assume this change of heart is due to the fact that Mark and Phil—who is from the FBI, after all—seem to be taking this so seriously. They've formally asked for Philadelphia's cooperation on the investigation, and it will take just a few days, Detective Aaronson assures me, to run through what she calls "the A list," those closest to me. After that, I can speak to them again. I can have a white wine with Lolly or a beer with Beau at Sherlock's, safe in the knowledge that they are not about to leap up and cut my throat

166 || LUCRETIA GRINDLE

with the pizza knife, or garrote me in the ladies' room, or run over me in the parking lot, or even try to poison my dog. In the meantime, however, I have to disappear.

The cab flies through a yellow light just as it turns to red, and I hear a screech of brakes behind us and a horn honking.

"Goddamn women drivers!" the cabbie says. He looks at me in the rearview mirror and laughs, and for some reason, I do, too. My duffel bag's in the trunk, and my portfolio is resting against my knee. I've called the vet school and arranged for Jake to stay there until I come for him. I've told them I have to go out of town. I've wiped all the messages off of my answering machine, and I've thrown the perishables out of the fridge. Eggs have gone into the garbage and milk down the drain. It's almost like I'm going on vacation.

"ALL OF IT?" THE GIRL SAYS. SHE'S CHUBBY AND, LIKE EVERY-one else who works here, dressed entirely in black. Her own hair has blue highlights, and the stud in her nose sports a stone of similar color. I want to ask her if it's a real aquamarine, but I'm afraid it might be rude. Her name is Joyce, I think, and she is holding a large hank of my hair in her hand. Her nails are blue, too, and when her eyes meet mine in the salon mirror, they're full of questions.

"Are you sure?" she asks, and I realize that she's not half as tough as she looks. She's probably a Penn student, just a nice girl studying art history and shaving people's heads to work her way through college. "This is a big step." Maybe she does some counseling on the side. Gives advice on tattoos and whether or not to drop French. "We could go by degrees," she points out, "give you bangs first and then try the color. Or go to shoulder-length and see if you like it."

I shake my head. "All of it," I say. "Right now."

"Okay," Joyce says. She drops my hair and stands back. "I usually cut dry," she says, "and then we do the color, and then I clean it up again after. Is that okay?" I meet her eyes in the mirror and nod, and a second later I hear the swish and click of scissors.

My hair makes a whispering sound as it slides over my shoulders and slithers onto the floor, where it lands in a thatch of copper, like the cut silk of dead corn. As I watch in the mirror, my neck, freed of its protective ruff, seems to grow longer, and my head and face appear stuck to the top of it. I emerge shorn. Like a stick figure in a child's drawing, I'm just as scrawny and ragged-looking as a baby chicken.

Detective Aaronson doesn't know I'm here. I didn't ask her permission because I was afraid she'd say no, so I came straight here in the cab. At least I've chosen a salon that I've never been to before. Not that I was fussy. I took the first one in the Yellow Pages that had an appointment open. It's called Avanti, which I think means "fast-forward," or something to that effect, and by the time Joyce has finished, I'm certainly streamlined.

She's done exactly what I asked her to, which is cut the hair all over my head to the same length as the fringe I was left with. Then she sent me to someone named Heather, who painted my head in a helmet of goo that she promised would turn it black.

"That looks really cool," the girl who hands me my credit card says, "really short hair is so sexy. You should come back for highlights."

I have trouble recognizing myself in the mirror behind the receptionist as I sign the receipt, which is exactly what I'd hoped for.

"Maybe I will," I say. "You could do them blue, to match my eyes." The girl grins, and I write in a big tip for both Joyce and Heather while she calls a cab for me.

SLEEP IS THE MOST WONDERFUL THING IN THE WORLD. BY eight P.M. I can barely stay awake to eat the chicken salad and drink the wine that I've ordered from room service, and by nine I've stuck the tray back out in the hall and climbed between the slightly stiff hotel sheets. I've brought Elena's sleeping pills with me, but there's not a chance on earth that I'm going to need them after the combined effects of today and spending all of last night awake. When I packed the bottle and thought of her, my hand shook. I would have given anything to run to the safety of her office with its dusty ficus tree and messy, stuffed shelves of books. I'd cursed her then for being in Vienna.

My head feels strangely light on the pillow when I turn over, and I'm aware that I miss the heavy drag of my hair. I wonder if I even have to brush the few spikes that I have left, or if I can just run my hand over it and be done, when I begin to drift off. Here in this anonymous room with its sealed windows and fifteen floors of people around me, I feel entirely safe. I feel as if I could sleep forever.

FROM WHAT I CAN SEE OF THE MORNING OUTSIDE, IT looks bright. I've just lifted a brush to my head when there's a knock on my door and a voice calling, "Room service." I'd forgotten that I ordered breakfast and the newspaper before I went to bed last night.

I can hear people walking up and down the hallway, and the ping of the bank of elevators around the corner as I go to the door. I think it's safe to open it. Even so, I look through the fish-eye, but all I can see is a piece of a small blond girl in a red uniform. When I undo the chain and swing the door back, she's facing me and holding a huge tray. On it is a coffeepot and a dish with a metal cover, and a neatly rolled copy of *The Philadelphia Inquirer.* There is also a basket of flowers.

"What's that?" I ask, pointing. I know it sounds unnecessarily brusque, but I can't help myself. I'm hoping this is a gift from the management, but even before the girl opens her mouth, I know it isn't.

"They just arrived for you, Mrs. Thompson," the girl says, using the not very inventive alias I checked in with. "The front desk sent them up with your breakfast order."

She smiles and starts to come into the room, but instead of backing up to let her past me, I reach for the basket. I don't actually want to touch it, so I grab the wicker with the very tips of my fingers, as if it might be toxic or hot enough to burn.

"Is there a card?" I hear myself ask.

By now the girl knows there's something wrong, and she just nods mutely. I turn the basket around gingerly, holding it by the handle. They're African violets, and nestled between their little purple faces and the broad spongy green of their leaves, I spot the white corner of an envelope. There's nothing written on the outside, and the message inside is computer-generated and printed on cheap paper.

"Bad girl. I don't like the hair at all. You should have asked me first."

I DID MANAGE TO BOLT THE DOOR AND SWING THE u-shaped security lock closed. It's not a big achievement, but it gives me a disproportionate sense of pride, as if I have the right to congratulate myself for moving at all. That was in my first moments of frenzy, when I couldn't do anything but move. Then, it seemed entirely possible that I might begin to scream, burst out of the door, and race down the hallway and out into the street. After I scribbled something on the bill and shooed the poor room-service girl out, I dragged the desk chair into the room's tiny hallway and shoved its back up underneath the doorknob. I drew all of the curtains. I yanked them together and crimped their gaps closed, as if I could stop someone from looking in, observing me through this panel of sealed, tinted glass twelve stories high.

After that, I picked up the telephone and dialed Detective Aaronson's number. Or tried to. The first two times I got it wrong. I forgot that I had to dial 9, and when the hotel operator asked in polite, cheery tones if she could help, I almost dissolved into tears. It was the cool sound of Detective Aaronson's voice on the answering system, the easy, clipped assurance in her syllables as she told me to leave a message or dial her pager number, that brought me around like a slap in the face and killed the words I had been so ready to babble.

As I looked at the telephone receiver in my hand, I was certain I could actually feel my blood turning viscous and heavy in my veins. "Take a deep breath," I told myself. It's the sort of thing my mother would have said. "Take a moment," I advised myself, "to consider the facts." Only four people know where I'm staying: Mark Cope, Phil Dorris, Rebecca Aaronson, and the vampire. This morning a basket of African violets and a note arrived on my tray. Someone who knew where I was and what name I was using had sent them.

The phone made a small, indignant chirp when I hung up.

The little patches of sweat that had bloomed across the back of my neck and between my breasts have cooled now and turned clammy. My shirt is sticking to them, and the room feels cold. I pick up the thermos of coffee and pour myself a cup. It's thick and inky brown, and it smells bitter, but I force myself to drink it anyway. It's not until the second cup that I remember to add sugar, which is supposed to be good for shock.

The flower basket is sitting in the center of the desk, and I stare at it. I can't take my eyes off it as I lift the cup to my mouth and swallow. The newspaper is on one side of the basket, and the thick block of the Philadelphia Yellow Pages is on the other, and it looks perfectly innocuous, even pretty. It hardly seems a threat. And maybe, I think, that's the point. On the surface, things look minor, innocent. It's what's underneath that counts.

Whoever killed Marina is close. I don't need Mark Cope or the FBI to tell me this. I can sense them just as surely as if they're looking through the keyhole. I put the coffee cup down slowly, reluctant to make any noise. I almost believe that if I closed my eyes, I could hear breathing.

"HOUSEKEEPING," THE MAID CALLS AS THE NOISE OF HER cart, which has at least one squeaky wheel, echoes down the long tunnel of the blue-carpeted hallway. I have been listening to it for the last half hour, standing behind the door and measuring the intervals between the clanks of cleaning buckets and the muttered words of Spanish as the staff pass one another in the hallway and rap on doors.

There has been no rap on my door, and no call, because I left the DO NOT DISTURB sign turned outward. Even so, the maid paused outside, and I could hear the small snifflings, the rustle of her, as she contemplated knocking. She thought better of it, and now I can tell that she's gone around the corner and parked up by the ice machine beyond the bend of the corridor. I lift the U lock and slide the security chain gently out of its berth.

I've abandoned my portfolio, and my duffel bag isn't very heavy. I check quickly to make sure that no one is around, and then I close the door behind me softly and hurry down the hallway. Almost as soon as I touch the button, the elevator door pings and opens, and I step in. It's empty, as I had hoped it would be at ten in the morning, and it whisks me straight into the basement parking lot, plummeting past eleven floors and the lobby.

When I get there, the hotel garage appears to be empty, too, except for the girl in the ticket booth, who looks like she's doing her nails. I lurk around for a good long time, and only when I'm certain I haven't been followed, that no one is shadowing me from behind concrete pillars or parked Windstar vans, do I slip out, walk up the ramp, and duck around the corner, heading for Independence Plaza and the Liberty Bell. A taxi is waiting right where taxis usually are, and I slide into the backseat and ask for the Rodin Museum.

Midmorning is a busy time for Rodin, which is what I've been counting on. When the cabbie lets me out, I cross the sidewalk and fall in with a bus tour from upstate that's pushing its way toward the entrance. A bunch of teenage girls are leaning against the wall, passing a cell phone back and forth. I scan the crowd but don't spot anyone I remotely recognize. Even so, I think as I hitch my bag up on my shoulder and duck around the corner of the building, I'll thread in and out of Fresh Fields before walking the six blocks north to Benjy's garage.

"DOLL, I PRACTICALLY DON'T RECOGNIZE YOU," BENJY SAYS when he sees me standing in the machine bay. "What the hell did you do? You have a wreck in the beauty parlor this time?"

I shake my head. I've made a decision to trust him, and I hope I'm right. "Benjy," I say, "I need a favor."

"For you, Miss Cheap," he says, "anything. Whadda you need? A new hairdresser? A Bose stereo, no questions asked?" He smiles when he says it, but I know he scents trouble and his antennae are up.

"No," I say. "I need to rent a car from you."

Benjy looks at me, and I look straight back at him. I can see him start to ask me what's going on, and then he changes his mind. He wipes his hands down the front of his incredibly filthy coverall and says, "How long are we talkin' here?"

I shrug. "Maybe a week, maybe two. I'd have to let you know."

"But not months?" Benjy says.

"No, nothing like that." Unless I'm dead, I think. In which case you'll probably get the car back anyway.

Benjy considers this, and then he says, "You need it now?" His eyes go to the bag at my feet, and I nod. "Okay," he says. "Lemme see."

The bulletin board behind Benjy's desk is covered in old bills and receipts and flyers from pizza places and Chinese takeouts. He stares at it for a second, as if he's looking for something in the hanging mess of paper, and then he spots it and grabs a set of car keys. He turns to me and holds them up and grins.

The car is an old-model pale blue Ford Taurus wagon parked behind Benjy's building. It's completely nondescript, and even better, it has Illinois plates.

"She's got some dings," Benjy says, "but she runs good." He bangs the hood of the car with the flat of his hand as if to prove this. "I got her for my sister's kid when she went off to Northwestern. I mean, a kid can't go to college these days without a car, right? Anyways, the kid's on junior year abroad, livin' with a French family, learnin' to eat snails. My sister's pissed she wouldn't go to Italy." He hands me the keys. "You get stopped, you just say she's your goddaughter or your niece or something. Registration's in the glove compartment."

"Thank you," I say. "I'll be careful with it, I promise." I reach for my checkbook, which I have ready in the pocket of my jacket, but when he sees it, Benjy waves it away.

"I don't know what my rental rate is yet," he says. "I'll think about it while you're gone." His face gets serious. "Just tell me one thing. You in trouble, Miss Cheap?"

I nod and swallow. Suddenly I'm afraid that if I actually try to say anything, I'll start to cry.

"This got anything to do with what happened to your door?"

"I think so," I manage to say.

Benjy nods and takes my duffel bag from me and throws it in the backseat of the station wagon. Then he opens the driver's door and holds it for me. "You need anything else? You got money?"

"I got money," I say, and for the first time we both smile.

I get in the car, and he closes the door. The ignition turns over on the first try, and I roll down the window. "Benjy," I say, "I can't tell you how much I appreciate this. But if anybody comes here, if anybody, even the police, ask—"

Benjy lays his index finger by the side of his nose. "I never saw you," he says.

THE WATER IN THE SHOWER AT THE PAOLI HOLIDAY INN IS hot, and I turn the pressure all the way up. I pour too much shampoo into the palm of my hand—I'm still not used to my brush cut—and rub it hard into my hair, sending a great froth of bubbles down over my body, as if I'm in a car wash. I scratch the top of my head on purpose. I dig my nails into my scalp and rake my fingers down my neck so when I dry off, there'll be red marks on my mottled skin.

I'm trying to make my body kick back against this weight that's descended on it like a virus. I have to jolt myself out of numbness. I'm fighting the rabbit reaction, the desire to freeze in the face of a predator, to just hunker down and hope not to get killed.

Before I got into the shower, I made myself do thirty push-ups. Then I did twice as many sit-ups. I want my arms to hurt and my stomach muscles to ache. If I could have turned the television up and screamed as loud as I could without attracting attention, I would have, just to feel the air going in and out of my lungs. Just to know I can still make that much noise. Instead I walked up and down the length of the room. I flexed my fingers as if they were claws.

When I get out of the shower, the room smells like Italian food. I stopped at a strip mall, the most nondescript, interchangeable place I could find, and drove around until I found an equally nondescript Olive Garden. I was so hungry that I thought about actually sitting down and eating right there, but Paoli is the sort of commuter suburb where I just might run into someone I know, so I ordered takeout. I'd already spotted the Holiday Inn out on the highway, and I wanted to get locked into a room where I could take the time to figure out what the hell I was going to do next.

My first priority is Jake. He's okay where he is right now, but I can't leave him at the Penn veterinary school forever, and it isn't safe for him to stay with me. I sit down on the bed with a towel wrapped around me and pick through the remains of my "Sampler Italiano," thinking that this is one of the things I hate the most, the fact that I have to be without Jake. Then I pull the phone book toward me and start making the only arrangements I can think of that will keep him safe. As for myself, all I can say so far is that I'm pretty sure no one followed me to Benjy's or here. That means that at least I've bought myself some time, so I may have a slight advantage over my opponent in this game. Now all I have to do is figure out how to use it.

SOMETIME AROUND OUR JUNIOR YEAR IN HIGH SCHOOL, Uncle Ritchie taught Marina and me how to play chess. Even at the time, the gift was unexpected. I found it strange and a little alarming that my perpetually overalled and overweight uncle, who seemed more interested in the workings of his John Deere than he did in the people who surrounded him, should be the keeper of such arcane knowledge. But in teaching us the opening gambits, the moves of knights and pawns and queens, Uncle Ritchie revealed an aptitude for strategy, and for devious and forward thinking, that neither of us had ever suspected he possessed.

Needless to say, Marina was better at the game than I was. At least initially. When it came to both the required concentration and the necessary ruthlessness, she was a natural. To be fair, every time she beat me, she went back and explained how she'd done it. Just as if she was winding back a film, my sister could reconstruct the board and point out to me exactly where I'd made the one irretrievable move that had led to my downfall.

At first I was amazed at how early in the game these gaffes could take place, and how inconsequential they could seem at the time. It seemed almost unbelievable to me, on reexamination, that in the wake of one of these cataclysmic moves I could continue to play, and even sometimes suffer the delusion that I was winning, when the game was already over.

But over time, and with Marina's tutelage, I got better. I learned the lessons she taught me, and I came to understand the two things that she had always known instinctively: no move is inconsequential, and in order to win, you have to take control of the board.

KATHLEEN HARPER'S WORDS HAVE GONE AROUND AND around in my head. "Determined." That was the exact word she used. She said that after Marina came back from Georgia, she was both smug and determined. I thought of this while I was doing push-ups; I repeated the word in time to my own motion, broke the syllables down and recited them in my head like the beats of a metronome.

The significance of Kathleen's phrasing had escaped me initially. I had assumed that she was merely describing my sister's ordinary knowing confidence and stubbornness, the all too familiar sight of Marina digging her heels in. It was exactly the sort of response that Marina would have had in the face of garbage being strewn all over her garden, so I had thought that what Kathleen told me was nothing out of the ordinary. But now, I suspect, I was wrong.

Now I suspect that something happened on Marina's last trip back to Georgia. Something that she either knew I would understand or wanted to ask me about. Something that caused her to feel smug and to call me one last time. Something that made her believe she could take control of the board.

THIS FEELS LIKE THE HARDEST THING THAT I HAVE EVER had to do, even though I know it isn't. It isn't as hard as burying

Momma, or seeing Marina on that mortuary slab, or watching George walk away through the yellowing glow of a streetlamp, his step already jaunty in anticipation of the Sainte Chapelle and copies of *Le Monde*.

But somehow I was prepared for those. This feels as if it's sneaked up on me out of nowhere. Last night even the Holiday Inn room had seemed empty without the slight rattle of Jake's snoring or the sound of him padding across carpets, and in the early hours of this morning, when I was jolted out of sleep into the darkness of a strange room, it had taken moments before I realized it was not an unknown presence but an absence that had set off the alarm bells in my head. The under-tow of loneliness was so profound and frightening that I felt tears welling and had to turn on the light and sit up in bed clutching a balled Kleenex and reassuring myself that I still existed.

Now I bury my face in Jake's ruff, and he's embarrassed. He doesn't like to be held this close, and he turns his face away, as if I'm doing something vaguely shameful. He wriggles away from me, and when I look up, I see the sun filtering through maple trees, pouring a thick golden syrup of light across the afternoon. Leaves drop. Red and lan-guid, they ride on the warm air and scatter themselves across the taste-ful gravel parking lot. The Val Marie Kennels are way up in the Brandywine Valley, over an hour from Philly. It's a place that specializes in high-strung gun dogs, setters and pointers who need to be spoken to and stroked and walked on a regular basis when their parents are away, and it's where I'm going to leave Jake, maybe for the last time.

This is the place Dr. Gurewich recommended when I called him from the Holiday Inn yesterday afternoon and explained that I needed somewhere to leave Jake for as long as a few weeks. I think in some crazy part of my mind, I had hoped that Dr. Gurewich would offer to take Jake himself, that he would say in his heavy Eastern European ac-cent, "But Ms. deBreem, I will take care of your beautiful dog," and would actually mean "But Ms. deBreem, I will take care of you."

That's how desperate I'm getting. I'm clinging to a fantasy about a vet at the Penn animal hospital because he's a doctor, if only for an-imals, and because his accent reminds me of Elena, and right now he's about the only person I can think of who I'm sure is not trying to kill me.

"Get a grip on yourself, Susannah," I mutter aloud, and I snap Jake's leash on and start toward the newly painted red door. A sign on the outside, shaped like a dog's head, reads OFFICE. But despite my best efforts, as we go up the steps and into the nice wood-paneled room, I feel queasy. When this woman who is getting up from behind a desk and smiling at me reaches out and takes Jake's leash, I will feel as if I'm letting go of everything.

I sign the papers and hand her his medical records, and I even smile. And then we go outside, and I hand Jake over and stand beside the Taurus and watch her walk him down a path that leads to a fenced-in set of runs. Jake looks back at me just once before he disappears. And then I feel as if I'm falling. As if I'm spinning in the darkness. Like Alice, I'm going down, down, down the rabbit hole.

THE HOUSE IS SHADOWED AND SMALLER THAN I REMEMBER it. Momma's lawn is spangled with dew, and puddles have formed in the driveway, so I guess it must have rained earlier. I stop the car on the far side of the dirt road and kill the engine. The silence around me seems total, and when I stick my hand through the open window, the air that lies in my palm is as soft and as thick as cashmere. No wind moves through the overgrown stalks that litter Uncle Ritchie's old field. In this suspended hour that comes between late afternoon and early dusk, I feel as if I've entered a dream world, a place where the past winds on and on and never reaches the present.

I'm tempted to turn the key again. I'm tempted to put my foot down and rev the engine, to turn around and race down the road, making for Louisiana and the Gulf beyond Baton Rouge, or for the riotous noise and fine decay of New Orleans. I could lose myself in either of those places. I could change my name and erase my life. I could bury my trail. Until whoever cut Marina into pieces and tried to poison Jake picks it up again.

I open the car door and step out gingerly, as if I'm afraid the ground might give way under my feet. And then I stand looking up at the house that I was born in. My eyes slide along the porch rails, across the clouded glass panes of the front door, and travel upward as if of their own volition, searching for the tiniest movement, for the twitch of a curtain or the motion of a drawn shade, anything that will betray the shadow of my sister, will reveal her looking down on me from the bedroom window where I left her standing fifteen years ago.

I got drunk last night. Well and truly, in a ground-floor room of a Red Roof Inn. I drank a bottle of red wine, the kind that makes your head throb and dries out the back of your tongue so it feels like fur when you wake. Anger drove me to it, I suppose. Just like I was a teenager again, or a college student, I threw one last petulant tantrum on the highway going south.

Before I fell asleep, tangled in cheap sheets and drifting on the endless hum of the room fan, I got up and went into the bathroom. The walls were white-tiled and as antiseptic as an operating theater, and the glass of water I drew was almost fizzy and tasted faintly of sulfur. I caught my own eye in the mirror as I raised it to my mouth, and the face that looked back at me was narrow and mean.

"Don't gloat," I said, and my voice was thick. A second later, while Marina was still looking back at me, I put down the glass and pointed at her. "You've got what you want," I said. "I'm coming home." And the tiniest flicker of a smile played across her face.

THE MAILBOX IS TILTED, AS IF SOMEONE HAS WHACKED AT it halfheartedly with a baseball bat. As I step past it, I reach instinctively to push it upright, and my fingers meet the outlines of letters that still read DEBREEM. This seems strange to me, since we haven't lived here for a long time. As I walk down the drive, I can see that the garage door has new hinges. They're shiny and silver against the graying wood. And although it's overgrown, Momma's main flower bed, which runs up the side of the front lawn, has been edged in big painted-white rocks. As I get closer to the house, I can see that a new bluestone square has been laid under the outside faucet by the kitchen door, and the step has been replaced, too.

For one terrible moment it occurs to me that maybe the Herveys have sold the place or rented it out and someone is living here, that even now they are watching me from inside or may be about to drive in. Any second they might come back from Piggly Wiggly and find me standing here. And then I look at the lawn, which is long and crab-grassy, and the puddles in the drive, and the padlock looped through a chain on the garage door, and I know the place hasn't been sold and the Herveys haven't rented it. No one is living here. No one has lived here since Marina was killed. The improvements that I'm seeing are hers.

I can see her here, shed of her expensive city clothes and crouched in the driveway, spray-painting rocks to line Momma's flower bed. She must have planted it in, too. She must have bought trays of pansies and marigolds from the hardware store. Sure enough, when I go over to the bed and part the thicket of weeds that have grown up there, I can make out the spear-shaped leaves of black-eyed Susans and the thick, woody stems of peonies. A bramble rose snags my finger, and creeping out across the white stones are the snaky stems of a clematis whose trellis has collapsed or been taken away. The blue star of its flower rests beside my shoe in the damp grass.

The porch must have been painted too, and not so long ago. Probably sometime in the autumn, or in the first days of that early spring before she died. The glider is gone. And outside the front door is a jute doormat in the shape of a fancy flat knot. As I round the corner of the porch, I can see, even after eighteen months of semi-neglect, that Marina had been at work in Momma's old vegetable garden as well.

She must have hoed, and tilled, and dug when she came down from Alexandria. The thought seems utterly bizarre, since I cannot once remember Marina evidencing any interest in the garden when we were children. At the same time, I know it's true. Looking at the chicken-wire fence and the overgrown tangle of squash and cucumber vines, suddenly I understand that this was my sister's secret life. She was re-creating the past. Month after month and year after year, she labored to turn back time.

My sneakers and the bottoms of my jeans are sodden from the long grass, but even so I pick my way toward the back of the house.

The pines that edge the back lawn and spread out behind the garage have grown dense. They block out what light there is left and throw a long cold wall of shadow. The back windows of the house reflect the trees. They're shiny, like ice, and anything could be behind them. It occurs to me suddenly that I have no idea how long I've been here. The air seems to have thinned and turned chilly, and it's almost dark. A tingling runs through my shoulders, as if someone's breathed on the back of my neck, and all at once I want to be back in the car with the doors locked and the radio on.

I'm tempted to run, to fling myself forward and sprint up past the kitchen door and down the driveway, groping for my keys and not looking back. But instead I make myself walk slowly, as if I don't care, as if with sheer bravado I can stare down the ghosts that lurk here. The bank of lilies that has always been against the garage wall has grown wild and unruly without supervision. It's so wide and dense that the path has been swallowed and bodies could be hidden in there as easily as a snake. I stop and realize that it will be impossible to pass through without losing sight of my feet. I look back, and I can see over my shoulder that the darkness has gathered in the pines. I tell myself not to be ridiculous, but even so, I don't want to walk back through the shadows behind the house. Beyond the lily bank, out on the road, I can see the pale gleam of the Taurus. It's maybe a minute away from me.

I don't take my eyes off the white shapes of my sneakers as they rise and then disappear, sinking down into the wet tangle of the leaves. I place each foot carefully and then lift it quickly. Intent on not tripping, I continue in this kind of high step until I'm past the edge of the garage. So it's not until then that I look up and see the figure standing in the driveway.

It's a silhouette, really. Just a solid shape between me and the car. I can't tell if it's a man or a woman. And I can't hear anything. No sound of footsteps, no engine in the road. And then a voice that I don't recognize says, "Hey, girlfriend. Long time no see."

"I DON'T UNDERSTAND HOW YOU KNEW IT WAS ME."

I sound more petulant than I mean to, and I smile to cover it up. I'm not sure if the whiny edge in my voice is because I'm tired, or because I just had the shit scared out of me, or because I never particularly liked Della Hervey and now I resent the fact that I'm sitting in her kitchen. My first instinct, when I figured out who it was, was to slap her. That, of course, was just adrenaline and would have been pretty stupid, since technically it was her property I was prowling around on in the dark. Even so, I don't like the idea that Della caught me red-handed, that she saw me so obviously terrified. And I hate being called "girlfriend." By anyone.

It's particularly inappropriate in Della's case, since when we were teenagers, Della was more Marina's friend than mine. That didn't mean that Marina really liked her, either. It just meant Della could be easily deployed as a weapon by Marina for use against me when she felt like it. Now, watching Della as she fiddles with a coffee filter, I can remember the two of them sitting on the bus a few seats ahead of me, whispering together. Their shoulders shake as they giggle. Then they twist around to look at me. They crane their necks, making sure I understand that I am being left out.

I hated Della on those afternoons, and later I would get my revenge on her by generously providing the wrong answers when she asked me for help on her math homework. She was thin back then, a pale girl with round brown eyes and fawn-colored hair that bleached almost to white in the summertime. She was always getting sunburned or having nosebleeds, and I also recall that she was remarkably stupid. So it really does annoy me that she managed to recognize me, given that it was dark and I've dyed my hair and all but shaved my head, and we haven't laid eyes on each other in fifteen years.

Irritation is bubbling up inside me. It's all I can do to sit still. I can't figure out if I'm exhausted, or if sitting in the Herveys' old kitchen, which doesn't seem to have changed one iota since we were little, is just freaking me out in general. Upstairs I can hear a television, and it reassures me. It seems somehow less likely that Della will turn around and beat me over the head with a rolling pin while her kids are upstairs watching some Baptist cartoon station or the Pokémon movie.

"Are you okay?" Della asks. I realize that she's been watching me as if I'm an interesting and potentially dangerous animal that's wandered into her kitchen.

I smile, way too brightly. "Oh, sure," I say. "It was a long drive. You know." I start to finger the heavy glass salt and pepper shakers that flank the paper-napkin holder on the table.

Della nods. "Well," she says, "I think I'd just know you anywhere, Shoo." I try not to stare at her in shock, and after I've gotten over the fact that she could tell what I was thinking, I figure she means this as a compliment, the same way she probably means to be friendly by using my baby name. "You know how it is," Della says gravely, staring back at me, "with people you grew up with and all." And then, before I can say I don't, she turns back to the coffee machine and flips a switch. In just a second there's the dribbling sound of water, and the whole room starts to smell like Maxwell House.

I could hardly get out of the invitation to "visit" after she found me standing in the driveway. She told me, walking back up the road, that she'd married some guy from Louisiana one summer twelve years ago, and after that her parents let them buy the farm cheap so they could go on down to Florida, where her aunt and uncle already had a place on the Gulf. "My husband, he's gone now," Della had said as we'd turned the corner and seen the lights of the Herveys' old house. "My brother, Tommy, you remember him? He was older than us. He does the farm. But we kept Mom and Dad's house, the kids and I," she added, as though this was the best that could be said for her marriage.

The kitchen is quiet. Della moves without making a sound. She doesn't crinkle paper, or knock into things, or bang the mugs down on the counter. Even the drawers she opens and closes don't make any noise. She's overcareful, almost stealthy, in her movements, and it's making me nervous.

"So what are your kids' names?" I ask.

"Shelby, he's ten," she says, reaching for a bag of Oreos. She starts to arrange the cookies in a circle on a plate. "And Karen. She's eight and looks just like her daddy."

"That's nice," I say, even though I suspect it isn't.

"Uh-huh." Della nods and puts the plate on the table. "They go to our old school and everything." She smiles at me. "They even ride the bus. Remember?"

"Oh, sure." I smile back.

"I used to be so jealous of you," Della says suddenly. She's still smiling, as though this is joyous news. "You two, with your long red hair. The way you could wear it in a big long braid and tie a ribbon on the end." Before I can stop it, my hand rises to my head, and Della starts to laugh. "I'm sorry," she says, "but it is just not how I think of you. You look sort of like a porcupine, Shoo. Like you did that time when you came home from college. Except now it's black." I can't really think of anything to say, so I reach for an Oreo while Della giggles.

"But you knew me anyways," I say after I've eaten my cookie.

"It's the way you stand, and walk, or something," Della says. "I just— Well, when I saw you coming through those lilies, I knew it had to be you. Nobody else was ever so terrified of those darned things."

Della's body has thickened. She's not fat, exactly, just wider. She looks as if she's been compressed, as if someone put a weight on the top of her head and things were forced to grow sideways instead of up. I can remember this look. It's as familiar as a smell or an old piece of clothing. My momma always said that one of two things happen to farmers' wives: they either get whip-thin and hard, so the sinews on their arms and necks stand out like wires under the skin, or else they muscle up. They turn solid and broad, like wrestlers.

"I knew you'd be comin' anyways," Della is saying. She's still smiling at me. "You know, after Marina died and all that stuff. I knew you'd show up here someday. So, when the kids said they saw a strange car over there, I thought I'd better go take a look. It's almost like I've been expecting you. People always seem to come home."

She slides a mug that has GOT MILK? written on it across the table toward me, and then she sits down and reaches for the sugar bowl. "So," she asks, "how long are you here for?"

I realize that I'm staring at her again, and I have to force myself to answer. "Oh, a day or two." I try to keep my tone matter-of-fact. "I've got work down in Florida, and I decided to drive. I thought it would be nice to see the place again."

Della nods as if this confirms something. She's stirring her coffee, and I can't figure out if she knows I'm lying. I'm afraid that any minute now, she's going to ask me what I'm doing here, exactly. But the idea doesn't seem to occur to her, and instead she jumps up and opens one of the kitchen drawers. When she sits down again, she pushes a set of keys on a pink plastic ring toward me.

"For the house," she says. "You can stay in it if you want."

The idea is so awful that I laugh. It's a kind of barking noise, and it's embarrassing, so I reach for another cookie and make sure my fingers avoid the key ring.

"So you haven't rented it or anything?" I ask.

Della shakes her head and takes an Oreo, peels it open, and bites one half. "No," she says. "It was the land, really. The well. The water. That's what we wanted. We owned everything on either side of it. Tommy says maybe Shel might want to live in it one day. Or Karen. That would be nice, wouldn't it?"

Actually, I can't imagine anything worse, but I'm grateful they bought the place from me so fast, so I keep my mouth shut.

"I haven't changed too much in there," Della's saying, as if I might be worried about that. "It's pretty much the way Marina left it. I mean, I threw food out of the freezer and stuff. That was kind of a shame," she adds, "because I'm sure a lot of it was expensive. But the kids won't eat that fancy stuff. You know, asparagus and stuff like that. They're real plain. Tommy goes and checks around in there every once in a while. We have some trouble with kids. You know."

"Yeah," I say. "I saw the mailbox."

Della nods. She drains her mug and gets up to reach for the coffee-pot again. "That," she says, "and a few broken windows at first. Noth-ing, really. They tell each other it's haunted, you know, like they see lights and things. But mostly they're 'fraidy cats and stay away. The video place in town is more interesting. You seen it yet?" She's offering me coffee, but I shake my head, so she pours some more for herself.

"I haven't been in to town yet," I say. "I figured I'd maybe go in to-morrow. Is the Coachstop still there?"

"You bet," says Della, "and just the same. We got a new high school, the old one's offices now, if you can believe that. But there's not too much to shock you. I don't think you'll get lost. Some of the old peo-ple are still around, too. Well, most of 'em, really."

"Like who?"

"Oh, I don't know," Della says. "BethAnn works in the bank. Dex Eames. He got married and owns the new pharmacy, and a couple of years ago he bought a food place, too. He's done pretty well. Sonny comes back from time to time. His mom's still alive, but they don't have the farm anymore."

"Don't tell me," I say, "you and Tommy bought them out?"

I meant it as sort of a joke, but Della says, "Oh, no. It went to some new people. Tom would have trouble working this place and the Delrays', too. Only kind of help we can get is those migrant workers. They come all the way up from Mexico. And they don't even speak English."

"Did you see Marina much?"

The question is out before I even meant to ask it, and it's a second before Della replies, as if she's afraid that I might break down in tears or there might be a right or wrong answer. Finally she picks up her half-eaten Oreo and shakes her head.

"No," she says. "Not really."

"But you guys were such good friends."

Della looks at me, then takes a tiny bite out of her cookie. "A few years back, four or five," she says, "I tried to be friendly, you know, when she came down. But she was real standoffish. I just got the feeling she wanted to be alone." The hurt has burrowed itself deep behind Della's face, but when she speaks, I can see it move. It brushes the surface of her eyes like a fish rising from deep water.

"I'm sorry," I say.

For a horrible second I think that Della might cry. There's no sound in the room. There's nothing between us except the distant echo of a cartoon gun being fired and some theme music, and then Della swallows her cookie and looks at me.

"You know, Susannah," she says, "even though I was mean to you sometimes, I never bought that stuff."

"What stuff?" I have no idea what she's talking about.

"About you and Marina." Della's voice has quickened and gotten louder. "All that stuff about how you two were just alike. 'Two peas in a pod.' " She does a surprisingly good imitation of my mother as she says it. "That was crap," she announces. A slight flush is creeping up her cheeks. "Excuse my French. But I knew that even then. You were the nice one. Oh, I know you could fool Sonny Delray. You could make him kiss either one of you until he didn't know which was which. But you didn't fool me. I knew. She was mean. That Marina was just plain dirty mean. And they're the worst kind."

I start to stand up. I try not to push the chair back, because I don't want to make any noise. My mouth has gone dry, and the sweetness from the Oreo is sticking to my tongue.

"Della," I say slowly, "I have to go." There's a loud crack from the television upstairs, and both of us jump. The chair almost tips over, but I grab it with one hand and reach for the keys with the other.

"Goodness!" Della exclaims. She shakes her head and laughs. "Look at the time. I've got to make dinner. Will you be okay walking back? Do I need to drive you?"

"No, no," I say, and in two steps I'm at the kitchen door. "Thanks for the coffee. I'll see you." The knob is slightly stiff, but it gives under my hand, and I step out onto the back porch just before Della reaches me. She looks as though she's about to try to give me a hug, or pat my shoulder, but I dive down the steps before she has a chance. When I look back, she's a solid bulk against the light.

"You take as long as you want, now," she says. "At the house. And don't be a stranger!" And then she waves and closes the door.

I stand there staring at the house as if it might move or something might jump off the porch at me. I can see Della inside the kitchen, but the rest of the windows are dark, except for one upstairs, where the lights from the TV flicker and shift against the ceiling. I can feel the keys in my pocket. I finger them and grasp the smooth-edged lozenge of the tag. Then I take a few steps backward, and by the time I turn around, I'm running. I'm out of Della's drive and into the road. I'm flying. I'm hitting potholes, and stumbling and recovering, and running as fast as I've ever run in my life, while my eyes search out the road, fasten on the dark strip that splits the fields and disappears into the high, solid band of the woods.

IN THE CLEAR LIGHT OF DAY, THE HOUSE LOOKS PER-
fectly ordinary. The first morning sun is spreading across the roof, and
it's early enough that the white porch railings are still faintly tinged
with pink. I've been up since before dawn, and by now the idea that I'm
going to miraculously unearth some key piece of evidence seems absurd. I feel like I should just drive back up to Della's and put the keys in
the mailbox before anyone's awake. Then I should go off to Sea Island
or to Savannah. I could go to the beach. I could watch the sun set over
the water and go out to dinner, and in the daytime I could look at nice
houses. The idea is tempting, and maybe I'll even do it. But the pink
plastic key ring in my hand is exerting a pull of its own. It's drawing me
up the front path and willing me onto the porch. It does seem pretty
dumb not to even go inside, since I've driven all this way.

The lock on the front door is stiff and refuses to turn, and finally I
give up and go around to the kitchen. The dew hasn't burned off yet,
and I leave dark footprints on the raw wood of the step. Maybe Della
gave me the wrong keys. I decide if the door doesn't open right away,
I'll leave. I'm actually half hoping this will happen when the key slides
into the lock and turns instantly, and the door swings open as if it's
been recently oiled.

I have no idea what I thought it would be like, but the first thing I notice is that the house smells different. I hadn't realized it, I guess, but when my mother was alive, it always smelled slightly of ginger. Even if bacon or fish or something else was cooking, there was always an over-lay of spice. It's gone now, and the place smells empty. There's a cool, disused feeling about it. Without even stepping into the kitchen, I can tell that nobody lives in this house anymore.

Blinds are pulled down over the windows, which is what must have made them look so blank and empty last night. The curtains have been taken down, and I can imagine Della doing this. I can imagine her slip-ping them off rails and piling them in a laundry basket to take home. I can see her ironing them and folding them and packing them away in plastic sleeves in case Shelby or Karen wants to use them someday.

I open a couple of the cabinets, but they're empty. The food has all been taken away, just like Della said, and the red-flowered Con-Tact paper has been wiped clean. I close the cupboard quickly and yank open a drawer. There are a couple of old wooden spoons and a can opener inside, and I rattle them, then bang the drawer closed, which makes me feel better. A radio/CD player is sitting on the counter, but when I try to switch it on, it's dead, which makes sense, since the Her-veys would hardly keep paying the electricity on a house that nobody lives in. The phone is dead, too. There's no sound on the line, but I stand there anyway, holding it to my ear like a kid pretending to make phone calls. Then I lift the window blind with one finger, and through the crack, I can see the garage wall and the lilies. I think that this must have been where Marina was standing when she called me that last time.

"What were you going to tell me?" I start to ask her, but I stop in midsentence when it occurs to me that I'm speaking out loud.

There's a jar on the windowsill full of pens and a couple of paper flowers on green wire stems that I think I made. Marina and I went through a heavy-duty origami phase when we were about twelve, and neither of us ever really outgrew it. When they finally let me clean out her town house, I found her desk drawers full of little white paper swans and horses and dogs. They must have been her form of doodling while talking on the phone. Her answer to hearts and arrows hitting bull's-eyes and endless shaded chains of interlinking squares. I recognize one of her creations tacked to the wall above the phone, and I put the silent receiver back and reach for it. It's a red-and-white flower, and only when I untack it and let it unfold in my hand do I see that it's a menu from a Chinese restaurant. I fold it back up and stick it in my pocket.

I don't know what I expected, but it wasn't this. I thought somebody would be living here, that I'd have to stand on the step and ask nicely if I could come in, and that when I did, everything would be changed. I didn't expect this strange, hollowed-out shell still littered with the pointless bits and pieces of our past. I imagined the rooms alive, and I imagined noise. A radio. TV. Kids. I imagined that I would have to peel back the layers of someone's new life in order to get a glimpse of our old one. I didn't think it would be presented to me quite so whole. Or quite so dead.

As far as I can tell, Marina didn't change anything in the living room. The two couches are still here, and the matching armchairs, and our mother's old rolltop desk. White shades are pulled down, the same as in the kitchen, so the light is murky and makes me feel as if I'm swimming in a big aquarium or a fishbowl where, instead of shipwrecks and mermaid's castles, the whole of my childhood is strewn across the fake ocean floor.

When I sit in Momma's desk chair and open the top drawer, I see her glasses looking up at me. Underneath them are a couple of pictures in frames. There's Marina and me, and Grandma, and Uncle Ritchie, and Momma. They used to sit on top of the desk in a row, and I guess Della must have dusted them and put them away in case anybody wanted them later. I thought that there was another one, too, one of Marina and me in our tutus and ballet shoes, but I can't find it. It probably got lost a long time ago. I can hardly believe that anyone would mind if I took them, so I drop the pictures into my bag along with Momma's glasses, and then I slide the rolltop up. It makes a clacking sound, like a train running on tracks.

I assume that the police went through the desk after Marina was killed, because there's no phone book here, or date book, or anything like that. I know they came down and looked around, but Mark Cope told me they didn't find anything useful. There's a stack of envelopes that are curling a little, and a couple of flyers in one of the pigeonholes. One's from a garden center and has a few things circled in red, and there's another take-out menu, from somewhere called Red's. "Easter Special," it says. "Ham Dinner and Biscuits, Two for One!" A couple of dishes are underlined, and across the top, Marina wrote what looks like "Halibut." Maybe, I think, it was "catch of the day" or something. I've always liked biscuits, so I fold the leaflet into a tulip and stick it in my pocket, too.

There used to be carpet on the stairs, but it's been taken up. The polished wooden steps are steeper than I recall, and slippery. The tenth step creaks loudly, just like it always did. I can imagine Marina stamping on it every night on her way up to bed, just for auld lang syne.

The upstairs hall is almost totally dark. A colored shade as thick as a blackout blind is pulled down over the single window, and I trip on the edge of the hall runner. For the first time, I feel the hair on the back of my neck stand up a little, and even though I tell myself not to be silly, I also think that after I've taken just one look at Momma's room, I'll leave. Then I bang into the hall dresser, which I'd completely forgotten about. There's the crashing noise of something breaking, and just in time, I catch one of a pair of antique hurricane lanterns before it hits the floor.

I remember them; they were pretty, with etched-glass funnels, and so was the glass plate that sat between them. It, however, is in two pieces at my feet. My eyes have adjusted by now, and I can see well enough to pick it up. I think it might have been my grandmother's, and I feel a sudden flash of irritation. Why the hell doesn't Della change this place around. Or sell all this stuff. Or give it to the Morgan Memorial. I'll suggest it when I drop off the keys. I'll tell her it's fine, and that nobody will care. I'll suggest she get one of those charities that come and clean out old houses and auction stuff off and keep the proceeds. If she isn't in jail. If Mark Cope doesn't come down and arrest her for cutting Marina into itty-bitty pieces with a carving knife. I put the two halves of the plate back and push them together, hoping nobody will notice.

Momma's room is just the same, too, although, thank God, none of her clothes are hanging in the closet. Marina must have gotten rid of those. But, I think waspishly, probably not before she'd taken to wearing them around the house. Some dust sheets have been thrown over the furniture, which is at least slightly more normal, but it gives me the creeps anyway, and I decide that I've had enough of this. I don't know what I thought I was doing here in the first place, or what I thought I'd find. All our old papers, if there are any, will probably be up in the attic, and I am definitely not going up there. Mark Cope can come down and go rooting for clues. It's his job.

I close the door to Momma's room and am on my way down the hall when I stop. The door to our room is closed, and I want to walk past it, but I can't. It's as if she might be standing behind it, as if I can hear her moving on the other side of this thin panel of wood. I almost call out to her, whisper her name in this darkened hallway, as if the nightspinning might still work. And then, with a kind of detached interest, I watch my hand as it reaches out and slowly turns the knob.

There are no dust sheets in here. It looks as if I could have walked out and left for Chapel Hill yesterday. Our beds are still on either side of the room, and our matching bureaus, and our desks and chairs. The cushions that our grandma made are in the window seat, and a thin strip of sunlight creeps through the edges of the blind and makes a stripe across one of her ugly afghans folded there. I run my hand down the quilt of my old bed and plump the pillow.

The bulletin board above Marina's desk is empty. There are brighter squares and patches where things must have hung before the police took them away. Mine still has stuff on it, and I get a better look; I see some drawings that I must have done in high school. There's a pastel of flowers. A galloping horse. A photograph of my mother, and of Grandma, and there are a couple of pale patches here, too, although I can't remember what might have covered them or why the police might have thought they held a clue. There's a tack on the board in the shape of a daisy, and a button that says SOLIDARITY. My hands are shaking when I start to take them down. All of a sudden I don't want them left here. I don't want this adolescent self of mine exposed.

I put my bag on the desk and am gently pulling the tacks out of the drawings when a voice behind me says, "Anything I can do for you?"

I spin around so fast, I almost fall over.

"Jesus!" I yell. "Goddammit!"

He's a big man, and I don't recognize him, and it takes me a couple of seconds to realize that he's backing out of the doorway, holding both hands in front of him like a surrendering prisoner, not coming toward me with a butcher's knife.

"I'm sorry," he's saying, over and over. And he looks as scared as I feel. "I'm sorry, I didn't mean to scare you. Della told me you might be over here, and I just wanted to see if you needed anything." He's wearing overalls and a T-shirt, and I realize that he must be Della's older brother, Tommy.

"I didn't hear the stair squeak," I say.

He smiles at this uncertainly and says, "I always step over it. Sorry."

"That's okay," I say. My breath is coming back now, returning in choppy little bites. "I'm Susannah. You must be Tom."

Now he comes forward rapidly and shakes my hand. "I'm sorry I frightened you," he says again. "You dropped all your stuff."

He's right. My bag has gone flying off the desk, and all the things in it, my glasses and lipsticks and keys and the pictures of us that I've pilfered from downstairs, are all over the floor. Before I can stop him, Tommy is on his hands and knees picking things up, and I end up taking them from him awkwardly, and thanking him, and telling him that he really doesn't have to do this. When his hand lights on one of the photographs, I can feel myself blushing.

"I'm sorry," I say when he looks up at me. "They were in the desk downstairs, and I didn't think Della or you would mind if I took them."

I feel as if I've been caught stealing, which I suppose technically I have. Although this is absurd, because it's my family, after all, and I can't see what the Herveys would want with a whole bunch of pictures of us. Even so, I feel sneaky and terrible, and to my utter horror, I'm afraid that I'm going to start to cry in front of this huge man with his balding head, and his fat reddened hands, and his overalls.

"That's everything," I say. "Really. Thank you. Thank you, so much." And then I grab my bag and dash for the stairs, going down them two at a time.

———

"NOT FUNNY, SUSANNAH," DETECTIVE MARK COPE SAYS when I finally get him on the phone.

It's just past seven A.M. and he's really angry. In fact, he sounds as if he'd be happy to save our psychopath the trouble and wring my neck himself, if he could get ahold of me. Not that that's going to happen, since I have no intention of telling him where I am. The last time I did that I ended up with a basket of violets.

I've even taken the precaution of driving to a White Hen Pantry to use a pay phone a good five miles from the motel where I checked in last night under the absurdly uninventive name of Mrs. Farmer. My voice had gone all nervous and squeaky when I'd done it, but the teenage desk assistant couldn't have cared less. She wouldn't have noticed if I'd checked in as Snoop Doggy Dogg. A tiny toy-size TV was half hidden under the counter, and she was watching reruns of *Buffy the Vampire Slayer* while she took the cash I counted out and grunted as she handed me the key.

Taking into account that Mark Cope is the police, I know sooner or later he'll figure out where I am. Probably sooner. It wouldn't exactly take Einstein. But I'm still freaked out enough by what happened at the Marriott that I'm not going to help him in the meantime. He knows this, and he's not happy about it.

"Susannah," he hisses into my ear while I lean against the grubby Plexiglas wall of the phone booth and watch pickup trucks pulling into the Dunkin' Donuts across the road, "you can't honestly think that I. Or Phil. Or Becca Aaronson. Or Paul Donovan. Murdered Marina? Or that we have more than an academic interest in murdering you?"

"Is that the vampire's real name?" I ask. I had him made as some kind of Eastern European. A Pole or a Latvian, maybe, but not an Irishman.

"What?" Cope asks.

"The flowers," I say. "The lovely little basket and the note. Sent to my room. That only the four of you knew about."

Mark Cope sighs. "They've gone to the lab," he says. "We don't have any fingerprints from the note, so we're trying to work through the florist. But it was an FTD order made on-line, so it's going to take some time."

I think about this, and then I ask, "Is Phil there? I mean, is he right there? Can I talk to him?"

"No," Mark Cope says, and he sounds momentarily confused, as if I've thrown him off his game plan. "I mean, he's not here. He's in court this morning. Why?"

"Could a woman have killed her?" There's a silence on the other end of the line. "Can you ask him?" I say. "I know that we went over this before, and I know he said it was possible. But can you ask him again if it's likely—psychologically, I mean."

"What's going on, Susannah?" Cope's voice quickens, and I can almost sense him leaning forward. I can see those fine hands of his, the lean fingers splaying out across the blotter on his desk. Or playing with a pen, tapping it angrily and then pausing in midair.

"I have a name for you," I say. "Della Hervey. I think her real name might be Adele. She comes from Petamill, Georgia."

I expect Mark Cope to be thrilled with this piece of news, so I'm surprised when his voice goes flat and not very interested. "Who is she?" he asks.

"We all grew up together," I say. "I sold the house to her. She and Marina used to be close. A long time ago. They seem to have had a falling-out." I remember the sound of Della's voice and the shape of her body as I say it. The power in her arms and shoulders. In her back. The way she had moved through the kitchen without making a sound.

"Susannah?" Mark Cope's voice in my ear makes me jump.

"I should go now." The phone booth is getting claustrophobic.

"Wait," he says. His voice has turned barky, and the pissed-off tone is back. "You know I can't make you cooperate. I have no jurisdiction over you at all. I don't even have the right to trace this call, incidentally, in case that's worrying you. You can do whatever you want. Frankly, I think you're a pain in the ass, and I don't have time for silly, fucking little games. But I also don't need you dead. You hear me?" I don't say anything, and a second later he goes on. "Do you have my new home number? I moved, and it's unlisted. I'm going to give it to you."

Part of me wants to hang up on him, but I resist the impulse and jam the receiver between my ear and my shoulder. I mumble at him to wait a minute, and finally I fish out of my bag the electronic diary that Lolly gave me for Christmas last year. I've had to rely on it since Detective Aaronson impounded my Filofax, and I barely know how to use the thing. It hasn't had the organizing effect on my life that Lolly had hoped for, but it seems better than scribbling Mark Cope's new number on the side of the phone booth.

"Shoot," I say, trying to make my voice sound normal, and he gives me the number twice and makes me repeat it back to him.

"Anything at all strange," he says, "and you call me." I can tell he's giving me his number because he feels bad for yelling at me. It's a peace offering, and I thank him.

"I mean it, Susannah," he says. "If you need me, you call. Okay? I know this is rough for you, but it's going to be over soon. We might be closer than you think." Then he asks, "What did you do with the dog? If you want, I can arrange—"

"It's okay," I say. "I put him in a kennel. He's fine. Actually, I told them to give him to you if I get killed."

There's a pause before Mark laughs at this, even though it's true. Then he says, "Thanks, Susannah, you're a peach."

"What did you mean," I ask, "about being closer?"

"Look, I don't want to get your hopes up, because I'm really not sure about this yet, but we're taking another look at Kathleen Harper's alibi for the Friday night when you think Marina was killed. It turns out she was in Philadelphia the day Jake was poisoned. She didn't get home until late. She says she had a doctor's appointment and then went out to dinner. But there are a few hours missing in there. We've got someone who's placed her near your apartment, and we're talking to her again. At the moment it's all circumstantial. We're taking another look at her divorce, too. But I am not saying," he adds, "that she did it. You understand?"

"You mean it's not over," I say.

"I mean," he says, "I still need you to be careful, if you insist on running around on your own."

Kathleen Harper's face swells up in front of me, and the phone booth is filled with the warmth and smell of her breath. I can see her hand, the long, strong fingers reaching out, grabbing at the edge of my car window.

"Susannah," Mark Cope says, as if he can tell what I'm thinking, as if he, too, can see the broad, flat bones of Kathleen Harper's face, "we're watching her. She's not going anywhere. And if it's of any interest to you, she's nowhere near Georgia."

After I put the phone down, I sit in the car. I'm holding the organizer with Mark Cope's number as though it's a good-luck charm. I'm turning it over and over, rubbing its smooth sides against my palms, while through the convenience-store window, I watch people buying coffee and cigarettes. There's a woman in there, and she's tall, and I'm suddenly sure she's Kathleen Harper. She turns to look at me through the glass, and I close my eyes. I squeeze them shut. And when I open them again, she's gone.

NO EX-PRESIDENTS OR CIVIL WAR GENERALS WERE BORN in Petamill, Georgia, and when I was growing up, it didn't even have an exit sign off the highway. It was a small, passably pleasant town surrounded by not very prosperous farmland, and it was on the way to nowhere. I suppose it was like a thousand other places with Memorial Day parades, and town picnics, and Fourth of July fireworks. Even in the seventies, it was the kind of town where almost everybody knew one another and went to church on Sundays.

Famous sons are not the only things that Petamill lacks. There is no Spanish moss, for instance, and the one plantation house in the area was burned in a fire in the twenties and stood derelict on the outskirts of town until a medical-services company finally bought it and turned it into a nursing home. So, as southern towns go, the Petamill of my memory, the place that I regarded as the prison camp of my teenage years, never was especially picturesque. But even so, I'm a little startled by the mini–miracle mile that has sprung up on its outskirts. There's a four-screen movie complex and a low-level mall flanked by a smattering of chain food places. An Applebee's. A Taco Bell. A Waffle House.

I've driven to the far side of town, so I don't follow the route that is burned into my memory, the one the school bus used to take and my mother drove every day to the Coachstop. Instead I come in over the railroad tracks, bumping over the old level crossing and passing the hardware-store building with its rickety staircase up to what had once been the Shall We Dance studio. The sign with the toe shoes and the star is no longer there, so I assume that no more ranks of hopeful little swans spend the afternoons turning out their toes and grasping the barre while the teacher claps her hands in time and the freight trains run by.

When I stop at the light, I notice a brand-new sign mounted above signs for the Rotary and the Lions Club: WELCOME TO PETAMILL'S HISTORIC CENTER. A pile of pumpkins and a Confederate flag have been arranged in the stone water trough in front of the town offices, and sawed-off barrels planted with chrysanthemums sit at the base of every lamppost on the main street. HALLOWEEN PARADE AND MINI-SPOOK DISCO, an announcement in front of the post office reads, PRIZES FOR THE BEST COSTUMES.

I've pulled into one of the spaces facing the town square, and I sit there feeling vaguely like a time traveler, somebody who's wandered— or, in my case, been shoved—straight out of one life and over a precipice into another. The Coachstop is directly across the square, and from the outside, at least, it hasn't changed at all. The sign with the four black horses and the red stagecoach still hangs over the door, and there's still the same gauzy, ruched white curtain across the big front window. Momma hated that thing. She said flies buzzed in there against the glass pane and got trapped in the folds of the material and died, and that it was very unhygienic. I can't read the sign from here, but I know what it says: OPEN LUNCH AND DINNER. NOON UNTIL LATE. MONDAY THROUGH SATURDAY. JOIN US FOR SOUTHERN HOSPITALITY EVERY DAY. COCKTAILS. I stare at it as if maybe I'm waiting for my mother to appear. As if maybe I've only been over to the library or up to the farm store, instead of gone for fifteen years, and any minute now she's going to come swinging through the door, her dark hair bouncing and her Peter Pan collar bright in the sunshine.

I HAVEN'T EATEN GRITS IN DECADES, BUT I FELT LIKE IT was the least I could do, a small gesture to mark my return to the

South, and suddenly I was hungry for them. When I got out of the car, I'd patted my pocket for quarters to feed the meter before realizing that a dime buys you an hour in towns like this, so I'd dropped in two and gone searching for somewhere that served breakfast. I found it fast, and it seems to be the local hot spot. It's called the Chicken-Fried Café, and it wasn't here when I was a kid.

The front door is lacquered scarlet and has a little bell above it that rings every time somebody goes in or out, just like the angels getting their wings in *It's a Wonderful Life,* and the walls are lined with paintings of chickens. There are big fat roosters crowing and red hens scratching, and sitting on fenceposts, and on golden nests of straw. It's actually not bad. I'm wondering how Lolly would like the idea. Retro diners are really hot, and this is the sort of place that college students and professors love. Booths make them feel both furtive and innocent at once, and the diner part reassures them that they're still cheap and honest. Blue-collar. Connected. Salt of the earth. I am stirring my third cup of coffee and seriously considering a proposal when BethAnn Evans walks through the door.

I haven't seen BethAnn since my mother's funeral, but you can't miss her. She looks just like those drawings of Alice in Wonderland. She did when we were kids, and when we were in high school, and she still does now. Her blond hair is pulled back with a headband and caught in a bouncy ponytail, and she's even wearing a blue dress and flat shoes that match. She waves to the cashier, and when she pauses to let one of the waitresses pass, she's so close to my little booth that I could reach out and touch her. She looks right at me, and her brow puckers a little, and as she decides that she doesn't recognize me after all, I say, "Hey, BethAnn. It's Susannah deBreem."

Since Della blew my disguise last night, it seems pointless to pretend that I'm not here. BethAnn stares, widening her big blue eyes until they look like marbles, and then she breaks into a smile and gives a little squeal like southern girls do when they meet somebody unexpectedly.

"Oh my God!" she says. "What did you do to your hair?"

BethAnn says she can't stay, that she's in a big hurry, but she's ordered a chocolate-chip muffin and coffee anyway, and she can't stop staring at me.

"I'm sorry," she says. "I'm really sorry. It just looks so strange. No"—she reaches out and touches my arm—"not strange. I mean great. It looks great, really. It's just so different from how I remember you!"

"That's okay," I say. "I'm different. I'm fifteen years older."

BethAnn rolls her eyes and breaks off a piece of her muffin. "Aren't we all," she says. "So what have you been up to, Susannah? Marina told me you were living in Philadelphia? Is that right? Or was it New York?"

"New York first," I say, "and then Philly." BethAnn's already told me how sorry she is about Marina, and I'm grateful to her that she can say my sister's name normally, that she can mention her in conversation without lowering her voice to a melodramatic hush. "What about you?" I ask. "What are you doing?"

"Small-town housewife," she replies. "No, that's not totally true. I work in the bank. I'm the loan officer."

"Yeah, Della told me something like that."

"Della." BethAnn rolls her eyes again. She's stirring sugar into her coffee, and I notice that her nails are painted pearl pink. "Now, there is one sad story."

"Oh?" Something inside of me quickens, and I wonder if BethAnn has heard the interest in my voice.

She looks at me and shakes her head. "That guy she married was a real no-good," she says. "A serious redneck. He was just all kinds of trouble, although those two little children are darling. Still, if you ask me, him walking out on Della was the best thing that could have happened. Of course," she adds, leaning forward and lowering her voice, "she has Sonny Delray and her brother to thank for that."

"She does?"

"Sure." BethAnn nods and eats another piece of her muffin. "They went and had a little talk with Mr. Harley, one weekend when Sonny was back visiting his momma and noticed that Della had a black eye, and right after that—poof!" She snaps her fingers, and I imagine the unseen Harley exploding in a little ball of fairy dust. "At least Sonny did that much for her."

I don't understand her last remark, and the look on my face gives me away.

"Well, you know she was sweet on Sonny for years," BethAnn says, "and I think it just got her hopes up again when he rode in like a white knight and got Tommy to kick that rat on out of there. Rumor says that Della had high hopes that something would come of it. But, no surprise, it didn't." She takes a sip of her coffee. "Mr. Delray has moved on. He's very citified now. And you should see the presents he gives his momma. He is not about to marry poor Della."

I find the idea of the chubby moon-faced boy with a grubby baseball cap permanently jammed on his head hard to reconcile with the picture BethAnn is painting, and I'm about to ask exactly how it is that Sonny has been citified when she winks at me and says, "Am I wrong in thinking that it was someone in your family who had sole possession of Mr. Delray's heart?"

"Wrong one," I say.

"Oh," she says. "Well, I was just teasin' you. But I still think Marina did not have to go and make things so bad for poor Della. I'm sorry"— BethAnn wags her finger at me—"but that was a naughty thing of your sister to do. I've never heard such nonsense. I can't imagine what got into her."

My stomach is sinking a little, and I'm torn between nodding and pretending that I know what she's talking about, and asking her to explain. In the end the latter wins out.

"What did Marina do?" I ask.

"Oh, Lord," BethAnn says, "of course she wouldn't have told you, because she was probably embarrassed when she came to her senses." I doubt it, I think. But I don't share this with BethAnn. "It was the craziest thing," she is saying, "even for Marina, who, I seem to recall, could be a little crazy."

"That's right," I say, "but I still don't know what you're talking about."

"Oh," BethAnn says. "Well, she accused Della of stealing things."

"Stealing things?" This seems so strange that it's almost impossible to believe, but BethAnn nods.

"That's right," she says. "You know, Della had a key to the house, in case of a fire or something while Marina was up in Washington, and Marina insisted that Della had gone in and taken things. I don't know what all, exactly." She picks at her muffin, pulling a chocolate chip out of it. "Marina made one big stink out of it. Went to the police and everything. Of course no one could believe it, and Chuck Hancy, he's the new police chief, he finally convinced Marina that nothin' had happened."

This story seems so bizarre that I can't think of anything to say. "Could it have been the husband?" I finally ask.

"Oh, no," BethAnn says, "this was after he was gone. This all happened about two, maybe two and a half years ago."

Six months to a year before Marina was killed, I think. Right around the time she started getting flowers and phone calls.

"I told you it was crazy," BethAnn is saying, and she's shaking her head, "but anyways, it all died down, although I think it was awfully hard on Della."

"Yes," I say, "I'm sure it was. What did you say the new police chief was called?"

"Chuck Hancy," says BethAnn. "He was hired about three years ago, used to be down in Naples, Florida, but said it got too big. You know, he was looking for somewhere to raise his kids that was civilized." She's digging chocolate chips out of the muffin and eating them one by one as she talks. "We were just so lucky to get him. And his wife is just the sweetest thing, too. We're in a book club together on Tuesday nights. I bet you are way too smart for that sort of thing, Susannah deBreem. You and Marina with all your gold stars. You girls were just too smart. The Straight A's, that's what we used to call you behind your backs at school."

"You did?" I say. "I didn't know that."

"Oh, we didn't mean it as mean." She reaches out quickly and touches my arm with the tips of her fingers. "Really. I think we were just jealous, if you want to know the truth."

"You didn't have anything to be jealous of, BethAnn," I say. "You were the most popular girl in the class."

"Oh, pooh," she says. "Look at me. Married and living in my hometown and working at the bank. How exciting is that?"

"I don't know," I say. "Excitement's relative. Who did you marry? Anybody I know?"

BethAnn shakes her head, and her ponytail bobs. "The bank manager," she says, and she starts to laugh again. "Well, somebody had to. He'd just come to town, and there he was all sad and lonely. And besides, I needed a job. That is a joke," she adds. "Sort of."

She finishes the remnants of the muffin, scrunching up the butter-colored crumbs, and looks at her watch. "Oh, Lord!" she exclaims, jumping to her feet. "Susannah deBreem, you are making me late. I had not counted on you, and now I will get fired and my babies will starve." She's gathering up her purse, and although it's only one small item, she manages to look as if she's in a flurry of activity.

"Now, don't you be a stranger," she says to me. "You come by the bank sometime, you hear? We can go to the Coachstop." She winks and adds, "I will buy you a cocktail."

And then BethAnn blows a kiss into the air and vanishes through the shiny red door, leaving nothing behind her but the bill and a bright tinkle of bells.

CHUCK HANCY HAS A PROMINENT ADAM'S APPLE. HE HAS agreed to see me only because he happened to walk out of the men's room and across the police-station lobby as I was asking for him. I had not planned to do this, but what BethAnn has told me is so strange that I can't leave it alone. I used her name flagrantly, giving the distinct impression that she would consider it a personal favor if Chief Hancy talked to me, and although he agreed, and has called me "ma'am" and asked me if I would like a glass of water or a Coke, I can tell he's not altogether happy about being buttonholed like this.

His uniform looks as if it's too big for him, but it's so stiff and so precisely pressed that the seams stand out in lines, and the heavy-looking badge on his chest that says CHIEF OF POLICE doesn't even drag his pocket down.

"Miss deBreem," he says as he ushers me into his office, "I want to tell you how sorry I am about your sister. That was a terrible thing." He shakes his head and gestures for me to sit down in one of the chairs in front of his desk. "We did everything we could to cooperate with Alexandria," he goes on, sitting down himself, "but I haven't heard that they've gotten anywhere."

"No," I say, "they haven't, really."

He blinks at me and smiles, and it occurs to me that I'm making him nervous. He can't figure out why I'm here.

"Cities are horrible places," he says, "you never know what's going to happen."

There are a lot of things that I could say in reply to this, but I don't bother. I'm not here to engage Chief Chuck Hancy in a debate on the relative merits of rural and urban life.

"Actually," I say, "I wanted to ask you about something else, I mean not the murder itself. I understand that my sister made some allegations, that she accused Della Hervey of breaking into the house."

"Oh, not breaking in, exactly," he says quickly. "Della had a key."

"All right," I say, "but she did think that Della had taken things?"

"Yes, yes, that's right," Chief Hancy says. He pinches the bridge of his nose between his thumb and forefinger and closes his eyes, and then he opens them and nods. "It was about two and a half years ago, almost a year exactly before your sister was murdered, I think. She hadn't been down here in a while, and when she did come down, oh, sometime before Easter, she came in and swore out a complaint against Della Hervey. Della was awfully upset, naturally."

"What was it that Marina said was missing?" I ask.

He looks at me as though he's summing up how much trouble I might be, and then he says, "Nothing of any value, really. Some photographs, I think. A scrapbook. Things that could easily have been misplaced, Miss deBreem."

"But Marina was sure she hadn't misplaced them?" I say.

"Well, yes," he replies. "I did suggest that to her, but she was emphatic. Very certain." He frowns at me as if certainty is a serious character defect. "She didn't strike me as an irrational woman, although I understand now, of course, that she was under great pressure."

I don't know how he figures this, since I doubt Marina had any inkling that in a year's time she was going to get murdered, but I let it pass and try not to let my newfound dislike of Chuck Hancy show on my face.

"Is there a list," I ask as quietly as I can, "of the things that she said were missing? Could I see it?"

I can tell that he's about to say no or remind me that the police are very busy and have to respect confidentiality. But then he remembers that Marina was murdered, and that I'm from out of town, and the combination of these things somehow makes me special, so instead he smiles and says, "Of course." He pushes a button on his intercom and asks for the file, and then he leans back in his chair. "We did tell the Alexandria police about this, of course."

"But they didn't think it was important?"

Chief Hancy shrugs, and when he does, his shoulders appear to move while his shirt stays still. "Miss deBreem," he says, "there was really no evidence that anything was missing. I went to talk to Della myself. You can imagine how upset she was. Reputations are still important things in towns like this, especially for a single woman. We looked all over Della's house. We didn't need a warrant; Della insisted. And there was nothing there."

He stares at me and I stare back at him, and although he does not say it, he wants me to know that Petamill had nothing to do with Marina's murder. This is what happens, his eyes say, to women who go up to the city, to places where reputations are not important. They step out of the safe circle. They stray too far. And then some lunatic hunts them down and kills them.

The file, when it arrives, is just a couple of pieces of paper in a buff-colored envelope. The sheet that Chief Hancy hands me is an official-looking form with a list of items in Marina's handwriting. It feels strange in my hand, and I imagine her standing in the old-fashioned lobby of this building, writing out these words with a fountain pen, itemizing the pieces of her past that had been taken from her. "One photograph, girl, aged fourteen, silver frame." "One scrapbook, blue vinyl with yellow flower on cover." "One diary, with lock, 1981." "One photograph, gold frame, girls, aged ten, in ballet clothes." And after this last item, in parentheses, Marina wrote, "Twins."

"Thank you," I say, and I hand the list back to Chief Hancy.

———

THE FLORIST IS CALLED KABLOOM. IT'S IN A ROW OF SHOPS a few blocks back from the police station, and its window is filled with large sprays of evergreen and yellow chrysanthemums and orange ribbons. A little black witch rides a broomstick that leaves a trail of baby's breath, and a tissue-paper ghost hovers over a bowl of paper-whites and says "Boo."

I should have taken flowers to Momma and Grandma earlier. I should have done it when I arrived yesterday. I tell myself that I haven't had time and that they'll forgive me. I also tell myself that I've intended to do this all along, that it didn't just occur to me because I happen to be passing this window, staring into it the way I've been staring into the Petamill General Store and the Kitchen Shoppe and about half a dozen other places, studying displays of candles and dish towels with pictures of Tara on them, trying to figure out if Della Hervey really could have killed Marina. And if so, whether she's trying to kill me. And if not, why Marina would have accused Della of stealing diaries and scrapbooks and photographs of us, and what Della might have done with them if she did.

When I open KaBloom's door, I'm bathed by a cloud of cool air. It's as chilly as a morgue inside, which I suppose is appropriate, since most of the flowers in here are technically dead and being given a semblance of life only by their buckets of water and little sachets of plant food.

There are roses and chrysanthemums, lilies and delphiniums, small, highly scented freesias and spice carnations, all stuck into silver metal buckets. On the whole, I'd prefer to take something living out to Momma and Grandma, but I'm told that the bowl of paper-whites under the ghost isn't for sale, and there's not much else apart from a small ficus tree and a couple of spider plants, which don't seem especially suitable. So I pick out two bouquets. I pluck the stems out of the buckets one by one and lay them on yellow patterned paper. The nice middle-aged lady in a pink apron and rubber gloves shoves their ends into little plastic tubes that she promises will keep them fresh, and when she's done, she ties each bouquet with a bow and loads me up.

My arms are so filled with flowers, I leave the store feeling like I'm going to a wedding.

I put the bouquets carefully on the front seat beside me, and I turn up the air conditioner, even though the Unitarian church is only a couple of miles outside of town and it's still blowing hot air when I get there. There is only one other car in the neatly graveled lot, and I pull in beside it, nosing into the shade of a tree. I had forgotten that the church was so desolate. It's a brick-and-glass box with a bad addition from the sixties. When I was a kid, it was the only alternative to the raucous hymn singing and dunking baptisms that went on in the Baptist chapel across the street. The Unitarian Meetinghouse, as they called it then, was so neat and so meticulously kept that it was hard to imagine people here at all, much less people praying, or weeping, or feeling anything as disorderly as exaltation, or grief, or joy.

My mother made us come here occasionally, on Easter and sometimes Christmas, but she never really went to church, and I always had the vague suspicion that this had something to do with us. I don't mean that we wouldn't have been welcomed because we didn't have a father; I just grew to suspect that our birth might have convinced Momma that life was not as high-minded, as orderly and benign, as the pastor liked to suggest.

The Baptist church across the street was altogether more rowdy and potentially more interesting, but we didn't go there. When I asked Momma why not, one Sunday morning when I was about ten and the Delrays and the Herveys had just driven by in all their best clothes with the kids waving from the backseat, she had yanked a weed out of the garden and replied sharply that she didn't believe in hellfire. Or, for that matter, salvation. "Dressing people up in nightgowns and dunking them in a bathtub," she said, "never saved anyone." Then she added, "But when you're older and have a brain of your own, then you can decide for yourself." I had slunk off after that, rebuked, and spent the afternoon wondering whose brain I did have if it wasn't my own.

Now, standing and looking down on Momma's grave, I wonder if she still feels the same way. Or if she's anywhere at all, feeling anything at all. Marina and I had been uncertain about what we should put on her headstone, since both of us were afraid of sentimentality. In the end, in one of our increasingly rare moments of agreement, we had done what she did for Grandma and put nothing at all except her name and the dates that had formed the borders of her life.

My grandfather is here somewhere, too, but I am not certain where. I do remember that when Grandma died, we discovered there was no space available for her to be next to him, because through some mix-up, one of his sisters had ended up in her spot. Momma had said at the time that this was typical, and she had not been at all happy about it, which was what prompted her to buy her own space when she bought Grandma's.

I'm pleased with the way the flowers look, even though I know that in a few hours they will wilt, and I think I should bring some for Grandpa, too. But that will mean finding him first. I don't think there can be many deBreems, and I wander backward across the neatly clipped grass, running my hand along the tops of the white stones and keeping my eye open for familiar names. Sometimes I pause to read the inscriptions: "Beloved Forever," they say. "Dear Wife and Loving Daughter."

A brick wall runs off from the side of the church, and the oldest graves rest there in the shade, along with the memorial plaques for those who could not make it home or were cremated but still remembered. I wander in this direction, making for a series of more weathered stones that look likely. Some of them are for boys who died in battles. "Iwo Jima," one says, and another reads "Da Nang."

I can't see any deBreems, and I think I must have missed Grandpa altogether and had better start again at the front and be more systematic, and then it occurs to me that he might not even be here. He might be across the street, and it might well have been my mother, with her lack of enthusiasm for hellfire and salvation, who decided that since there was no room for Grandma, we would take up residence, so to speak, with the Unitarians. The more I think this, the more likely it seems, and so I walk back up the lines of stones and cross the gravel lot, making for the white clapboard house of God on the other side of the road.

This graveyard is more haphazard in its design. The stones range across the thick green grass as if they've tumbled there from heaven of their own accord, or simply been wedged in where there was room. A lot of them have flowers planted around them. Roses seem popular, and some of the more impressive ones boast calla lilies and little pots of trailing ivy. There are more monuments here, too, mainly angels, their faces turned to heaven and their hands held out. Right away I see some Herveys and Charlie and Dex Eameses' parents, and I really have to wonder whether Momma was right or not, whether maybe Grandma wouldn't have been happier buried here with these people she'd known all her life.

I weave my way among the stones, looking for Grandpa and his sister, and every once in a while I have to be careful not to step on one of the small, flat ones that are just rectangles sunk into the earth. It's well past noon now, and hot, and I'd kill for a beer, and when I find that I've come the wrong way and ended up amid a whole bunch of newer stones, I think I'll give this up and let Grandpa rest in peace. And then I see our name, which is weird, since these dates are more recent.

It's one of the plaques, down in the ground, and I catch it just out of the corner of my eye, so I have to look again to be sure. I crouch down in this crowded space so that my back scrapes against a white cross and my shoulder rests against a tablet that proclaims, "He Will Rise Again." It's only then that I can see the whole inscription, that I can be certain of the name. There are capital letters carved into the pale marble, and they're garish, bright and shiny with gilt. "Rest in Beauty," they proclaim. And underneath they say, "Marina deBreem, Born into This World, August 30, 1965—Called to God, March 19, 1999."

21

IT'S THE HEAT, I TELL MYSELF, THAT'S MAKING MY HEAD swim. It's the bright sun that I'm no longer used to. I close my eyes, but when I open them, the bright gold letters are still there, sunk into the ground in front of me. This is still Marina's grave, here in the Baptist cemetery in Petamill, Georgia, even though I buried her ashes myself in Reston eighteen months ago.

I get to my feet too quickly and back up, anxious to get away. I bang into the marble cross behind me and trip on a pot of flowers that falls over. I right them, stuffing them back in their pot, and when I'm done, the moist, dark loam clings to my hands. I wipe them down the sides of my jeans, rubbing them against my thighs as I weave back through the maze of stones. When I finally reach the front of the church, even though the parking lot is empty and I know there's probably nobody here, I go up the steps and bang on the door, which is locked.

There's a notice board in a glass-fronted case on the wall. An advertisement for a domestic-abuse help line, a couple of flyers, and a schedule of services and events are pinned to its corkboard. A diet group meets in the basement every Tuesday at noon. "Slim for Him!" the notice exhorts. But beyond that there's nothing, not even the pastor's name or a phone number or any clue when he or she might be back.

The car I noticed before in the Unitarian parking lot is still there, but when I cross the road and try the church doors, they're locked, too. I think about driving into town and going to the chamber of commerce, or looking for an information booth, or even going to the bank to ask BethAnn who runs the Baptist church and where I can find them. But the inside of my mouth has a thick, sour taste, and my eyes are gritty, so instead I unlock the Taurus and get in and turn the air-conditioning on full.

It clicks and whines in protest, and I lower my face to the vent. I bend over until I'm half lying across the furry gray fabric of the front seat, and I wait for the stream of warm air blowing onto my eyelids and my forehead to turn cold. I move my face in it, twisting so it blasts first one cheek and then the other. Then I open my mouth and breathe in the air. I gulp and swallow as if it can somehow fill me, as if it can rush down my lungs and into my stomach and make me clean.

"WELL, I DON'T KNOW," THE GIRL SITTING AT THE FRONT desk of Sweet Memories is saying. "How would you expect me to know? What do you think I am, Lennie? A mind reader?" She's tapping her fingers on the desk in exasperation, but when she sees me standing in the doorway, she lowers her voice and says, "Lennie, I have to go. I'll see you tonight." And then she puts the phone down and smiles. "Welcome to Sweet Memories," she says to me. "My name is Laurel. How can I help?"

I'm a little surprised. She's good at this. In about two seconds, she's gone from haranguing the unfortunate Lennie to being a model of sympathy and discretion. Even her eyes have turned from hard to limpid, and when she reaches up to straighten her hair, giving it just the slightest pat, she does it with a demureness that suggests not vanity but modest deference to the depth of my presumed grief.

"I don't know if you can help me," I say. "I'm trying to find out who bought a headstone for my sister." At this Laurel looks momentarily confused. I sit down in the guest chair and help myself to one of her Kleenexes.

Sweet Memories is the third memorial store I've been in this afternoon, and I'm hoping that the third try will bring me some luck, because so far I've drawn a complete blank. The first place I tried was Gulliver's, where Momma bought Grandma's stone, and where Marina and I bought Momma's stone. It's a dark little storefront down by the old railroad depot in Petamill, and once it used to belong to old Mr. Gulliver, who did all his own carving and engraving and wore suspenders and had eyes that looked perennially sad and hands as calloused and hard as hooves. He must be long gone now, because the young man I talked to today looked at me blankly when I asked after him, and had hands so pale and fine that they hardly looked as if they'd ever done a dish, much less picked up a chisel or a mallet. He had eventually, and grudgingly, led me into the office and let me sit there while he very slowly turned the pages of the company's order books and made clicking sounds with his tongue, finally telling me that they had no record of anything remotely like the plaque bearing Marina's name.

The second place I tried, Millet's Memorials for All Occasions in Sefton, the next town over, had produced the same result. Although that time a middle-aged woman had searched the back orders, and she had done it on a computer.

There are six local memorial places that I got from the Yellow Pages I consulted at the Applebee's in the mini-mall, where I stopped to wash my face and get a Coke. I had considered a beer, but I'd been afraid that if I sat down in the electric twilight of the bar and started eating chips and drinking Heinekens, I might never move again. My first thought, once I got over the shock of seeing Marina's name there, had been Kathleen Harper. But surely she would have told me. Not out of consideration for my feelings, but because she wouldn't have been able to resist it. And besides, she knew where Marina was buried; she had stood there while the urn was lowered into the ground. If she hadn't done it, I had no idea who might have, but I had to try to find out.

Sweet Memories is hidden in the back of an office park in the middle of nowhere, one of those places that house FedEx depots and tax accountants, and the buildings look so temporary that you imagine them erected or removed overnight. Stunted fir trees are placed around the parking lot in tubs, and all the offices have plate-glass doors and signs that look new. I've drawn a radius, and moved steadily away from Petamill through the course of the afternoon, and sitting here at Laurel's desk, toying with her Kleenex, I'm really hoping that my luck has changed, because it's almost five and the other places on my list are much farther away, which means I'll have to wait until tomorrow to check them out.

Despite my best efforts here, and my story about how I really want to thank whoever did this for my sister, Laurel is looking a little dubious.

"Well, I don't know," she says. "I mean, I understand what a dilemma this must be for you. But we do have to respect our clients' privacy." She looks at me and blinks. "Death is a very delicate matter."

"Look," I say, taking out my driver's license and putting it on her desk. "This is me. I know my hair looks different, but really, it is. And here's my MasterCard, too." I slide my credit card, which has my picture on it, toward her. "DeBreem is not a common name," I add, "and it's the name on my sister's headstone. Marina deBreem. Couldn't you possibly just look through your records for March '99 and see if there's a stone that had that name on it?"

Despite their earlier tiff, Laurel wants to get home to Lennie, I can tell. She's eyeing the clock behind my head. I take the twenty-dollar bill that I've had ready in my pocket and slide it under the edge of her desk blotter.

"I know it's a lot to ask," I say, "but I'd be really, really grateful."

She looks away from the money, and then she picks up the credit card and the driver's license and inspects them carefully. "Philadelphia," she says, "that's a long way away." And then she puts them down and swivels her chair around to her computer terminal. "It was 1999, you said? March?"

I nod, and Laurel clicks the mouse a few times. Without taking her eyes off the screen, she reaches out and pulls the bill out from under her blotter and slips it into her pocket. She spends the next few minutes scrolling through what I presume are back orders and squinting at the screen so closely that I wonder if she needs glasses. Then she stops.

"Hmmmn," she says. "This is it. A plaque, white marble, twelve by twenty-four inches. Gold lettering."

"That sounds right," I say.

"Marina deBreem," she goes on, and then she pauses. "Oh. 'Rest in Beauty.' " She looks at me and smiles. "That's so nice. Is it part of a poem?"

"I guess so," I say, forcing myself to smile. "I don't really know. Now you can see why I'd like to know who it is that did this for her. I'd really like to thank them, and I can't call all her friends asking if it was them, can I? I mean——"

"No," Laurel says. "I see what you mean." She turns back to her screen. "Let's just see what I can do." She clicks the mouse a few more times and types in some numbers. The twenty and the mushy epitaph have touched her heart.

"Here we go," she says. She looks at me and beams while the screen loads. "That's one of the beauties of Sweet Memories. We have outlets all up and down the East Coast. Some people think a chain is tacky, but it means you can order your own personalized memorial in any one of them, and then the outlet closest to the cemetery of your choice orders the stone and installs it for you. It makes it a lot easier on people, you know." She looks back at the screen. "So, here we go. Your sister's stone was ordered in Washington, D.C. Then we fulfilled the order and had it placed in Petamill."

I guess this shouldn't surprise me. But even though it's muggy in this office, and Laurel doesn't have the air-conditioning on, I can feel myself going cold.

"Washington, D.C.?" I hear myself say.

"That's right." Laurel nods. "Does that help?"

"She worked there," I say. "She had a lot of friends. Can you give me anything else?" I push another twenty across her desk. This time I don't bother to hide it, and she doesn't make any pretense about not seeing it. She picks up the bill and folds it in half. Then she makes a few more clicks.

"Um," she says, "it was ordered on the twentieth of March."

"The twentieth," I say. "A Saturday. Is that right?"

Laurel shrugs. "I guess so," she says. "We're open on Saturdays. Nine to five. Sunday's the only day we close." Through the open window, I hear a door slam, and a car starts and backs up.

"Does it say who bought it?" I ask.

"Well," Laurel says, "it was paid for in cash, and—" Her voice falters. She stops talking and frowns at the screen, then turns and looks at me. "Is this a joke?" she asks. "Are you trying to set me up or something?"

I shake my head. The cold feeling is getting worse. There's a sound like the patter of running feet in my head. "What does it say?" I ask. "Please tell me."

Laurel sees my face and looks worried. She turns back to the screen. "Susannah deBreem," she says. She falters and looks at my driver's license again. "Our records say you bought this stone on March twentieth, 1999. In Washington, D.C. You paid in cash."

"SHE SAID SHE WAS ME," I SAY, AND MY VOICE IS HIGH AND whiny, as though this is the worst affront, the worst thing, this person has done: walking into Sweet Memories on K Street the day after Marina was killed and pretending to be me.

Mark Cope makes a humming sound. "Okay, Susannah," he says, "good. This is really good. The name of the place is Sweet Memories, on K Street. Right?"

"Right," I say, and neither of us actually mentions Kathleen Harper, although I know we're both picturing the way she walks, what she wore, how she pushed the door open. We're both hearing what she must have said.

I paged Mark Cope, and he called me back in about two minutes. While I was waiting, standing beside this phone booth bolted to a telephone pole across the parking lot from the Sweet Memories storefront, I could see Laurel. She was closing up the office, and she kept glancing at me while she straightened things on her desk and shut down her computer. I'd made her write down the K Street address of the Washington store, even though all she wanted to do was get me out of her office. By then she'd figured out that something was really wrong, and she still thought that somehow I was setting her up, that I was going to get her fired for taking my money. When she closed the window, she stared at me through the glass, then she pulled the blinds.

"It's after five now," Mark is saying. "But we'll get somebody down there tomorrow, first thing. We'll try to get an ID. Why didn't we get this?" he mutters, more to himself than to me.

"Wrong graveyard," I say. "My family's all in the Unitarian's. This is across the street with the Baptists. And besides, it wasn't there when you guys were down here. Apparently it takes as much as a month for the stones to get made and placed. I'm going to talk to the pastor tomorrow, try to find out—"

Mark Cope cuts me off. "No, Susannah. What you've done is great, but let us do our job now, okay?" When I don't answer right away, he says, "Susannah, I mean it. Really. I don't want you messing around with this anymore."

"Okay," I say.

"Promise me," he says.

"I promise," I say.

There's a pause before he says, "Do you feel like telling me where you're staying yet?" His voice has softened, and the question makes me feel silly. As if I'm some stupid Nancy Drew character he's been indulging.

"Sure," I say. "The Green Hills Motel, in Sefton, Georgia. I'm Mrs. Farmer."

He gives a low whistle. "Inventive," he says. And then he adds, "Hey, Susannah, make me another promise."

"What?" I ask.

"Take yourself out for a drink tonight," Mark Cope says. "On me."

"CALLED TO GOD." "REST IN BEAUTY." I HEAR THE WORDS spoken out loud, and in my dream, I run my fingers along the edge of the stone. I scrabble for a corner that I can dig underneath, and when the marble tablet still refuses to move, still lies heavy and stuck, welded to the earth, I get up and run to the car and find a jack and a tire iron so I can pry it loose. I wrestle and sweat, and finally the gravestone pops free. It lifts into my hands as easily as a top off a beer bottle, and when I carry it, it's light. It might as well be papier-mâché. With the clear logic of dreams, I understand that this is because Marina is not there, her body never anchored it to the earth.

I am barefoot, but I do not feel the heat that rises off the road as I walk down it, and I know I don't have far to go. The big sign rises ahead of me, filling the sky, and the blond man with his hands upraised stares vacantly. I throw the stone. I fling it, and it flies as easily as a Frisbee or a bird. Marina's plaque arcs through the air, and when it hits the billboard, the blond man shatters. His face crumbles, and his hands fall to his sides, and on the road there is nothing but a heap of letters that once spelled "Jesus Saves."

The blood is rushing to my head, making me dizzy when I wake up, and when I close my eyes again, I see Marina. She revisits me as I saw her last. Bruising around both eyes and across her cheeks, dull purplish against the putty color of her dead skin. Broken nose. Cut forehead where she fell against a table. The sheet, bright white against the gray of her face, is pulled up tight under her chin. I can't see the broken nails or the marks on her arms that I know are there, or the gash that stilled her voice. I can't see the long slice where the blade came across her throat, opening her like a sacrificial animal so the blood poured out.

Called to God. Rest in Beauty. I'm convinced the words are going to make me sick. I sit up in the double bed in the Green Hills Motel and wrap my arms around my knees. I lay down for only a moment when I came back, but now the room is dark, and the electric clock on the bedside table says it's past seven. I'm queasy and my head aches, but I know it's not the nap that's left me feeling like this. It's not even the dream, the fury that coursed through me as I dug up that stone, or the vision of Marina in the morgue. It's not any of those things. It's the date. It's the gold letters reading "March 19" that make my stomach heave.

When I buried Marina, when I had a gray granite stone polished and cut for her, I told them just to carve "Deceased" and "March 1999." Because until last week, there was no time of death and no date. Nobody knew whether it was the night of Friday, March 19, or sometime on Saturday the twentieth, or even very early in the morning on Sunday the twenty-first, when she was "called to God." Nobody, that is, except the person who killed her, and me.

CHAPTER 22

RED'S IS A BIG BARN OF A PLACE SET BACK OFF THE ROAD.
Even before I open the door, I can hear the noise from inside, a twangy
beat of country-western music and the purr and hum of voices, and I'm
glad that I ordered takeout and didn't try to reserve a table. I'd dug Marina's red-and-white origami flower out of my pocket, and it was only
after I'd started to dial that I realized the restaurant, Mau's China
Palace, was in Virginia, not Georgia. Then I'd remembered the tulip
that I'd made out of the menu I found in Momma's desk, so I dug that
out and unfolded it to see if it was local, which it was.

When I get inside, it's obvious that the place is doing pretty well. It
looks like they have at least three dining rooms. They aren't doing the
ham-and-biscuit special anymore, but they have a whole range of barbecue and things like catfish, and gumbo, and dirty rice. Sitting in my
motel room just reading the names made me realize how hungry I was,
so I've probably ordered way too much food. The hostess is wearing a
cowgirl outfit with a little fringed jacket, and when I give her my name,
she apologizes for the fact that my order isn't ready yet and suggests
that I have a seat in the bar while I wait.

The bar is actually a little quieter, and I find a free stool and order
a beer, which comes ice-cold in a frosted mug. I realize, as I'm raising it
to my mouth, that I'm thinking of Beau, and as I take the first long, cold

swallow, I wish I'd bought myself a pack of cigarettes. Then I remember that it's not as much fun if you don't have somebody to blow smoke rings at. I'll call him, I think. I'll finish my beer, and then I'll go find a pay phone and call him while I'm waiting for my food. I wonder if he'll be at Sherlock's, or if he'll be home trying to figure out how to heat up a frozen pizza. Or maybe he has choir practice tonight. I don't even know what day of the week it is, and I'm just about to wave to the bartender and ask him when I see him looking over my shoulder, and then a voice says, "Lou, this lady's order is on the house!"

At first I don't recognize Charlie Eames's older brother, Dex. It's not until he's taken my hand and is pumping it and saying, "Hey there, sugar, how are ya?," and the bartender's saying, "Yes, Mr. Eames," that I realize who he is and that this must be the "food place" Della told me he owned, and that's why Marina had the menu in the desk.

"Dex, hi," I say, and he beams at me and claps me on the back. Dex is bigger than I remember, in all senses, and prosperity seems to have agreed with him. He's as round as a Santa Claus, and he's wearing round glasses, and a checked shirt and bolo tie with a silver cow's head at his throat. I can't see anything of Charlie in him. There's no ghost of the tall, skinny boy Marina once loved in his older brother.

"You look great," I say, "really."

"Well, so do you, Miss Susannah," he says. "Although I admit that I would not have known you without that red hair, if I hadn't been watchin' for you. Saw your name on the order list in the kitchen." Dex winks at me. "I haven't seen you in a coon's age, girl. Mind if I have a seat?" And without waiting for me to say anything, he pulls out a bar stool and slides onto it. "Listen," he says, "I want to tell you, that was a terrible thing that happened to your sister. Just god-awful. We all felt so terrible about it down here when we heard. We're just damn sorry, that's all."

"Thanks," I say. The bartender brings Dex something that looks like bourbon on the rocks with a twist and sets it in front of him.

"Another for the lady," Dex says, and I don't stop him. "Tell me," he goes on, "they ever get the son of a bitch did that?"

"Not yet," I say. "They're working on it."

"Well, here's to 'em," Dex says, raising his glass. "Bastard like that ought to be wiped off the face of the earth. She was one beautiful woman, your sister." We clink glasses, and on the sound system, Linda Ronstadt sings "Heart Like a Wheel."

"This place is great, Dex," I say. "It looks like you've done well."

He nods his head a few times and pushes his glasses up onto the bridge of his nose. There's something about him that reminds me slightly of a fat Jerry Lee Lewis. I can imagine him jumping in the air and singing "Great Balls of Fire." "The Good Lord has been good to me," Dex says. "He surely has, Susannah." He looks so serious while he says this, so totally convinced of God's personal benevolence, that for a second I envy him. "Yes, sir," Dex adds, grinning, "I am blessed with a wonderful wife who's smart as a whip and doesn't take any crap from me, and three wiseass kids. Oldest one's applying to colleges next year. Can you imagine that?" He shakes his head. "Makes me feel old." Somehow I don't think he really minds. "What about you?" he asks. "Married? Kids?"

I shake my head. "Neither," I say. "But I have a great dog."

Dex laughs at this as the bartender puts my second beer in front of me and slides a basket of popcorn shrimp down to us.

"What about your parents?" I ask. "How are they?"

"Oh, Daddy died about five years ago," Dex says. "A heart attack. Real quick. Hope I go like that. I sold the farm for Mom after that and moved her into one of those assisted-living places. She was happy, I think, the last years of her life. She died about a year ago," he adds.

"I'm sorry," I say.

"Well," Dex says, "I guess it happens to the best of us."

"It looks that way," I agree, and then, more to make conversation than anything else, I ask, "Did you guys ever hear anything from Charlie after he went away?"

Dex shakes his head. "No," he says, "and you know, it's so strange you should ask that. Marina asked me the same thing. She came in here lookin' for me, oh, God, it must have been just right before she died, and that's the only thing she wanted to know about, whether we'd ever heard anything from Charlie."

I don't know why this should surprise me, but it does. As far as I can remember, I never once heard Marina mention Charlie Eames after the week he disappeared, and I suppose I'd assumed she forgot all about him, consigned him to the graveyard of faintly embarrassing teenage romances. Or filed away his memory in the catalog of early loves that most of us keep well buried, and only care to remember when we are drunk and weepy with longing for some imagined past. It certainly never occurred to me that he might have been someone she still thought about.

"You're kidding," I say. "She came here to find you? And to ask that?"

"Yup," Dex says. "I mean, she was hardly what you'd call a regular, but she'd been in here a few times over the years. Never mentioned Charlie, not before that night. And then she turned up on a Saturday. I remember, 'cause we had a big party on, and she said she was down from D.C. for the weekend. And that was all she wanted to know about, whether we'd ever heard from Charlie. Whether we'd ever tried to find him." He thinks about it and adds, "Yeah, it must have been damn close to when she was killed. It was fresh in my mind when I heard the news. I mean, I'd just seen her, just been talking to her a week or so before. Made it even more weird, you know?"

"Yeah, I do know," I say, and Dex nods. He assumes that I'm talking about the strangeness of seeing somebody very much alive one week and hearing that they're dead the next, but that's not what's going through my mind. What's occurred to me is that Marina must have come here either just before or just after she called me in Philadelphia on the Saturday before she died. I imagine her sitting at one of the tables in the bar, a beer in front of her and a basket of nibbles on the table. The image is so real that I almost expect to look over my shoulder and see her. A sudden pulse of excitement runs through me, and if I still believed in nightspinning, I might think she'd just whispered in my ear.

"Can you remember what time it was, Dex," I ask, "when she came in that night?"

If he thinks this question is odd, he doesn't say so. Instead he just nods and says, "Oh yeah, early. It would have been about six, I think. 'Cause I'd just gotten here, and I had time to have a beer with her. Things hadn't gotten busy yet."

He swirls the ice cubes in his glass and takes a swallow, and I can smell the sweetness of the bourbon. I think about what he's just said and realize that it means Marina must have called me afterward, possibly because of something she'd heard from Dex.

"Can you remember what she was like that night?" I ask. "If she was upset, or sad, or—"

"Well, she didn't want to eat anything," Dex says, "I can tell you that much. It's what restaurant owners remember, honey. Terrible, isn't it?" He laughs and slaps me on the shoulder, and then his face sobers at the memory. "I told her I could get her a table, even though it was a weekend," he says, "but she wasn't interested. So I bought her a couple of drinks, and I finally got her to nibble on some wings or something. She was too thin, that girl. We talked about some other stuff, maybe the house, your grandma's old farm, but she kept comin' back to Charlie. I mean, I know they were sweet on each other and all, but it was kind of strange after all this time. I told the police all about it. I mean, they came in asking right afterward, tryin' to trace her movements and all. Of course, it would have been different if she'd been killed down here."

I'm not sure quite why, so I let the comment pass, and instead I ask, "Did you ever try to find Charlie?" I slide my second beer toward me and pick at some of the popcorn shrimp.

"Oh, sure," Dex says. "Just as soon as Daddy died. Hired a private detective and the whole nine yards." He signals for another drink and turns to me. "You see, Mom never did believe that Charlie burned that barn down, and neither did I. Hell," he adds, "I don't think even Daddy believed it." He grabs a shrimp and tosses it into his mouth, diving for it so he looks like a terrier catching a treat. "Dad and Charlie just didn't get along, is all." A wave of sadness passes over his face.

"But he thought so at the time?" I say. "I mean, your dad thought he'd torched the barn?"

"Oh, yes and no." Dex shrugs. "You know what men are like. You know what teenagers are like. Hell, there are times when I want to wring my own boy's neck, but I just love him to death. Daddy had a lot wrapped up in that farm, times weren't too good, and he had to be mad at somebody, so he fastened on Charlie. Charlie was going through a bad phase that summer. Running around. Never where he was supposed to be when he was supposed to be there." Dex smiles at me. "Your sister probably had something to do with that, although we didn't know it at the time. And then there were those weird little brushfires that made everybody so jumpy."

I can see my mother standing on the porch in the summer dark, her body a still column of shadow and her arms crossed while she stared out over the field, scanning the boundary of our woodland for any bright leap of flame.

"They ever find out who set them?" I ask.

"Oh, I don't know," Dex says. "Dickhead did come around just before the barn went up and talked to all those boys, Charlie and Sonny and Tommy Hervey, about playing with matches, which was of course what stuck in Daddy's head, and there was gossip going around about something called a firebug club, but I didn't pay too much attention to it. You guys were all too young and dumb for me to spend my time on, remember?"

"I remember," I say.

Dex laughs and slaps me on the back again, and I narrowly avoid spilling my beer. "You always were a good sport, Susannah," he says. "Anyhow, after Charlie left, everybody blamed him. So that was the end of that, even if he didn't do it."

"You know he didn't light the fires?"

Dex shrugs, pulls the twist of lemon rind out of his drink, and bites it in half.

"Well, not all of 'em, for sure. He was with me over in Sefton when one broke out. I figure it was a bunch of kids, that's how things usually work." And suddenly I can remember Sonny Delray staring at Marina on the afternoon when he told us that Charlie had disappeared and saying "Crackle, crackle," and her opening her mouth and closing it again, like a guppy. Maybe, I think, it wasn't just the boys that Dickhead should have talked to.

"Did you ever find out anything about him? Where he went or anything?" I ask.

Dex shakes his head and sighs. "Nope," he says, "not a thing. Daddy wouldn't let Mom do anything about it while he was alive. Pride, you know. Although I think it hurt him plenty, inside. I think right to the end, he always hoped we'd hear something. But we never did. Not a peep. And pretty soon after Daddy died, I knew it was eating away at Mom, so I went and hired a private detective. Hell, I could afford it by then. A good guy, name of Hal Burton."

I start to laugh, and Dex looks at me. "I'm sorry," I say. "You told Marina about that, didn't you?"

"Sure did," Dex says, although he clearly doesn't get the joke.

"She wrote his name down," I explain, "on the top of one of your menus. I thought it said 'halibut.' "

"Oh," Dex says. "Well, halibut or not, he didn't find anything. 'Course it had been the better part of fifteen years then, and trails go cold."

"So nothing?"

"Zippo," Dex says. "Not a trace. Damn sad thing. It's like one Sunday afternoon he just ceased to exist. No record of him anywhere. That's not so unlikely with a sixteen-year-old. They can change their name, disappear into the oil fields or out on some cargo ship, or God knows where. If a person doesn't want to be found, it's not that hard. We just never reckoned that was Charlie, that's all. You know how moms are. She just always thought he'd turn up. Truth was, so did I."

"I'm sorry," I say.

"Yeah," Dex says. He pushes the last piece of the lemon rind around the edge of his glass, and then he says, "Funny, him and Marina, isn't it, in a way? That God should see fit that they both end in a mystery." I'm not sure what to say to this, but then Dex says suddenly, "I wonder if she knew, if she had some kind of premonition or something, and that's why she came asking for Charlie then, like she was tying up a loose end."

I wonder, too, but it's what sort of premonition she had that interests me. Somehow I don't think Dex and I are thinking the same thing. "You told Marina, right?" I ask. "Everything you've just told me?"

"Oh, sure," Dex says, "and then some. She could have been a prosecuting attorney, your sister. She cross-quizzed me like you wouldn't believe. But the end result was the same. As far as we know, when Charlie got on that bus, he vanished off the face of the earth." His glass is empty, and he rattles his ice cubes around, but when the bartender moves to bring him another one, Dex waves him away.

"And you know what else is strange?" he says. "After I told Marina, after she questioned me up and down and sideways, and after we went 'round and 'round and came out at the same place, it was like she was happy."

"Happy?" I ask.

"Yeah," Dex says, nodding, "happy. It was like I'd told her something that she really wanted to believe."

I'm still thinking about this last statement, and about what Kathleen Harper told me, when the hostess comes over and mutters something in Dex's ear.

"Oh, right, honey," he says, and then he turns to me. "Susannah, you are gonna have to excuse me. I have a big private party coming in. Now, are you sure I can't get you a table? Your order is ready and bagged and all, but we can serve it up for you right here if you want."

I shake my head. All I really want to do now is get back to my room. "No, but thanks," I say. "I will next time, I promise." I get up and start to walk back to the front of the restaurant with Dex, and after he's handed me the bright white bag with RED'S! written on the side of it and refused to let me pay the bill, I ask him one last question.

"Hey, Dex, you all went to the Baptist church growing up, right?"

"Well, sure thing," he says. "Everybody on our road, except for you Uni-tar-ians."

"But not that Sunday?" I ask. "At least not Charlie. Not on the day he left?"

Dex looks at me. "Well, no," he says. "As a matter of fact, that was part of Charlie's actin' up that summer. One of the things that made Daddy so mad, that he wouldn't go to church."

"And Sonny Delray, too," I say. "I mean, he didn't go to church either that day, and Charlie must have known that. Didn't he ask him for a ride to the bus?"

"Yeah," Dex says, "I guess so."

I shrug and smile at him. "I just don't remember them as being real good friends," I say.

Dex laughs. "Poor old Sonny," he says. "I don't think anybody was his real good friend back then. But that's what you get for being the fat kid. Doesn't youth suck? But no more!" he crows. "No more!" He beats out a little tattoo on his stomach. "Bigger is better. And that's the truth of it. Now, you get on the other side of that barbecue! All you city girls are way too skinny!"

DEX IS RIGHT ABOUT THE BARBECUE, IT'S DELICIOUS, AND I'm not surprised that his place is a success. By the time I'm finished with it, my room smells like a giant sloppy joe, and I open the windows and go sit on the little plastic lawn chair outside my door while it airs out.

I've been thinking over my conversation with Dex Eames, and as I sit in the dark, it's clear to me that Marina must have believed Charlie had come back into her life. I wonder what it was that tipped her off. Some special signal? Some private thing she remembered that reappeared in one of the gruesome gifts he sent her? Maybe it was the wording on the Valentine or something about the flowers. But clearly she thought she'd figured it out and came down here that last time to try and find out if anyone knew for sure where he was.

But none of that explains why she should have been happy after talking to Dex, and I can't figure that out for the life of me. Surely her conversation with him would have just increased her frustration, not given her something she really wanted to believe, as Dex said, or filled her with the calm sense of determination that Kathleen Harper described. And nor does it explain the headstone in the Petamill Baptist cemetery, unless Charlie Eames has taken to wearing a wig or has become a transvestite and was able to walk into Sweet Memories on K Street and pretend that he was me.

I get up to go back inside. The night air is turning chilly now, and it's late enough in the fall to want a jacket on after dark. I think next week is Halloween, and I remember how Momma and Grandma used to work for days when we were little to dress us up as lions, or witches, or princesses, or whatever it was Marina and I fancied ourselves as that year. Then Mr. Delray, or Mr. Hervey, or even Uncle Ritchie sometimes, would collect all us kids and load us into the back of one of their farm pickups and drive us around from house to house so we could ring the doorbells and yell "Trick or treat!" and make all our mothers pretend they were scared and didn't know it was us.

I can't remember when that stopped, but I do remember the sadness of it, the strange, empty feeling of being at odds with your own body when you realize that you're too big to dress up, when painting whiskers on your face or pinning a tail on your pajamas and carrying a fairy wand just makes you feel dumb instead of magical. And I wonder now if that's the moment when we all start to get mean, when we start to figure out that we're stuck, that there's no magic, no costume we can put on that releases us from what we are.

When I go back inside, I lock the door and the windows. And after I put on the chain, I prop a chair under the doorknob. Then I go into the bathroom and pull back the shower curtain and loop it up and tie it in a knot. I leave the closet door open, too. I've done this in strange rooms for years, not just since Marina was killed. Life is tough enough without having to wonder who's behind things if you have to get up and go to the bathroom in the night. When I get into bed, the sheets are cool, and the pillows smell slightly of pine and fabric softener, and after I turn off the lamp, I hear the occasional car going by on the road and see the reflection of headlights on the ceiling.

It's not long, then, until I fall asleep. I hear a voice in the parking lot. A dog barks and a door slams, and then I'm dreaming. I'm floating above a darkness that stretches out as dense and soft as the sea. I hover there all through the night. I hang above the ocean, and above fields, and above thick tangles of trees and brambles and rosebushes. And when I eventually come to earth, I walk, but my feet do not touch the ground. And I am surrounded by the bright flicker of fireflies, and lured onward by distant yellow leaping tongues of flame.

CHAPTER 23

"IT'S OVER." LIGHT SEEPS BETWEEN THE EDGES OF THE curtains and the wall. "They brought Kathleen Harper in early this morning, and they're going to charge her later today." The clock on the bedside table clicks, and the green numbers read nine-thirty.

"I said it was over. Did you hear me, Susannah?" Mark Cope asks, and when I finally say yes, my voice is furry with sleep.

Something that I can't quite grab is lingering in my mind. It's shifting in and out of focus like the hangover from a dream. Pictures and bits and pieces of information that all meant so much in sleep are receding and threaten to mean nothing in the mundane light of day. Somewhere in Alexandria, Virginia, I can hear what sounds like a car alarm going off or a telephone ringing.

"Did you get the ID?" I ask. "From the memorial place on K Street?"

There's an infinitesimal pause before Mark Cope answers, and then he says, "Not yet. But we will. It turns out the order for the stone came in by fax. The payment arrived in cash by FedEx an hour later. It was sent from a mailbox place, and the name on the envelope was yours."

"So—" I'm trying to understand the implications of this, but my mind seems sluggish, unable to turn itself in any useful direction. Before I can finish the question that I haven't asked, Mark Cope answers it for me.

"We're not charging her with Marina. Yet," he says. "But it's only a matter of time, Susannah. In the meantime, Becca Aaronson can hang on to her, because we've got her tied to you."

"To me?" The room comes into sharper focus, and I reach for the second pillow to stuff it behind my back and sit up.

"Yup," Mark says. "She talked her way into your building the night your hair was cut. One of your housemates let her in. She claimed she was a really good friend of yours. Knew all about you and even produced a key to your apartment but said she didn't have one to the front door."

"My apartment?"

"Yes, ma'am," Mark says. "She's even admitted it. Says she was there about nine P.M. and wanted to talk to you. Claims she knew you wouldn't let her in, so she lied. Then says you wouldn't answer the door, so she left. But we know she didn't."

I'm trying to understand how Kathleen Harper could have gotten ahold of a key to my apartment. I'm trying to remember what I did with my bag while I was at her house, where exactly I put it down and for how long. I'm trying to figure out how she could have taken a key without my noticing it. Or did she somehow take an imprint of it, press it into Play-Doh or Silly Putty the way people used to in the movies. I shake my head quickly, like a dog coming out of water. Most probably she just flashed any old key at the front door and banked on the fact that she could get me to let her into the apartment once she got upstairs. Or that she could jimmy the lock, or use a credit card, or something. And then she got lucky, since I took a sleeping pill and forgot to lock the door.

"What time was this again?" I ask.

"She turned up at about nine, nine-fifteen," Mark Cope says. "We think she spent the intervening time hanging out in the basement, waiting until it was late enough to give you a haircut. We've got forensic people down there now, just in case she doesn't cop to it."

I'm imagining this, how easy it would have been for Kathleen to convince Cathy—always so concerned about the poverty of my social life—that she was an old friend, when I realize that Mark Cope is still talking.

"Breaking and entering," he's saying, "we've got her on that, and assault maybe. Probably the stalking stuff, too, but that depends on Pennsylvania law, which isn't my specialty. Anyway, I wanted to be the one to call and tell you."

"Thanks," I say.

"You're going to have to come back. The DA's office is going to want to talk to you. And we're going to need you, too."

"Okay," I say. He pauses, as though this is easier than he'd anticipated, as though he thought he was going to have to fight with me, and he's about to say something else. I can hear him thinking about it, and when he doesn't say it, I ask, "What? What is it?" I can almost see him shake his head.

"Nothing," he says. "It's just—" His voice lingers, and then he says, "Why didn't you tell me? About Marina?"

"What?" I ask.

There's a silence, and then his voice rises in exasperation. "Why didn't you tell me she was gay?"

I turn this over in my mind the way you finger a stone. I'm watching the sunlight that's reached the carpet and crawls across the end of the bed, and finally I say, "I didn't know." Which is the truth.

I can hear him breathing on the other end of the phone, a faint rasping sound, and for the first time I wonder if he smokes.

"It would have helped," he says. He clearly doesn't believe me.

"I'm sorry," I say.

"Well, apparently she was," Mark says. "Certainly according to Kathleen Harper's ex-husband."

I think about this, and then I say, "It's not something I ever really thought about."

Dust motes are drifting through the bars of sunlight that sneak past the curtains as Mark Cope considers this. Then he says, "Okay, Susannah. You drive carefully, all right?"

———

IN THE DARK, I HADN'T BEEN ABLE TO TELL WHAT COLOR Della Hervey's house is painted. Now I can see that it's dark green with white trim, which is unusual; most of the houses down here are white. I guess because of the heat. I can't see anybody in the yard when I drive up, although there's a car parked in the driveway that I figure must be Della's. I was faintly surprised, when I went to check out of the Green Hills Motel this morning, to discover that it's Saturday. Which probably explains why Red's was so busy last night, and why Della's car is in the drive at eleven in the morning. It also means that her kids must be home from school. As I get out of the car and walk to the kitchen door, I can hear music playing through an open upstairs window.

Della's waiting for me, standing just behind the screen, and she has an apron on over her jeans. "I'm making a Halloween cake," she says as she pushes the door open and lets me in, "for Karen to take to school on Monday. They're having a bake sale for the class dance."

The kitchen is warm and smells of cinnamon, and there are a pile of bowls and the beaters from a mixer in the sink.

"I just came to give back the key," I say.

"Oh." Della's opening the refrigerator, but she turns to look at me. "So you're going? That was fast."

"Yeah," I say, "I have to go back to Philly."

I put the key in an uncluttered place on the counter beside the telephone and watch Della while she moves eggs and butter and a carton of milk from the kitchen table back to the fridge.

"Della," I say, "I'm sorry."

She stops and fingers the back of one of the kitchen chairs.

"I'm sorry about what Marina did."

Della looks up at me and says, "I didn't steal nothing. Ever. I don't know where those things went, but I didn't steal them."

"I know that," I say. "I know you didn't." She nods and looks down at the chair, and I'm not sure what else, if anything, I can say to make her feel better, to salve the hurt and humiliation that she must have felt.

"Listen," I say, "I saw Dex last night. We talked some about Charlie. And about that summer when he took off."

"Charlie," Della says. She shakes her head. "I never knew him real well, did you?"

"No, not really. I mean, I guess I was kind of out of it that summer. I wasn't really hanging around with you guys. Dex said something about a firebug club, do you remember that?"

Della laughs and pushes the chair away from her. "That was Sonny," she says. "I thought everybody knew that. That was his secret club."

"Was Marina part of it?" I ask, and suddenly the answer seems incredibly important to me, even though I know what it's going to be.

"Sure," Della says. "Marina, and Sonny, and me, and Charlie, and a couple of other people, I guess. The Firebug Club. We had a clubhouse and everything. Up in the woods. We all signed in blood. Well, made an X."

The sting is as sharp as if I'm fifteen again. Where was I? How come I didn't know? Della's chuckling to herself at the memory.

"So you all set those fires?" I ask. "That summer?"

"Sure," Della says. "That was the initiation rite. You had to set a brushfire, just a little one, and not get caught in order to become a member."

"And the Eameses' barn?"

"Oh, I don't know," Della says. "I don't know 'bout that. I guess that must have been Charlie, but things got out of control."

" 'Cause the other fires were all at night," I say.

Della nods. "Oh, yeah, that's when we'd meet. And you'd have to go off and set your fire, and the others would watch, like from far away, to make sure you did it and didn't just say so. And then we'd put 'em out and git before the police came. We didn't mean no harm," she says. "Not like the Eameses' barn. That was different. We were just havin' fun, you know, the way kids will. But I guess that's where Charlie got the idea."

"Yeah," I say, "I guess so."

"Things might have been different," Della says suddenly, "if he hadn't gone away." At first I can't figure out what she's talking about, and then I remember what BethAnn said.

"Della," I say, "there was nothing, ever, between Sonny Delray and Marina." She's staring at me, and a stubborn look comes over her face. I can remember it now from when she was a kid. "Honestly," I say. "There wasn't. Really."

"That's not what he thought," she mutters.

"Well, it's true. Believe me. I know. And it was a long, long time ago."

Della stares at me, then smiles. Her mouth stretches over her teeth in an arc. "Well, you are right there," she says. And something goes out of the room, dispels, like a breath that's been held. Della wipes her hands quickly on the front of her apron and brushes past me and into the hallway. "Karen!" she yells up the stairs. "You come on down now. Like we talked about. Miss deBreem is here!"

I can't imagine what this is about, but a second later a thin little girl with dark hair comes down the stairs. At first I can just see her feet, and the legs of her jeans, and then she walks ahead of her mother down the hallway and into the kitchen, where she stops in front of me. She's carrying a book about the size of a photograph album, holding it in two hands a little away from her, the way you might hold a tray or a present.

"Go on, Karen," Della says. She's standing in the doorway as if to block any escape that the child might try to make back up the stairs. Karen seems overcome with shyness. She's staring at the floor intently, and I'm about to say something to her when she shoves the book toward me.

"This is yours," Karen says. "I took it out of your room."

It's a turquoise vinyl album. On the front is a pink flower and the words "My Scrapbook by Susannah," spelled out in purple letters that I painstakingly stuck on one afternoon shortly after my thirteenth birthday when Uncle Ritchie gave it to me. Marina had been given a matching one with a yellow flower, one of the items on the list I read in Chief Hancy's office yesterday afternoon. I don't think, however, that she stuck her name on the front of her album, and that was something that I later felt she did on purpose, and only after I finished mine, so I would regret it and wish I could peel off the purple letters.

Karen is looking up at me now.

"She took it when we were cleaning up the house," Della says.

"After we bought it. I told her she could. But she thought maybe you might want it back."

"Thank you," I say, and I take the scrapbook out of Karen's hands.

Della walks me out to the car. "They're good kids," she says. She kicks a stone in the drive, and it skitters into a flower bed that's thick with violet-faced asters and edged with pieces of driftwood that Della's kids must have collected on trips to the beach or down on the creek. "They mean the world to me," she adds. "Even if their daddy was a son of a bitch."

"Will you thank Karen again for me?" I say. "Will you tell her how much I appreciate it?"

Della nods.

I'd tried to thank Karen myself but without much success. She'd looked at the floor and nodded a few times, and then she'd asked her mother if she could be excused and had run back upstairs. Now the music's playing again, and this time I recognize Sheryl Crow, because I'm pretty sure Cathy has the same CD.

I zip the album into my duffel bag, and when I slam down the hatch and look back at Della I see she's dug both hands deep into her jeans pockets and is staring off across the field toward the big low barn. We can hear the whine of Tommy's tractor.

"You do whatever you want with the house, Della," I say. "It's yours. All of it. I mean, I appreciate the scrapbook. But don't worry about what I'll think. There's nothing there I want anymore."

"Okay," Della says. She smiles, and I open the car door. "You drive carefully, Susannah," she says. "And you come back and see us."

"I will," I say, although both of us know this isn't true, and then I slide into the front seat and start the Taurus. I roll down the window so I can wave, and then I back out of the drive and start down the road. It's a clear, bright day and in the rearview mirror, I watch Della. Her apron blows a little in the breeze, and just before I reach the band of the woods, she raises her hand to wave.

JAKE LEAPS IN THE AIR. HE LANDS AND WHEELS AND THEN races back to me. He shoves his face into my stomach and wags his tail so hard that his whole body swings back and forth. Ever since I picked him up from the kennel this morning, he's been reluctant to let me out of his sight, and although he's thrilled to be at the dog park, he needs to keep coming back to me, to keep flinging himself up against me just to reassure himself that I'm solid and not someone he's imagined. Now he turns his face up to me and speaks in his low singsong dog voice, telling me how happy he is to see me. I grab him on either side of his face and shake him until he growls. I bury my hands in the deep fur of his ruff and kiss the black triangle on top of his head.

The sun is setting, and the sky behind Penn is turning orange and then crimson as the darkness bleeds into it. By the time we leave the dog park, the streetlights are coming on. A nimbus of light hovers around each one and picks up the faint chilly mist that is gathering in the air. All day long it's drizzled but hasn't yet been able to work up to rain.

The street that Jake and I walk up is quiet, but there's a background cacophony of honking and the buzz of rush-hour traffic. The houses here are tall and narrow and old. Each of them is three floors high and two windows wide, and their front doors are painted glossy greens and blues and reds. The houses are larger than they look from the street. They are two and sometimes even three rooms deep, and many of them have been remodeled and have fancy basement kitchens that open through French windows onto tiny walled gardens that trap the sun and shut out the city.

I know all of this because when the lease for our apartment came up for renewal, George and I briefly considered buying. For several weeks we trailed from house to house in the wake of a real estate agent. Now, as I walk Jake up the cobbled street, I find myself hoping that a for-sale sign will be posted in front of one. For the first time since Marina was killed and George left, I think that perhaps I would like more than one room and a bedroom, and that Jake should have a garden, no matter how tiny, and that I wouldn't mind the yoke and harness of a mortgage. Maybe, I think, I'll stay in Philly after all. Beau will laugh at this, I know, when he hears. He will tell me that I am getting old and bourgeois, and then he will ask me if my new home has an attic where he could leave some of his things. And if it's anywhere near a decent bar.

I haven't been able to get ahold of him since I got home last night, and when I look at my watch and see that it's past five, I decide that Jake and I could both use some more exercise. We'll walk uptown and bang on Beau's door. We'll throw a pebble at his window. Stand in the alley and call his name. He should be home from work by the time we get there. We'll send out for pizza or, if he invites us, we'll watch *The Simpsons* with him.

I can hear music as Jake and I come up the stairs. It's the piano, something with a faint boogie-woogie beat, and I can picture Beau playing. He'll be perched on the old-fashioned piano stool, bent over, his forehead creased with concentration, with a sooty lock of blond hair falling over it. Jake pushes ahead of me, impatient to see if Beau has a new tennis ball or a Frisbee, and the music pauses. Beau plays a few notes over, and then he starts the piece again. This is why he hasn't been answering the phone. I've called four times, and all I get is the answering machine. Sometimes, when he's playing the piano, Beau puts his telephone in his sock drawer and leaves it there for days at a time.

The music breaks, and I knock on the door. "Beau," I call. "Beau, it's me, Susannah."

He hits a few notes, high and plinking, and then he yells, "It's open."

I push the door and see that the two lamps on either side of Beau's big disorderly couch are on. The light they cast is so bright that the rest of the room seems unnaturally dim, and in the white pools, I can see an overturned shoe, a plate with a fork on it sitting on a side table, and the sleeve of a sweater hanging over the edge of a chair like a disembodied arm. Housekeeping has never been Beau's strong point.

Jake gives a little yip of joy. He jumps away from me almost as soon as I have the door open, and rushes toward Beau's wide back. The shades on the big loft windows haven't been pulled, and the wall of the warehouse opposite is shadowed by a streetlight from the alley below. Beau says something to Jake that I can't quite make out and reaches down with one hand to rub his ears while, with the other, he picks out a little tune of single notes. He doesn't turn around and look at me.

"Hey," I say, coming as far as the couch. "How are you?"

"I'm fine," Beau says. "How are you?" His hand still moves over the keys, and he seems to be watching it intently. I expect him to make some smart-ass comment about my hair, but he doesn't even look at me.

"I'm okay," I say. I've never seen Beau behave this way before, and I'm not certain what's going on.

"They've arrested Kathleen Harper," I say. "I left a message on your machine. Maybe you didn't get it." I look down at the coffee table and see Beau's phone sitting on top of an old newspaper. The little red message light says "4."

"Beau," I say, "haven't you listened to your machine? Didn't you get my messages?" He nods, but he still won't look at me. I wonder suddenly if something bad has happened at work, or to his parents, and if he's been drinking.

"Sure," he says. "I got them." His hand stops moving over the keys, and the last note he hit hangs in the room. "I got the ones from today, anyway. If there were others, I guess I missed those."

So that's what this is about. He's mad at me because I didn't call him while I was down in Georgia. A flash of anger runs through me. I see the basket of violets on my breakfast tray at the Marriott and the lock of hair taped to my bathroom mirror. I feel the cold thing that happened to my heart when I saw Della Hervey standing in the driveway at the house, and I remember the metallic taste that came into my mouth. I see the sharp bright edges of the gold letters on a headstone that I didn't buy for my sister.

"For Christ's sake, Beau," I say. "Somebody was trying to kill me!"

At this he swings around on the piano stool so fast that Jake jumps backward in surprise. "Yeah," Beau says, "well, it wasn't me!"

We're staring at each other like two kids on a playground before they start hitting and pulling hair.

"I know that," I say.

"Do you?" Beau asks. The words are hard and clear, and even in this half-lit room, I can see that Beau's face is mottled, his color high, as if he has a fever or has been running in cold air. "Is that why I found out about it from the police? Because you trust me so much? Is that why they came to my office and started asking where I'd been, and who saw me, and if I could prove it?"

"I'm sorry," I say. "I guess that's what they have to do."

"And what do you have to do, Susannah?" Beau asks. "Did you have to just disappear? Just vanish off the fucking face of the earth without saying a word?"

A groundswell of anger is rising between us, and like an earthquake, it shakes the air.

"Yeah!" I realize that I'm yelling now. "Yeah, that is exactly what I had to do, as a matter of fact." Jake whines at the level of my voice. He pins his ears back against his head and looks from me to Beau. "Beau," I say, and take a deep breath, "somebody tried to poison Jake. They almost killed him. Somebody came into my apartment and cut off my hair while I was asleep. Somebody—" But I don't get to finish my litany. Beau cuts me off before I can go on.

"And you thought it was me," he says. The words hang in the air between us. "You thought I could have done that," he says. "To you."

We look at each other for a long time, and I don't know what to say. Jake creeps across the floor and shoves the tip of his nose into my hand.

"You didn't even trust me enough, Susannah, not to think that I was trying to kill you." Beau turns back to the piano. He picks out a few notes. "Well," he says, "I'm glad they got whoever it was." And then he starts to play again.

The music ripples out of the shadows and dances across the room. It reaches me and flows on either side of me as if I'm an island in a river, or a stone. I can feel tears rimming at the edge of my eyes, and I stand there watching Beau's back, and the way his head bobs and his hands move, and then I pick up Jake's leash. When we get to the hallway, I pull the door shut behind us. The music swallows the sound of our footsteps as Jake and I go back down the stairs.

"ARE YOU ALL RIGHT?" GORDON ASKS, AND HIS VOICE makes me jump. I'm sick of people hanging around in shadows and sick of them asking me if I'm all right all the time. I was sniveling on the way home and wiping my nose on the arm of my jacket, and I feel irritable and slightly embarrassed.

"There's not enough light in this goddamn place," I say, and Gordon laughs.

"Yeah," he says, "but it's very authentic." Without meaning to, I smile, and Gordon grins, too, and reaches down and rubs Jake's ruff. Jake tolerates it for second and then sidles away.

We're standing in the entry hall, and Gordon has obviously just come home from work. He's carrying a briefcase and wearing a long dark overcoat and a suit, and he looks so ordinary and familiar that I'm happy to see him. This surprises me, and I turn around quickly to lock the vestibule door so he won't see the look on my face.

"You've got some mail here," he says. "You want it?"

"Do I have a choice?" I ask.

"Sure," Gordon says. "We can throw it out. Or write 'no known address' and go outside and stick it back in the mailbox." He's smiling at me, and I realize I've never really been very nice to him.

"Listen," I say awkwardly, "I, I wanted to thank you."

This is the first time I've seen Gordon since Detective Aaronson told me earlier today that it was he who let Kathleen Harper into the building. I had been so certain that it was Cathy that when Aaronson told me otherwise I had simply stared at her until she finally stopped talking and tilted her head a little to one side and asked if I was all right. Then she'd explained to me that I'd be hearing from the prosecutors at the DA's office, and that they had already spoken to Gordon, who has agreed to testify if we go to trial.

Becca Aaronson had gone on to explain that the woman who works in the video store down the block only saw Kathleen Harper standing on the corner when she went out for a cigarette that night and didn't actually see her come up the steps and into the house. Which means Gordon's the only person who can place her inside, and we should love him for it.

This is even more important because forensics didn't turn up zip in the basement. Aaronson had taken a deep breath after telling me this last fact, and then she had told me that they were still waiting for the results to come back on fibers that they'd collected from my apartment. She'd glanced away from me as she'd said this, but even so, the implication had been clear. It was possible that Kathleen had gotten into my apartment. That she had been there all along, hiding under my bed, or standing in my closet, listening while I poured a drink, watching while I took my clothes off, and waiting until I fell asleep so she could slither out into the darkness and cut off my hair.

Now Gordon says, "I'm sorry. I just feel so awful that I let her in."

"Don't," I say quickly, "really. Don't. You couldn't possibly have known. And I'm sure she was very convincing."

Gordon nods. "That doesn't make much difference, though, does it?" he says, and then, before I can reply, he gestures toward the stairs. "Susannah, would you like a drink? I hate to say this, but you look like you could use one, and I've got a cold bottle of wine."

I'm sure I do, I think. I'm sure my eyes are red-rimmed and my face is blotchy. And although I've moved on from feeling sorry for myself to being mad at Beau for being mad at me, I still don't feel like being alone. Besides, I really am grateful to Gordon, and I know I should allow him to make amends. Testifying will probably be a major pain in the ass, and he could hardly have guessed that Kathleen was a murderous psychotic. So I say, "Thanks. That would be really nice."

I HAD STARTED TO TAKE JAKE UPSTAIRS, BUT GORDON TOLD me he was invited, too, so now he's sprawled at my feet. I can see that he's leaving a pale nap of hair across Gordon's rug, which is a newer and much more expensive variation on mine. This newer and more expensive look characterizes his whole apartment, and I wonder if he insisted on additional renovations before he moved in, and paid for them, or if Zoe just did them herself and charges him a lot more.

The walls of Gordon's living room are painted bright white, which makes the wooden paneling on the window seat and the ornate fireplace look buttery-soft and almost black, as if they are carved from shiny dark chocolate. The lighting fixtures are more modern than mine, too. They're bounce lights, little upturned dishes of frosted glass, and they don't really do enough for the two big abstract canvases that hang on either side of the massive mantel. The furniture suite is leather, and all at once I can see Gordon buying it, picking it out from one of those already arranged living rooms displayed at the malls in King of Prussia. I can see him standing there with a young salesman who shows him how the couch and the loveseat and the two armchairs were featured in the latest *Esquire*.

I know I'm being mean, but there's something about Gordon that eggs me on, something that positively invites me to do this. "Stop it," I tell myself, and Jake lifts his head from the rug and glances up at me as if he can read my mind.

A phone starts to ring, and I realize that it's mine and the sound is coming from upstairs. It's Beau, I think, and I almost start to get to my feet. But that would be impossibly rude, so instead I start to fidget. I count the rings. There will be five of them before the machine kicks in.

"Do you hear me much?" I ask Gordon as the last ring dies above us. My living room is directly overhead, and I've never even thought to ask before. He's in the kitchen, where he's doing something that I can't see, so I'm not sure if he's heard me.

But then he replies from beyond the door. "Oh, not much. Just the odd patter of footsteps, or should I say paws, sometimes." He comes out of the kitchen and is carrying a tray that has two glasses on it, and a bottle of white wine stuck in an ice bucket, and a little bowl of olives and another one of macadamia nuts, and suddenly I feel utterly self-conscious. I remember that my face is probably grubby from crying, and that I haven't combed what's left of my hair, and that these are the jeans I wore to the dog park.

Gordon sets the tray on the glass coffee table, which doesn't have a speck of dust on it. He lifts the bottle out of the ice and pours the wine. When he hands me my glass, it's heavy in my hand, and I realize that it's crystal.

"Cheers, Susannah," Gordon says. "Welcome home."

THE BARS OF THE SECURITY GATE ARE A BLACK CRISSCROSS against my pale paint, and from inside the apartment, it looks like you could play tic-tac-toe on the door. I don't know if Zoe and Justin have seen it yet. At the moment, they're on their way to Paris. They left this morning very early, and Cathy and I stood on the front steps and promised that the house would be fine and waved while they drove away. When they were gone, Cathy turned to me and sighed. "Paris," she said. "Wow. I love Paris." And I nodded and thought that before they got back, I'd have to get the security gate taken down. After all, I don't need it anymore. I have the locksmith's number out. I've opened the Yellow Pages to his ad and underlined it in red pen, and I should be calling him now, or working on the drawings for the museum tearoom, or seeing if I have anything to wear to the lunch I'm having with Lolly this afternoon, but instead I'm sitting at my desk and leafing through the scrapbook that Karen Hervey gave me.

There are photographs pasted onto pages of thick colored paper. "Swamp!" I've written under one in green felt-tip pen. I've decorated the letters with drippy tendrils and drawn an alligator with big teeth. The snapshot is from a school trip to the Okefenokee Swamp. We stayed overnight in a motel and ran up and down the halls and ate peanut-butter snack crackers from the vending machine.

In the picture, a group of kids whose faces I can't make out line up against the railing of a walkway that spans greasy water. They're sticking out their tongues and waving, and behind them, long ropes of Spanish moss fall from the top of the frame. There are some pressed flowers on the next page. Almost all of the color has left their petals, which look translucent and threaded by tiny veins, and I can't remember where they're from or why they were important to me.

On the next pages, six valentines are glued side by side in a center spread, and I've written "February 14!!!" and drawn a bow and an arrow that pierces a heart. One card is in the shape of a heart, with silver writing on it, and another has a wreath of flowers and a fat Cupid with wings that look far too small to keep him in the air. One says "Be Mine!" in block letters on the front, and I remember it because it was not given to me. It was sent to Marina by Sonny Delray, who left it in our mailbox in a red envelope. After she opened it, standing in the middle of our bedroom, she threw it into the air, laughing, and said, "Here, you might as well keep it, since he doesn't even know which of us is which!"

When the phone rings, it's so loud that I jump. I start to answer it, but instead I let my hand hover over the receiver. Last night when I came back upstairs after finishing Gordon's wine, I saw the message light as soon as I came through the door, and I hit the button, certain I would hear Beau's voice. But there was nothing there, just the sound of empty air.

For half a second I had thought that I'd heard someone speaking, had heard the sound that a voice makes when it is cut off, and I had wondered if it was Beau, and if he had started to say something to me and then had changed his mind. I played the tape back three times, bending over it as if I could sense him there, as if his reflection were somehow imprisoned in the little box on my desk and I could divine it if I tried hard enough. But in the end I decided I was wrong and that there was nothing, and I erased the tape.

Now the voice is Benjy's. He doesn't ask if I'm all right, which I'm grateful for. He did that just once, when I returned the Taurus. When I said yes, he just looked at me and nodded. "You're a smart cookie, doll," he said. "You know how to take care of yourself." Now he's telling me that he has a new door for my Mercedes, one that will actually match, and that I should bring the car in ASAP. I listen to his voice, and when he hangs up, I close the shiny covers of the scrapbook with a snap.

"DO NOT, I REPEAT, DO NOT, BE LATE," LOLLY HAD SAID. "Do you hear me?"

"Do not pass go. Do not collect two hundred dollars," I had replied.

"What?" Her voice had sounded genuinely confused, and then she had sighed. "Susannah," she had said, "I should kill you, but I won't because I'm glad you're back. This reservation was very hard to get." And so I am making a special effort not to be late. In light of this, and because I'm dressed up, I've taken a cab uptown instead of walking, and I've allowed enough time for it to drop me at Stratus, which is one of the better toy stores in the city.

"Toy," insofar as it relates to children, is a misleading term. This place is filled with all sorts of stuff, from every Stieff animal ever made to enough science kits and telescopes to keep most adults happy. They sell the best kites I've ever seen, birds and airships and dragons in wild, bright colors with streamers attached to their tails. George and I went through a kite phase, and I'm tempted to walk through that department now, but I don't have time. I head for art supplies instead.

It takes me only a few minutes to find what I'm looking for, and I try not to get sidetracked amid the endless rows of stickers and fluorescent pens. There are scrapbooks in all sizes here, and they range from plain to very fancy. Finally I pick out a big one that comes in a box with a silver pen and a gold pen, and press-on letters, and colored glitter that you can use with a glue stick. Then I take it down front and stand in line, and when I pay for it, I arrange to have it wrapped and shipped to Miss Karen Hervey at 727 Rural Route One in Petamill, Georgia.

THE LUNCH, LOLLY TOLD ME, IS TO "SIZE UP THE COMPETITION," which, in this case, is a very expensive Thai restaurant that's just opened on the roof of one of the huge waterfront blocks. It's getting excellent write-ups, which gives Lolly fits.

Normally Richard, her husband, or whatever he is, would go with her on one of these expeditions into enemy territory, but he has a meeting today, so Lolly has asked me. We're going for lunch rather than dinner because, Lolly insists, lunch is when you can really tell what a place is about. "Everybody puts on the dog for dinner," she said to me on the phone, "but lunch is when you can tell whether or not it's really a quality act."

"I hope it revolves," she hisses at me as we get into the elevator. "If it revolves, it will be really tacky."

"Even if it doesn't," I say, "maybe there will be Buddhas."

There are, but they're not as bad as they could have been. They're small and carved out of dark wood and made into a screen that hides the register. The place is called Chiang Mai Orchid, and the waiter, who is almost certainly a kid from Penn wearing a Thai silk cummerbund, leads us to a table by the far wall, which is made entirely of glass. The view of the river is stupendous, but I wouldn't advise this seating arrangement for anyone who suffers from vertigo. Before she sits down, Lolly moves her chair almost imperceptibly inward.

"The 'Orchid' is too much," she mutters, leaning toward me after the waiter has gone. " 'Chiang Mai' would have been much better left alone. They couldn't help gilding the lily." The thought of this makes her happy, and she orders us a bottle of champagne.

"What's this for?" I ask after the waiter has fussed around with an ice bucket and the bottle.

"For you," Lolly says, raising her flute to touch the edge of mine. She takes a sip, and then she says, "Now, does buying you a bottle of Moët give me the right to know what the hell's been going on?"

"No," I say. "But I'll probably tell you anyway."

Her eyebrows, which are plucked into two perfect half-moons, are raised, and they almost disappear into her bangs. She's had her hair cut in a pageboy since I saw her last, and it makes her look a little like Doris Day.

"I had a visit from a Detective Aaronson," she says, "who, incidentally, has all the charm of a prison warden. Some other specimen came to visit Richard. Reminded him of something out of *Tales from the Crypt*."

"Philadelphia's finest," I say. "They were only doing their job." There's a terrible inevitability to this, and I wonder if Lolly's mad at me, too, and if she's going to fire me, and that's why she ordered champagne. Little bubbles fizz and explode on the back of my tongue. "I'm sorry, Lolly," I say. "I'm really sorry. I should have told you myself." And then I tell her about the phone calls, and the flowers, and Kathleen Harper, and my hair, and someone singing "Shoo, fly" in the basement.

"Jesus Christ," Lolly says when I'm finished. She reaches for the bottle and pours us each another glass, and this brings the waiter running. He pretends to be full of remorse, but secretly he's very irritated with us for touching the bottle on our own, because now the maître d' is glaring at him.

When he finally goes away, Lolly points at my head. "That, by the way," she says, "is hideous. Where did you have it done? Someplace on campus?"

"Just about," I say.

She shakes her head as if this confirms her worst fears about me. "Well," she says, opening her menu, "at least you won't need a costume tonight."

"It's not that bad," I protest.

She raises one eyebrow at me. "I'm taking you to New York next time I go."

I realize I should maybe be insulted by this, but I'm not. Actually, it sounds fun. "Lolly," I say, "are you going to make a fashion plate out of me?"

"Well," she says, flipping a menu page, "there's always hope."

WE'VE FINISHED OFF A PLATE OF A CONFUSED CROSS BE-tween dim sum and sushi, and we're on the last glass of the champagne and picking at a selection of marzipanlike little cakes when Lolly pats her lips with her napkin and drops it on the table.

"So," she says, "are they sure it's this woman?"

"Kathleen Harper," I say. "I think so. I mean, they think so."

"What do you think?" Lolly asks, and I realize that it's the first time anyone has asked me this question.

"I don't know," I say.

The words have an unsettling effect on my stomach, but at the same time it's a relief to actually say them. I look out at the river, at the piers and at the tiny shape of the *Moshulu,* which was once a four-masted bark and is now a restaurant and a nightclub for tourists. When I look back at Lolly, she's watching me.

"I was so certain that it had to be something in Georgia," I say. "That Marina must have found something down there. But maybe I had to believe that because it was the only part of her life I knew. Maybe I couldn't really grasp the fact that she had another life, one that had nothing to do with me. And that I insisted on it. I made it that way. I don't know. I guess deep down I still needed to believe that no matter what happened between us, we'd always be the nightspinners." Lolly raises her eyebrow again. "Nothing," I say, "it's just a name that we had for ourselves when we were kids." I drain my glass and shake my head. "I was wrong, that's all. I mean, the only person who ever led me to believe Marina discovered anything in Georgia was Kathleen herself, who may not be exactly reliable."

"Not just Kathleen," Lolly says. "There was the conversation with Rex—"

"Dex."

"Rex, Dex, whatever. But, more important, Marina, too. She called you from down there, didn't she?"

"Yeah," I say, "she did." And I can hear the sound of her voice, first demanding and then whispering. "You know it won't do any good, Shoo," and I think, well, she was right. Nothing I've done has done any good.

"You could not have saved her," Elena has said to me how many times, leaning through the dusty air in her office. "There is nothing you could have done to save her." But now, looking out through this glass wall at the waterfront and the hundreds of tiny cars and people scurrying by below, I wish I could be so sure.

"I just thought," I say to Lolly, "that it must have been someone she knew, and that when she went back there, she figured out who it was, and it reassured her, made her think she could handle them, and that's why she opened the door."

"Well, probably it was," Lolly says. "Probably it was this Kathleen. Maybe that's what Marina figured out down there. Maybe she needed to get away from her to see it. I mean, this guy says he let her into your building, right?"

"Yes," I say, "I know. She even admits to being there. So it must have been her. And why would she come after me like that if she hadn't killed Marina?"

"They're sure it's the same person?"

"I'm sure," I say. "I can feel it."

"Well, anyway," Lolly says, "you don't have to worry anymore." She reaches out and covers my hand with her own. "You've got to try to move on, Susannah. It's over now."

IT'S THREE-THIRTY BY THE TIME WE GET IN CHIANG MAI Orchid's express elevator. The compartment is paneled halfway up and padded the rest of the way with blue-and-green-striped Thai silk, so the effect is slightly like being inside a small aquarium. We're joined by a party of four middle-aged men in dark suits and overcoats. They murmur among themselves and suck on toothpicks while the doors snap shut and we fall back down to earth.

Lolly offers me a ride home, and for one guilty moment I think of Jake, and I'm tempted to accept. But then I tell her I'd rather walk. The champagne's gone to my head a little, and our lunch was so fashionably light that I feel the need to sober up. We kiss the air beside each other's cheeks, and I watch Lolly as she darts across the street and hops onto the far sidewalk, landing like a bird on a branch.

I'm only three blocks from Beau's apartment, and at first I don't mean to go there. But as I start walking, I can't help it, and suddenly I'm filled with an urgent, almost weepy need to see him. I know, of course, that he's at work, but I cross at the lights and cut over to his street anyway, as if standing outside his door will somehow make me feel better.

The florist company that Beau lives above is going out of business.

It was a big place, a wholesale supplier with just a small shop in front that I guess sold the leftovers, the odd groups of stems and pieces of foliage that they couldn't fit into those towering arrangements for hotel lobbies and front tables of places like Tiffany's. On some weekend mornings, the warehouse doors have been open, revealing a cave of blooms, bright blobs of color that melt back into a cavern of brick. This afternoon, however, the doors are closed, and through the plate-glass window of the shop, I can see a woman packing pieces of Styrofoam into a box.

I push the security code on Beau's street door, and it occurs to me that I'm trespassing. But since he's not here, I can't see that it makes any difference. Inside, the fluorescent light above the hall buzzes, and when I start to climb the stairs, I pause, almost hoping I'll hear music. But there's nothing. Only dead silence, and then the sound of my shoes on the stairs.

By the time I get to his door, I'm feeling foolish. I have a key, and I could go inside. But I don't. Instead I decide to write a note, but when I dig a pen out of my bag, I don't know what to say. So finally I just fold the piece of paper into the shape of a dog that might be Jake. And then I wedge it in the crack of the door and leave quickly, before anybody knows that I was here.

Back on the street, I notice a bank of dark clouds and realize that what I had thought was a light mist is about to turn to rain. Four o'clock is a quiet time of day, and there are no cabs in the street. People who have been coming and going for lunch are back at the office, and rush hour hasn't started yet. I want to get home in time to take Jake for a good run in the park before it starts to pour, and I decide that the fastest thing to do is cut down the alley beside Beau's building, which will bring me out on a busier cross street, where I should be able to find a taxi.

It's too early for the streetlights to come on, and the brick walls of the warehouses rise so high that it seems like there's just a narrow wedge of cloud above. If I stood with my back pressed against the opposite wall and looked up, I could see Beau's line of windows. I could check to see if light is shining through, and if maybe he's hiding up there after all. Once, when I was drunk, I threw gravel at them and actually hit some of the thick, wavy panes. But there's no gravel lying around today, and I'm not about to lean against the warehouse wall, which smells of urine.

There are no sidewalks in the alley, which is barely wide enough for a car. I suppose that originally it was nothing more than a passage, dating from the days when people used horses. I pass an old door that looks like a coal hole, and the first heavy splashes of rain plummet through the gap between the roofs and hit the pavement. I can see the big, soft gray drops, and I realize that I'm going to be walking Jake in the rain, which he hates. He folds his ears down and slinks, and sometimes I have to coax him even to come out of the vestibule and onto the street. I am thinking about this, and wondering what effect the rain will have on trick-or-treating, and what I will say to Beau when he finds my origami dog and calls tonight, when I hear the footsteps.

At first I think they're an echo I haven't noticed before. But then I realize they're not. I hold my breath and I can hear them. They're measured and not loud. But they're there, a little ways back and constant. As if someone entered the alley a minute ago and is slowly gaining on me.

I'm about halfway down now, and the walls ahead of me seem to converge like the endpoint of a tunnel. I don't know if I can reach it even if I run, and I'm trying desperately to remember what's on the cross street ahead. There may be stores, and there should certainly be traffic, although I can't hear it. All I can hear is the sound of my heels on the pavement and the echo that moves in perfect time. I don't want to make an obvious motion, but I pull my bag in front of me and reach for my keys. I know I could scream, but there are no windows in the wall of the warehouse opposite Beau's, and his is the only loft in his building. I walk faster, and the steps behind me speed up.

They sound as if they're drawing in. I'm sure they're getting louder and growing closer, and the end of the alley seems just as far away. I slip my bag off my shoulder and grab it halfway down. It's not heavy enough to do damage, but I might be able to swing it once, hit someone in the face hard enough to momentarily confuse them. Inside the soft leather, I wrap my other hand around the keys so their points stick up through my fingers. The eyes, I think, you aim for the eyes. And then, in mid-stride, I stop and wheel around. In one motion, I brace my feet and swing my arm back. My breath comes out in a long rush.

But there's nothing there. The alley is empty. No one stands between me and the gray block of light on Beau's street.

"I'M A MARTINI!" CATHY ANNOUNCES AS SHE TWIRLS ACROSS the landing. "This is the rim of the glass"—she holds out a circle of silver wire that hangs from her shoulders—"and my lipstick is the pimiento. What do you think?"

She is wearing a silver leotard and silver spray-painted ballet slippers. Silver sparkles dust her cheeks and the bridge of her nose. Her hair is covered by a fuzzy green hat that has a cardboard dowel sticking out of either side of it, so her head looks like an olive impaled on a giant toothpick.

"It's great," I say. "Are you gin or vodka?"

She stops twirling and puts her hands on her hips. Now she looks like an angry martini. "Come on," she says, "don't be a party pooper. Come with us. Jill is going as a margarita, it'll be fun."

I make a face at her. "I don't have a costume."

"I have an extra one," she counters. "Shawn was going to wear it before he decided to take off early for Mexico. You can come as a tequila sunrise."

"Beau's coming over," I say, which as far as I know he isn't, but it's a trump card anyway. In Cathy's world, boyfriends take precedence.

She narrows her eyes at me. She suspects that I'm lying, but she doesn't want to say so. "Well," she says finally, "then you get to be on trick-or-treater duty." She picks up the big mixing bowl of Tootsie Rolls and mini Snickers bars sitting on the landing table and thrusts it into my hands. "Gordon is hopeless," she adds. "I tried to get him to do it last year, and he wouldn't even go downstairs after the first few times. And besides, I think he ate all the peanut-butter cups."

"Okay," I say. "I don't even like peanut-butter cups."

Cathy's intercom buzzes, and she pulls her door closed and starts down the stairs. Then she stops and looks back at me. "Are you sure?" she asks. "You don't even have to wear a costume." She's frowning with concern because I'll be left out, sitting home on Halloween by myself, when I could be at a Northwest Airlines party dressed as a cocktail. The buzzer goes again, and she raises her eyebrows.

"Trick-or-treaters," I say, and I follow her downstairs, hefting the giant bowl of candy and telling Jake to stay because he gets too excited and barks and knocks little kids over.

The rain has slowed to a drizzle, and a coven of tiny witches is standing on the top step. I lower the bowl so they can grab handfuls of candy, and over their heads, I watch Cathy skip toward the waiting cab. The back door opens, and I get a glimpse of someone inside dressed in green who I figure must be the margarita. Cathy squeals when she steps in the edge of a puddle by the curb, and she has trouble adjusting her wire hoop and ducking her head low enough so her toothpick doesn't get caught on the cab's roof, but then she slides into the backseat and slams the door, and they're gone.

The mother of the little witches thanks me, and as I close the heavy front door, they run down the steps and join a mini Darth Vader and an angel with pink wings. I stand in the vestibule looking out through the etched panels onto the street. The pattern of swirls and arabesques and a garland of flowers superimposes itself on the dark band of the sidewalk and on the cars that cruise past. People appear as fuzzy outlines in the frosted glass. They come briefly into focus and vanish again, moving silently in and out of sight.

The front hall is so quiet that I feel almost like I should tiptoe, and instead of closing the big doors to the vestibule and shutting out the glimpse of the street, I prop them open. Zoe would frown on this. The inner doors are always supposed to be locked, as a security measure, so if some bad guy makes it through the front door, he can be locked into the marble-floored entry, trapped in the high cage of Zoe's midnight-blue walls until the police can arrive and take him away. As far as I know, this has never happened. And, I think to myself as I wedge the doorstop home, it certainly didn't deter Kathleen Harper. On either of her visits. This makes me wonder if I should go down to the basement and check the back door to the garden, but one look down the stairs decides me against it. It's dark and spooky down there. I content myself with locking the door that leads up into the hallway, which is uncharacteristically flimsy compared to the rest of the house, but it makes me feel better.

THE BUZZER GOES THREE TIMES IN THE NEXT TWENTY minutes, and each time I take my bowl and run dutifully downstairs and stand on the damp top step in the misty rain and offer Tootsie Rolls to wizards and little monsters. Between trips, I find a bag of Mars Bars and some Hershey's Kisses on top of my refrigerator and I add those to the bowl, too. The second time I let Jake come with me, but he barks at a tiny green dinosaur who recoils against his father and looks as if he might cry, so after that I close the security gate and leave the door open so he can sit in the apartment and watch me as I go down. I hate to do it because when I come back he's lying down with his nose and front paws sticking through the black iron grid, and he looks like he's in prison. "As soon as the kids go," I tell him, "you can get out of jail free."

Beau doesn't call. It's almost eight o'clock, and I wonder if he's out at a Halloween party, dressed up as a doctor or a pumpkin. I should call him, I think. I should leave a message in case the paper dog got blown into the stairway or stepped on when he opened the door. But then the buzzer distracts me, and commanding Jake to stay, I take up my bowl again and skitter down the stairs.

This time the ghosts and princesses are a little older, and the mother waits at the bottom of the steps and waves to me when they leave. I notice when I close the door that there seem to be fewer trick-or-treaters now, and I suppose that soon they'll all be hustled home and only the bigger kids who throw eggs and spray shaving foam, and the cops who watch them, will be left on the streets. My bowl is half empty, and as I go back up the stairs, I wonder if we'll get through it all, or if some will be left over for Cathy to use next year, although she probably wouldn't ever do anything that cheap. The Snickers bars have been going the fastest, and I'm counting them up when Gordon pops his head out of his door like a jack-in-the-box and says, "Susannah, hi!"

He's been so quiet that I didn't even know he was here. I'd assumed that I was in the house alone, and seeing him is momentarily disconcerting.

"Hi," I say, and I realize that I'm holding the bowl out in front of me like an offering. "I've been doing the trick-or-treating. For Cathy. She went to a party. As a martini."

"I know," Gordon says. "Last year she went as a zebra." I can see Cathy covered in stripes with a pair of long ears made of wire and tissue paper mounted on her head. "It was an African theme," Gordon adds. "The guy who went with her was a Masai warrior." He pauses, and then he opens the door wider and says, "Come on in." I think of Jake, and of whether I'll be able to hear the buzzer. "They're tailing off anyway," Gordon says, reading my mind. "Do you have any peanut-butter cups in there?"

"No," I say, and just to make sure he doesn't steal the last of the Snickers bars, I put the bowl down on the stairs before I step inside.

He's got the gas fire lit in his big fireplace, and it's much more impressive than mine. His actually looks like flames. The bright red tongues climb up over a pile of painted glass logs and make them glow from inside. The lights must be on dimmers, because the room is more shadowed than it was last night, and the low light suits it. The walls don't seem as white, and the paneling looks clubby and very male.

"This house must have been magnificent," I say, "don't you think?"

"Oh yeah," Gordon says. He's pulling the curtains across the bay window and the window seat, shutting out the sparkle and glare of the streetlights. "I love these places. I've always dreamed of being able to afford one. You know, the whole thing, to do it up. I used to walk down these blocks, picking out which one I'd want." He smiles at me, and I imagine him as a little boy, looking into lighted windows.

"Did you grow up in the city?" I ask. I realize as I say it that I know absolutely nothing about him, that in the year I've lived here, I've never bothered to ask.

He shakes his head. "No," he says. "Well, not this one, anyway. I was born in D.C. We didn't have nice things," he adds. "Not like you, I bet."

There's an awkward pause. I can't think of anything to reply to this, except to say that we didn't have nice things, either, but before I can get the words out, Gordon says, "Can I get you a drink? Some wine?" He seems excited and kind of fidgety, like a child who has a secret. I hesitate, and then I remember how good the bottle of chardonnay that he opened last night was. A glass won't hurt, I think, and besides, it'll help me get up my nerve to call Beau.

"Sure," I say. Gordon grins and ducks into the kitchen, then reappears with a bottle and two of the heavy crystal glasses. I take the glasses from him, and while he pours Gordon says, "This is getting to be a habit." I force a halfhearted smile.

"Happy days!" Gordon says, raising his glass. And then, while I take a sip of the chilly straw-colored wine, he vanishes into what I guess must be a hallway or his bedroom.

The lights are on in Gordon's kitchen, and I wander over to the door and look in. It's about the same size as mine but much more modern and expensive. The whole room is white, with a tiled floor and walls and a white refrigerator and a fancy halogen stove set into a white wood island that looks like it's never been used. In fact, the whole kitchen looks like it's never been used, and it occurs to me that I can't remember one cooking smell ever wafting up from Gordon's apartment. I imagine there's a microwave somewhere in one of these white cabinets, and that if I opened the fridge, I'd find bottles of white wine and beer and things like salsa and pickled-herring treats and gherkins and olives.

The walls are empty except for a Sierra Club calendar and a magnetic strip that holds a pristine set of knives whose blades are so new that they sparkle under the lights. The phone is one of those sleek panels with a little computer screen and lots of buttons for preprogrammed numbers. I remember what Shawn said about him probably calling porn lines, and now it seems slightly ridiculous. Even so, I take a look at the frequent-number panel on the phone. There are no names penciled into the little white slots, and when I look around, I realize there's not even a menu for a Chinese restaurant or a pizza-delivery service stuck on the refrigerator. Suddenly the place makes me uneasy. Gordon's loneliness permeates it, and I feel embarrassed that I've noticed, as if I've opened a door and found him with no clothes on or sitting on the john.

"Here!" Gordon says. "I found it!" His voice startles me, and I spin around more quickly than I mean to. Some of my wine spills over the edge of my glass, and I wonder if I look guilty. I can feel my cheeks begin to color. Gordon doesn't seem to notice. He's standing in the kitchen doorway holding a round orange card in his hand as if it's a trophy, and he's put on a jacket. It's obviously new, an expensive-looking mossy tweed, and it's not quite right over his black turtleneck and jeans. He waves the card at me, and I can see now that it's supposed to be a pumpkin. It has black slit eyes and a snaggletoothed grin.

"It's a party uptown," Gordon announces. "I was going to ask you, you know, if you wanted to come? We could go for a while and then go get some dinner. I made a late reservation at Monique."

I know Monique. It's a wildly expensive French bistro up in the historic district that features things like open fireplaces and overly cozy little tables frilled with that flowery neo-Provençal material that gives me a headache. It's frequently billed as romantic in the tourist guides and is the sort of place bankers take their girlfriends on first dates or when they're going to propose. I can't imagine sitting in one of those stuffy little rooms across from Gordon, and I have no idea what to say. He's watching me, grinning in expectation, and I notice for the first time that when he smiles, his face is as round and smooth as a child's.

I start to say something about the trick-or-treating, or Jake, or Beau, but before I can get the words out, Gordon is talking again. He has switched now from excited to sincere. He creases his brow and lowers his eyes a little bit, and when he looks at me again, there's something sneaky in his face. He has a secret, and he's about to share it with me.

"I'm really, really sorry about your sister," he says. "It must have been horrible for you."

I stare at Gordon. I've never told anyone in the house about Marina. A thin prickle of sweat spreads across my chest, and when I speak, my tongue feels leaden. "How did you know?"

"The policewoman," Gordon says. "She told me why it's so important that they get this conviction." I try to decide whether he's lying, whether Becca Aaronson really would have told him this. Before I have a chance to make up my mind, he adds, "I knew there was something anyway. I mean, I guessed. I can tell usually, you know, like when someone's been really hurt. I think people recognize that in each other. And I feel like it's sort of, you know, fate."

The air in Gordon's kitchen seems suddenly condensed. "I don't really want to go to a party," I hear myself say.

But Gordon isn't paying any attention. He's talking about fate. "I mean, when all that stuff started happening to you. It was like I was supposed to be here. I don't know how to say this, Susannah, but I want to take care of you. I really do."

I put my glass down on the island and step backward. I can feel the cool white tiles of Gordon's kitchen wall through my sweatshirt.

"Gordon," I say, and my voice sounds strange, as if I'm talking from far away.

"I won't tell anybody," he says quickly. "About your sister, I mean. I understand about stuff like that, really."

I nod, and Gordon takes this as a signal that everything's okay.

"It's not a fancy-dress thing," he says. He's smiling to reassure me. He's holding out the pumpkin, offering it as proof that I won't have to put a sheet over my head and say "Boo" or wear a witch's hat. But all I can see is his arm coming toward me, backing me up into the corner of the kitchen. "It's just drinks and maybe a random vampire or two. Then we can get away and talk." His body blocks the door. I try to take a deep breath. But even so, I feel as if at any second, I might begin to scream.

"I have to go!" I say.

I push past Gordon into the living room. As I move toward the door, I try not to dart. It seems important to go slowly, to keep my eyes on him, and I try to make myself walk, although I'm aware that I must be sidling like a crab.

"Susannah," he says, "please." He's following me with his hands stretched out, and I step away from him and into the open doorway.

"I can't, Gordon," I say. "I'm——" I want to say that I'm involved with someone, that I don't want him to care about me or even to be anywhere near me, but before I can get the words out, he takes my arm.

"Susannah," he says, "please. I don't want you to be upset. I just want——"

"No!" I say, and I try to jerk away from him, but he hangs on to me. "Let me go, goddammit!" I wrench my arm away and spin around, and that's when I see Shawn coming up the stairs. He's taking them two at a time.

"Let go of her! Right now!" Shawn yells. "What the fuck do you think you're doing?" Upstairs, Jake barks once in alarm, and Gordon drops my arm and his face colors.

"Why the hell don't you mind your own goddamn business, just for once?" Gordon says. "She's just fine. Ask her."

Before I can say anything, Shawn grabs Gordon by the lapels of his new jacket and pushes him against the wall. I jump backward and knock the candy bowl off the stairs, and Snickers and Tootsie Rolls spill out onto the red rug. Shawn is sticking his face close to Gordon's, twisting the lapels in his fists. "You stay the fuck away from her, you pervert. You hear me?" he hisses.

I start to step toward them, to try to stop Shawn from punching Gordon, which he looks like he's about to do, but before I can do anything, Gordon reaches out and shoves Shawn away. "Get off me, you asshole," he says. "This'll cost you your job!"

"My job?" Shawn jabs Gordon in the chest with his index finger. "I know all about you, you fuckin' weirdo. You've got a prior for soliciting and harassment. You like to follow girls around, don't you?" There's a moment of dead silence, and then Shawn says, "It's true, isn't it? Go ahead, tell her." Gordon is turning sheet white, and I feel my stomach contract. "I've seen the note from your community-service officer in Zoe's files," Shawn says. "The one that he wrote so you could rent this place. The one that says you're not 'a danger to society.' Well, maybe they'd like to think again. Maybe they'd like to talk to Susannah."

"I don't have to put up with this," Gordon says. He steps away from Shawn, and although his skin has blanched and I can't swear that he isn't shaking, he looks right at me. "I'm going out to dinner, Susannah," he says. "I'd like it very much if you'd come with me."

I shake my head. I can't stop staring at him, can't stop wondering if this round baby face is what Marina saw when she opened her front door. "No," I hear myself say.

"There," Shawn says, "you've got her answer. Now leave her alone."

Gordon is still staring at me. He starts to say something but decides not to. Instead he steps past me and reaches inside his apartment and flicks off the lights. Then he closes the door. "You have a good night," he says to me. And then he pulls his jacket straight and steps past Shawn and goes down the stairs. A second later we hear the front door open and close.

"Shi-it," Shawn says. The word comes out as if he's been holding his breath. "Are you okay?" he asks, turning to me.

"Yeah," I say, "I'm fine." I can hear Jake whining upstairs, and I call up to him. His whine fizzles out, and I hear him thud down onto the hall floor.

We stand there staring at the stairway as if Gordon might material-ize out of thin air any second. "Is that true," I ask finally, "about the prior conviction?"

Shawn nods. "Yeah," he says. "I didn't find out until this afternoon or I would have warned you sooner. I found it in Zoe's files while I was looking some stuff up." I don't ask why Shawn was going through Zoe's files on her tenants, or why he's here at all, for that matter, since he's supposed to be in Mexico. Right now I really don't care. I'm just glad he's here.

"The conviction came up when they ran a security check on him. They have one of those services do that before they rent to anybody," Shawn is saying. I try to remember if Zoe and Justin informed me about this before I considered signing a lease, but I can't. "His community-service guy squared it," Shawn goes on, "or at least he must have con-vinced Zoe and Justin that Gordy was a reformed man. And them being them, they decided to give him a chance. Admirable, I guess, but maybe none too smart. That's why I'm here, incidentally. Zoe called from Paris just before I was due to leave. They've screwed up some big bid—

FedEx messed up the delivery—and she offered me enough money, so I said I'd stay and fix it for her."

"I'm glad you did," I say.

"Yeah," says Shawn. "So am I."

"Should we have let him go?" I ask, nodding toward Gordon's apartment.

"What?" Shawn says. "We were going to detain him? Tie him up with the light cord? You and me? Besides, do you want him in the house?"

I shake my head. "I should go call Mark Cope," I say. "He's the detective. The one who's handling all this."

Shawn nods. "Okay," he says. He turns and starts to go down the stairs. "I'm down at Zoe and Justin's if you need anything."

I figure I should pick up the Snickers bars and the Tootsie Rolls, and I bend down to start collecting them, then let them drop onto the rug again. I'll do it later. Right now what I want is to hear the sound of Mark Cope's voice. I'm not even sure what I'm trying to tell him, what it means about Gordon, what the implications are for Kathleen, but, I decide as I start climbing the stairs, I'll let him figure that out. I'm a little pissed he didn't tell me about Gordon himself, and all I can figure is that maybe he didn't know. Maybe Becca Aaronson never told him, or she didn't find out until after they'd picked up Kathleen. By that time it wouldn't have mattered, and now that I think of it, I'm pretty sure that the police can't just run around telling people that kind of stuff anyway.

Jake is lying flat on my hall floor with his nose and front paws shoved as far through the bars as he can get them. He wriggles and moans at me while I turn the locks, and it takes me a minute to convince him to back up far enough so I can swing the gate open.

"Good!" I say, and kiss him on the top of his head while I pull his ears. "Good, good boy!"

All of a sudden I'm feeling shaky and a little giddy, the way you do when you've just skidded in a car and narrowly missed running into something or going off the road. I pull the security gate closed behind me, and Jake and I go into the bedroom to get my bag. My organizer is buried in the bottom of it, and it takes me a second to open it and figure out how to retrieve what I want, but eventually I pull up Mark

Cope's listing. I prop the thing against my alarm clock and punch his home number into the bedroom phone, but when I hold it up to my ear, there's nothing but silence.

I look at the phone and see that its little battery light isn't even on, much less green.

"Damn," I say out loud. I probably pulled the plug out by mistake when I was making the bed this morning. I put it down and take the organizer and go into the living room, but there's no dial tone on that phone, either.

Halloweeen, I think. Some jerk's screwed with the wires somewhere, and now the phone's dead. Cathy's been telling me to get a cell for ages, and so has Lolly, but I hate the things. I'll have to walk up to the video store, I think, and use their phone. But then it occurs to me that Shawn's here, and he's definitely the sort of person who would carry a cell. I close the organizer and slip it into my sweatshirt pocket.

When I unlock the security gate, Jake follows me out onto the landing. It seems too mean to lock him up again, but at the top of the stairs I order him to lie down and stay. I don't want him shedding all over Zoe and Justin's apartment.

"Good dog," I say, "you stay." Jake gives me a long look, but he flops down on the landing like I tell him. Then I start down the stairs, calling, "Shawn? Hey, Shawn, are you there?"

ZOE AND JUSTIN'S APARTMENT IS BIGGER THAN I EXPECTED. I've been in their downstairs office, which is on the other side of the main hallway, but I've never been in here before. The living room and kitchen must have been the original dining room or possibly even a ballroom. It runs across the back of the house, and between its big sets of bay windows that look over the garden is a set of French doors that open onto a deck. White blinds hang above the black panels of glass, and the effect, combined with bright white walls, makes the room look monochrome, as if the color's been bleached out. I would have added some red, I think, or maybe even a deep purple for contrast. Anything to lift it out of this expanse of black and white that is supposed to look minimalist and trendy but in the final analysis is dull.

The lights don't help. They're spots that fall in pools and leave shadows washed up in the corners like splashes of dirty water. There's music playing, something classical, maybe Brahms or Beethoven, and I don't see Shawn right away. I step inside, and the door swings shut behind me. It's not until I call him that he appears out of what I guess must be a bathroom or maybe a bedroom, and by that time I've already picked up the telephone that's sitting on a table by the couch. It's dead. I'm still holding it in my hand when he walks in.

"Hey," he says. "Did you reach your detective? Have they put out an APB? I've always wondered what that stands for. APB. They say that a lot on cop shows. You want a beer?"

"All points bulletin," I say. "Sure. And the phones are dead, so I couldn't call. Do you have a cell I can use?"

He's wearing motorcycle gear tonight, a black jacket with lots of pockets and complicated-looking zippers, so his color scheme fits right in with the rest of the room. It crosses my mind that maybe he planned it that way.

"Have a seat," he says, and waves at the high half-back stools pulled up to the breakfast bar. They're stainless steel and go with the rest of the kitchen, which is open-plan and takes up the back of the room. Shawn opens the shiny fridge and takes out a couple of bottles. I slide onto a stool, which is uncomfortable and probably cost a fortune, while he rummages in a drawer for an opener. Watching him, I remember what he said about being Zoe and Justin's wife. He moves around this place like he owns it.

"Pretty weird about our friend Gordy, huh?" he asks. "I tried to tell you earlier, but you weren't here."

"When was it?" I ask. "The soliciting thing?"

"About two years ago," Shawn says. "I couldn't tell too much about the details from the letter. Just that he got community service, really, and that it happened."

"Well, I'm glad you showed up when you did," I say.

"Think nothing of it." He grins at me over his shoulder. "I'm just glad I poked my nose into those files."

The music swells and falls again, and Shawn pops the caps on the bottles.

"Thanks," I say when he hands me one. "Here's to being nosy."

"Here's to the Day of the Dead," Shawn says.

I get my organizer out of my pocket and try to find Mark Cope's number again. "I can never work these damn things." I take a sip of the beer and press the right button, and as if by magic, the number flashes onto the little black screen. "Eureka!" I say. When I look up, Shawn is leaning against the edge of the stove watching me. He raises his bottle, then starts to dig around in his pockets for what I presume will be his cell phone, but when he finds what he wants and pulls it out, it's a pack of cigarettes.

"Want one?" he asks. Somehow I don't think Zoe would like us smoking in here, and I shake my head. Shawn lights up and blows a thin stream of smoke toward Zoe and Justin's beautifully restored ceiling.

"Cell phone?" I ask.

"Oh, right, the cell phone. Sure."

He stands there smiling at me and holding the beer and the cigarette, and for the first time I wonder if maybe he's high on something. There's a funny glazed look in his eyes that I didn't notice when we were upstairs, and I wonder what he was doing in the other room before I came down. I feel a little ripple of unease and think that maybe this really wasn't such a great idea. Stoned people are a pain in the ass.

"You know," I say, taking a swallow of the beer, "don't worry about the phone. Jake needs to go out anyway, so maybe we'll just walk up to the video store."

"Oh, no," Shawn says quickly. "I'm just not sure what pocket it's in." He smiles at me, and then he puts down his bottle and starts to unzip his jacket. "Maybe it's in here," he says, and all at once I understand.

There was no call from Zoe in Paris. The dead phone line isn't a Halloween trick. And he isn't here to fix a bunch of papers. What he's here to do is kill me.

I know I should run. Or at least throw something. Or kick. Or scream. But I can't. I can't move. My whole body has seized up. My muscles have clenched, and my mind has, too. Like a clock whose hands have been stopped, I've come to a complete halt. I'm frozen in time. All I can do is stare at the necklace.

He's wearing a black T-shirt that makes the gold chain glitter, and the medallion that hangs from it seems smaller than a quarter. Its wavy edges look like someone drew them in with an unsteady hand, but even from where I'm sitting, some ten feet away, I can see the picture clearly. It's exactly as I remember it. The big man stands in the river, one leg in front of the other, and on his shoulders he carries the baby Jesus.

The last time I saw it, I felt a similar rush of paralysis and confusion, because then, like now, it was not where I had intended it to be. It was not guarding Marina, guaranteeing her safe journeys as Mrs. Pease at the jeweler's had promised me it would, but hanging from the neck of the boy she had loved.

"Charlie?"

I say the name almost without meaning to, but even before the man standing in front of me shakes his head, I sense that I am wrong, that the Saint Christopher medal had not guarded Charlie any more than it had guarded Marina.

"Ironic," he says, "isn't it. Now you're the one who can't tell us apart."

But I can. All at once the pieces slide into place, and the past is reconstructed in front of me.

When did she guess, I wonder. Did a card come with the flowers? Was there something in the wording of the Valentine? Or was it just a hope that turned into a conviction? A hope that Charlie Eames would never do this to her, would never torment her like this, even after all these years; and a conviction that blossomed and grew into the certainty that if it wasn't Charlie, it still had to be someone we'd known a long time ago.

I see Marina sitting with Dex Eames. I see her smiling because he's confirmed what she already suspects. And then I see her calling me. She stands in the kitchen and twists the phone cord around her hand, she's calling to discuss her next move with me, and to tell me that Charlie Eames never left Petamill at all.

Shawn's watching me the way a cat watches a beetle. He caresses the neck of the bottle, and his lips curve upward. I can remember kissing them. I can remember the soft, mushy feel of those lips, and the voice that whispered through them at that Memorial Day picnic twenty years ago, "I love you, I love you." I see my sister as she stops in the alfalfa field just before dawn, her head coming up fast like a deer's when it scents a hunter. A tiny light glows in the dark by the tangle of old rosebushes.

"You followed them," I say. "That night. And you watched. Then you killed him."

He sighs as if this story is boring. "I told him to leave her alone, but he wouldn't listen to me," he says. "That Sunday morning, I was down digging a ditch by the silo, and I saw him coming. He stood there and said he'd tell about the barn, and about the rest of the fires, about everything, unless I stopped following her." The man who used to be Sonny Delray shakes his head at how unbelievable this was. "Somebody had to take care of her. Somebody had to make sure she was saved."

Saved? I think. Saved from who? From what? And I see the Delrays driving by our house in their best Sunday clothes, and I remember the billboard with its promises from Jesus.

"Is that why you bought her the plaque?" I ask. "So she'd be saved?"

My body seems to be thawing and may be capable of moving again. I tighten my grip on the beer bottle's neck and wonder if I can use it as a weapon. My keys are in my jeans pocket, and I can't get to them without standing up. I don't want to look away from him, but I don't think I saw a knife block, or a set of boning shears, or even a skewer, in the pristine kitchen. Even Jake can't get to me, because Zoe and Justin's door is closed. I slide my feet down from the rung of the stool, feeling for the floor, and Shawn smiles at me as if I've said something clever.

"I hope you liked the inscription," he says. "I thought of it. I didn't want to take the chance that God would forget her."

"No." I try to force myself to sound normal. "I can understand that."

I'm gauging the distance between me and him and the door to the balcony, wondering if it's locked and if I could get to it before he could grab me. Even if I could, I don't know how I'd get over the garden wall. I'd be trapped. I can't tell where his knife is, but I'm betting on a pocket in his jacket.

"How did you know where to find her?" I ask. My toes brush Zoe's polished floor.

"I always knew," he says. "I kept track. I'm good at that." I imagine Sonny keeping track of us for years. Looking up our names in the phone book. Walking by the apartments where we lived. And I imagine him romancing poor Della the way he romanced Cathy, getting up close so he could find phone numbers, and ask questions, and get inside.

"I saw her a couple of times," he's saying, "in Petamill. I even ran into her once. On the street. I asked her if she wanted to go for coffee, but she said she was in a hurry. I don't think that was very nice, do you?"

"No." I shake my head.

"After that, I watched her," he says, "when she was home. I kept an eye out for her, just to be sure she was okay. Oh, she never knew," he answers the question that must be in my face. "But she looked so sad, up there all alone. I couldn't abandon her, not like you did." I hold my breath, but he doesn't move. There's no flash of a blade, or lunge toward me. Yet.

"I didn't tell her," he says. "I had to get ready."

I don't want to hear this, but I know that if I'm going to have any chance of staying alive, I have to keep him talking. His pauses are terrifying.

"Until you were ready," I prompt, and he nods.

"I mean," he says, "I had to have something to offer her. Something good enough. I went to college, you know. Vo-tech. Not like you guys did, but I did better than anybody thought." He's proud of this, and he preens a little as he says it. Then he takes a drag on the cigarette and drops the butt into the beer bottle. "And I got a job, too, a good one." I remember BethAnn calling him citified and saying he'd never marry Della. "A condo," he's saying, "in Falls Church. I had it all ready for her. Furniture and everything. I got a blue rug. Blue was her favorite color." I nod, trying to choke down the nausea that's rising in my stomach.

"When I called her, I used to sit on that rug," he says. "I used to imagine how happy she'd be when she saw it. I liked to hear her voice." I remember the shrill, empty ringing of the telephone in my apartment, and I don't want to know where he was sitting when he called me. "I sent her flowers. And a Valentine. A big one, Godiva. I wanted her to know that she wasn't alone on Valentine's Day. That she shouldn't be sad, because she'd never have to be alone."

"That was nice of you," I say.

He shrugs. "I wanted her to be happy."

"So why?" I ask. "Why did you kill her if you wanted her to be happy?" My voice barely comes out at all, and I think he might not have heard me.

Then he says, "You know."

I shake my head. "No," I say. "I don't." As much as I'd like to look away from him, I can't. I have to encourage him to keep going.

"Because," he says. "You know. Because of what she was doing." Color is rising up his cheeks, and he can barely say the words. It takes me a second to realize that he's talking about Kathleen Harper.

"Because of Kathleen?" I say. "You killed her because her friend was a woman?"

"She wasn't her friend!"

I don't know if deliberately throwing Kathleen in his face is a good idea, but I can't seem to stop myself. My heart has suddenly gone from being dead to hammering, and my mouth seems to be working on its own, possibly without too much advice from my brain. But maybe, if he gets worked up, he'll get distracted, which is the only chance I've got.

"You, of all people, should understand," I say.

His face colors again, and he laughs. "What?" he says. "What?" He slams his beer down on the counter and pulls on his jacket collar. "You think this is all there is to me?"

His voice goes soft, almost seductive, but the anger underneath it radiates until I can feel it on my face.

"You thought about it, didn't you?" he asks, and I remember the night at Bruges, the mixed signals, the smell of sex that hung in the air. "You wondered, just like Cathy." He's come up close to me and he has his face down close to mine. I can feel tears welling. They spill over and dribble down my cheeks. "You didn't know whether all that talk about Jake, and travels in Europe, and whether people can reinvent themselves, made you want to fuck me or tell me all about your sad little love life. And that's the trick," he says, "that's where I'm good. I keep you wondering what you're going to get, a best buddy or a good fuck. And you never have a chance to wonder who I really am." His voice rises until he's almost shouting. "I'll tell you a secret, Shoo Fly," he shouts, "women never take men like me seriously. If you let them talk about their hair and their makeup and their pathetic little heartaches, they'll never see you coming."

Shawn's face is red, and the cords in his neck are standing out like taut strings. He stops and takes a breath, and it's shallow and ragged, like he's run a long way. I've slid myself forward so I'm off the stool, but when he starts talking again, I freeze.

"Don't get me wrong, though. I wouldn't put up with that sort of shit from her. I wouldn't put up with her flaunting around like that, with her being a goddamn queer." He's shaking his head as if he still can't believe that Marina could have done this to him, and his voice almost quavers, as if he might cry.

"It's a sin," he says. "You go to hell, you know. I couldn't let that happen. Not to her. I told her I could save her. And do you know what she did?"

He's leaning toward me, so close I could reach out and touch him. Spit trembles at the corners of his mouth, and I can see tears at the edges of his eyes. I try to move, and the sharp edge of the bar bites into the small of my back. "She laughed," he whispers. "I told her I could save her, and she looked right at me, and she laughed."

I see Marina. I see her thinking that this is only Sonny Delray, and that even if he did kill Charlie all those years ago, he's nothing she can't handle. As far as she's concerned, he's nothing at all. He never has been. I see her looking right at him. I see her listening to his offer of a blue rug, and of salvation, and then I see her laugh.

"I'm sorry." My voice doesn't want to come out properly, but I force it to, and I think that maybe, maybe if I can make a connection with him, I'll survive this. "I'm sorry," I say again, "I'm so sorry, Sonny——" But they're the wrong words.

"It isn't even my fucking name!" he yells. "You never even knew my fucking name!" And then he hits me, hard.

The bar holds me up, and I swing my arm back and aim for his head with the beer bottle. At the same time I scream as loud as I can. And I go on screaming. I scream and scream, forcing the noise out of me, hoping that somebody, somewhere, will hear me.

The bottle connects with the side of his nose. It probably startles him more than anything else, but automatically he raises a hand to his face. It gives me time to kick the stool toward him and run, but not before I see his other hand reach into his pocket and come out with a knife.

My socks slip on the floor, and as I reach the couch, he grabs at my leg and I feel a sharp pain. A lamp falls over and crashes, but I get to the door just before he does. I yank it open and feel his hand on my waist. He grabs for my head. I feel his fingers slipping, and I scream, twisting and throwing myself forward, my arms flailing, but he's got me around the neck.

There's pressure, sharp pain, and a choking feeling, and when I try to scream again, no sound comes out of my mouth. My feet are still moving, though. They're slipping and scrambling, and the two of us lurch forward into the hallway. I hit the sideboard, and a pile of magazines spills onto the floor. Shawn's yelling something, but I can't tell what, and then, out of the corner of my eye, I see Jake.

He's bounding down the stairs, coming as fast as he can, and in the brief glimpse that I get of him, I see that his ears are pinned down and his lips are curled back, exposing his big canines in an ugly grin. I want to yell at him, to stop him, because I know Shawn will kill him, too. But I can't, and he leaps, and I fly sideways.

I need to keep both hands on my throat. It's hard to breathe, and I can't see Jake. I'm afraid he's been stabbed, that he's lying somewhere and I can't help him. A lot of blood is seeping through my fingers. It keeps coming no matter how hard I press. I can feel it on my arms and running down my chest, and I know that I have to get to the door and out onto the street. Because Shawn has cut my throat, and I'm dying.

I get up and take a step and almost fall. Black smears rise and shift in front of my eyes. My legs don't work, and I grab for the edge of the sideboard. I'm aware of broken china, and a piece of something that must have been a vase crunches under my hand. I can see the white panels of frosted glass in the front doors ahead of me, and when the sideboard ends, I feel for a split second as if I'm falling into nowhere. Then I half step and half slide across the parquet, and collide with a chair, and the marble of the vestibule floor swings up to meet me.

My head is too heavy to lift. Something moves beside me, and I feel Jake's fur against my face. I see flashes of light, and then there's a loud ringing and a child's high voice shouting "Trick or treat." Someone is hammering on the glass and yelling. But I can't breathe, and I feel myself getting smaller and smaller, as though I'm being sucked backward out of time. And just before I disappear, I hear Jake bark.

28

I CAN SMELL FLOWERS. SOMETHING LINGERING AND SWEET. Freesias. Their perfume clouds my dreams. It drifts across the fields to the farm, where I can see the sun lighting the steps of the front porch and the windows thrown open. As I come closer, I see the white curtains pushing against the gray mesh of the screens as if they're trying to escape. They flutter and throb to the hidden pulse of fans. By the garage, the lilies are blooming in a bank of flame, and the glider rocks, restless in the wind. The front door opens, and someone is standing there, beckoning me in. But before I can make out who it is, I am awake again.

That is how it happens every time. The nurses say this is because of the morphine dripping into my blood, but I am not so certain. In the last moments on the vestibule floor, as I was growing smaller and smaller, shrinking to nothing but a point of light, I heard Marina's voice. "Come home," she whispered, "come home."

Lolly bends over me. "I have Jake," she says. "He's fine. Don't you worry." She squeezes my hand.

The perfume is coming from my nightstand, and I can see color out of the corner of my eye. Bright purple and gold and a velvety magenta splash against a pale square of the wall.

"I don't know who they're from," Lolly says. "There's no note, but they're beautiful. Somebody's spoiling you." She picks up the vase, which is crowded with freesias and holds it up so I can see. "There's just this," she says, "taped on. I wonder who did it. It's so cute. It looks like Jake."

The door opens, and a nurse in pink scrubs swims into my vision. "I'm sorry," she says to Lolly, "but you'll have to leave now." The nurse is plump and blond, and with her apple cheeks and blue eyes, she looks like someone out of a children's story. I can hear the wheels of the cart she's pulling. She parks it beside my bed and ducks out of sight as she locks it into place.

"We have to change the dressings," she announces when she pops back up. Lolly nods and puts the flowers back on the bedside table.

"I'll be back tomorrow," she says to me. "I have to go now, because Richard and I are taking that dog of yours out to Fairhill. Richard bought him a Frisbee." Her hair tickles my face as she kisses me on the forehead, and I hear the click of her heels as she slips out of sight. The door closes, and there's a snap as the nurse pulls on plastic gloves. Out of the corner of my eye, I see the flash of steel.

"Don't worry," she says, "this shouldn't hurt."

I feel a tug and hear a snipping sound. Shawn only got one good slice at my throat, and they tell me that it wasn't really enough to do any serious damage. If I hadn't been moving so fast, though, and if Jake hadn't appeared, it might have been different. As it was, I almost bled to death.

I roll my eyes sideways until I can see the edges of the flowers. I breathe in their smell and watch their melting blur of color. And even when I feel a sharp tear of pain across my neck and hear the nurse mutter under her breath, I keep concentrating on the vase of freesias and on the little origami dog taped to its rim.

THAT WAS THIS MORNING. NOW MARK COPE IS STANDING by the window in my room. His shirt is a crisp, bright blue against the gauzy white rectangle of the sky, and he's moving his finger back and forth along the windowsill, tracing its edge as if he's found dust there and is going to complain to housekeeping. When he looks at me, he frowns, and I know what he's going to say before he says it.

"They found the body a couple of hours ago," Mark Cope says. "Right where you said. Near the old silo hole."

I had guessed that Charlie would be there because the Delrays had torn down the silo that summer, and the hole and the rubble would have been ready-made, a grave waiting for him when he walked across the summer fields to find Sonny Delray that Sunday morning twenty years ago.

I had whispered this to Becca Aaronson yesterday, croaked it in her ear when she bent so close to me that I could see the stitching on her white silk collar and smell the mix of shampoo and perfume that clung to her hair. She and the vampire were here when I woke up, and she was the one who told me about the trick-or-treater who peered through the glass panels of the door, and about his father, who had a cell phone and dialed 911.

"You were lucky," Becca said.

Now I look at Mark Cope and close my eyes. I see Chief Hancy. And Dex Eames. And blue lights flashing down the farm road. I see a group of men standing over the sinkhole of the Delrays' old silo, and I think of Charlie, who never made it to the Gulf, or to the oil fields, or anywhere else, despite the medal that he wore tucked inside the collar of his shirt.

"They say they think Delray burned down a barn," Mark Cope says. "Does that make any sense to you?"

I nod and open my eyes. "He did," I whisper. "It was a warning. For Charlie to stay away from Marina."

"Well," Mark Cope says, "it's all unrolled like a ball of string. Sonny—his real name actually is Shawn, by the way—never got over her. He went off to the vocational college at Macon and did pretty well. He was a smart kid, made his momma proud. She still doesn't believe this, of course. Says her boy never hurt a fly. Anyway," Mark goes on, "he got a job in Atlanta, and we're trying to see what we can find out there. He doesn't have a record, but there's a spate of Peeping Tom incidents that happened around the time he was in town and stopped about when he left." Mark Cope shrugs. "It might have been him. All the women were single, and several of them had red hair."

He looks out the window as though he's studying something or has seen someone he knows in what I guess must be the parking lot or the street below. Then, without turning around, he goes on telling me about Shawn.

"He left Atlanta after about five years at the same company. He was a product manager for some farm equipment manufacturer. The personnel director said they were sorry to lose Shawn, but he said he was relocating to D.C. with his fiancée, who had just started a job there. They gave him a great reference and a modest golden handshake." Mark Cope thinks about this, then says, "We figure he watched Marina for maybe a year, possibly two, before he ever did anything. He had another pretty good job in Bethesda in product management again, and that's when he started to become the Shawn you knew. He had a friend he played squash with, a guy who never believed he was gay and called him on it. Shawn said he played the part because it made things 'easier.' He had a female boss at work who he cozied up to. He told his buddy that women were never threatened by gay men."

I close my eyes again, and Mark Cope goes on talking.

"Eventually, he outlasted his boss, took her job, and bought the condo in Falls Church in August. We figure he made his first call to Marina about a month later. Della Hervey thinks she might have given him the number. And the new one after Marina changed it. Della's sure he must have used her keys to get into your old house. Incidentally, when he went down there, he ditched the gay routine."

Mark's words flow over me, and even though I close my eyes, he knows I'm listening. He's talked to me this way in the day and a half since I've been here, swaddled in my hospital gown and my white turtleneck of gauze. He has come every couple of hours and told me everything. He's laid out every minute detail that the police have discovered about Shawn, as if he owes it to me, as if it is the least he can do for failing to protect me. Now he says, "He sold the condo a year ago and quit his job. In fact, his company wanted to downsize, so he took voluntary redundancy and got paid for it. That's what he's been living on in Philly. He found out where you were from Della, too, sometime after Marina was killed. Said he wanted to send you flowers." He pauses while this sinks in, and then he says, "We think he must have watched the house awhile, trailed Cathy, joined her gym. They became friends, she'd invite him over, he had what he needed. Getting hired by Zoe and Justin was pure luck, icing on the cake. Now he had keys to the whole house. We found a screwdriver in his apartment that we expect to have blue paint traces on it. He'd been following you. He knew where you worked."

There's something else he wants to say, I can tell even with my eyes closed, and I wait. After what seems like a long time, I hear his voice again.

"Clearly Marina's relationship with Kathleen Harper tipped Shawn over the edge, took him from stalking to homicide. Although if she hadn't rejected him so totally, if she hadn't laughed at him when he said he wanted to save her, maybe he wouldn't have killed her. According to Phil Dorris, at least."

"No," I say, but I don't open my eyes.

"That's what I think, too," I hear Mark say. "I think he was going to kill her anyway. Sooner or later. It was the only way he was ever going to be able to keep her."

"Save her," I say. "He wanted to save her."

"Right," Mark says. "I should have seen the pattern with you. When Beau spent the night, things accelerated. Shawn's wire tripped. The haircut was a final warning, just like the barn burning and Marina's trash cans. I should have figured it out. I was so focused on Kathleen Harper that I didn't see what was right under my nose."

"Neither did I," I say.

"Yeah," he says, "but you're not a policeman."

At first I thought it was unfair to let him go on this way, to let him feel so guilty for the blossoming of something that set its roots so long ago, something that had been growing, creeping, through the years, its buds of envy, and love, and pain finally swelling to the bursting point. But then I realized it's the only thing he can give me now, and it seemed churlish to turn down the gift. This talking, this testifying, is Mark Cope's atonement for the fact that Shawn has gotten away.

I first suspected this yesterday, when neither Becca Aaronson nor the vampire mentioned him, and my suspicions were confirmed by the cop posted outside my door. I was not supposed to know he was there, but I glimpsed the uniform and heard Becca's lowered voice when she spoke to him. But I didn't know the details until Mark Cope told me how Jake had attacked Shawn, who fled into the basement, where he got out through the garden door and climbed the wall that we never did top with razor wire or broken glass.

The police found blood on the basement stairs and on the garden door, and yesterday Mark assured me that they would catch him. That now that they knew who he was and had gone through his apartment, and were questioning his friends, and tracing his movements, it was only a matter of time, hours even, before Shawn would be in custody. In all probability, Mark said, he had more than one serious dog bite that would need treatment, which would only make the search easier. Every hospital, every clinic and drugstore, had been alerted. But the day had passed. And this morning had passed. And when I finally open my eyes, Mark Cope has his back to me.

"I have bad news, Susannah," he says. "I didn't want to tell you until we were sure." He sits down in the plastic armchair at the foot of my bed so I can see him, and for the first time since I've known him, he looks tired.

"He was one step ahead of us," Mark Cope says. "He got a plane out of Kennedy early yesterday morning. To Mexico City. He bought the ticket here in Philly three weeks ago."

Something is rising inside me, so unfamiliar that it takes me a moment to realize that it's laughter. It's painful, and when it hits my chest and my throat, it brings tears to my eyes. Mark is talking about extradition after they find him, which of course they will, when he notices that I am making small, strange sounds. I sound more like a gerbil or a bird than a human being.

"Susannah," he asks quickly, "are you all right?" His hands move toward me, although they don't know what to do. He jumps up. "Do you need a nurse?" he asks. But I shake my head.

He watches me as the sound subsides, and when I gesture, he hands me the pad and the blue Bic by my bed. I can talk, sort of, but when it hurts too much, I've taken to writing things down. "Water," I've written, and "Beau." Now I write "November 2" and hold the pad out to Mark Cope, who takes it.

He looks at me but doesn't understand. "Yeah," he says, "that's today." When I don't say anything more, or gesture for the pen again, he decides I must be getting tired and puts down the pad.

"Listen," he says, "you get some rest. I'll be back later." I watch him as he walks to the door. He pulls the cuffs of his shirt down in a fussy little gesture, as if he's straightening himself up before he faces the world again.

"KATHLEEN HARPER WANTS TO SEE YOU," BECCA AARONSON says. "She's outside. Do you feel okay about that? You can say no." Becca has dropped by to tell me they don't know anything new about where, exactly, in Mexico Shawn might be, but they do know that he must have been in the house and followed my cab when I went to the hair salon and the Marriott. A girl in the newspaper kiosk had ID'd him from the photo.

Then Becca told me how he poisoned Jake.

"It was ordinary household mouse killer," she said. "We found it in his apartment, and two sausages laced with the stuff that he hadn't bothered to throw out were in his freezer. That afternoon he probably just hung around and followed you down to the dog park. Jake knew him, so it wouldn't have been so tough."

I remember how Jake struggled when Shawn picked him up to carry him to the car. He'd even growled. I'd been too stupid to guess. But Jake knew. The idea of this brings tears to my eyes, and I reach for a Kleenex. Becca thinks I'm worried about Kathleen and says, "I can stay while Kathleen's here. If you want. Or I can tell her to leave."

"I'm okay," I whisper in my strange nonvoice.

Becca nods and straightens up. I can tell that she doesn't like this much, that she's afraid Kathleen might do or say something to upset me even more. If talking were easier, I'd point out that I'm pretty much on the far side of being upset. Becca goes to the door and opens it. My guardian cop is gone now; he's back on traffic duty now that we know Shawn is in Mexico. Becca looks back at me and says, "I'll be right out here if you need me."

A second later, Kathleen Harper is standing at the end of my bed. She's holding a bouquet of asters. Their stems are bound in Saran wrap and tied with a ribbon.

"They're the last from the garden," she says, and she puts them down on top of my fake wood bureau. She's wearing a suit. It's navy blue and looks like it fit her once, but now it's all loose and baggy in the wrong places because she's lost a lot of weight.

"That night," she says, "the night I came to your house. I lied to get in. I showed them some old key and said you gave it to me. I didn't think you'd let me in, and I needed to see you again." She pauses and looks at me, and I think she's going to cry, but she doesn't. "I wanted to apologize," she says, "for being such a total bitch to you when you came out to the house. And I wanted to explain about me and Marina."

I look at her, nod a little bit, which hurts, and gesture to the chair, telling her to sit down.

She shakes her head. "I can't stay," she says. She fingers the bunch of asters, and suddenly I wonder if Marina planted them or if they planted them together. "It was my first time," she says, without looking at me, "with another woman. Hers, too, I think. I met Allen right after college, and we got married and had the kids. We were happy. Sort of. But when Marina came to work at the bank, I just knew." She looks at me. "You know what she was like. She pulled you in, made you feel like everything else was pale in comparison. I really loved her, you know. I wanted us to be together. I felt like she owned me. But I never felt like I owned her."

I watch her. I don't know what I would say even if I could.

"I was so jealous of you," Kathleen says. "I still am."

She goes to the window and stares down. The tips of her fingers rest on the sill, tensed and waiting, as if she's a pianist about to play. From behind, she looks as if she might be holding her breath.

"He killed her because of me, didn't he?" she says, and I realize that in some horrible way, she needs this to be true. She needs to believe that if she could not be utterly central to Marina's life, then at least she was utterly central to her death.

When I don't answer, she turns around and looks at me. She's willing me to give her this last thing, this last piece of Marina.

"I don't know," I whisper, and the words hurt. Each one of them.

CATHY COMES TO SEE ME. BEAU IS HERE WHEN SHE AR-rives, and we're watching *The Simpsons*. "D'oh!" Homer says, and the door pops open and a bunch of Mylar balloons fly in. Cathy's still wearing her uniform, which means that she's come straight from the airport. She's trying to be perky, but she's having a hard time. Finally she starts to cry. Beau puts his arm around her and makes her sit in the plastic chair and brings her a glass of tepid water from my bathroom.

"I didn't know," she says over and over again. "He was so friendly at the gym. He seemed harmless. He was funny. I didn't know. I just didn't know."

Beau tells her that it's okay. He pats her shoulder and says that nobody could have known. "Susannah didn't know," he says. "And she'd known him all her life!" At this, Cathy laughs a little bit and nods. Beau gets her some Kleenex and she blows her nose and then wads the tissue up into a little ball.

"I know," she says. "But it's different. I mean, I made friends with him. He let me even have a crush on him. He let me think maybe—"

"He's a psychopath," Beau says. "Manipulating people is what he does." When he's not killing them, I think. Cathy and Beau look at me, and I know they just thought the same thing, but none of us wants to say it.

ZOE COMES, TOO, WITH JUSTIN. THEY BRING ROSES AND A split of champagne, with a straw, that I can't drink. Zoe twists her hands back and forth and says she's sorry for hiring him, and Justin says they should never have given him keys. Later that night Lolly arrives and drinks the champagne.

"Don't you worry, kiddo," she says, waving the straw at me, "we're going to get you all fixed up in no time. I have this dynamite plastic surgeon."

MY NECK STILL HURTS, AND I WHISPER AND WRITE THINGS down, but they've moved me off morphine and on to Percodan, and this afternoon they are letting me go home. Lolly is picking me up and taking me to Beau's, where Jake and I are going to be staying for a while, and where he and Cathy are serving a dinner that is supposed to be a surprise. Lolly has told me this because she knows I won't be able to eat any of it, and I don't like surprises. She says she'll get them to call it off if I want, but I know that Zoe and Justin are coming and that Beau's even invited Benjy, so I tell her it's okay. She is still worried, though, and she has bought me a pair of Chinese silk pajamas and a kimono so I'll have something to wear. They're gorgeous, and I am fingering the heavy silk, tracing the pattern of chrysanthemums and dragons and wondering if I can wear anything this beautiful, when Mark Cope comes into the room.

He is carrying a large paper bag from somewhere like Saks Fifth Avenue or Filene's, and he smiles at me and says, "Hey, looking good!"

It is not the sort of comment that comes naturally to him, and I grimace and push away the kimono. I'm a little surprised to find that I'm happy to see him.

"So, you're going home," he says. "That's good." He holds the bag out to me. "If this ever gets to trial, this will be material evidence, but we found it in Shawn's apartment, and I thought you'd want to see it."

I take the bag, and when I look inside, I see photo frames and recognize the pictures that were taken from Momma's desk in Petamill. Under them is something wrapped in white plastic that feels like a book. I catch a glimpse of bright turquoise, and when I unwrap the parcel, Marina's scrapbook lies in my lap, the bright yellow daisy on its cover as round and unblinking as an eye staring up at me.

The album's covers are smooth and slightly puffy under my fingers. I notice that the binding is cracked, as though someone's opened it over and over again, and the edges of the colored paper pages are soft and worn and slightly grubby from being turned. The words "BALLET" and "RIDING" are written at the tops of facing pages. The letters are a childish attempt at calligraphy, in green ink, with too many swirls and tails. A silver ribbon that has "LEVEL II" printed on it in blue letters is glued down on the ballet page, and below it is a picture of all the girls from that dance class clustered around our old teacher. Marina smiles from the center of the group. On the facing page there are pictures of Uncle Ritchie's old horse Jewel, and of Marina and me riding double. In one we sit back to back like a pushmi-pullyu. Marina holds Jewel's mane, and I rest my hands on the horse's rump, laughing.

A few pages later there is a junior high school portrait of Marina. It's one of those bad studio pictures taken against a cloudy blue background that makes the subject look like they're giving off steam. I don't remember ever having seen this picture before, but I would say it must have been taken just before the summer of the fires, and I'm surprised she was still putting pictures in by then. She stares straight at the camera. Her long hair is combed, uncharacteristically, straight back in a headband, and she is scowling. She looks almost as if she has a widow's peak.

But it's not Marina's face that holds my eye. It's the gold necklace she's wearing. I look at it lying in the indent of her collarbone. I touch it with the tip of my finger. And I think that this photo must have been taken just weeks before she gave the necklace away.

Marina was not the chronicler I was. She didn't have my belief in souvenirs, and many of the pages in the album are blank. I flip through them almost mechanically, and then, toward the end, I see more pictures. These are grainy and black and white. The quality is poor, but they've been arranged carefully on the pages and are held down with professional mounting tabs, as if they're valuable.

At first I don't understand, and I look at Mark Cope for an explanation, but he's staring out the window. I look back at the top picture. There's something blurry at the foreground, and beyond it is something that looks like a stage with two figures on it and columns down one side. I squint a little, and then suddenly I see. It's Marina and me on our front porch.

We used to practice ballet out there sometimes in the evenings.

Momma would turn on the stereo for us and let the music drift through the open windows, and we'd use the porch rail as a barre. Our pink leotards would become damp with sweat and soft as flesh as we sank on our knees, and rose, and pointed, our toes flicking up and down in our shiny black slippers. If we were being swans, we would wear our tutus, and they would rustle like dead leaves when we moved.

The other pictures are as fuzzy and as distant, but there's the same strange intimacy to all of them, and I understand that they were taken without our knowledge. They're moments that were snatched from us long ago without permission, and now they're pinned down on this page like butterflies. When he took these, Shawn must have been hiding behind the corner of the barn, possibly even crouching in the dense bank of lilies.

There's a single shot of one of us, I can't tell which, sitting on the glider, reading. But in all of the others, we are together. There are several pictures of us on the porch, and in one we stand at the bottom of the steps, obviously quarreling. Marina reaches for what looks like a book in my hand, and I am caught in the moment of swinging it away from her. Looking at the picture now, I can hear the tone of her voice. I can almost feel the warm air move with the swipe of her hand, but I cannot recall what we might have been fighting about or why.

I imagine the comfort that Shawn must have taken in studying these pictures, these stolen glimpses of my sister. It was the best way he had of getting close to her. Undisturbed by reality, he must have spent hours alone with them, planning her salvation. And then after he'd killed her, when he could no longer hear her voice on the phone or follow her through the streets, there was nothing left. Nothing but these photographs and me.

These blurred little moments of possession that Shawn had hoarded so carefully and for so long are giving me a strange feeling in the bottom of my stomach.

"He watched us," I say. "Always." The words come out in my croaky whisper, as loud as I can make them, and Mark Cope turns from the window.

"We'll get him, Susannah," he says. "I promise you, we'll get him."

———

THAT WAS A YEAR AGO. NOW BEAU, JAKE, AND I LIVE IN another city. It's a smaller place in the flat Midwest, somewhere where strangers will stand out. I still work, but I have changed my name, and I fly from city to city. On the whole, I don't like to be away from home for long.

Lolly was as good as her word, and I'm sure her plastic surgeon would have been excellent. I met with him twice, but in the end I decided not to have anything done. So for now I wear high collars and turtlenecks. Elena would say that this is a sign that I am not ready to part with my past yet, and perhaps she would be right. Beau says we'll do something about it when I'm ready.

I still hear from Mark Cope. He calls every couple of months, and before he hangs up, he always repeats his promise: "We'll get him, Susannah. We'll get him." But nothing has been seen or heard of Shawn for a year now. He has vanished, and probably transformed himself, buried himself in a new persona and a new wardrobe, just as surely as he buried Sonny Delray in the punky weight lifter with the mahogany hair. This presents me with a problem, since beyond a medal that assures safe journeys, I have no idea what or who I should be watching for.

It is cold now, and soon the snow will fly. Two nights ago, tiny witches and ghouls made their way up the lighted path to our front door by the dozens, and Beau and I handed out Hershey's Kisses and mini bags of M&M's. Today I saw a Christmas tree in the drugstore window, and next week they're turning on the lights around the Madonna and the shepherds and the baby Jesus in the park. The phone rings, and downstairs I hear Beau go to answer it. Seconds later I hear his footsteps again, and when I lean over the stairwell and ask who it was, he stops with his newspaper in his hand and smiles up at me and says, "Just someone trying to sell us something, doll. I hung up on them."

I am running the water for a bath. It steams slightly and bubbles, and when I get in, I let my hands float across the top of it. I make swirls on the soapy blue surface and imagine that my hands are not my own until they gravitate to my collarbone and finger the tapering edge of the scar that I wear like a medallion.

I lean my head back and, through the skylight above me, watch the dark patch of sky. There's a thin veil of cloud tonight, and the lights from town reflect off it and make it shimmer like smoke. But somewhere up above it are stars and possibly a moon.

It's the Day of the Dead today, and I wonder if Shawn can see the stars where he is now. I wonder if he is buying sugar skulls. I imagine him preparing for his annual second chance with the dead, laying out his feast and inviting Charlie and Marina to his table. And then I wonder if all the places are taken, or if, when Shawn makes his plans, he still thinks that someday he will lay a place at his table for me.

ABOUT THE AUTHOR

LUCRETIA GRINDLE was born in Sherborn, Massachusetts, and graduated from Dartmouth College. She has lived and worked as a freelance journalist in England, Canada, and the United States. She and her husband currently divide their time between Devon, England, and Massachusetts.

THE ENCYCLOPEDIA OF PSYCHOACTIVE DRUGS

IN 25 VOLUMES
Each title on a specific drug or drug-related problem

AMPHETAMINES

THE ENCYCLOPEDIA OF PSYCHOACTIVE DRUGS

AMPHETAMINES

Danger in the Fast Lane

SCOTT E. LUKAS, Ph.D.

Assistant Professor, Harvard Medical School
Research Pharmacologist, McLean Hospital

1985
CHELSEA HOUSE PUBLISHERS
NEW YORK

SENIOR EDITOR: William P. Hansen
ASSOCIATE EDITORS: John Haney, Richard Mandell
CAPTIONS EDITOR: Richard Mandell
EDITORIAL COORDINATOR: Karyn Gullen Browne
ART DIRECTOR: Susan Lusk
LAYOUT: Carol McDougall
PICTURE RESEARCH: Susan Quist

First Printing

Library of Congress Cataloging in Publication Data
Lukas, Scott E.
    Amphetamines: danger in the fast lane.

    (Encyclopedia of psychoactive drugs)
    Bibliography: p.
    Includes index.
    Summary: Examines the history, effects, and medical and legal aspects of
amphetamine use and abuse.
        1. Amphetamine abuse—Juvenile literature.
2. Amphetamine—Toxicology—Juvenile literature.
[1. Amphetamines.   2. Drugs.   3. Drug abuse]   I. Title.
II. Series.
RC568.A45L85   1985   615'.785   85-476

ISBN 0-87754-755-6

Chelsea House Publishers
Harold Steinberg, Chairman & Publisher
Susan Lusk, Vice President
A Division of Chelsea House Educational Communications, Inc.

Chelsea House Publishers
133 Christopher Street
New York, NY 10014

Photos courtesy of AP/Wide World Photos, Kaethe Kollwitz, SmithKline
Corporation, D.C. Public Library, UPI Bettmann Archive, *Journal of Applied
Psychology,* U.S. Drug Enforcement Agency, Museum of the City of New York,
National Institute of Mental Health, CIBA Pharmaceutical Co., Terry Stevenson,
and *Inter-Clinic Information Bulletin.*

CONTENTS

Amphetamine use produces heightened sensitivity to visual, auditory, olfactory, and tactile stimulation. The auditory threshold, for example, may be so lowered that not only does the user hear sounds normally inaudible, but these sounds may cause extreme discomfort.

FOREWORD

In the Mainstream of American Life

The rapid growth of drug use and abuse is one of the most dramatic changes in the fabric of American society in the last 20 years. The United States has the highest level of psychoactive drug use of any industrialized society. It is 10 to 30 times greater than it was 20 years ago.

According to a recent Gallup poll, young people consider drugs the leading problem that they face. One of the legacies of the social upheaval of the 1960s is that psychoactive drugs have become part of the mainstream of American life. Schools, homes, and communities cannot be "drug proofed." There is a demand for drugs—and the supply is plentiful. Social norms have changed and drugs are not only available—they are everywhere.

Almost all drug use begins in the preteen and teenage years. These years are few in the total life cycle, but critical in the maturation process. During these years adolescents face the difficult tasks of discovering their identity, clarifying their sexual roles, asserting their independence, learning to cope with authority, and searching for goals that will give their lives meaning. During this intense period of growth, conflict is inevitable and the temptation to use drugs is great. Drugs are readily available, adolescents are curious and vulnerable, there is peer pressure to experiment, and there is the temptation to escape from conflicts.

No matter what their age or socioeconomic status, no group is immune to the allure and effects of psychoactive drugs. The U.S. Surgeon General's report, "Healthy People," indicates that 30% of all deaths in the United States

9

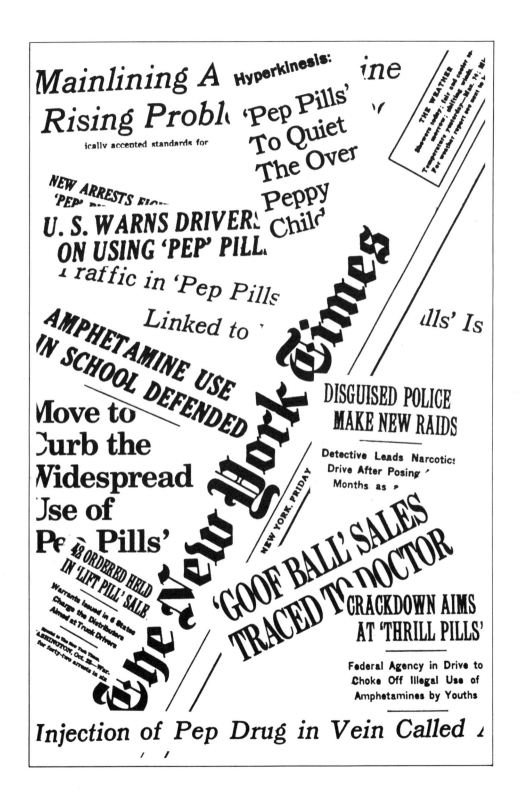

are premature because of alcohol and tobacco use. However, the most shocking development in this report is that mortality in the age group between 15 and 24 has increased since 1960 despite the fact that death rates for all other age groups have declined in the 20th century. Accidents, suicides, and homicides are the leading cause of death in young people 15 to 24 years of age. In many cases the deaths are directly related to drug use.

THE ENCYCLOPEDIA OF PSYCHOACTIVE DRUGS answers the questions that young people are likely to ask about drugs, as well as those they might not think to ask, but should. Topics include: what it means to be intoxicated; how drugs affect mood; why people take drugs; who takes them; when they take them; and how much they take. They will learn what happens to a drug when it enters the body. They will learn what it means to get "hooked" and how it happens. They will learn how drugs affect their driving, their schoolwork, and those around them—their peers, their family, their friends, and their employers. They will learn what the signs are that indicate that a friend or a family member may have a drug problem and to identify four stages leading from drug use to drug abuse. Myths about drugs are dispelled.

National surveys indicate that students are eager for information about drugs and that they respond to it. Students not only need information about drugs—they want information. How they get it often proves crucial. Providing young people with accurate knowledge about drugs is one of the most critical aspects.

THE ENCYCLOPEDIA OF PSYCHOACTIVE DRUGS synthesizes the wealth of new information in this field and demystifies this complex and important subject. Each volume in the series is written by an expert in the field. Handsomely illustrated, this multi-volume series is geared for teenage readers. Young people will read these books, share them, talk about them, and make more informed decisions because of them.

Miriam Cohen, Ph.D.
Contributing Editor

Amphetamine especially appeals to women, who are constantly bombarded by the current notion that the "ideal woman" is extremely thin. In addition to aiding in weight loss, the euphoric effects of amphetamine may also make a woman feel thinner and thus artificially increase her self-confidence in her attempt to achieve that "ideal."

INTRODUCTION

The Gift of Wizardry
Use and Abuse

Jack H. Mendelson, M.D.
Nancy K. Mello, Ph.D.
Alcohol and Drug Abuse Research Center
Harvard Medical School—McLean Hospital

Dorothy to the Wizard:

"I think you are a very bad man," said Dorothy.
"Oh, no, my dear; I'm really a very good man; but I'm a very bad Wizard."
—from THE WIZARD OF OZ

Man is endowed with the gift of wizardry, a talent for discovery and invention. The discovery and invention of substances that change the way we feel and behave are among man's special accomplishments, and like so many other products of our wizardry, these substances have the capacity to harm as well as to help. The substance itself is neutral, an intricate molecular structure. Yet, "too much" can be sickening, even deadly. It is man who decides how each substance is used, and it is man's beliefs and perceptions that give this neutral substance the attributes to heal or destroy.

Consider alcohol—available to all and yet regarded with intense ambivalence from biblical times to the present day. The use of alcoholic beverages dates back to our earliest ancestors. Alcohol use and misuse became associated with the worship of gods and demons. One of the most powerful Greek gods was Dionysus, lord of the Underworld and god of wine. The Romans adopted Dionysus but changed his name to Bacchus. Festivals and holidays associated with Bacchus celebrated the harvest and the origins of life. Time has blurred the images of the Bacchanalian festival, but the theme of drunkenness as a major part of celebration has survived the pagan gods and remains a familiar part of modern society. The term "Bacchanalian festival" conveys a more appealing image than "drunken orgy" or "pot

13

party," but whatever the label, some of the celebrants will inevitably start up the "high" escalator to the next plateau. Once there, the de-escalation is difficult for many.

According to reliable estimates, one out of every ten Americans develops a serious alcohol-related problem sometime in his or her lifetime. In addition, automobile accidents caused by drunken drivers claim the lives of tens of thousands every year. Many of the victims are gifted young people, just starting out in adult life. Hospital emergency rooms abound with patients seeking help for alcohol-related injuries.

Who is to blame? Can we blame the many manufacturers who produce such an amazing variety of alcoholic beverages? Should we blame the educators who fail to explain the perils of intoxication, or so exaggerate the dangers of drinking that no one could possibly believe them? Are friends to blame—those peers who urge others to "drink more and faster," or the macho types who stress the importance of being able to "hold your liquor"? Casting blame, however, is hardly constructive, and pointing the finger is a fruitless way to deal with problems. Alcoholism and drug abuse have few culprits but many victims. Accountability begins with each of us, every time we choose to use or to misuse an intoxicating substance.

It is ironic that some of man's earliest medicines, derived from natural plant products, are used today to poison and to intoxicate. Relief from pain and suffering is one of society's many continuing goals. Over 3,000 years ago, the Therapeutic Papyrus of Thebes, one of our earliest written records, gave instructions for the use of opium in the treatment of pain. Opium, in the form of its major derivative, morphine, remains one of the most powerful drugs we have for pain relief. But opium, morphine, and similar compounds, such as heroin, have also been used by many to induce changes in mood and feeling. Another example of man's misuse of a natural substance is the coca leaf, which for centuries was used by the Indians of Peru to reduce fatigue and hunger. Its modern derivative, cocaine, has important medical use as a local anesthetic. Unfortunately, its increasing abuse in the 1980s has reached epidemic proportions.

The purpose of this series is to provide information about the nature and behavioral effects of alcohol and drugs, and the probable consequences of both their moderate use and abuse. The authors believe that up-to-date, objective information about alcohol and drugs will help readers make better decisions as to whether to use them or not. The information presented here (and in other books in this series) is based on many clinical and laboratory studies and observations by people from diverse walks of life.

Over the centuries, novelists, poets, and dramatists have provided us with many insights into the beneficial and problematic aspects of alcohol and drug use. Physicians, lawyers, biologists, psychologists, and social scientists have contributed to a better understanding of the causes and consequences of using these substances. The authors in this series have attempted to gather and condense all the latest information about drug use and abuse. They have also described the sometimes wide gaps in our knowledge and have suggested some new ways to answer many difficult questions.

One such question, for example, is how do alcohol and drug problems get started? And what is the best way to treat them when they do? Not too many years ago, alcoholics and drug abusers were regarded as evil, immoral, or both. It is now recognized that these persons suffer from very complicated diseases involving deep psychological and social problems. To understand how the disease begins and progresses, it is necessary to understand the nature of the substance, the behavior of the afflicted person, and the characteristics of the society or culture in which he lives.

The diagram below shows the interaction of these three factors. The arrows indicate that the substance not only affects the user personally, but the society as well. Society influences attitudes towards the substance, which in turn affect its availability. The substance's impact upon the society may support or discourage the use and abuse of that substance.

SUBSTANCE
(ALCOHOL OR DRUG)

PERSON ←——————→ SOCIETY

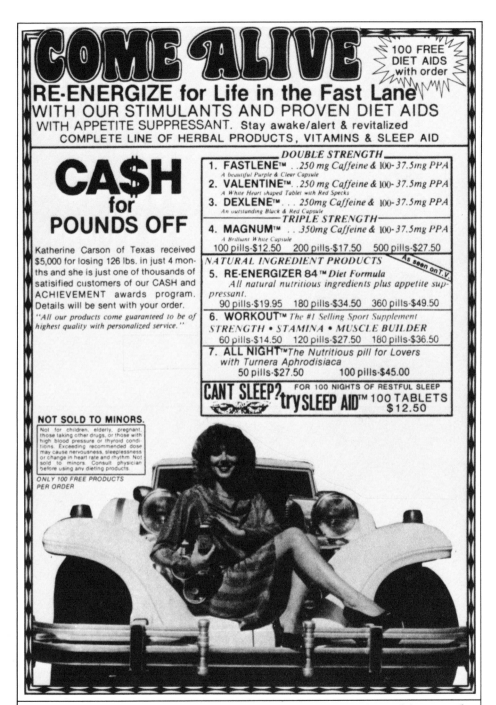
This ad in a women's magazine perpetuates certain myths and ignores the dangers of drug use, seductively linking dieting, exhilaration, enhanced love-making, and even economic success with drugs.

Although many of the social environments we live in are very similar, some of the most subtle differences can strongly influence our thinking and behavior. Where we live, go to school and work, whom we discuss things with—all influence our opinions about drug use and misuse. Yet we also share certain commonly accepted beliefs that outweigh any differences in our attitudes. The authors in this series have tried to identify and discuss the central, most crucial issues concerning drug use and misuse.

Regrettably, man's wizardry in developing new substances in medical therapeutics has not always been paralleled by intelligent usage. Although we do know a great deal about the effects of alcohol and drugs, we have yet to learn how to impart that knowledge, especially to young adults.

Does it matter? What harm does it do to smoke a little pot or have a few beers? What is it like to be intoxicated? How long does it last? Will it make me feel really fine? Will it make me sick? What are the risks? These are but a few of the questions answered in this series, which, hopefully, will enable the reader to make wise decisions concerning the crucial issue of drugs.

Information sensibly acted upon can go a long way towards helping everyone develop his or her best self. As one keen and sensitive observer, Dr. Lewis Thomas, has said,

> "There is nothing at all absurd about the human condition. We matter. It seems to me a good guess, hazarded by a good many people who have thought about it, that we may be engaged in the formation of something like a mind for the life of this planet. If this is so, we are still at the most primitive stage, still fumbling with language and thinking, but infinitely capacitated for the future. Looked at this way, it is remarkable that we've come as far as we have in so short a period, really no time at all as geologists measure time. We are the newest, the youngest, and the brightest thing around."

By the middle 1950s there were at least eight different inhalers which contained amphetamine or its derivatives. All could be purchased without a prescription and were easy to break open.

CHAPTER 1

HISTORY OF AMPHETAMINE USE AND ABUSE

*T*he term "amphetamine" refers to a group of chemically related drugs, all of which produce similar behavioral and physiological effects. Every drug in the amphetamine group is a psychostimulant, or a drug that increases the activity of the brain. Unlike many other frequently abused drugs, amphetamines do not occur in nature but can only be made in a chemical laboratory. (The various amphetamine drugs are described in Appendix 1.)

Since amphetamine is a synthetic drug, it does not have the long history of use and abuse that many other psychoactive drugs have. Originally synthesized in 1887 by a German scientist, amphetamine was then largely forgotten until 1930, when it was discovered that the drug could increase a person's blood pressure. Three years later amphetamine was found to be helpful in treating lung congestion. In 1932 a pharmaceutical company, Smith, Kline & French, marketed a nasal inhaler containing amphetamine. It shrank the mucous membranes of the nose and thereby relieved the discomfort of nasal congestion due to colds, hay fever, and asthma. At the time, the powerful stimulating effects of amphetamine, when taken internally, were unknown.

By 1935 amphetamine's stimulant effects had been recognized by Smith, Kline & French, and reports appeared of its effectiveness in treating narcolepsy (uncontrollable sleepiness) and Parkinson's disease. When the American Medi-

cal Association (AMA) approved the use of amphetamine for these disorders, a mild warning was added which cautioned that "continuous overdosage" might cause "restlessness and sleeplessness," but physicians were assured that "no serious reactions had been observed." A year later the first reports of nonmedical use of amphetamine appeared.

Exaggerated publicity and claims about the drug's psychological effects contributed to the public's increased interest in amphetamine. Between 1932 and 1946 the pharmaceutical industry developed a list of 39 generally accepted clinical uses for amphetamines. Some of these uses included the treatment of schizophrenia, morphine and codeine addiction, "nicotinism" or tobacco smoking, heart block, head injuries, infantile cerebral palsy, radiation sickness, low blood pressure, seasickness, persistent hiccups, and "caffeine mania." Amphetamine was promoted as being effective without the risk of addiction. Since nearly every abused drug was originally thought to be "nonaddictive," this claim is not surprising.

The trends in amphetamine abuse have changed over the last 40 years. Despite official statements to the contrary, amphetamine or the "pep-pill" was commonly used by the

A balcony view of the wholesale drug firm of Smith, Kline & French. In the early 1930s F.P. Nabenhauer, the company's chief chemist, made discoveries which led to the production of the Benzedrine inhaler.

military during World War II. It has been estimated that approximately 200 million tablets were supplied to American troops. At the end of the war many soldiers who had used amphetamine returned to the United States and spread the news about this invigorating drug.

In the 1950s college students, athletes, truck drivers, and housewives, in addition to soldiers, were using amphetamine for nonmedical purposes. Even race horses were given amphetamine since it was believed that it made them run faster. Use of the drug expanded all across the United States during this decade, as production of amphetamine increased significantly. It was being marketed to treat obesity, narcolepsy, hyperkinesis, and depression, but people were taking it primarily to increase energy, decrease the need for sleep, and elevate mood.

In the 1960s some people began using amphetamine intravenously, that is, injecting it directly into the bloodstream. Most often this was accomplished by obtaining from legal or illegal sources small sealed containers containing amphetamine in solution. At that time heroin addiction was being treated with intravenous amphetamine. As a result

World War II saw the widespread use of both legally authorized and black-market amphetamines. German Panzer troops used the drug to eliminate fatigue and maintain physical endurance, and some historians have even linked many of the German atrocities to the abuse of amphetamines.

amphetamine in injectable form was readily available.

Japan and Sweden faced a crisis of amphetamine abuse at about the same time as the United States. There are numerous similarities between these three countries with respect to this problem.

The Amphetamine Epidemic in Japan

Japan was the first country to have an epidemic of amphetamine abuse. The problem began after World War II when large amounts of amphetamine were made available on the Japanese market. A vigorous advertising plan by the pharmaceutical companies promoted this stimulating drug as "wakeamine" and as a necessary addition to the medicine cabinet in every home. These advertisements were aimed at helping individuals to cope with the hardships caused by the social, cultural, and industrial upheavals of the postwar period. Pills were the first form of amphetamine to be widely abused.

Amidst the devastation, hardship, and rebuilding in postwar Japan, more than two million people were using amphetamines. Japan's successful crackdown on amphetamine abuse has been attributed to strict law enforcement methods—sweeping arrests, stiff prison sentences, and a curtailment of supplies.

However, intravenous use also soon increased to epidemic proportions. At the height of the epidemic in 1954 it was estimated that there were over 2 million amphetamine users in a population of 88.5 million. During this period, reports of the drug's toxicity first began to appear.

Education and treatment programs began in 1954. The epidemic subsided when the penalties for sale and use were increased and more strictly enforced. It is possible that the epidemic may have been short-lived even if these measures

In 1969 horse racing, which gained the reputation for its widespread use of drugs, was the only major American sport to have imposed strict drug regulations.

Table 1

Demographic Characteristics of Crisis-Contact Clients								
DRUG	NUMBER	MEDIAN AGE	RACE: WHITE	RACE: BLACK	MALE	EMPLOYED	SOURCE: STREET	SOURCE: LEGAL PRESCRIPTION
DAWN: Emergency Rooms, May 1976 to April 1977								
amphetamine (Benzedrine)	1196	24½	80%	16%	57%	30%	58%	27%
dextroamphetamine (Dexedrine)	260	25½	76%	22%	45%	31%	29%	56%
methamphetamine (Methedrine)	143	23¾	83%	12%	59%	27%	65%	21%
methylphenidate (Ritalin)	538	28½	44%	53%	58%	15%	42%	52%
"speed"	689	22½	83%	14%	62%	27%	83%	0%
DAWN: Crisis Centers, May 1976 to April 1977								
amphetamine (Benzedrine)	1641	23	78%	20%	54%	35%	83%	9%
dextroamphetamine (Dexedrine)	875	25½	90%	8%	60%	53%	73%	19%
methamphetamine (Methedrine)	528	25	86%	10%	70%	43%	81%	11%
methylphenidate (Ritalin)	353	26¾	57%	38%	73%	25%	61%	23%
"speed"	1253	22¼	84%	13%	52%	29%	95%	0%
CODAP: Admissions, July to September 1976 Amphetamines	2444	22.6	83.7%	11.7%	70.5%	26%	—	—

had not been introduced, since amphetamine abusers often become increasingly violent and involved with crime, and either "burn out" or are institutionalized.

Detecting Amphetamine Abuse

The Drug Abuse Warning Network (DAWN) is a project sponsored by the National Institute on Drug Abuse (NIDA). It is a data collection system that focuses on how often a drug is involved when people are brought to a hospital emergency room or when a death is reported by a medical examiner. The major objectives of DAWN are: to identify substances associated with drug abuse; to monitor patterns and trends of drug-taking; to assess drug abuse-related health

Table 2

The Drugs Most Often Cited in Emergency Admissions (quoted by hospital physicians in descending order of frequency)	
DRUG NAME	BRIEF DESCRIPTION AND/OR TRADE NAME
Alcohol in combination	depressant in alcoholic beverages
Diazepam	sedative used for anxiety; Valium
Heroin	opiate, narcotic
Aspirin	nonnarcotic painkiller
Cocaine	stimulant
Marijuana	hallucinogen
PCP (angel dust)	hallucinogen
Acetaminophen	nonnarcotic painkiller; Tylenol
Flurazepam	sedative used for sleep
Methaqualone	depressant; Quaaludes
Amitripytyline	tranquillizer
Hydantoin	anticonvulsant
Phenobarbital	depressant
Acetaminophen with Codeine	painkiller; Tylenol
Chlordiazepoxide	sedative used for anxiety; Librium
Pentazocine	narcotic painkiller
Methadone	narcotic for treating heroin abuse
Propoxyphene	narcotic painkiller
Amphetamine	stimulant
OTC sleep aids	sleeping pills
Chlorpromazine	tranquillizer; Thorazine
Speed	stimulant
Thioridazine	tranquillizer
Oxycodone	narcotic painkiller
Amitriptyline	tranquillizer
Ethchlorvynol	depressant
Haloperidol	tranquillizer
Doxepin	tranquillizer
LSD	hallucinogen
Chlorazepate	sedative used for anxiety
Diphenhydramine	antihistamine
Lorazepam	sedative used for anxiety
Butalbital	depressant
Codeine	narcotic painkiller
Meperidine	narcotic painkiller; Demerol
OTC Diet Aids	stimulants

Table 3

Percent of Drug Abuse by Age Group					
AGE	AMPHETAMINE	SPEED	METHAMPHETAMINE	OTC DIET PILLS	COCAINE
10–17	11.7	15.0	7.0	34.8	2.9
18–19	11.4	13.2	10.0	13.7	5.2
20–24	28.0	31.6	36.5	19.4	21.7
25–29	23.8	21.1	25.1	12.9	28.8
30 +	24.9	18.5	21.3	19.0	41.2

hazards; and to provide data for national, state, and local drug abuse agencies so they can formulate policy and plan programs.

A second major source of information comes from independent studies that randomly poll members of various age groups. The questions typically focus on the individual's personal drug preferences, frequency and history of use, and their perceived harmfulness of a drug. The major drawback of this type of study is that there is no way to verify that the answers are completely honest or that the drugs taken were indeed the ones *thought* to have been taken, since there are many "look-alike" drugs on the street.

The Client-Oriented Data Acquisition Process (CODAP) is the third major source of information for tracking drug abuse patterns. In essence, while emergency rooms, crisis centers, and medical examiners report to DAWN, treatment programs report to CODAP. Some individuals may seek help at a treatment center. Others may be required to attend as a result of a court order. Either way, the drugs of abuse are recorded.

Prevalence of Amphetamine-Related Incidents

Table 2 lists the top 36 drugs mentioned in emergency room reports. As can be seen from this table, cocaine ranked 5th, amphetamine 19th, speed 22nd, and over-the-counter (OTC) 36th. All of these drugs are stimulants.

Table 3 shows the data in terms of specific age groups. This table reveals an interesting pattern. The 10- to 17-year-old group accounted for 35% of the over-the-counter (OTC) diet pill mentions, indicating that the greater availability of these drugs may contribute to their misuse among minors.

Table 4

Percent of Drug Abuse by Motive					
	AMPHETAMINE	SPEED	METHAMPHETAMINE	OTC DIET PILLS	COCAINE
Psychic Effect	29.1	43.1	45.7	24.6	34.4
To Satisfy Habit	44.3	27.6	33.1	5.8	51.9
Suicide	16.2	16.7	7.5	54.4	5.7
Other	1.0	0.8	1.2	1.4	0.5
Multiple Motives	2.7	3.3	3.6	0.8	3.6
Unknown	6.8	8.6	8.9	13.0	3.9

The 20- to 24-year-old group accounted for most of the mentions of all stimulants. However, these differences may simply reflect a greater number of individuals in this age bracket who end up in the emergency room.

Table 4 provides information from the DAWN data on the motives that led to the abuse of the various drugs. Again, the OTC diet pills were mentioned quite frequently, especially with regard to suicide attempts. Amphetamine and cocaine were most often used to maintain addiction while speed, methamphetamine, and other stimulants were commonly used to get high. These data reflect the differences in perception about the effects of these drugs.

Results from national surveys on the medical and nonmedical use of amphetamine have uncovered some in-

Publicity about heroin and opium abuse by troops has obscured their widespread use of amphetamine. Between 1966 and 1969 the U.S. Army consumed more amphetamines than the entire British or American Armed Forces during World War II.

AMPHETAMINE   PHENYLPROPANOLAMINE

Amphetamine consists of (1) a phenyl ring; (2) CH3, a methyl group; (3) a two carbon side chain; and (4) NH2, an amino group. Any alterations change, reduce, or eliminate the effects. Phenylpropanolamine, for example, has no central nervous system stimulating effects.

teresting attitudes and trends. The main findings for 1982 as compared with the previous 10 years were as follows: almost 7% of youths, age 12 to 17, reported nonmedical experience with amphetamine as compared to 4% in 1972. For young adults from 18 to 25, the increase was from 12% in 1972 to 18% in 1982. Only 2.9% of youths and 4.3% of young adults reported ever having medical experience with amphetamine.

Attitudes and Beliefs about Amphetamine Abuse

A major survey conducted in 1981 measured changing trends in the incidence of drug abuse and its degree of acceptability among peers, and found that nearly one-third of high school seniors reported using amphetamine at some time without medical supervision. This is the highest rate for any illicit drug except marijuana. Only 25% of the users reported that they had used the drug just once or twice. Those reporting that they used amphetamine daily represented 1.2% of the respondents—again second only to daily marijuana use. No significant differences were found between males and females with respect to prevalence of use, which between 1975 and 1978 remained stable. Beginning in 1979, however, use of amphetamine began accelerating.

Another aim of the 1981 survey was to assess trends in the degree and duration of "feeling high." Individuals were asked, "When you take amphetamine how high do you usually get?" and "How long do you stay high?" The data were divided into two groups: recent users (within the last

In 1969 the United States military establishment was still "flying high" by remaining one of the largest purchasers of amphetamine. The Navy required the most (21.1 pills per person per year), followed by the Air Force (17.5) and the Army (13.8).

30 days), and all individuals responding to the question. A very interesting trend was discovered. A much smaller percentage of the class of 1981 reported that they got high after taking amphetamine as compared to the class of 1975.

A similar shift was observed in the duration of the drug's effects. While many students in the class of 1981 reported that the effects lasted only 1–2 hours, most students of the class of 1975 reported that they lasted 7–24 hours. It is possible that these differences in effects and duration are due to the changing chemical content of street

Many people enjoy the thrill of speed and the sense of impending danger. But while "speed" may cause euphoria and elation, when the drug's direct effects wear off the user may abruptly experience mental depression and fatigue.

Table 5

Street Names for Amphetamines and Related Drugs		
A	dex	oranges
AMP	dexies	orangies
AMT	diet pills	pap pills
A's	doe	peaches
bambita	eye-openers	pep pills
bams	fives	pills
B Bomb	footballs	purple hearts
bean(s)	forwards	reducing pills
bennies	gas	rippers
benz	goofballs	roses
Black Beauty	grads	sparkle plenties
Black birds	green hornet	sparklers
bombido	greenies	speed
bombita	head drugs	speedball
bottles	hearts	splash
box of I.	jam	splivins
brownies	jam Cecil	stuka
browns	jellie babies	sweets
cartwheels	jolly-beans	thrusters
chalk	jugs	truck drivers
chicken powder	leapers	turnabouts
coast-to-coast	lid poppers	uppers
co-pilot	lid proppers	uppies
crank	love drug	ups
crink	ludes	wake-ups
crosses	meth	whites
crossroads	methadrine	yellow bams
crystal	meth freak	

preparations purported to be amphetamine. With less and less amphetamine available, the tendency is for sellers to substitute a less potent drug.

The reasons for the increase in use over the past few years are not completely known or understood, but trends in attitudes about the harmfulness of amphetamine probably contributed. Whereas 35% of the class of 1975 felt it harmful to try amphetamine once or twice, only 26% of the class of 1981 concurred. The perceived danger of taking amphetamine on a regular basis also dropped, but not as much as that for the perceived danger of occasional use. As expected, fewer individuals disapproved of experimental or recreational use of amphetamine. It must also be remembered that those individuals who regularly use amphetamine are also more likely to promote its benefits, downplay its risks, and report that their parents and friends approve its use.

CIAO! MANHATTAN

Speed. Madness. Flying saucers.

During the filming of Ciao! Manhattan, *a medical doctor gave amphetamine injections to the entire cast to maintain a high pace and create a false sense of community. This led to the fatal overdose of actress and model Edie Sedgwick (above).*

WHEN USE BECOMES ABUSE

Drugs have become easily accessible and therefore widely used and abused in our society. One of the most difficult decisions facing young people in the 1980s is whether or not to experiment with drugs.

Drug abuse refers to the use of any drug for nonmedical reasons. Very few people are capable of questioning the value of a drug that makes them feel good. Because of factors such as poor self-esteem, the need to be part of a group, and depression, the results of drug-taking can seem so beneficial in the eyes of the user that occasional experimentation can become compulsive drug use and, ultimately, abuse. So drug abuse is really not about drugs. It is about people and their problems in dealing with society.

Amphetamine Abuse:
Effects on the Individual, the Family and Society

The individual may ignore the effects of his behavior on those around him. The issue of becoming addicted rarely enters the drug user's mind. He insists that he is not "hooked" or than he can "quit at any time," but why should he when the drug makes him feel so good? Some people take certain drugs because they look on these drugs as status symbols. For example, cocaine abusers typically look down on those who take heroin. They rationalize the difference by claiming

that they are not "hooked on coke." Heroin is addictive, they say, while cocaine is just a habit.

Members of the amphetamine abuser's family are either the first or the last to know about the problem. While they frequently suspect that something is wrong, they may be reluctant to interfere. Unfortunately, by the time drug abuse makes an impact on the family, the amphetamine problem is already quite serious. The family may need to seek professional help in the form of family counseling. Other times, if violence is involved, the police must be called in.

A drug abuser can be dangerous not only to himself but to others. A drunk driver who commits manslaughter is a common example. Every locality in America has laws to deal

Drugs are often purchased in places such as shopping malls, where illegal activity is hidden by the hustle and bustle of automobile and pedestrian traffic. The amphetamine may be pure and from a highly controlled laboratory, or adulterated and from an amateur's kitchen.

with drug abuse. Typically, the law makes distinctions between possession, local distribution, and manufacturing of drugs and imposes different penalties for each.

Patterns of Amphetamine Abuse

Amphetamine abuse often follows one of three basic patterns: (1) occasional low-dose use, (2) sustained low-dose use, and (3) high-dose use by intravenous injection. In the first pattern, individuals may take 5 to 20 milligrams (1 to 4 tablets) of amphetamine about once or twice a week. The purpose of taking the drug is usually to avoid fatigue, to recover from a hangover, to elevate mood while performing tedious, unpleasant tasks, or to "get high." This pattern of abuse is most common among students and truck drivers who usually obtained the drug from a friend. In such cases, the drug-taker's life does not center around the use of amphetamine or other stimulants.

The differences in abuse patterns of amphetamine and cocaine may be due to the length of time it takes each drug to work. Since cocaine acts very quickly, a person would have to take it about every 30 minutes in order to maintain a "high." In contrast, the effects of a single dose of amphetamine last for hours. A person who takes it will not experience rapid changes of mental state from euphoria to depression and back to euphoria like a cocaine user. So the two compounds are generally used for different reasons. Cocaine is rarely used as an aid to staying up late studying since its effects are not noticeable half an hour after taking the drug. This may be the reason for cocaine's popularity with executives on their lunch breaks.

Those who fit the sustained low-dose category usually obtain their amphetamine from a physician for weight control, but take 3 to 4 times the prescribed dosage in order to sustain a state of euphoria. In some cases, the individual visits two or more physicians in order to get enough amphetamine to maintain this pattern of abuse. As the use of amphetamine becomes part of the patient's daily routine, he begins to believe that survival without the drug is impossible. Sleep is increasingly difficult, and he may try to compensate for insomnia with depressants such as alcohol or barbiturates. This pattern of stimulant-depressant-stimulant abuse is very dangerous.

The last pattern, high-dose intravenous abuse, is the most dangerous. The speed cycle consists of three phases: injection of the drug, exhaustion, and reactive depression. This cycle may be repeated numerous times a month. After the injection of from 400 to 1,000 milligrams of amphetamine, a "rush" or "flash" immediately follows. The injection may be repeated every two or three hours for several days, and bizarre or violent behavior may result. Ultimately, fatigue becomes so great that the individual stops injecting and falls into an exhausted state. Continuous sleep for one or two days is not uncommon. Signs of depression, lethargy, and weakness occur next, and may last from a few days to several weeks. It is during this time that the amphetamine user may decide to avoid the depression by self-injecting again.

Amphetamine Abuse by Professionals

We often hear about amphetamine abuse among sports and show business figures. The great pressures of these two careers are similar. Those who pursue careers in these fields are in the public eye and playing for high stakes. They dream of stardom, fortune, and recognition for their accomplishments. Surprisingly, it appears that older, more established athletes frequently abuse amphetamine, perhaps in order to feel young and prolong their athletic careers. In show business, those who achieve early success are more likely to become involved with stimulants. One reason given is that they become so euphoric without drugs during a performance that when the show is over they do not want to lose the feeling. They search for artificial ways to bring back the applause and the spotlight.

Amphetamine abuse among professional football players has been studied scientifically, and a phenomenon called the "Sunday Syndrome" was identified. This refers to the use of amphetamine to kill pain from injuries, to overcome the sleepiness produced by other pain medication, and to get "psyched up" for the game. Prior to the Controlled Substances Act of 1972, a law which more closely regulated amphetamine and other substances, athletes in many sports regularly used amphetamine, but currently the drugs are less available.

Table 6

Incidence of Amphetamine Use by Professional Football Players Interviewed				
POSITION	YES	NO	OCCASIONALLY	DOSE RANGE (MG. PER SUNDAY)
Quarterback	1	8	0	10– 15
Wide receiver	6	5	2	5– 15
Offensive line	10	4	0	15–105
Running back	8	3	2	5– 25
Tight end	2	2	1	10– 30
Defensive line	9	0	1	30–150
Linebacker	5	4	1	10– 60
Defensive back	7	4	2	5– 20
Totals	48	30	9	5–150

SOURCE: Dr. Arnold Mandell

Throughout the 1970s professional football players increasingly turned to amphetamines to heighten their aggressiveness. Dr. Arnold Mandell, locker-room analyst, observed pacing, obscene swearing, vomiting, diarrhea, and rage. He claimed that fans were "buying tickets to see speed freaks try to kill each other."

While students sometimes use amphetamines as an aid to studying and exam-taking, their results are usually disappointing actual achievement does not correspond with the user's sense of efficiency. Most studies have shown that amphetamines cause the speed of reaction to increase but the accuracy of work to decrease.

CHAPTER 3

BEHAVIORAL EFFECTS OF AMPHETAMINE

*A*mphetamine increases physical activity and produces restlessness in many individuals. Users are fidgety and unable to sit still. If confined to a small room the user appears to be very anxious about being restricted to a small area and may insist on going out for some fresh air. In some cases, this is an attempt to conceal amphetamine use. Often a student will take amphetamine in order to study or work on a paper late into the night. Upon completing the project he is usually still wide awake and must find a way of expending this extra energy. Persons on amphetamine often repeat simple acts such as tapping a pencil on a glass, polishing and repolishing shoes, or throwing a ball against a wall. The individual may repeatedly assemble and take apart an object such as a jigsaw puzzle. He may also finger his hair or clothing to the point of pulling out strands or ripping a hole in the cloth.

Amphetamine also causes users to talk more than usual, and they talk about many different and odd topics. At first the individual will appear simply to be excited, but he will talk so fast that it becomes very difficult to understand him. He may jump from subject to subject in such a way that the discussion makes no sense at all and keep talking until he is interrupted.

Table 7

Effect of Benzedrine Sulphate on Reading, Multiplying, and Analogies Scores.		
	BENZEDRINE GROUP MEANS	SUGAR GROUP MEANS
Words read per minute	458.0	453.0
Seconds required to multiply six problems of four-place digits	368.0	318.0
Number of analogies attempted	24.4	22.9
Number of analogies correct	19.2	18.3
Percentage of accuracy for analogies	79.0	82.0

SOURCE: Charles D. Flory and Jane Gilbert, "The effects of benzedrine sulphate and caffeine citrate on the efficiency of college students." J. Appl. Psychol., 27(1943), 122.

Effects of Amphetamine on Performance

The effects of brain stimulation by amphetamine include euphoria, increased alertness, and increased self-esteem and self-confidence. As a result, the individual feels less tired and more capable of thinking clearly. This is one reason students use amphetamine while studying for exams. However, even though amphetamine users think their performance has improved, their mental performance is actually decreased. Under the influence of the drug, a person generally feels good about everything. Students are disappointed, however, when grades do not match their expectations.

Amphetamine improves performance on simple but tedious tasks that do not require a lot of thinking, such as sorting and stapling pages together. Tasks like these can be done faster and with less fatigue after taking amphetamine. The effect depends upon the amount taken. Low doses such as 5 milligrams decrease the need for sleep and the individual may actually be unable to fall asleep for 8 to 10 hours after taking a single 5 to 10 milligram dose of amphetamine.

This effect is often misinterpreted as enhancing mental performance since one can remain awake for longer periods of time. Unfortunately, the work performed during this time is unchallenging and mechanical. It is important to remember that amphetamine interferes with performance involving thought and creativity.

Effects of Amphetamine on Driving

Amphetamine has profound effects on motor vehicle driving performance. The effects are dependent upon the dose of amphetamine taken as well as the simultaneous use of other drugs. It has been shown that alcohol impairs driving ability and that low doses of amphetamine will restore driving performance to normal. This is apparently because alcohol, a depressant of brain activity, impairs driving performance even at low doses due to a mental clouding and a decrease in reaction time. Amphetamine, when given to a person who has taken alcohol, reverses these effects by stimulating the brain. The driver becomes more alert and his reaction time is restored to normal. This effect of amphetamine on driving performance after drinking does not occur in all people and only occurs after specific doses of alcohol and amphetamine are given. Thus, people who are driving should not attempt to counteract the effects of alcohol with amphetamine. The best thing to do in such a case is to avoid driving until the effects of the alcohol have worn off.

Amphetamine has also been used by drivers who are fatigued from lack of sleep. The use of the drug to ward off fatigue has been a major problem for truck drivers, who typically drive long distances without stopping to rest. Amphetamine may help maintain alertness for a short period of time, but a person can go only so long without sleep, regardless of any drug that he may be taking. Eventually the person will not only become fatigued, despite the amphetamine, but his judgment will be grossly impaired as well. This is frequently a cause of accidents among truck drivers

Amphetamine may give a driver a sense of confidence, but this is often a distortion of actual mental competence. Euphoria and elation, masking slow reaction time and improper judgment, can lead to fatal accidents.

and others who drive for long periods under the influence of amphetamine. Therefore, it is not recommended for the sleepy driver. The effects of amphetamine taken alone can be very dangerous. Because of the euphoria and exaggerated sense of self-confidence the drug causes, the user is much more likely to take risks. This is particularly dangerous while driving a motor vehicle. For example, there are numerous cases of people under the influence of amphetamine being hit by trains while driving an automobile because they were convinced that they could beat the train.

In conclusion, there is no justification for taking amphetamine while driving. If the driver is in a mentally fatigued state, whether due to alcohol, some other depressant drug, or lack of sleep, he should get the sleep he needs and allow the effects of the other drug to wear off before resuming

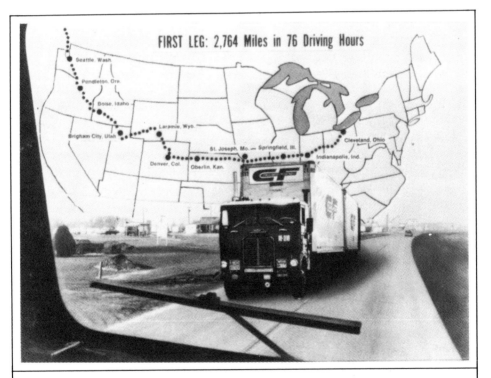

Occupational pressures often demand that truck drivers go for long periods without sleep. While initially amphetamine does improve the user's performance of simple tasks, it has little effect on the user's emotional and intellectual functioning during a crisis.

Table 8

Behavioral and Psychological Effects of Amphetamine	
Increased physical activity	Increased performance on simple, tedious tasks
Anxiety	Impaired performance on tasks involving creativity
Repetitive movements	Impaired driving ability (at high doses)
Talkativeness	Increased sexual desire (at low doses)
Euphoria	Impaired sexual performance (at high doses)
Increased alertness	Irritability
Increased self-esteem	Slurred speech
Increased confidence	Enhanced reflexes
Insomnia	

driving. Amphetamine increases the probability of having an accident by producing euphoria and increasing the willingness to take risks in an individual who is not already tired.

Amphetamine's Effects on Sexual Performance

There are a number of fallacies concerning amphetamine as an aphrodisiac (sexual stimulant). Scientists have found that the effects of amphetamine on sexual desire and activity depend on the dosage. When people consumed low doses they reported a stimulant-like euphoria and an enhanced desire for sex. Men experienced erections for longer periods and delayed ejaculations, while women reported an enhanced desire for sex and variable effects on their ability to achieve orgasm. Higher doses of amphetamine consistently disrupted sexual function. Men's ability to maintain an erection and the ability of both sexes to have an orgasm decreased. This indicates that amphetamine increases sexual drive at low doses, but decreases sensation at higher doses.

A second factor in determining the drug's effect on sexual function is whether the amphetamine is taken orally or intravenously. This finding is complicated by the fact that intravenous users typically take higher doses. In some individuals the more intense high resulting from intravenous injection of amphetamine seemed to take the place of sexual desire. In rare cases where both partners were injecting amphetamine, all sexual activity, and even physical contact, decreased dramatically. Others have reported that they participated in sexual activities they did not usually practice when they were drug-free, such as group sex, sexual marathons, or homosexual acts.

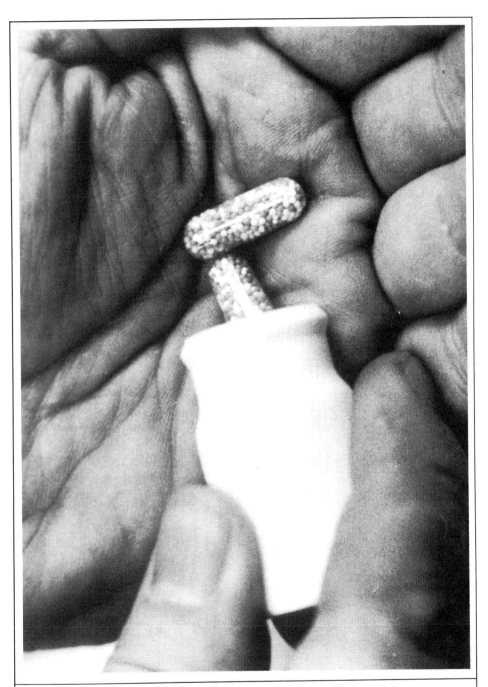

Research has shown that amphetamine, sometimes dispensed in capsules containing hundreds of colorful and harmless-looking globules, can cause constriction and/or deterioration of small blood vessels, which, if the effects are massive and in the brain, can lead to a stroke.

CHAPTER 4

THE EFFECTS OF AMPHETAMINE ON THE BRAIN AND BODY

*T*he brain is composed of specialized cells called neurons. These neurons are grouped in specific patterns and locations and function as relay stations which regulate the various activities of the body. The different areas of the brain are interconnected by a complex array of neuronal axons. Messages are transmitted by electrical impulses along these axons. Upon reaching the end of an axon the message is transferred chemically to the next neuron. This process is depicted in Figure 1. It is this alternating electrical-chemical system which transports a message from one part of the brain to another.

The chemicals used in this process are called neurotransmitters because they transmit or communicate between neurons. About 30 different types of neurotransmitters have been found in the brain. The chemicals most important in producing the effects of amphetamine in the brain are noradrenalin and dopamine. When amphetamine comes in contact with the axon terminal an excess of these chemicals is released, causing a stronger response or effect. Since amphet-

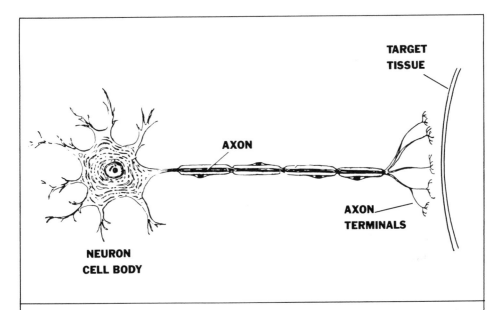

Figure 1. *Drawing of a neuron. Electrical activity is generated within the cell body and transmitted down the axon to the axon terminals. Here, in response to the electrical signal, the neurotransmitter, a chemical substance, crosses the synaptic gap to the target tissue.*

amine is slowly inactivated by the body, it takes longer for the extra noradrenalin or dopamine to be inactivated, resulting in a longer effect.

Amphetamine modifies the actions of these two neurotransmitters which are normally found in neurons and body tissues. Noradrenalin and dopamine are essential for the proper functioning of the brain and other organs.

Amphetamine's Effects on Heart and Blood Vessels

The effects of amphetamine on the heart and blood vessels depend upon the dose taken. After small doses of 5 to 10 milligrams of amphetamine, blood pressure is increased. The elevated blood pressure is sensed by the brain, which in turn sends signals to the heart causing it to beat more slowly. Doses of amphetamine greater than 25 milligrams act directly on the heart to increase the rate and force of contraction. It is this effect that many individuals identify as a pounding of their heart. Irregular heart beats can also occur, but usually only after high doses such as 100 milligrams.

Extremely high doses of amphetamine can cause permanent damage to the blood vessels in the brain.

Other Effects of Amphetamine

Amphetamine can also cause dilated pupils, dry mouth, increased breathing rate, and increased use of the body's stored energy. These signs may help to identify an individual who is using amphetamine. The most obvious sign is dilated pupils, which at times may be so open as to look as if they

Because amphetamine causes pupil dilation, users are often extremely sensitive to light and compensate by wearing sunglasses, even indoors. Actor John Belushi, who was given to every kind of excess, died of a drug overdose in 1984.

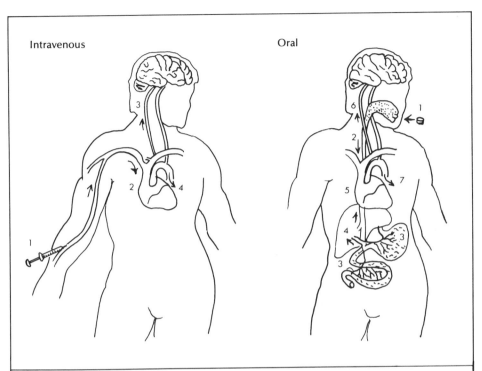

Figure 2. *Comparison of intravenous and oral ingestion of a drug. Intravenous: The drug is injected directly into a vein (1) and travels to the heart (2) where it is pumped into the arteries and carried to the brain (3) or the rest of the body (4). Oral: The drug is taken by mouth (1) and travels down the esophagus (2) to the stomach (3) or intestines. It is then absorbed into the bloodstream and travels to the liver (4) and the heart (5). From here it is pumped to the brain (6) and the rest of the body (7).*

might pop out. Since they are so open, more light enters the eye. As a result, the individual becomes very sensitive to every kind of light. Many amphetamine users compensate by wearing sunglasses not only during the day, but at night as well. The dilated pupils sometimes cause blurred vision. An increased breathing rate is not nearly as noticeable since it is often easy to attribute this to the person's increased level of activity. The increased use of the body's energy stores affects the user by "thinning" the body. In time the individual can lose up to 20% of his normal body weight. This effect, however, does not occur with everyone. The effects of amphetamine on the body are summarized in Table 9.

Table 9

Physical Effects of Amphetamine	
Increased blood pressure	Dry mouth
Increased heart rate	Headache
Increased body temperature	Nausea
Irregular heart beats	Vomiting
Increased breathing rate	Blurred vision
Damage to blood vessels	Increased blood sugar
Dilation of pupils of the eyes	Sores and abscesses on the skin (from intravenous use)
Increased use of energy	Decreased pain sensitivity
Weight loss	Salivation (at high doses)

Detecting Amphetamine in Body Fluids

The exact amount of amphetamine in the body can be measured by a urine or blood sample. The results can be used in four basic areas: research, treatment, identifying drug abusers, and law enforcement.

Once a drug enters the bloodstream, it moves about in basically the same way, regardless of how it was taken. The only difference between taking a tablet and injecting the drug is that the tablet must pass through the stomach and intestines before it reaches the bloodstream. An injected drug enters the bloodstream directly. The passage of a tablet through the system is shown in Figure 2. Once swallowed, it travels to the stomach where it dissolves. It is then absorbed by the lining of the stomach or passes into the intestines where it is absorbed into small blood vessels. From here the drug is transported to the liver, which functions mainly to degrade chemicals and prepare them for excretion. After acting on the brain and body, about 30% of a dose of amphetamine is metabolized to inactive compounds. The rest is excreted unchanged in the urine.

After passing through the liver, amphetamine reaches the heart, which sends it out to all of the body's organs. Amphetamine injected intravenously goes directly to the heart and to the rest of the body. This accounts for the rapid onset of effects. Most amphetamine will go to the brain and heart, causing the various effects described earlier. The amphetamine is eventually transported to the kidneys where it is separated from the blood and enters into the urine.

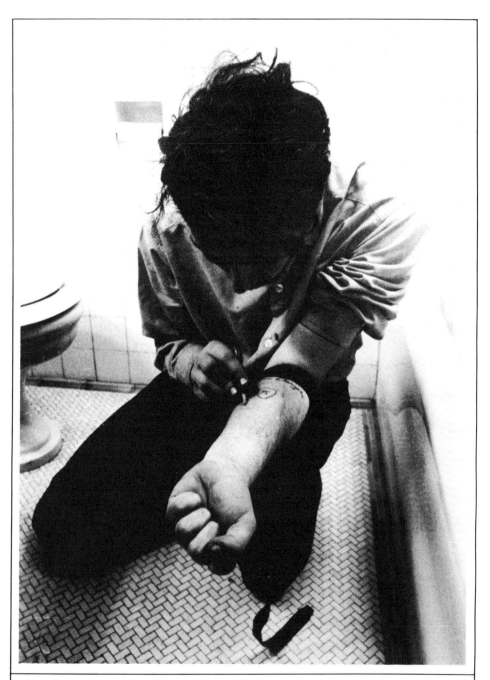

Amphetamine was first injected intravenously by American servicemen in Korea and Japan during the early 1950s. After the Korean War the custom was introduced into the United States, though it was not seen as a problem until it became widespread in the 1960s.

CHAPTER 5

ADDICTION TO AMPHETAMINE

*T*he term tolerance refers to a state in which the same dose of a drug no longer produces the effect it did initially. In order to achieve the original effect, the dose must be increased. If a person continues to take amphetamine, tolerance develops to a higher dose. Thus a cyclic pattern of drug-taking is set in motion.

Tolerance to amphetamine represents a decreased sensitivity to the drug, though it is important to remember that tolerance does not develop equally to all its effects. In fact, the degree of certain effects never decreases even after weeks and months of drug use. Tolerance appears to develop to the euphoria and feelings of well-being produced by amphetamine. The amphetamine abuser may systematically increase his dose 50 to 100 times the initial dose over a period of time for a more intense effect. Tolerance to the adverse effects of amphetamine on the heart definitely occurs. People who do not take amphetamine could not possibly survive a dose of the drug that the amphetamine abuser typically takes.

The mechanisms for tolerance are complex and not completely understood but mostly reflect changes in the neurons in the brain or enzymes in the liver. Initially, a

certain dose of amphetamine will cause a particular number of neurons to be activated. After repeated exposure to the same dose of amphetamine, hardly any of these neurons are activated. If the dose is then increased the original response is regained.

Addiction and Withdrawal

Addiction is sometimes associated with tolerance, but not always. Addiction refers to the body's need for a drug in order to function properly, following continuous use of that drug. If the drug is withdrawn, then various behavioral and physical disturbances occur which together are called the withdrawal syndrome. Under most circumstances, these withdrawal symptoms end completely and abruptly when the drug is readministered.

The classical physical signs of heroin withdrawal—abdominal pain, cramps, muscle weakness, nausea and vomiting—are not always observed, even in heroin addicts.

Drug addiction includes an endless cycle of highs and lows, craving and satisfaction. Even after an addict has lost the craving for amphetamine for as long as 15 years, if even a small amount is ingested the addiction may continue at its previous advanced stage.

Since there are different degrees of addiction, withdrawal symptoms can range from mild discomfort and inability to sleep to some of the more severe reactions listed above.

Addiction to amphetamine is not as obvious as with some other drugs. The degree of discomfort can vary over a wide range from a mildly unpleasant feeling to an over-whelmingly powerful need for more of the drug. The signs of mild amphetamine addiction are often mistaken for sim-ple enthusiasm or poor judgment. In fact, many individuals conceal their addiction from friends or relatives by attribut-ing their behavior to overwork, temporary irritation, or an upcoming cold. It is the overall pattern of the amphet-amine abuser's behavior that will identify him.

At the other extreme are those so addicted to amphet-amine that they exhibit signs of mental illness such as psychosis, attempted suicide, and other antisocial behavior. Unfortunately, these signs indicate a problem so severe that complete recovery, even with excellent health care, is difficult.

Judy Garland, screen and television star who first gained fame as Dorothy in The Wizard of Oz, *began taking amphetamines to combat her weight problem. However, her need to use barbiturates for sleep created a poly-drug syndrome which finally led to severe depression and suicide.*

Thus, the importance of recognizing the early signs of amphetamine abuse cannot be overemphasized.

With newer techniques, it has been possible to identify an amphetamine withdrawal syndrome. These signs include increased sleepiness that persists for weeks after "crashing," enhanced appetite, and abnormalities in the electrical activity of the brain as determined by an analysis of the EEG (electroencephalogram, or brain wave pattern).

During the initial phase of withdrawal the individual may sleep almost continuously for up to three days. Since this is a natural response to the prolonged periods of intense stimulation induced by amphetamine abuse, it should not be interrupted. A state of depression then follows which may last for more than two weeks. During this time the individ-

An amphetamine user's mood varies, depending on whether he or she is high or coming down. During the "crash," the heavy user may be irritable and selfish, argumentative over insignificant matters, and even violent.

ual is irritable, apathetic, and experiences episodes of anxiety, extreme fears, and obsessions. Sleep disturbances, depression, and apathy may persist for months. Unlike opiate (for example, heroin) addiction, the symptoms of withdrawal from amphetamine are usually not relieved by taking more amphetamine.

An additional hazard to amphetamine abusers is that typically they begin using alcohol or other depressants such as barbiturates in order to mitigate the overstimulation produced by the amphetamine. This practice of using amphetamine during the day and depressants at night can very quickly develop into what is called poly-drug abuse. This is particularly dangerous because the potential for drug interactions and overdoses is increased and addiction to the depressant can easily develop.

In conclusion, repeated use of amphetamine results in tolerance to the drug. When tolerance develops the user will increase the dose to obtain the desired effects. The higher dose of amphetamine produces stronger tolerance, and the cycle continues. Eventually the person becomes addicted to the drug and will experience serious withdrawal symptoms when use of the drug is stopped.

In one experiment a rhesus monkey self-administered amphetamine directly into a vein by pressing a lever. The drug had a reinforcing effect and thus strengthened the lever-pushing behavior. Studies such as this help us to understand amphetamine craving and addiction.

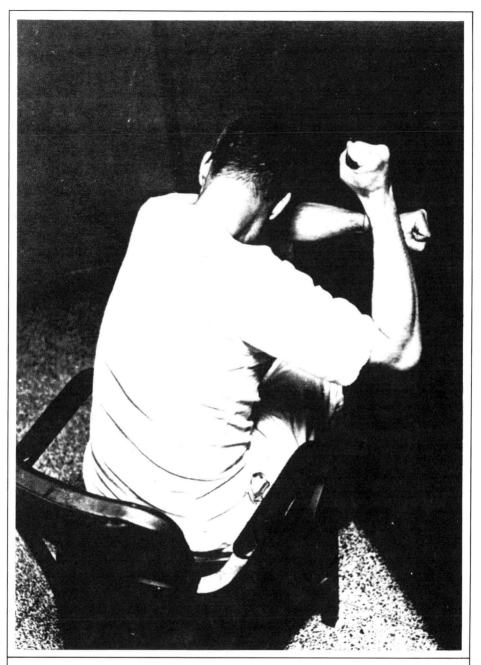

Paranoid psychosis, which can result from a single large dose or chronic moderate doses of amphetamine, is characterized by feelings of persecution and omnipotence, and the sense that people are talking behind one's back. Unlike paranoid schizophrenics, the "speed freak" is usually aware that these feelings are drug induced.

CHAPTER 6

AMPHETAMINE PSYCHOSIS

A chronic amphetamine user develops physical, mental, and behavioral signs of toxicity, or harmful effects of the drug. His general health and personal hygiene deteriorate, and, if he is an intravenous user, he will exhibit track marks from needles, infections, and abscesses. Behavioral signs of amphetamine toxicity include nervousness, irritability, and restlessness due to the almost constant overstimulation the drug provides. This leads to stereotypic compulsive behavior, exemplified by the common tendency among amphetamine users to spend hours taking an object apart, sorting out the pieces, and then putting them back together again. When these chronic users are not dismantling something, they are pacing back and forth across the room. During conversation they tend to analyze ideas in a stern but repetitious manner.

The more extreme manifestation of toxicity is a state of paranoia called amphetamine psychosis. During this phase of toxicity the individual becomes suspicious of everyone and thinks that people are "out to get him." He is physically exhausted and will appear to be confused. At any moment he may become violent and physically injure himself or someone around him. If the abuse pattern persists, he may suffer hallucinations and delusions and could easily be mistaken for a paranoid schizophrenic. These hallucinations tend to differ from those induced by LSD in that a person on

LSD typically is aware that his "visions" are being caused by a drug.

The individual who is intoxicated with amphetamine cannot be convinced that a drug is responsible for his perceptions. The paranoia he displays appears identical to that observed in schizophrenia. Other behavioral aspects of amphetamine psychosis include heightened awareness, curiosity, and an overwhelming fear or terror.

Amphetamine-Induced Hallucinations

Most people experiencing amphetamine psychosis report both auditory and visual hallucinations. It is this feature which indicates that the condition is not due to LSD or paranoid schizophrenia. Psychedelic drugs such as LSD usually produce lucid visual displays without sound. The hallucinations of the paranoid schizophrenic are generally confined to voices and other sounds. Amphetamine psychosis pro-

The paranoid speed freak may feel that he or she has been cheated of his or her drug. With a gun under the jacket and unable to accurately identify the imagined culprit, addicts have been known to run through the streets terrifying innocent people.

duces similar auditory hallucinations, most often appearing as vague noises and voices. Occasionally, the individual will actually have a conversation with the voices.

One particularly unique feature of amphetamine psychosis is the occurrence of tactile hallucinations. This means that the individual may believe that he has worms or lice on his body, or he may "feel" small animals brushing against him. In more severe cases, the person says that he can "feel" the amphetamine crystals under his skin. His constant picking and scratching can result in numerous sores which can easily become infected. Some sufferers have taken knives or razor blades and severely cut their skin in an attempt to remove the offensive organisms.

The confusion between paranoid schizophrenia and amphetamine psychosis began in the 1950s. Numerous case reports have verified cases in which people were hospitalized and treated for schizophrenia for up to three years

Though a person might seek a safe amusement park ride to satisfy a desire for controlled terror, in cases of extreme amphetamine psychosis one may experience uncontrolled terror and feelings of persecution. One man claimed that he was being watched, that searchlights were always focused on his bedroom, and that cars were following him to and from work.

when, in fact, they had been ingesting amphetamine all the time in the hospital, prolonging their psychosis. At the time electroshock therapy and insulin coma therapy were widely used to manage schizophrenics yet these measures had little effect on amphetamine-induced psychosis.

Cause of Amphetamine Psychosis

It was once believed that because psychosis occurs after chronic heavy use of amphetamine, the psychosis may be due to lack of sleep, overstimulation, or the uncovering of an existing schizophrenic state. Recent scientific studies have demonstrated that amphetamine psychosis can be induced in approximately four days in human volunteers. All people developed the same basic symptoms. The people were carefully screened to exclude anyone with a history of psychosis. Only one night's sleep was lost in a few subjects, and therefore it does not seem likely that loss of sleep is the cause of the amphetamine-induced psychosis.

In some cases a person suffering amphetamine psychosis will be hospitalized after an unsuccessful suicide attempt. It is critical that the proper diagnosis be made at this time. A urinalysis will detect the presence of amphetamine, and if the patient is kept off the drug, the psychosis usually disappears within a week. If the patient is mistaken for a paranoid

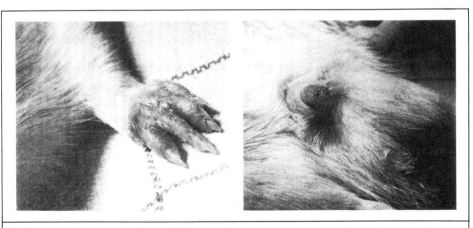

In experiments, rats self-administering amphetamine often chew on their own bodies. Human abusers may develop dermatitis from unconsciously rubbing, picking, and digging at their hands and faces.

schizophrenic and continues to take amphetamine in the hospital, then his condition will persist.

It is important to emphasize that all of the drugs in the stimulant class *including* cocaine can produce psychosis. The ease with which tolerance, addiction, or toxicity develops is determined by a number of factors. These include the amount of drug taken at a given time, the method by which it is taken, and frequency of use. Taking 5 milligrams of amphetamine once a week does not pose a serious drug threat to one's health. Unfortunately, because the drug's psychological effects are so intense and pleasurable, very few people who try them have the self-control to maintain a once-a-week pattern of use.

In a Cleveland hospital, the first prescription computer system was designed to identify customers with drug abuse records. A system such as this would make it difficult for a drug user to fill various doctors' prescriptions for the same drug.

In the 1967 Tour de France, which involved a precipitous 6,000-foot climb in 90-degree heat, bicyclist Tommy Simpson (right) began to zigzag across the road and then collapsed in a coma and died. The autopsy showed that he was heavily drugged with methamphetamine.

CHAPTER 7

OTHER TOXIC EFFECTS OF AMPHETAMINE

When a doctor prescribes a drug for a patient the dose is carefully selected. The drug abuser, on the other hand, can never be sure of either the content of the drug he takes, or the dose. Only relatively low doses of amphetamine produce increased alertness and vigor. Higher doses result in toxic effects which prevail over the more pleasurable ones.

Toxicity from amphetamine can occur after a single dose or after chronic use. The major difficulty in treating amphetamine-induced toxicity is identifying it correctly in the first place. Symptoms of an amphetamine overdose can be mistaken for signs of heroin withdrawal. The clinical signs also differ from person to person. Someone who rarely uses amphetamine will experience more severe toxic effects than a chronic abuser. Very few chronic high-dose intravenous abusers die from amphetamine overdose because their high level of tolerance seems to protect them. The relatively inexperienced user is more likely to take an extremely high fatal dose.

Toxic Effects of a Single Dose of Amphetamine

Acute toxicity refers to those harmful effects occurring after a single, high drug dose. They include severe headaches,

Table 10

Methamphetamine and "Speed" Abuse and Trafficking Indicators					
	1979	1980	1981	1982	1983*
Hospital emergencies reported through the DAWN System** of which:	1,443	2,087	2,552	2,380	1,866
Philadelphia	313	363	466	372	314
San Francisco	58	52	55	132	142
New York	90	384	475	341	137
Detroit	60	87	85	118	104
Los Angeles	22	35	52	82	94
Methamphetamine/"speed" related deaths	30	37	38	40	60
Laboratories seized	136	126	89	133	119
Prices:					
Wholesale (oz.)	—	$900-1,400	$900-1,400	$1,400-1,800	$1,000-2,000
Retail (gm.)	—	$65	$65	$80–100	$60-120

*1983 data regarding hospital emergencies and deaths are provisional.
**Data represent the total DAWN System. The cities listed are the five leading cities based in 1983 Data.

SOURCE: Project DAWN annual reports and DEA enforcement statistics.

excessive sweating, dry mouth, large pupils, a rapid but weak heartbeat, tremors of fingers or hands, rapid breathing, nausea, dizziness, and increased heart rate and blood pressure. When amphetamine is combined with strenuous athletic activity these effects can be seen after much lower doses.

Death from acute overdose is usually preceded by an elevated body temperature, cardiovascular shock, and convulsions. Amphetamine quickly raises the body temperature by altering the activity in the brain's temperature-regulating center. Also, increased muscle activity generates heat that remains in the body and raises its temperature. A moderate dose of amphetamine during strenuous physical activity in hot weather will cause heat exhaustion and even heat stroke. Amphetamine intoxication can also cause hemorrhage of blood vessels, especially in the brain, due to high blood pressure. This can be fatal or, at very least, cause a stroke which may leave the individual permanently paralyzed.

While amphetamine psychosis usually occurs only after chronic high doses, as discussed in Chapter 6, there have been a few occasions in which individuals have experienced hallucinations followed by a paranoid attack after a single large dose of amphetamine.

Treatment for Amphetamine Overdose

In cases of acute amphetamine overdose, treatment aims to decrease the body temperature, control the convulsions, and remove the amphetamine from the body. The patient is usually placed in a cold water bath or a full body ice pack. The convulsions seem to be associated with the high body temperature and are treated with Valium. If the drug was taken in pill forms, pumping the stomach may help to reduce the amount of amphetamine that reaches the bloodstream. However, this must be done relatively soon after the drug is taken. As a final measure, the excretion of amphetamine can be speeded up by making the urine more acidic.

After such treatment, the patient should be moved to a quiet, dimly lit room to prevent any noise or stimulation from adding to his agitation.

Amphetamine and Violent Behavior

The earliest reports of amphetamine-related violence appeared in the late 1950s when abuse of the drug became widespread in California. Amphetamine was available by legal prescription and was relatively cheap. As intravenous use of amphetamine grew, so did its reputation for producing bizarre, violent behavior. Law enforcement officials were able to eliminate the legal sources of amphetamine by 1963. This resulted in an illicit market, complete with backyard chemists who found the drug easy to make and the ingredients easy to find.

Speed, as it is sometimes called, was used by large groups of people in "flash houses." Intravenous use was popular at these gatherings, and the usual practice was for the "speed freak" to inject himself with a high dose which brought on delusions and paranoia. Many of these drug abusers carried weapons and incidents of senseless violence were common.

Most members of this group engaged in armed robbery, drug dealing, and homosexual prostitution to obtain money. They stole speed from each other or tried "burning" a fellow user by selling him the drug in heavily diluted form. In some cases another substance such as cleaning powder was passed off as speed. These acts, once discovered, provoked swift retaliation. During the first three months of

1968, the crime statistics for the Haight-Ashbury district in San Francisco were staggering: 17 homicides and scores of assaults, robberies, shootings and knifings, forced drug overdoses, and gang rapes.

This violent behavior was not unique to those who used amphetamine intravenously. High-dose oral use also resulted in aggression which often victimized innocent bystanders. Numerous well-publicized cases of multiple homicides or shooting sprees have been studied in an effort to determine the factors that led the killer to act out his amphetamine-induced delusions. Certain personality traits, poor impulse control, unstable social adjustment, and a criminal history all indicate the potential for violence which is enhanced by the use of amphetamine.

Unexpected Toxic Reactions

The buyer of amphetamine or cocaine can never be sure what he is getting. Recent studies have shown that the typical bag sold on the street as cocaine is only 5 to 15% cocaine. Amphetamine samples have varied in their purity from a high of 55 to 60% in the early 1970s to about 12 to 15% since 1975. The rest of the sample is made up of either active drugs or inactive fillers. The most common active drug substitutes include caffeine, ephedrine, dyphenhydramine, barbiturates, phentermine, iron, diethylpropion, and theophylline. Other substances found include acetaminophen, pemoline, atropine, and methapyrilene. Occasionally vitamins, strychnine, benzocaine, procaine, and diphenylhydantoin are added to the drug.

Sometimes fillers called dilutants are added to drugs. Typically, they are sugars. These compounds are inactive and are not dangerous to the individual. The more filler present, the less active drug there is. This is a common complaint among drug users.

One risk of taking "amphetamine" of unknown content is that the individual will have an allergic reaction to one of the compounds in the mixture. When this occurs it can be fatal. The early signs of an allergic reaction include redness of skin, sweating, fever, and sometimes local swelling, especially if the drug was injected. The symptoms progress rapidly and include a tightness in the chest, runny nose, and difficulty in breathing. In extreme reactions, the trachea will

close off completely, preventing air from reaching the lungs and causing death by suffocation. The entire response can occur within only a few minutes or over a few hours, so the afflicted person must be taken to an emergency room at the first sign of symptoms. Since the mechanism of the allergic response is due to a massive release of histamine in the body, antihistamines will usually help.

Injection of the drug can cause a different toxic reaction. The sale and distribution of hypodermic needles and syringes are restricted to hospitals and pharmacies, so it is difficult for the amphetamine user to obtain sterile needles. When the hypodermic needle first became a widespread method for administering drugs, the needles were usually made of very thick stainless steel and the syringes of finely ground glass. After each use, the pieces were separated and then sterilized for use again until they wore out. This practice has been abandoned for the safer and more economical method of using disposable needles and syringes. The syringes are made of plastic and the needles are made of very thin steel so that the needle diameter is much smaller, decreasing the discomfort of an injection. These changes in

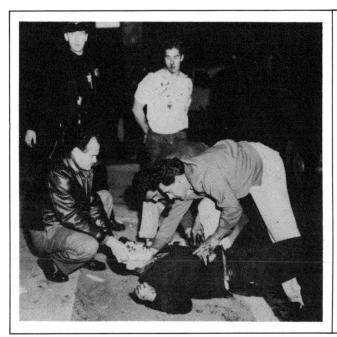

Though working within the black-market environment feeds the speed freak's paranoia, mixing speed and barbiturates which decrease inhibitions and produce surliness and aggressiveness can produce highly irrational and violent behavior.

the hypodermic needle make it difficult to reuse the syringe and needle. The point of the needles becomes dull quickly and is easily bent. Hospitals have special devices which destroy all needles and syringes to prevent them from falling into the hands of drug abusers.

Obtaining a fresh needle and syringe for each injection is virtually impossible, especially if the abuser is involved in an amphetamine "run," that is, injecting every few hours for days. When a drug is taken orally, any foreign particles, dirt, or bacteria are usually destroyed by the strong acids and enzymes in the stomach. This is not the case when a drug is injected. It is for this reason that infections occur so frequently, ranging from local abscesses under the skin that appear as hard lumps to more dangerous infections of the liver (hepatitis) or the inside of the heart (endocarditis).

Amphetamine and Pregnancy

Women of child-bearing age who use amphetamine have a special concern. Many women, especially teenagers, do not suspect they are pregnant until they miss a menstrual period, and even then the woman may discount the missed period as simply an irregularity. Drugs often have disruptive effects on the menstrual cycle.

During the early stage of pregnancy the embryo grows and develops quickly. Any disturbance during this phase can

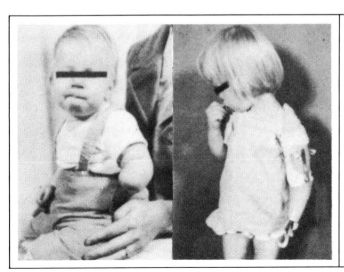

In 1962 the British Medical Journal *published the case history of a woman who, after taking Preludin (an amphetamine-like drug prescribed for obesity) for the first six weeks of pregnancy, delivered a child with one hand and deformities of the lower limbs.*

lead to embryotoxicity, malformations, and a number of less serious abnormalities in the offspring. The fetus is also vulnerable to drugs because it is so small and the drug dose is proportionally large. The liver has not developed enough to inactivate the drug so exposure is increased. The effects of amphetamine on the fetus are irreversible. Stopping the drug one or two months after conception will not undo the damage.

People might assume that once a woman discovers that she is pregnant she will stop abusing drugs. This assumption is false. A surprisingly large number of women continue to take amphetamine and other drugs throughout their pregnancy.

In a study done in Sweden in 1981 the effects of amphetamine abuse were investigated in 69 pregnant women. The women were divided into two groups: those who stopped using amphetamine early in their pregnancy (Group I) and those who continued to take amphetamine (Group II). Only 25% of the women fell into Group I while 75% were in Group II. Those women who continued to take amphetamine had 25% more premature births and 7.5% more infants who died just before birth and up to four weeks after birth than the women who had stopped taking amphetamine.

All of the babies in Group I remained with their mothers. Forty-six percent of the babies of Group II mothers had to be transferred to pediatric wards for medical or social reasons. These newborns were denied the emotional and physical support of their natural mother during the difficult first weeks of life.

Unfortunately for the children, the consequences of being born to a mother who abused amphetamine did not end at birth. The children of women who stopped taking amphetamine were still with their mothers one year later. One-third of the children born to mothers who continued to take amphetamine throughout their pregnancy had to be transferred to foster homes.

Babies of women who had taken prescribed amphetamine for weight reduction very early in their pregnancy had more oral clefts such as harelips than babies born to mothers who were drug-free. But the toll amphetamine takes on an infant is due not only to the drug itself but to the poor maternal care the child often receives.

Ads for obesity-fighting drugs, such as Tenuate, not only emphasize the need for complete weight-loss programs, which should include drug use, calorie restriction, and counselling, but also warn doctors to avoid addiction in their patients by discontinuing rather than increasing the dosage if tolerance develops.

70

CHAPTER 8

MEDICAL USES OF AMPHETAMINE

Amphetamine was once used widely to treat several ailments. During the 1930s and 1940s, when there was no legislation against it or medical challenge to the unproven claims about the drug, many people assumed it was safe for anyone to use. There are now only three generally accepted medical uses for amphetamine. A well-trained and experienced physician can use it effectively in the short-term treatment of obesity, narcolepsy, and the hyperkinetic syndrome, and in rare cases for depression, pain management, and epilepsy. Regulation of the drug was due primarily to the establishment of the Food and Drug Administration (FDA) and the Drug Enforcement Administration (DEA). Their task is to ensure that drugs are safe and that illegal use and distribution is stopped.

Obesity

The use of amphetamine to treat obesity has been controversial. Certainly an extremely overweight person should receive treatment for obesity if he has high blood pressure, heart disease, or diabetes. Even if he doesn't yet have one of these disorders, obesity is a risk factor for disease and should be treated preventively. But when should someone receive amphetamine for the purpose of weight reduction? The FDA

recommends that amphetamine not be the first choice in the treatment of obesity. Only those who have had no success with alternative methods such as diet, group therapy, and other less harmful drugs which suppress appetite should be treated with amphetamine.

Most scientists agree that the currently available preparations of amphetamine are effective in producing short-term weight loss. The issue, however, is whether long-term use of amphetamine is effective in maintaining lower weight. Even if it is, a drug abuse problem may develop.

Initially, it was believed that no tolerance developed and thus amphetamine could be used to treat obesity over a long period. It is currently felt that when used as prescribed by a physician, amphetamine is effective in reducing food intake and body weight over a one- to two-month period. In most cases, no further reductions in weight are seen and this has been attributed to tolerance.

However, if the patient also receives counseling directed at his eating habits and his emotional state, the weight loss continues for longer periods with no sign of tolerance. It appears that amphetamine may help the obese patient establish new, more restrained eating patterns, but then he must maintain them without the drug.

There are currently a number of drugs other than am-

After recognizing amphetamine's addictive properties and toxic side effects, in 1971 Dr. Charles C. Edwards, commissioner of the Food and Drug Administration, appealed to drug manufacturers and doctors to limit sharply the use of the drug.

phetamine used to suppress appetite. Fenfluramine is perhaps the most popular and appears to remain effective over the long term. Because it does not produce the pleasurable effects of amphetamine it is an unlikely candidate for abuse. But not all individuals respond to fenfluramine, so amphetamine is often used as an alternate treatment. In some cases, a very obese person who is depressed over his inability to lose weight may actually benefit from the euphoria provided by amphetamine during the early treatment stages.

Ultimately, the success of any weight reduction program depends on control of the diet. Without it, both drug and behavioral therapies will fail. Unfortunately, few overweight people are able to adhere to a strict diet program and additional aids are needed. Weight reduction, like any medical treatment, must be tailored for the individual, taking into account his specific needs, limitations, and goals.

Hyperkinesis

The hyperkinetic syndrome, also called minimal brain dysfunction, occurs in children. A short attention span is a telling sign of this condition. The child is constantly moving about, and easily distracted, and is unable to focus his attention for more than a few minutes. As a result, the child has difficulty learning and often acts in socially unacceptable ways. Many hyperkinetic children also experience bouts of drowsiness between episodes.

Amphetamine has the unexpected effect of calming hyperactive children. They become less restless and impulsive, and more aware of their surroundings. They concentrate better and their behavior improves. The most successful programs combine drug treatment with psychotherapy and parent counseling. The treatment of the hyperkinetic syndrome is a long-term process. Once the drug is stopped, the child's performance tends to deteriorate. But because the stress of school seems to aggravate many of the problems, many physicians recommend stopping the treatment over summer vacations, to avoid the adverse side effects frequently encountered.

Tolerance to the calming effects of amphetamine in hyperactive children does not seem to develop. However, children may experience sleep difficulties, headaches, stomach cramps, and irritability, and perhaps excessive crying

and depression. One potentially serious side effect is that children who begin amphetamine treatment at a young age tend to grow more slowly. They are shorter and weigh less than other children of the same age.

Studies have shown that long-term use of amphetamine and other stimulants to treat hyperactivity does not lead to drug abuse. Treatment is usually stopped as the child reaches adolescence, since the symptoms of hyperkinesis tend to disappear at this time.

Narcolepsy

The symptoms of narcolepsy include attacks of severe sleepiness, episodes of lost muscle tone, sleep paralysis, and auditory or visual hallucinations. The attacks of sleepiness occur throughout the day. A person suffering from narcolepsy may fall asleep every few hours and each episode may last 30 minutes. To observers, the sleep appears to occur abruptly, but people who have these attacks report feeling drowsy and falling asleep only after resisting the urge for some time. They awaken feeling refreshed, but within a few hours they become sleepy again.

A sudden, often complete, loss of muscle tone is the second sign of narcolepsy. These episodes occur when the person is fully awake and last a few seconds to a few minutes, varying in frequency from one per week to a dozen per day. The attacks are often precipitated by sudden, strong mood changes and outbursts of laughter, crying, or anger.

Sleep paralysis, the third sign of narcolepsy, is an abrupt loss of muscle tone that occurs when the person is about to fall asleep and lasts only a few seconds to minutes. The paralysis, especially the first few episodes, is a particularly frightening experience and is often accompanied by hallucinations. Touching the person is usually enough stimulation to end the episode.

Another sign of narcolepsy is an hallucination that is described as hypnagogic. This means that the hallucinations are vivid and intense and can be visual, auditory, or tactile. The frequency of these hallucinations among narcoleptics is not well documented, but they are almost always unpleasant.

Amphetamine controls most of these symptoms in narcoleptic patients. However, the drug cannot be used for

long periods of time due to the development of tolerance and consequent need to increase the dose, ultimately leading to toxic side effects.

In conclusion, the usefulness of amphetamine in treating obesity, hyperkinesis, and narcolepsy is limited and these disorders are often better treated by other drugs. Amphetamine is rarely used for the treatment of depression, pain or epilepsy, since better drugs are typically used to treat these conditions.

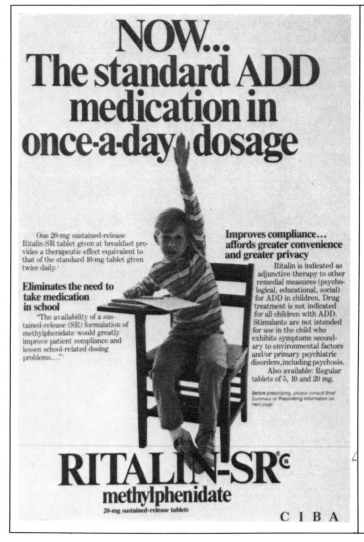
In 1970, according to Dr. Ronald Lipman of the FDA, as many as 200,000 hyperactive children were being treated with stimulants, such as Ritalin. However, a follow-up study of 83 teenagers showed that while 60% exhibited some overall improvement, over 75% still had poor concentration, impulsiveness, and defiance, and 25% were involved in antisocial activities. Low self-esteem, worthlessness, and difficulties with schoolwork also persisted.

Law enforcement and arrests have served mainly to raise prices and thus contribute to the spread of the amphetamine black market.

CHAPTER 9

AMPHETAMINE AND THE LAW

*I*n 1970, Public Law 91-513, known as the Controlled Substances Act, or CSA, was enacted. This law gives the Federal Drug Enforcement Administration (DEA) power to supervise every person who legally handles controlled substances, including about 500,000 physicians, pharmacists, scientists, and drug manufacturers.

Soon after the CSA became law, a comprehensive series of regulations was issued by the former Bureau of Narcotics and Dangerous Drugs. These regulations have been amended hundreds of times as new and different procedures, substances, and exceptions to the rules appear.

Drug Enforcement Administration

The DEA, an agency within the United States Department of Justice, is responsible for enforcement and regulation of the CSA. Its purpose is to prevent the illegal use of controlled substances, and to ensure their use only by legally registered handlers.

The U.S. government has issued the Controlled Substances Handbook for licensed handlers of abusable substances. This handbook contains all the rules and regulations for the proper handling of drugs of abuse. It also contains the drug schedules.

Drug Schedules

The CSA divides drugs into five different lists, or schedules, labeled I–V in order of decreasing potential for abuse. The decision to place a drug in a particular schedule is based largely on data obtained from human and animal experiments. There are, however, other factors involved.

Schedule I.
Drugs belonging to this schedule are characterized as having a high potential for abuse. In general, they are either opiates, opium derivatives, or hallucinogens. These drugs have no currently accepted medical use in the United States, but may be used in research projects or in educational programs. Examples of drugs in this schedule include: heroin, marijuana, and the hallucinogens (peyote, mescaline, psilocybin, and LSD).

Schedule II.
Drugs in this schedule do have some accepted medical use, but have a potential for addiction. Amphetamine and the majority of the amphetamine-related compounds are Schedule II drugs.

Schedule III.
This schedule is made up of preparations that contain limited quantities of certain opioids and non-opioids, and some preparations that contain amphetamines. Abuse of substances in this class may lead to moderate or low addiction.

Schedule IV.
A drug which results in only limited degrees of tolerance and addiction is placed in this schedule. It includes sedative/ hypnotic drugs such as the barbiturates and Valium, as well as drugs such as Darvon.

Schedule V.
Drugs in this schedule have less potential for abuse than those listed above. The preparations contain moderate quantities of certain opioids that are generally used to control coughs or diarrhea. They may be obtained without a prescription provided that they are dispensed by a pharmacist and only a limited amount is provided in any 48-hour period.

A drug's place in the schedule determines its availability for both medical and nonmedical applications. The sched-

ules also indicate the penalty for illegal use, which can range from a mild warning to heavy fines and imprisonment. However, a drug's status in the schedule can change as new information about the drug is discovered.

The information about abuse liability is most often obtained from data by scientists and trends observed in the DAWN data. Not all drugs are thoroughly tested before being placed into one of the schedules. Given the number of drugs and preparations available, this would be impractical. However, if a new drug's basic chemical structure resembles that of a drug known to have potential for abuse, then it may be assumed that the new drug will be similar to the standard drug and should be placed in the same schedule.

These classifications can serve the population as a whole by preventing individuals from obtaining and abusing harmful drugs. Sometimes a potentially valuable drug for treating a disease or symptoms can be incorrectly scheduled, and because of its classification as a controlled substance its usefulness may never be realized. The opioid Temgesic is an excellent example of such a problem. Its pain-killing properties occur at doses below those that cause any significant side effects. In addition, this drug may be quite useful in the treatment of heroin dependence because the addict can be weaned from the drug without abrupt and disturbing with-

During the 1960s Dr. Max Jacobson (left) administered amphetamine to celebrities, such as Tennessee Williams, to lift their moods. These "magic pills," however, may mask serious underlying psychological problems which should be cared for with professional counseling.

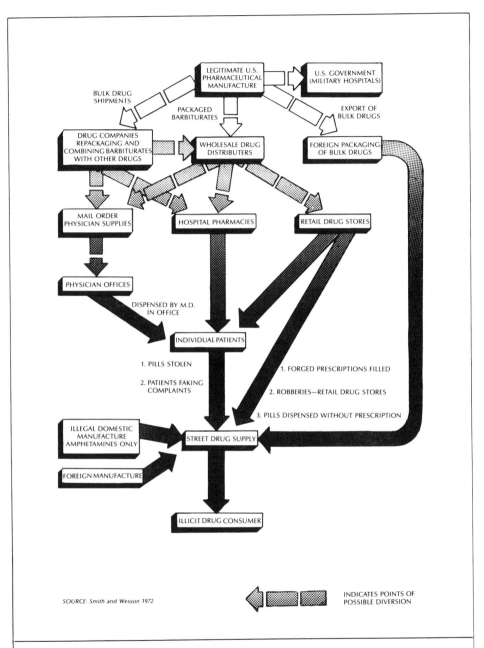

Figure 3. *The complexity of the legitimate and illegitimate distribution routes of amphetamine, complicated by its legal and needed medical use, makes it easy for drug abusers to acquire the drugs yet difficult for federal agents to control successfully the drug traffic.*

drawal effects. There is no way to prevent this type of inconsistent treatment of drugs. However, since drug scheduling is a dynamic process and can change due to new information, improper decisions can be corrected.

The Effect of Scheduling on Amphetamine Abuse

Following the introduction of the drug schedules and subsequent enforcement, there was a decline in the amount of legally manufactured amphetamine and related compounds. The impact of scheduling amphetamine, however, will never be fully known because so many other changes occurred at the same time. An increase in drug education, free evaluation and treatment services, and hotlines, as well as increased law enforcement and increased penalties have all contributed to the decline in amphetamine production.

The schedules provided the legal basis for arresting any unlicensed person for possession, use, and distribution of drugs. Physicians were made to register with the DEA in order to write a prescription for a controlled substance. For doctors, this meant a lot of paperwork and the need for special security systems, both of which contributed to a decrease in the number of prescriptions written for amphetamine. Once the legal sources of amphetamine dwindle, other sources make up for the loss. This is exactly what happened when amphetamine became a Schedule II drug in 1972.

In the 1940s and 1950s there was little need for an illicit market in amphetamines. Legally manufactured tablets could be sold wholesale at a price of about fourteen pills per penny—a staggering 75 cents per thousand. Once amphetamine was scheduled, the door was opened for a profitable illicit market. Illegal laboratories ranged from one-room operations producing an ounce or two of amphetamine per week to full-scale, highly organized groups producing 25 pounds per week. The illegal amphetamine quickly filled the void created by the scarcity of legally produced amphetamine. Around this time, many people began to use cocaine and other stimulants such as Ritalin.

The Effect of Scheduling on the Practice of Medicine

When the CSA Handbook was first released, amphetamine and related drugs were placed in Schedule III. In 1971, with the support of the American Medical Association, these drugs

81

were transferred to the more stringent Schedule II category. In 1978 the following statement was issued by the Council on Scientific Affairs:

> When administering drugs of the amphetamine type for any medical reason ... the physician should weigh their therapeutic efficacy against the disadvantages of abuse.
>
> The physician should be especially alert to aspects of his patient's current and past behavior that indicate risk of substance abuse or drug [addiction]. Dosages should be set as low as possible, the duration of therapy kept as short as possible, and drug holidays provided as often as possible. There is always the chance that the efficacy of a stimulant in helping a patient achieve a therapeutic goal may predispose him to look upon amphetamine-type drugs as desirable rather than hazardous substances, and open the door for future drug abuse.

Amphetamine abuse was lower during the first two years after its reclassification in Schedule II, but a significant amphetamine problem still exists. The FDA is considering a proposal to prohibit amphetamine use in the treatment of obesity, since four out of every five prescriptions are written for this purpose. It is doubtful that such an action would seriously affect the level of abuse, since most of the current sources are illegal laboratories and foreign suppliers. Though a small minority of physicians called "script doctors" sell prescriptions for a profit, amphetamine abuse seldom occurs when the drug is prescribed for a therapeutic reason.

One argument in favor of the proposal is that if amphetamine is no longer used to treat obesity, production could be reduced by 80%, which would significantly limit the script doctor's supply. Black market prices might very well become so high that the demand for amphetamine would disappear. Unfortunately, Canada tried such an action and soon discovered that abuse of numerous amphetamine-like compounds rose.

In the author's opinion, physicians should not be prohibited from prescribing amphetamine for obesity. Some people may need a weight reduction program built around a

strong, effective drug. For them, amphetamine may be the only hope. What is truly needed is better education for the practicing physician and more stringent laws to identify and inactivate the script doctor. In this environment, the risks associated with amphetamine would be lessened.

Attitudes and Knowledge about Amphetamines

The history of amphetamine abuse indicates that "scare tactics" are ineffective. While a national policy on drug abuse is necessary, it is not sufficient. The specific problems of each individual community must be addressed. Parents, teachers, and local officials need to be involved and educated as much as teenagers and pre-teens.

There are national, state, and local policies that have made drug abuse even more dangerous than it would be otherwise. One result of scheduling is an economic environ-

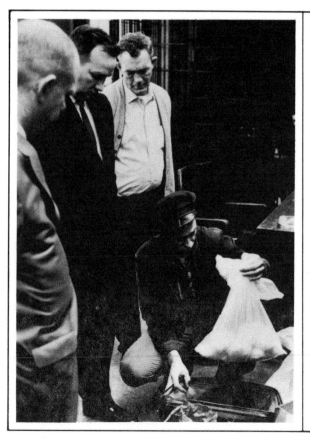

The federal Drug Enforcement Administration (DEA) often uses undercover agents to track down and arrest users, distributors, and manufacturers of amphetamines. Here an agent examines 300,000 pills confiscated during a single arrest.

ment that supports illegal laboratories, in which the quality, purity, and content of the amphetamine preparations are unregulated. The penalties for selling adulterated drugs are no different from selling the very pure products that have been diverted from legitimate sources.

The law that makes the sale or possession of hypodermic needles a criminal offense leads to the dangerous practice of using and sharing nonsterile needles, causing widespread outbreaks of hepatitis and other potentially fatal infections. Unfortunately, many policies intended to deter drug abuse have failed.

Drug abuse is regarded by many as a disease. The pain, tragedy, and severity of endogenous depression cannot be appreciated by those who have never experienced it. Psychiatric illnesses such as depression are terribly difficult to live

Over-the-counter drugs such as NoDoz are sold as wake-up potions in gas stations, drugstores, and supermarkets. Containing concentrated doses of caffeine, 10 tablets, equal to about seven to 10 cups of coffee, are enough to cause acute toxicity, which may include mild delirium, insomnia, restlessness, excitement, and ringing in the ears.

with. For some, drug abuse may be an attempt to relieve the signs and symptoms of these disorders. But is amphetamine too effective? Does it reverse the depression so well that the user will ruin his health in the quest for a never-ending high?

Of course, not everyone who tries amphetamine ends up an addict. But drug abuse is also an economic issue. First, the drug abuser has difficulty in keeping a job and being productive. This can have serious consequences in families where money is tight and everyone is expected to help. When a family member abuses drugs to the exclusion of everything else, it can cause a great deal of resentment and tension at home.

On the national scale, amphetamine abuse is not very significant when compared to the abuse of alcohol and tobacco. These two drugs alone account for more loss of life, damage of property, and misery than all of the so-called "hard" drugs combined. But alcohol and tobacco are backed by powerful agricultural industries. These industries provide many jobs and federal, state, and local governments receive much needed revenues from taxes on the sale of these products. The drug laws we have may be necessary, but one should not lose sight of the double standard society promotes by outlawing some drugs and embracing others.

Summary

Amphetamine is a synthetic drug that causes considerable stimulation of the brain. It was once recommended for the treatment of a wide variety of medical disorders. Today, however, its only three recognized medical uses are for the treatment of obesity, hyperkinesis in children, and narcolepsy. Amphetamine is widely abused because of its potent psychological effects: it produces euphoria or a "high," increases self-esteem, self-confidence, and alertness. The drug can improve performance on repetitive, tedious tasks, but interferes with thought and creativity. Repeated usage of amphetamine results in tolerance and addiction. If the drug is taken away from an addicted person, a withdrawal syndrome appears. The acute and chronic effects of amphetamine can be life-threatening. One of the most serious of these effects is the development of psychosis. Long-term use of amphetamine may also result in permanent damage to the brain and other organs of the body.

APPENDIX 1

AMPHETAMINE-RELATED PREPARATIONS

There are a number of compounds which are related to amphetamine—that is, they have similar properties. There may be differences in the degree of brain stimulation or appetite suppressant activity, but they are not dramatic enough to warrant choosing one drug over the other. A brief description of these preparations follows. All of these drugs are Schedule II compounds unless indicated otherwise. Manufacturers are listed in parentheses after the trade name.

Amphetamine

Amphetamine is marketed under the trade name of Obetrol (Rexan). Dextroamphetamine, the more active form of amphetamine, is marketed as simply Dextroamphetamine Sulfate (Rexan) and as Dexedrine (Smith, Kline & French). Dexedrine can be prescribed as a 5 milligram, heart-shaped, yellow, uncoated tablet, as a Spansule, sustained, release capsule, or as a liquid. The tablets are stamped with the manufacturer's initials and product code "SKF E19." The capsules contain either 5, 10, or 15 milligrams of dextroamphetamine and the liquid contains 5 milligrams and 10% alcohol in each dose of 5 milliliters. Approved uses include treatment of narcolepsy, hyperkinesis, and obesity.

Benzphetamine

Benzphetamine is marketed as Didrex (UpJohn) as round, yellow tablets containing 25 milligrams and round, orange, uncoated tablets containing 50 milligrams. The tablets have "DIDREX" stamped on one side and "UPJOHN" stamped on the other. Didrex is approved for use in the short-term treatment of obesity.

Diethylpropion

Diethylpropion is marketed by three manufacturers as Diethylpropion Hydrochloride (Schein), Tenuate (Merrell Dow), and Tepanil (Riker). Tenuate comes in 25 and 75

milligram doses. The smaller dose is a round, white, uncoated tablet and the larger dose an oblong, white, uncoated tablet. Both have "MERRELL" stamped on one side and the product code "697" on the round tablet and "698" on the oblong one. The 75 milligram dose is a controlled-release tablet marketed as Tenuate Dospan. Tepanil is also provided in the same two dosage forms but both are round, white, uncoated tablets stamped "RIKER" on one side and "TEPANIL" on the other. The 75 milligram dose is called a "Ten-Tab" and is about twice the size of the 25 milligram dose. Diethylpropion is approved for use in the short-term management of obesity and is a Schedule IV compound.

Fenfluramine

Fenfluramine is marketed as Pondimin (A.H. Robins) in a 20 milligram dosage form. It is a small, orange tablet with "AHR 6447" stamped on one side. Fenfluramine is approved for use in the short-term management of obesity. It is also a Schedule IV compound because numerous studies have shown it to possess a minimal abuse liability.

Methamphetamine

Methamphetamine is marketed in tablets as Desoxyn (Abbott) or Desoxyn Gradumet. The latter tablets contain an inert plastic matrix from which the drug is slowly released as it passes through the gastrointestinal tract. Desoxyn Gradumet comes in 5, 10, and 15 milligram doses as small, white, orange, or yellow tablets, respectively. Desoxyn is supplied as a small, white tablet containing 5 milligrams for immediate release. Each tablet is stamped with the manufacturer's logo, which is a squared-off letter "a" and looks like a backward "6."

Methylphenidate

Methylphenidate is marketed as Ritalin (CIBA) and is supplied in small, round, uncoated tablets that are color-coded by the dose: bright yellow contains 5 milligrams, white contains 10 milligrams, and tan contains 20 milligrams. Each tablet is stamped with "CIBA" on one side and either "7," "3," or "34" on the other side, identifying the 5, 10, and 20 milligram doses, respectively. CIBA also markets Ritalin-SR,

in 20 milligram sustained-release form. This preparation is a small, white coated tablet with "CIBA 16" printed on one side. Ritalin is approved for use in hyperkinesis and narcolepsy.

Phendimetrazine

There are currently 17 different preparations of phendimetrazine manufactured by 11 different companies. They are as follows: Bacarate Tablets (Reid-Provident), Bontril PDM and Bontril Slow Release (Carnick), Dyrexan-OD Capsules (Trimen), Hyrex-105 (Hyrex), Melfiat Tablets (Reid-Provident), Plegine (Ayerst), Prelu-2 Timed Release Capsules (Boehringer Ingleheim), SPRX-105 Capsules (Reid-Provident), Slyn-LL Capsules (Edwards), Trimcaps and Trimtabs (Mayrand), Trimstat Tablets (Laser), Wehless-105 Timecells (Hauck), and X-Trozine Capsules and Tablets and X-Trozine LA-105 Capsules (Rexan). All preparations are supplied as either tablets containing 35 milligrams for immediate release or 105 milligram capsules for sustained or timed release, in various sizes and color combinations. Phendimetrazine is approved for use in the short-term management of obesity.

Phenmetrazine

Phenmetrazine is marketed as Preludin (Boehringer Ingleheim). The standard immediate release preparation contains 25 milligrams and is a diamond-shaped, white tablet with "BI 42" stamped on one side. A prolonged-action tablet containing 75 milligrams is a larger, round, pinkish tablet with "BI 62" stamped on one side. Phenmetrazine is approved for use in the short-term management of obesity.

Phentermine

Phentermine is manufactured by six different companies. The currently available preparations include: Adipex-P Tablets (Lemmon), Fastin Capsules (Beecham), Ionamin (Pennwalt), Oby-Trim 30 Capsules (Rexan), Phentermine Hydrochloride Capsules (Schein), and Teramine Capsules (Legere). Fastin is supplied as a 30 milligram blue-and-clear capsule and Ionamin is supplied in either 15 or 30 milligram doses as a gray-and-yellow or all-yellow capsule, respectively. Phentermine is approved for use in the short-term management of obesity and is a Schedule IV compund.

IF A FRIEND IS IN
TROUBLE WITH AMPHETAMIN

Someone might read all about the signs and symptoms of amphetamine abuse, but still be the last to realize that he is a victim. If confronted, he will most likely deny the problem or claim that he has it under control. The abuser's only hope is that a friend or family member will recognize the signs and care enough to do something about it.

Some of the earliest signs of amphetamine abuse include changes in daily habits. The user may sleep through most of the day and stay out all night, or simply appear a bit edgy or nervous. He may blame his behavior on tension from school, or trouble with a friend, or any number of reasons. In fact, there is more truth to these excuses than meets the eye. They may be the tip of the iceberg for a deeply troubled individual who uses drugs to escape reality. Identifying the problems which led to the drug-taking is the first step in reaching out to the abuser.

When the pattern of amphetamine abuse is intermittent low doses, the individual may begin to lose interest in his personal appearance. He may shower less often and pay little attention to his hair and clothing. Sunglasses may be worn in order to shield light-sensitive eyes. He will look quite tired between periods of drug-taking. If he does admit to using amphetamine, he will usually try to justify it by saying "speed is the only thing that keeps me going," or "if you think I look bad now, you can imagine what I'd look like without it."

At this point the user may be argumentative and short-tempered. He probably has a new set of friends. The break with a close friend is often a sign that he has made a choice to avoid those who do not approve of amphetamine use. The appearance of strangers at the house who are shuttled into his room behind a closed door may be a sign that drugs are being sold or shared. The drug user may even sell household items to finance his habit. All of this, of course, is done in complete secrecy.

At the first sign of violent behavior, which may be directed at inanimate objects such as walls and doors, the

individual may be approaching a very dangerous turning point. He may be on the verge of experiencing the acute psychotic reaction that occurs after higher doses of amphetamine. It is imperative that professional help be sought at this time to prevent the user from hurting himself or others.

The treatment of amphetamine psychosis and the management of withdrawal is best left to drug–abuse crisis centers or hospitals. The psychosis is best treated by leaving the individual alone, preferably in a padded room, without any kind of stimulation that might set him off in a rage. He may be given drugs to make his urine more acidic, which will increase the rate at which amphetamine is eliminated from the body. This acute phase usually abates within a few days after all the amphetamine has been excreted from the body.

The first phase of withdrawal is characterized by extreme exhaustion, sleep disturbances, and irritability. But this phase, unpleasant though it is, is the easy part of the treatment. The next step is for the patient to confront and analyze the problems that led him to amphetamine abuse. The process of learning to live in one's environment can be painful and full of frustrations and setbacks, but escaping from reality with amphetamine or any other drug does not solve problems, it only delays the recovery.

CASE STUDIES:
ACUTE AMPHETAMINE EFFECTS

Case 1

A healthy 41-year-old woman was given 5 milligrams of amphetamine before meals because of mild depression and fatigue. Ten minutes after taking the first dose she complained of a feeling of impending death, headache, giddiness, fast heartbeat, and general discomfort. She was pale, cold, and clammy. Her body temperature was low and her pulse rate 90. She was given phenobarbital and put to bed. Seven hours later she was still clammy, her headache was still present, pulse rate 100, and blood pressure normal. Although the patient was rational she felt "miles away." The next day the patient was well except for a feeling of weakness. A subsequent test dose of 2.5 milligrams of amphetamine produced a similar but much less severe reaction.

Case 2

A 30-year-old widow with anxiety and depression was given 10 milligrams of amphetamine intravenously for exploratory purposes. After a few minutes the patient began to scream that she was being watched, and that the doctor wanted to kill her on orders from the church. She was suspicious and hyperactive, but clear-minded. Later she developed visual and auditory hallucinations and vivid fantasies. These acute psychotic symptoms disappeared after two days.

Case 3

A 33-year-old unemployed bartender ingested 250 milligrams of amphetamine. Half an hour later he had intense headache, cold sweats, hyperexcitability, dryness of the mouth, fast and irregular heart beat, and abdominal pain. This was followed by loss of consciousness, violent convulsions, especially of the upper limbs, drooling, paleness, fast pulse, and dilated pupils. The blood pressure was very high (220/145). After sedation the symptoms disappeared rapidly and the next day the patient was relatively normal, clear-minded,

and calm, but felt back pain and bled from the mouth. The patient was discharged and recovered after eight days.

Case 4

A 31-year-old man ingested most of the contents of an amphetamine inhaler (325 milligrams) over a six-hour period because he was feeling depressed and knew amphetamine "pepped you up." He became restless, began walking the streets, and spent the night in a park. He spent the next day looking for gold in the park. In the evening he thought he heard people talking about him and he was sure they were going to kill him. He also thought that cars and people were following him. Finally he climbed on a roof to get away and began to throw tiles at the crowds he imagined in the streets below. He was taken by the police to the hospital. He was overactive, trembling, agitated, and terrified, but after three days he became calm and relaxed, and the delusions or hallucinations ceased. He had never suffered hallucinations or delusions of persecution before. He drank heavily but not continuously and was not an amphetamine addict.

Case 5

A 36-year-old physically normal soldier, undergoing psychotherapy because of periodic feelings of depression accompanied by heavy drinking, was given 5 milligrams of amphetamine daily. During one of these periods of depression he decided to commit suicide by taking an overdose of amphetamine. He was admitted to the hospital in a dazed condition. His pulse was slow and strong and he had an intense headache. At 11:30 P.M. his right leg and arm became paralyzed and he had difficulty breathing. Except for a rise in pulse rate to 80 per minute the condition remained unchanged until 4:00 A.M. when he vomited. The rectal temperature was 103.8°. Despite caffeine and sodium benzoate and oxygen, the respiration became labored and his pulse rate rose to over 100. The patient's condition became steadily worse until he died at 4:55 A.M. Autopsy revealed that the immediate cause of death was hemorrhage of the blood vessels in the brain.

APPENDIX 4

CASE STUDIES:
CHRONIC AMPHETAMINE EFFECTS

Case 1

Before her admission to a hospital, a 21-year-old woman had taken amphetamine for six years and large doses of it for several months. Her symptoms increased gradually and consisted of insomnia, loss of appetite, weight loss, and headaches. Some weeks before admission ideas of persecution appeared. When seen at a hospital she was agitated, anxious, and disoriented, and had developed speech difficulties. Withdrawal of amphetamine and administration of sedatives diminished the agitation and anxiety but not her thought and mood disorders. She improved after insulin coma therapy, but was readmitted a year later to another hospital despite abstinence from amphetamine.

Case 2

A 39-year-old man upon admission to a hospital complained that a number of persons were plotting against him. About four months earlier he had begun to take amphetamine daily in doses of up to 90 milligrams. Two months before admission he began to develop an elaborate system of paranoid delusions. When admitted he was suspicious of hospital staff but talked freely about his ideas of persecution. His senses were clear and there were no hallucinations. The patient's pre-psychotic personality had a distinctly paranoid trend. Although earlier he had used alcohol excessively and had had one episode of delirium tremens with paranoid delusions, he had not drunk at all for a year prior to admission. After a two-month period of observation and conservative treatment his condition remained unchanged. It appears that in this case amphetamine was an important agent in precipitat-

ing psychosis in a patient who was emotionally predisposed to paranoid thinking.

Case 3

A 27-year-old chemist was admitted to a hospital two and one-half years after he started to take amphetamine. The drug had been prescribed for weakness, fatigue, and other symptoms. In initial doses of 18 milligrams per day, it produced great improvement in mood and capacity for work, but tolerance soon developed and the patient began taking doses averaging 180 milligrams daily. The beneficial effects were not maintained, but marked side effects, such as insomnia, weight loss, and irregular heartbeat appeared. He became inattentive, slow-thinking, restless, irresponsible, and could not continue working. When marked obsessive-compulsive behavior and sensory illusions of various types developed he entered the hospital voluntarily. After 12 days of withdrawal, the compulsions and illusions disappeared but the physical signs persisted for two to three weeks. Eventually the patient made a complete recovery. His pre-toxic personality was psychopathic and probably contributed to the particular psychic symptoms which appeared during the period of intoxication.

Case 4

On admission to a hospital a 49-year-old lawyer was exhibiting somatic, visual, and auditory hallucinations which had begun four months earlier. He had been taking amphetamine in steadily increasing doses for six years. The drug had originally been prescribed (40 milligrams per day) for fatigue but later, without the consent of his doctor, he continued to use it in doses of up to 250 milligrams daily. Amphetamine enabled him to give up the use of alcohol which he had been drinking since age 17. He was also a heavy smoker and excessively fond of sweets. The first symptoms were insomnia and restlessness followed by delusions of persecution and hallucinations. He became so fearful and unable to sleep that hospitalization was advised. On admission he was agitated, hallucinated, and deluded (refusing food for six days), but physical examination was essentially negative. He was oriented, but had no insight and protested violently that he had been committed illegally. After four

weeks in the hospital his insight was good and he was discharged as recovered with a diagnosis of psychosis due to drugs.

Case 5

A 38-year-old doctor, on being admitted to a hospital, was experiencing hallucinations and ideas of persecution, but was aware that he was intoxicated with amphetamine. He had begun taking 20 milligrams of amphetamine intravenously some months earlier because of personal problems. At first, with doses of 50 milligrams daily he experienced hyperactivity, marked but not unpleasant insomnia interrupted by periods of deep, almost comatose sleep, disturbances of the personality, loss of appetite and weight, and dilated pupils. A few attempts to give up the drug at this time failed: "I needed my injections to regain my calm." Progressive increase in dosage to 500 milligrams per day was accompanied by the development of delusions of persecution. He became isolated, seclusive, and jealous. Despite a decrease in dosage to 200 milligrams per day his delusions persisted, and in addition visual hallucinations appeared. Voluntary abstinence for 48 hours abolished the symptoms but a single injection brought them back. He was then hospitalized. After four days in the hospital the hallucinations and delusions disappeared completely.

Case 6

A 35-year-old married man had been taking amphetamine for two years in doses of up to 300 milligrams per day. For the past three years he had become increasingly aggressive, solitary, jealous of his wife, and preoccupied with religious subjects. On admission he was very tense, talked about religious matters in a rambling and almost incoherent manner, and thought that a bearded fellow patient was John the Baptist. There was no clouding of consciousness. When his condition settled he was released but his psychotic symptoms, including paranoid delusions, reappeared. This time they lasted about 36 hours and for the following five days he was depressed. Both on admission and during this relapse his urine tested positive for amphetamine. The patient was well a year after discharge from the hospital, although the diagnosis of paranoid schizophrenia had been considered.

Speed kills

Contrary to the belief spread by posters such as this, though speed may lead to fatal accidents, rarely is it the direct cause of death.

APPENDIX 5

STATE AGENCIES
FOR THE PREVENTION AND TREATMENT
OF DRUG ABUSE

ALABAMA

Department of Mental Health
Division of Mental Illness and
  Substance Abuse Community
  Programs
200 Insterstate Park Drive
P.O. Box 3710
Montgomery, AL 36193
(205) 271-9253

ALASKA

Department of Health and Social
  Services
Office of Alcoholism and Drug
  Abuse
Pouch H-05-F
Juneau, AK 99811
(907) 586-6201

ARIZONA

Department of Health Services
Division of Behavioral Health
  Services
Bureau of Community Services
Alcohol Abuse and Alcoholism
  Section
2500 East Van Buren
Phoenix, AZ 85008
(602) 255-1238

Department of Health Services
Division of Behavioral Health
  Services
Bureau of Community Services
Drug Abuse Section
2500 East Van Buren
Phoenix, AZ 85008
(602) 255-1240

ARKANSAS

Department of Human Services
Office on Alcohol and Drug Abuse
  Prevention
1515 West 7th Avenue
Suite 310
Little Rock, AR 72202
(501) 371-2603

CALIFORNIA

Department of Alcohol and Drug
  Abuse
111 Capitol Mall
Sacramento, CA 95814
(916) 445-1940

COLORADO

Department of Health
Alcohol and Drug Abuse Division
4210 East 11th Avenue
Denver, CO 80220
(303) 320-6137

CONNECTICUT

Alcohol and Drug Abuse
  Commission
999 Asylum Avenue
3rd Floor
Hartford, CT 06105
(203) 566-4145

DELAWARE

Division of Mental Health
Bureau of Alcoholism and Drug
  Abuse
1901 North Dupont Highway
Newcastle, DE 19720
(302) 421-6101

DISTRICT OF COLUMBIA
Department of Human Services
Office of Health Planning and
 Development
601 Indiana Avenue, NW
Suite 500
Washington, D.C. 20004
(202) 724-5641

FLORIDA
Department of Health and
 Rehabilitative Services
Alcoholic Rehabilitation Program
1317 Winewood Boulevard
Room 187A
Tallahassee, FL 32301
(904) 488-0396

Department of Health and
 Rehabilitative Services
Drug Abuse Program
1317 Winewood Boulevard
Building 6, Room 155
Tallahassee, FL 32301
(904) 488-0900

GEORGIA
Department of Human Resources
Division of Mental Health and
 Mental Retardation
Alcohol and Drug Section
618 Ponce De Leon Avenue, NE
Atlanta, GA 30365-2101
(404) 894-4785

HAWAII
Department of Health
Mental Health Division
Alcohol and Drug Abuse Branch
1250 Punch Bowl Street
P.O. Box 3378
Honolulu, HI 96801
(808) 548-4280

IDAHO
Department of Health and Welfare
Bureau of Preventive Medicine
Substance Abuse Section
450 West State
Boise, ID 83720
(208) 334-4368

ILLINOIS
Department of Mental Health and
 Developmental Disabilities
Division of Alcoholism
160 North La Salle Street
Room 1500
Chicago, IL 60601
(312) 793-2907

Illinois Dangerous Drugs
 Commission
300 North State Street
Suite 1500
Chicago, IL 60610
(312) 822-9860

INDIANA
Department of Mental Health
Division of Addiction Services
429 North Pennsylvania Street
Indianapolis, IN 46204
(317) 232-7816

IOWA
Department of Substance Abuse
505 5th Avenue
Insurance Exchange Building
Suite 202
Des Moines, IA 50319
(515) 281-3641

KANSAS
Department of Social Rehabilitation
Alcohol and Drug Abuse Services
2700 West 6th Street
Biddle Building
Topeka, KS 66606
(913) 296-3925

KENTUCKY
Cabinet for Human Resources
Department of Health Services
Substance Abuse Branch
275 East Main Street
Frankfort, KY 40601
(502) 564-2880

LOUISIANA
Department of Health and Human
  Resources
Office of Mental Health and
  Substance Abuse
655 North 5th Street
P.O. Box 4049
Baton Rouge, LA 70821
(504) 342-2565

MAINE
Department of Human Services
Office of Alcoholism and Drug
  Abuse Prevention
Bureau of Rehabilitation
32 Winthrop Street
Augusta, ME 04330
(207) 289-2781

MARYLAND
Alcoholism Control Administration
201 West Preston Street
Fourth Floor
Baltimore, MD 21201
(301) 383-2977

State Health Department
Drug Abuse Administration
201 West Preston Street
Baltimore, MD 21201
(301) 383-3312

MASSACHUSETTS
Department of Public Health
Division of Alcoholism
755 Boylston Street
Sixth Floor
Boston, MA 02116
(617) 727-1960

Department of Public Health
Division of Drug Rehabilitation
600 Washington Street
Boston, MA 02114
(617) 727-8617

MICHIGAN
Department of Public Health
Office of Substance Abuse Services
3500 North Logan Street
P.O. Box 30035
Lansing, MI 48909
(517) 373-8603

MINNESOTA
Department of Public Welfare
Chemical Dependency Program
  Division
Centennial Building
658 Cedar Street
4th Floor
Saint Paul, MN 55155
(612) 296-4614

MISSISSIPPI
Department of Mental Health
Division of Alcohol and Drug Abuse
1102 Robert E. Lee Building
Jackson, MS 39201
(601) 359-1297

MISSOURI
Department of Mental Health
Division of Alcoholism and Drug
  Abuse
2002 Missouri Boulevard
P.O. Box 687
Jefferson City, MO 65102
(314) 751-4942

MONTANA
Department of Institutions
Alcohol and Drug Abuse Division
1539 11th Avenue
Helena, MT 59620
(406) 449-2827

NEBRASKA
Department of Public Institutions
Division of Alcoholism and Drug Abuse
801 West Van Dorn Street
P.O. Box 94728
Lincoln, NB 68509
(402) 471-2851, Ext. 415

NEVADA
Department of Human Resources
Bureau of Alcohol and Drug Abuse
505 East King Street
Carson City, NV 89710
(702) 885-4790

NEW HAMPSHIRE
Department of Health and Welfare
Office of Alcohol and Drug Abuse
  Prevention
Hazen Drive
Health and Welfare Building
Concord, NH 03301
(603) 271-4627

NEW JERSEY
Department of Health
Division of Alcoholism
129 East Hanover Street CN 362
Trenton, NJ 08625
(609) 292-8949

Department of Health
Division of Narcotic and Drug Abuse
  Control
129 East Hanover Street CN 362
Trenton, NJ 08625
(609) 292-8949

NEW MEXICO
Health and Environment Department
Behavioral Services Division
Substance Abuse Bureau
725 Saint Michaels Drive
P.O. Box 968
Santa Fe, NM 87503
(505) 984-0020, Ext. 304

NEW YORK
Division of Alcoholism and Alcohol
  Abuse
194 Washington Avenue
Albany, NY 12210
(518) 474-5417

Division of Substance Abuse
  Services
Executive Park South
Box 8200
Albany, NY 12203
(518) 457-7629

NORTH CAROLINA
Department of Human Resources
Division of Mental Health, Mental
  Retardation and Substance Abuse
  Services
Alcohol and Drug Abuse Services
325 North Salisbury Street
Albemarle Building
Raleigh, NC 27611
(919) 733-4670

NORTH DAKOTA
Department of Human Services
Division of Alcoholism and Drug
  Abuse
State Capitol Building
Bismarck, ND 58505
(701) 224-2767

OHIO
Department of Health
Division of Alcoholism
246 North High Street
P.O. Box 118
Columbus, OH 43216
(614) 466-3543

Department of Mental Health
Bureau of Drug Abuse
65 South Front Street
Columbus, OH 43215
(614) 466-9023

OKLAHOMA

Department of Mental Health
Alcohol and Drug Programs
4545 North Lincoln Boulevard
Suite 100 East Terrace
P.O. Box 53277
Oklahoma City, OK 73152
(405) 521-0044

OREGON

Department of Human Resources
Mental Health Division
Office of Programs for Alcohol and
  Drug Problems
2575 Bittern Street, NE
Salem, OR 97310
(503) 378-2163

PENNSYLVANIA

Department of Health
Office of Drug and Alcohol
  Programs
Commonwealth and Forster Avenues
Health and Welfare Building
P.O. Box 90
Harrisburg, PA 17108
(717) 787-9857

RHODE ISLAND

Department of Mental Health,
  Mental Retardation and Hospitals
Division of Substance Abuse
Substance Abuse Administration
  Building
Cranston, RI 02920
(401) 464-2091

SOUTH CAROLINA

Commission on Alcohol and Drug
  Abuse
3700 Forest Drive
Columbia, SC 29204
(803) 758-2521

SOUTH DAKOTA

Department of Health
Division of Alcohol and Drug Abuse
523 East Capitol, Joe Foss Building
Pierre, SD 57501
(605) 773-4806

TENNESSEE

Department of Mental Health and
  Mental Retardation
Alcohol and Drug Abuse Services
505 Deaderick Street
James K. Polk Building, Fourth Floor
Nashville, TN 37219
(615) 741-1921

TEXAS

Commission on Alcoholism
809 Sam Houston State Office Building
Austin, TX 78701
(512) 475-2577

Department of Community Affairs
Drug Abuse Prevention Division
2015 South Interstate Highway 35
P.O. Box 13166
Austin, TX 78711
(512) 443-4100

UTAH

Department of Social Services
Division of Alcoholism and Drugs
150 West North Temple
Suite 350
P.O. Box 2500
Salt Lake City, UT 84110
(801) 533-6532

VERMONT

Agency of Human Services
Department of Social and
  Rehabilitation Services
Alcohol and Drug Abuse Division
103 South Main Street
Waterbury, VT 05676
(802) 241-2170

VIRGINIA
Department of Mental Health and
  Mental Retardation
Division of Substance Abuse
109 Governor Street
P.O. Box 1797
Richmond, VA 23214
(804) 786-5313

WASHINGTON
Department of Social and Health
  Service
Bureau of Alcohol and Substance
  Abuse
Office Building—44 W
Olympia, WA 98504
(206) 753-5866

WEST VIRGINIA
Department of Health
Office of Behavioral Health Services
Division on Alcoholism and Drug
  Abuse
1800 Washington Street East
Building 3 Room 451
Charleston, WV 25305
(304) 348-2276

WISCONSIN
Department of Health and Social
  Services
Division of Community Services
Bureau of Community Programs
Alcohol and Other Drug Abuse
  Program Office
1 West Wilson Street
P.O. Box 7851
Madison, WI 53707
(608) 266-2717

WYOMING
Alcohol and Drug Abuse Programs
Hathaway Building
Cheyenne, WY 82002
(307) 777-7115, Ext. 7118

GUAM
Mental Health & Substance Abuse
  Agency
P.O. Box 20999
Guam 96921

PUERTO RICO
Department of Addiction Control
  Services
Alcohol Abuse Programs
P.O. Box B-Y Rio Piedras Station
Rio Piedras, PR 00928
(809) 763-5014

Department of Addiction Control
  Services
Drug Abuse Programs
P.O. Box B-Y Rio Piedras Station
Rio Piedras, PR 00928
(809) 764-8140

VIRGIN ISLANDS
Division of Mental Health,
  Alcoholism & Drug Dependency
  Services
P.O. Box 7329
Saint Thomas, Virgin Islands 00801
(809) 774-7265

AMERICAN SAMOA
LBJ Tropical Medical Center
Department of Mental Health Clinic
Pago Pago, American Samoa 96799

TRUST TERRITORIES
Director of Health Services
Office of the High Commissioner
Saipan, Trust Territories 96950

Further Reading

GENERAL

Black, J. "The 'Speed' that Kills—or Worse." *The New York Times Magazine,* June 21, 1970. An easy to read description of the dangers of amphetamine abuse.

Louria, D.B. *The Drug Scene.* New York: McGraw-Hill, 1968. Interesting reading about the legal and illegal use of amphetamine and other psychoactive drugs.

Ray, O. *Drugs, Society and Human Behavior.* St. Louis: C.V. Mosby, 1978. A very good book about amphetamine and other commonly used drugs, including discussion of the social, cultural, and historical factors that relate to drug use and abuse.

Smith, R.C. "The World of the Haight Ashbury Speed Freak." *Journal of Psychedelic Drugs,* 1969. An interesting description of the lives of amphetamine addicts.

TECHNICAL

Bell, D.S. and Trethowan, W.H. "Amphetamine Addiction." *Journal of Nervous and Mental Diseases,* 1961. A description of the process of tolerance and addiction to amphetamine following chronic usage.

Connell, P.H. *Amphetamine Psychosis.* London: Chapman & Hall, Ltd., 1958. A detailed description of the psychological effects of chronic amphetamine abuse.

Costa, E. and Garattini, S. *International Symposium on Amphetamines and Related Compounds.* New York: Raven Press, 1970. A comprehensive description of the biochemical, metabolic, behavioral, and physiological effects of acute and chronic administration of amphetamine and other stimulants.

Kramer, J.C., Fischman, V.S., and Littlefield, D.C. "Amphetamine Abuse." *Journal of the American Medical Association,* 1967. A description of the problems of amphetamine abuse by physicians who have worked with these patients.

Glossary

acetaminophen: a minor pain reliever not containing aspirin

acute: having severe symptoms and a short course

addiction: physiological or psychological dependence on some agent with a tendency to increase its use

American Medical Association (AMA): a national organization which oversees the training of medical students and the activities of practicing physicians

amphetamine: a behavioral stimulant

analgesia: insensitivity to pain without loss of conciousness

aphrodisiac: a drug that arouses sexual desire

asthma: a condition characterized by difficult breathing

atropine: a psychoactive drug that has hallucinogenic properties at high doses

barbiturate: a class of chemically related sedative-hypnotic drugs

benzocaine: a drug used topically as a local anesthetic

burn-out: a state of exhaustion which occurs in individuals after prolonged amphetamine abuse

caffeine: a behavioral stimulant found in coffee, tea, cola drinks, and chocolate

caffeine mania: hyperresponsiveness resulting from excessive ingestion of coffee or other caffeine-containing beverages

chronic: persisting over a long period of time

clinical: pertaining to treatment of a patient

cocaine: a behavioral stimulant

codeine: a sedative and pain-relieving agent found in opium which is related to morphine but is less potent

Controlled Substances Act (CSA): a law enacted in 1970 that is designed to control the manufacture, sale, and use of potentially dangerous drugs

depressant: any agent which slows any bodily function

diethylpropion: a drug used to diminish appetite

diphenylhydantoin: an anticonvulsant compound

dopamine: a neurotransmitter in the brain

Drug Abuse Warning Network (DAWN): an organization that monitors trends in drug use and abuse in the United States

Drug Enforcement Administration (DEA): a branch of government that oversees the legal use of drugs for medical and research purposes and enforces laws concerning illegal drugs

drug schedule: a classification system of drugs based on their medical usefulness and potential for abuse

dyphenhydramine: an antihistamine

electroshock therapy: therapy involving the application of electric current to the brain

ephedrine: an amphetamine-related stimulant

epilepsy: a disorder characterized by convulsive seizures and/or disturbances of consciousness which are associated with disturbance of electrical activity in the brain

euphoria: a pleasant feeling of well-being

fenfluramine: an appetite-suppressing drug

Food and Drug Administration (FDA): an organization which regulates the purity of food and drugs for consumer protection

hallucination: a sensory impression that has no basis in reality

hallucinogen: an agent capable of producing hallucinations

heart block: a lack of muscular coordination between two chambers of the heart so that they beat independently of each other

heroin: a semisynthetic opiate produced by a chemical modification of morphine

histamine: a body chemical involved in pain responses, swelling, respiratory disorders, and allergic reactions

hyperkinesis: a condition of abnormally increased motor function or activity

hypnagogic: occurring during sleep

illicit: illegal

insomnia: the condition of not being able to sleep

intravenous: within a vein

marijuana: a hemp plant that contains cannabinol, or THC, a habitforming intoxicating drug

methapyriline: an antihistamine substance for treatment of allergic symptoms attributed to histamine

morphine: the major sedative and pain-relieving drug found in opium

mucous membrane: a tissue that lines the openings to the body, such as the mouth and nose

narcolepsy: recurrent uncontrollable desire for sleep

National Institute for Drug Abuse (NIDA): a subdivision of the National Institute of Health that monitors patterns of drug use and research in the area of drug abuse

neuron: one of the cells that comprise the nervous system

neurotransmitter: the chemical found in neurons which carries an electrical message from one neuron to another

nicotinism: poisoning by tobacco or nicotine

noradrenaline: a neurotransmitter in the brain

opiate: any drug whose effects on the body are similar to those caused by morphine

paranoia: a mental disorder marked by delusions of persecution

Parkinson's disease: a disorder of the motor system characterized by involuntary movements, tremor, and weakness

pemoline: a stimulant used to treat hyperkinesis in children

pep pill: slang for amphetamine

pharmaceutical: pertaining to drugs

pharmacology: the study of drugs, their sources, preparations, and uses

phentermine: an appetite suppressant similar to amphetamine

Preludin: a drug used to reduce appetite

preservation: persistence of one reply or idea in response to various questions

procaine: a local anesthetic

psychedelic drug: a drug with the ability to alter sensory perception

psychosis: a major emotional disorder with derangement of the personality and loss of contact with reality, often with delusions, hallucinations or illusions

psychostimulant: a drug that increases brain activity

Ritalin: a stimulant drug used to treat hyperkinesis in children

schizophrenia: a chronic psychotic disorder with predominant symptoms such as paranoia, delusions, and hallucinations

speed: a group of drugs that produce brain stimulation

stimulant: any drug that increases behavioral activity

strychnine: a convulsant drug

synthetic drug: a drug that does not occur in nature but rather is man-made

tactile hallucination: a hallucination of touch

Temgesic: a pain-killing drug similar to morphine

theophylline: a drug used as a smooth muscle relaxant and diuretic

tolerance: decrease of susceptibility to the effects of a drug due to its continued administration

toxicity: the quality of exerting deleterious effects on the body or body parts

Valium: a drug that eliminates anxiety

wake-amine: slang for amphetamine

withdrawal: the physical and psychological effects of discontinued usage of a drug

Photo by John Giorno

William S. Burroughs, Jr., (right) son of Beat generation writer William S. Burroughs (left), was greatly influenced by the Beat generation's insatiable thirst for extreme experiences. In Speed, **his first, autobiographical novel, Burroughs, Jr., describes his plunge into the world of amphetamine addiction and his physical and mental deterioration. At 33 years old he died from liver collapse due to a life of drug abuse and alcoholism.**

Index

Dr. Scott E. Lukas received his Ph.D. in pharmacology from the University of Maryland. He was a post-doctoral fellow and assistant professor at The Johns Hopkins University and received a National Research Service Award from the National Institute on Drug Abuse. He is currently both assistant professor of psychiatry (pharmacology) at Harvard Medical School and research pharmacologist at the Alcohol and Drug Abuse Research Center, McLean Hospital in Belmont, Massachusetts.

Solomon H. Snyder, M.D., is Distinguished Service Professor of Neuroscience, Pharmacology and Psychiatry at The Johns Hopkins University School of Medicine. He has served as president of the Society for Neuroscience and in 1978 received the Albert Laster Award in Medical Research. He has authored *Uses of Marijuana, Madness and the Brain, The Troubled Mind, Biological Aspects of Mental Disorder,* and edited *Perspective in Neuropharmacology: A Tribute to Julius Axelrod.* Professor Snyder was a research associate with Dr. Axelrod at the National Institute of Health.

Barry L. Jacobs, Ph.D., is currently a professor in the program of neuroscience at Princeton University. Professor Jacobs is author of *Serotinin Neurotransmission and Behavior* and *Hallucinogens: Neurochemical, Behavioral and Clinical Perspectives.* He has written many journal articles in the field of neuroscience and contributed numerous chapters to books on behavior and brain science. He has been a member of several panels of the National Institute of Mental Health.

Jerome H. Jaffe, M.D., formerly professor of psychiatry at the College of Physicians and Surgeons, Columbia University, has been named recently Director of the Addiction Research Center of the National Institute on Drug Abuse. Dr. Jaffe is also a psychopharmacologist and has conducted research on a wide range of addictive drugs and developed treatment programs for addicts. He has acted as Special Consultant to the President on Narcotics and Dangerous Drugs and was the first director of the White House Special Action Office for Drug Abuse Prevention.

19958

WITHDRAWN

19958

ABOUT THE TYPE

This book was set in Perpetua, a typeface designed by the English
artist Eric Gill, and cut by the Monotype Corporation between
1928 and 1930. Perpetua is a contemporary face of original design,
without any direct historical antecedents. The shapes of the roman
letters are derived from the techniques of stonecutting. The larger
display sizes are extremely elegant and form a
most distinguished series of inscriptional letters.